IRON HEARTS AND DRAGON MAGIC

OF FIRE & FAE I

IRON HEARTS AND DRAGON MAGIC

DAY LEITAO

SPARKLY WAVE

MONTREAL, 2022

CONTENTS

Fernick
Karsal
Formosa
Royal Manor
Vastfield
Varana
Umbrar
Haven
Eaglehold
Greenstone
Wolfmark
Wildspring
Mount Prime
Iron Citadel
Ironhold
Frostlake Castle
Frostlake
N

SUMMARY OF BOOK I
WHAT HAPPENED IN FROZEN HEARTS AND DEATH MAGIC

This story is on the small continent of Aluria, where there are eleven kingdoms, and, in most of them, the royal families have magic.

On a rainy night, something drew Irinaia, or rather, Naia, out of her bedroom and into the woods surrounding her manor. She found a fae, unconscious and cold. A white fae, to be more precise. These fae usually had pale blond hair, pointy ears, horns, and long nails. The one she found had brown hair, though. Now, the issue was that these fae hadn't been seen in almost twenty years. Another problem was that, before disappearing, they had been in a horrible war with humans, so bad that an entire human city had been destroyed.

Even then, Naia decided to bring him to her bedroom and not alert her father or brother, fearing they would hurt the fae. As a human from a royal family, Naia had magic—iron magic, or iron-bringing, in her case, which she used to bend the bars from her window and to move a large tray to carry the fae inside. She wanted to save him, but she also wanted to know who he was and what he was doing there.

When the fae woke up, Naia tried to pry answers from him, but got very little. He claimed his name was River and evaded her questions, but he told her to ask for something in return for saving his life. Her first choice was obviously life servitude, but apparently that wasn't allowed or something, and she was half kidding anyway. And then, the fae was so beautiful, so alluring, she didn't think she'd ever be alone with someone like that, so she ended up asking for a kiss. The kiss she got was magical, except that he stopped it, then stared at her in horror, and asked, "What have you done?" before disappearing.

A year after that, Naia was about to visit another kingdom for the first time, to go to the gathering, when royals from all over Aluria met. Naia was a princess from Umbraar, the kingdom where they had deathbringing, even if she and her brother were iron-bringers, able to control metal. Her father was a deathbringer, and in theory could kill someone with a stare, and yet despite being so powerful, Naia noticed he was anxious on the way. He explained that he was afraid that too many princesses would make advances on her brother Isofel, or Fel, and that he didn't want Naia to show off her magic or let anyone know about it.

In the last year, she had found a different kind of magic—fire. She could produce flames with her hands. No royal in Aluria had ever had it. Instead of being happy about her unique power, her father seemed worried or bothered by it. Naia found it unfair. For years now, she had been used to being the sibling with the weak magic, since her twin brother, Fel, was such a powerful iron-bringer. Now that she had her own magic, it didn't seem to matter.

It was true that her brother had a very good reason for being so good. He had been born without hands, and ended up using his ironbringing to compensate for that, eventually having false hands made of pieces of metal that he could control. It didn't change the fact that he sometimes felt uneasy about his disability, and didn't quiet down the eventual whispers calling him "cripple".

Although sometimes marriage matches were made in the

gatherings, their father didn't want either of them to pick partners there. He thought that Naia didn't need to get married, that she could become Fel's advisor, and that Fel could choose a commoner from Umbraar instead of a princess.

One thing Naia was looking for in this gathering was to learn more about her mother, who had died when she and Fel were born. Her father refused to say anything about her, claiming it caused him grief. Her mother had been from Ironhold, and they hated Umbraar for some reason. Naia also wondered if she could learn more about the fae, and understand what had happened to River. She still hadn't forgotten him. That said, there were some mysterious attacks happening in some villages in Aluria, and people were saying the fae were returning. Naia wondered if it had something to do with River, and wondered if she should have told someone she'd seen a fae.

Frostlake was the kingdom receiving the other royals. Despite its name, the magic there was necromancy. The king and his wife had only one heir, princess Leandra, or Leah. Leah often had strange dreams and nightmares. Her solace was a silver dragon, a constant companion in her dreams, bringing her comfort and joy. And she needed comfort! Her mother wanted her to pick a husband in this gathering, in such little time.

The first ball was going to be that night, but the royal delegations sometimes had activities for the princes and princesses during the day. Leah's mother didn't want her to participate in them. She was very strict about Leah keeping her honor, and yet very vague about what exactly she meant by that. Still, Leah's father had a close advisor, Kasim, who was like a second father to her, who decided to take her to the first activity, which was going to be ice-skating. He wanted her to have some fun and to get to know some of the princes outside the formalities of the balls.

Leah was excited to meet the royals from the other kingdoms, but in the end, the only people present were the Umbraar twins. She was quite curious to meet them because her mother spoke about that kingdom dismissively, and all the kingdoms hated them. She knew that Ironhold hated Umbraar because the king had eloped with an Ironhold princess years before; the twins' mother. That said, the twins were nice. Actually, the prince was more than nice, quite stunning, even if he was using his metal magic rather than properly skating. Umbraar was north, therefore warmer than Frostlake, so Naia and Fel had never ice-skated before.

Then as Leah was ice-skating, a watersnake breached the ice. These creatures shouldn't be able to reach a lake, let alone a frozen lake. Leah almost fell in the cold water, but Fel took care of the watersnake, scaring it, and caught her with his metal hands. Kasim, who was there, rushed them to the carriage to return to the castle. Leah was quite impressed with Fel's magic. Impressed with everything about him, in fact. They bonded quickly on the way back talking about their favorite books, but their conversation was cut short when they arrived at the castle.

Kasim then took Leah aside and told her that while it was fine for her to interact with the Umbraar twins, she should never consider Fel a possible match. Kasim was the greatest rule-breaker in the family, so this was odd. He wouldn't explain to her the issue with Fel, mostly stating that it had something to do with his father, whom Kasim despised.

When Leah was getting ready for the ball, her mother came to her for a private conversation, telling her the story of a woman who let a man into her room and lost her honor. It was very vague, but her point was that Leah should never trust any man.

While waiting for her turn to enter the ball, Leah heard a song she liked and stepped in, then Fel found her and they danced. Barely breathing by being so close to him, she was visibly nervous. He asked if she was worried about the introduction, when the young ladies would show off their magic. Leah explained that she wouldn't do necromancy because it would be morbid, that she would play the flute instead. Fel said that she would look graceful even resuscitating a dead rat, and that it would scare all potential suitors. "Except you," she said, and after this slip, there was no more denying their mutual attraction.

Naia felt odd at the ball because her father didn't interact with anyone and nobody even looked at her. Her cousins and uncle from Ironhold didn't even acknowledge her or Fel. Then, with the Ironhold delegation, she saw River, without his pointy ears or horns, but definitely him. Soon he left the ball, though.

In the young women's introduction, Naia noticed how Leah and Fel looked at each other and realized they were in love. Leah's reawakened a dead rat for a few seconds for her presentation, scaring some people in the audience.

Naia, Fel and their father left the ball early. In her room, Naia lit a flame wondering where River was, and then saw him standing by the fireplace.

River thought Naia had tried to kill him on purpose with their kiss, when he had absorbed some iron magic. He was immune to iron now. As they talked, he realized she had never tried to harm him. Naia then tried to get some answers from him, wondering about the watersnake and the attacks in the villages, but he evaded the questions, then asked her to marry him. Naia was stunned by the question and trying to understand his motivations, but then he left, telling her she had two days to make up her mind.

Leah, still at the ball, danced with three possible suitors, but didn't like them. One of them was one of the Ironhold princes, and she didn't mind dancing with him because Ironhold didn't usually have marriage alliances.

Later that night, Fel showed up by Leah's window. Even though it was high up in the castle, he could float using his metal magic as well as open her bars. Still, her mother's talk about the danger of letting a man into her room was still in her mind, so he took her out instead. They floated above the city together and kissed. Afraid of heights, Leah ended up asking him to return to her room.

Fel then asked her to marry him and she said yes, but he soon left before their kisses got too heated, promising to speak to her mother the next morning. Part of her was glad he had left before anything happened, but part of her wished he had stayed and done everything that was forbidden. She ended up dreaming about her dragon, lulling her into a pleasant sleep with his tongue.

In the morning, Leah watched the meeting between kingdoms, when they discussed the attacks in villages. Ironhold suggested sending forces to all the kingdoms, and King Azir from Umbraar opposed it. Leah's father had been neutral in it, and the discussion ended up postponed.

Meanwhile, Fel spoke to Leah's mother, Queen Ursiana, who said she would pass on the proposal. The queen, however, later lied to Leah, saying he had never spoken to her. Worried about it, Leah wrote a note asking Fel what was happening.

Fel, however, got a different note, stating that Leah was looking for someone with physical integrity. Ashamed of being rejected for his disability, he was furious, and yet wrote a response, since the messenger requested it.

Leah received a note from Fel wishing her good luck in her marriage prospects, and didn't understand what was happening. At a dinner with all the royal families, Fel didn't even look at Leah. She was sitting beside prince Venard, the youngest Ironhold prince, who had proposed, and was pleasant and friendly.

When the families were moving from one room to another, Naia saw several white fae, armed with bows and arrows, appearing in the room, surrounding them all. At the same time, all the mirrors were broken, shards flying towards every single fae. That was Fel's work, in a quick reflex. Then everyone stopped, frozen in place, and the mirror shards fell on the floor.

River appeared, telling Naia he could stop this attack, to which she reminded him that all the fae were about to be hit by shards. River then told her it would be dangerous if other kings understood the extent of her brother's power, and offered to make the fae disappear if Naia left with him to the part of the underworld where he lived. Naia, partly intrigued, agreed, but asked him to return at dawn, so she would have time to say goodbye to her family.

The attack then stopped, the fae disappeared, and so did River. Not everyone noticed what had happened, but everyone was rushed back to their rooms. On her way to hers, Leah told Kasim she was considering accepting Venard's proposal.

Fel slept in the same room as Naia. When she saw her brother asleep, she wrote notes to him and her father. River showed up, and was attacked by Fel, who pushed him against a wall using iron pokers. Eventually, after Naia said she was leaving with him out of her own will, and after River promised to honor her, Fel agreed to let them go, not that his magic could stop them, but for Naia it was important to have her brother's approval, even if reluctant.

River took Naia through a strange blackness, called the hollow, and they ended up in a clearing with a little house. He explained it would be temporary, that eventually they would have something better. Still, it was a lovely, colorful cottage and Naia liked it, despite being disappointed that it was so isolated, since she'd been expecting to learn more about the fae.

Her disappointment was huge, however, when River told her he had to go, and that she would spend her days alone. He'd been spying on the Ironhold family, and claimed he couldn't just leave his post. He also told her they would wait to marry, so that she could make up her mind, and that he would wait to touch her, including kisses. Another disappointment, of course. He didn't answer any of her questions properly, which was upsetting, since one of the reasons she had come was to understand what was happening to the white fae, which he called the Ancients. Before leaving, he told her not to go into the woods surrounding the clearing, which she felt was exactly what she had to do.

When Naia's father received her note, he was furious, promised to find her, and told Fel to go to the king's meeting in his place. In the meeting, the kingdoms agreed to have Ironhold send reinforcements to all kingdoms, except Umbraar, since Fel refused their help.

Leah agreed to marry Venard, anxious that she would be married in a few months, but then her mother told her the wedding would take place in that same afternoon, after which, she would spend some time in Ironhold.

Naia's father appeared in the clearing by River's house and confronted her, but she refused to go with him. Naia yearned for freedom, she wanted to make her own destiny, and not simply do whatever her father told her. Her father eventually left, but not after disowning her and telling her she was not his daughter. River then appeared and comforted her.

Leah was so nervous in her wedding that she vomited, causing a commotion. Her father later told her that everything was fine, and it only meant the consummation would be postponed, without explaining what that entailed.

At the house in the clearing, since Naia and River spent the day together, he did answer some questions, but he said he didn't know if the fae were returning, for example, which only made Naia even more confused. After some heated kisses, Naia fell asleep. River had given her a drink to make her pass out, as he'd been afraid of what could happen between the two of them and wanted to keep his word.

As he watched her, he considered that he'd been frozen in time for nineteen years only to wake up and meet her, and what a coincidence or strike of destiny it was. He recalled the time almost twenty years before, when he'd refused to help in the war between fae and humans, believing the humans would be defeated easily, and yet his cousin died.

Leah took a carriage with Venard and his grandmother, Lady Celia, to Ironhold. Traveling between kingdoms in Aluria didn't take long, as most kingdoms had a portal hub, from which they could teleport to the other kingdoms.

This trip was horrible, though. The old woman confronted Leah, threatening her in case she was pregnant. When Leah protested that her word was being questioned, Celia made Venard slap her and restrain her using his metal magic, but he whispered in her ear, begging her to be quiet, and although Leah couldn't forgive him for hitting her, she thought he wanted to protect her. When she arrived at the Ironhold castle, called Iron Citadel, she found it enormous and monstrous, all made of metal.

They got off the carriage, and a girl came running towards them, upset that Venard was getting married, and was strangled with her necklace. Horrified, Leah screamed "no" and tried to help the girl, but was taken by two guards and dragged to a room. There, Venard asked her to scream as if she were receiving a beating from him. After seeing them murder someone in cold blood, Leah didn't hesitate to do what he asked of her, horrified that his family would expect him to do that.

Locked in her room, she wondered how she could warn her parents, how she could escape this castle. Leah felt hurt and betrayed as well. She had trusted her family, trusted her parents' advice, and now she was in this situation. In the morning, she asked to send her family a note, and used a code to tell them she needed help. Lady Celia, the grandmother, caught the note, and Venard's older brother, Cassius, burned Leah's hand with a not knife to make her confess about the code. They then sent her to a cold cell as a punishment.

Naia tried to go into the woods, but whenever she did it, she ended up in the house, with no recollection of what she had just tried.

In Umbraar, Fel was ambushed by three assassins, one of them an ironbringer. With a lot of difficulty, he managed to kill two of them by using his magic. Having lost his weapons and with no metal available, he had to remove one of the assassin's blood by focusing on the iron in it. The third assassin killed himself so as to not get caught. River then showed up, claiming he was there to help, and asked Fel to announce to the other kingdoms that he was dead. Fel agreed, but asked River to help Leah in case she needed it.

When Naia realized there was some enchantment keeping her from the woods, it was late, and soon River arrived. She tried to ask him about it, but he dodged the question. Still, they spent some sweet moments watching the stars.

In the morning, Naia tried to go to the woods again, this time using her fire magic and keeping a flame all the time. On the other side, she found houses, a city and a castle, but everyone in it was asleep—a magical sleep from which they couldn't wake up. She felt bad for River, seeing the state of his people. When she got back, she found him worried about her. Still, she confronted him, and found out he hadn't been in that place, called the Ancient City, in a long time. He didn't even know if anyone was dead there. Determined to learn what he was doing in Ironhold, she tried to bargain an answer for an answer, but he got agitated, worried about the fae. Naia offered to help, but he told her he loved her, then made her unconscious.

River felt bad about doing that to Naia, but he didn't want her to get hurt. He thought back to almost twenty years before. The fae were losing the war, and his father mentioned a staff that could counter human magic. This staff was kept by the dragon lords, in the continent of Fernick. Fae could not go there through the hollow, but River was good at glamouring himself and still didn't have horns, so he was going to travel in a human ship.

In the Iron Citadel, Leah had a strange dream about a place with a child who turned out to be a creature with sharp teeth. She was rescued by a woman, who showed her that Ironhold had an army of ironbringers, not from the royal family. This could be a threat to other kingdoms, if they sent ironbringers among regular soldiers. During the day, Leah learned to remain quiet and stoic even when humiliated, so as to prevent physical punishment, but she wanted to kill them all, especially Cassius, the older brother. Venard wasn't bad, but he was too scared to speak up and defend her.

After another wedding ceremony in Ironhold, Venard informed Leah that they would return to Frostlake soon, unless she did something foolish, and that they should consummate their marriage. She asked him to wait, and he said he'd return in one hour. It wasn't what she meant. Anxious, Leah closed her eyes and tried to imagine her connection to her silver dragon. From a beautiful meadow, she ended up in a room with maps on the walls and many books on various tables. Fel was on a bed, and smiled when he saw her. Nothing was forbidden in a dream. They soon kissed, undressed, but then she remembered it was a dream and felt sad. At that moment, he pulled his metal hands and pinched her, telling her this was real. She was in his real room in the Royal Fort in Umbraar and they had almost gone too far.

Leah couldn't believe it was real, couldn't believe she had shown up there. Their meeting soon turned from surprise and shock to bitterness and resentment, since he was still upset she had married someone else and she was upset he had rejected her. Worried about her parents, Leah wanted to go back to Ironhold. Fel then took her to his father, who, as a deathbringer, was capable of teleporting. He was very agitated, and asked her twice if she was really a necromancer, but agreed to take her back to Ironhold.

Luckily enough, nobody noticed Leah's absence. The issue was that Venard came to her room and told her to wait for him in the dark, so that they would consummate their marriage. Leah kept the candles on, planning to speak to him. He'd been understanding enough that she trusted he would agree with postponing this. But when the door opened, it was Cassius, not Venard, and he didn't have any good intentions. Leah ended up using her powers and killing him. She then tried to escape, but was chased by guards. River showed up, took her to a safe room, and then disappeared.

After leaving Leah in Ironhold, Fel's father, Azir, went to Frostlake. There, he found the king dead, and Leah's mother, Ursiana, about to be attacked. He slipped with her through the hollow, something that was considered dangerous to do with another person, and found himself stuck.

In the Royal Fort in Umbraar, Fel waited a long time for his father, and then sensed some danger and prepared for an attack.

River recalled his past almost twenty years before, when he had gone to Fernick. Travelling with humans made him bond with them. In Fernick, he found the dragon temple and the staff easily, but then was encased in ice. A beautiful young woman rescued him, then rescued him again on the way back, after his ship sank. When he arrived at the Ancient City, he learned that a human city had been destroyed, and was disgusted to see his brother Forest taking credit for it.

In the present, Naia couldn't move or do anything, as if she were stuck in her dream. Then she recalled how her fire had countered the enchantment keeping her away from the woods, so she lit a flame in her hand—and woke up.

Leah was able to teleport to Frostlake, where she dreamed again about that place by the mountains where she had almost been attacked by shape-changing creatures. This time, they took her to a cave where a "queen of darkness" offered to help Leah gain power, but she was not interested and then left the dream and woke up in the place she was hiding in the castle.

Stuck in the hollow, Azir and Ursiana (Leah's mother) talked. They had been involved many years before, when, according to Ursiana, he had used her and abandoned her. He believed she had betrayed him. She ended up confessing that Leah was Azir's daughter and she feared that she and Fel were siblings.

Azir explained that he had never met Fel and Naia's mother. He had received messages from her as she was dying, before giving birth, then, at her request, went to Ironhold to see the babies and ended up taking the twins home and pretending they were his children. He did that because he needed heirs and didn't want to get married anymore. He also wanted to protect Fel, as he feared what Ironhold would do to him, considering he didn't have hands. After explaining this, Azir apologized to Ursiana, and was willing to die to save her. When it was time to try to leave the place where they were stuck, Ursiana remained behind, sacrificing herself to save him.

Twenty years before, River was about to use the staff to counter human magic, when he realized it would instead kill every human in Aluria, and instead, used the magic of the object to destroy itself. When River returned to the Ancient City, he found out one of his sisters had died trying to attack Ironhold. His father, the king, then exiled him. His other sister gave him a scrying mirror, through which he saw dragon lords confronting his father about the destruction of the human city. Forest denied having done it, but the king tried to attack the dragon lords and they isolated the city.

River, knowing that the city would not survive in isolation, found the dragon lords and asked them to investigate the destruction, claiming it might have been Ironhold. The dragon lords just told him to go back to his city. Stuck between the dragon lords' command and his father's exile, River got suspended in the hollow. Before that, he found a way to freeze in time everyone in the city, just to make sure they wouldn't die while being isolated.

In the Royal Fort in Umbraar, Fel fought Ironhold forces, who even had ironbringers, who melted the fort's gate. Still, Fel was able to defeat them using his metal magic. The problem was that, after the attackers were dead, they got up again and were hard to kill. Fel was alone outside the fort, using his metal magic to protect himself, but severely outnumbered.

Leah was called to Fel, appeared beside him, and called something from other worlds to help them.

Naia, now free, walked to the Ancient City. This time everyone was awake and she asked to see the king. He imprisoned her in a magical cell, claiming she was a dragon. Some strange, hooded fae, caused her imaginary pain. River sensed she was in danger and found her. In the magic cell, the king used the hooded fae to try to make him rip out Naia's heart. River then asked naia to order him to take her home. His life-debt magic kicked them back to their little house in the clearing. Understanding that she could make River do anything she wanted, Naia made him tell her what he'd been doing. He told her about the past, the staff, and the dragons, and told her that he was creating illusions for Ironhold, temporary illusions that would be undone in a few months.

Naia was upset for what he'd done to her, but released his life debt and told him that destroying was easier than creating, that a relationship took effort, and that she wanted to see him making that effort, which he promised he would do. She asked to go back to Umbraar and then he told her about the attack. Naia was understandably furious he hadn't told her anything, and convinced River to take her there. She saw Arry, Fel's friend, and asked him what happened.

Leah dreamed about Fel, human Fel, who said they could no longer be together because he was different now. She woke up on the back of a silver dragon: Fel, in his other form.

To everyone who's had the courage to forgive.

I

THE IRON DRAGON

Light gleamed on those marvelous, iridescent scales. Leah's dragon was real—and was flying over the rippling sea, headed to Fernick, that mysterious, unreachable continent. The feeling would be dream-like, if it weren't for her fears; her kingdom, her people, her mother, they were all in danger. And then she couldn't forget the dreadful deaths she had caused—without a single shred of remorse.

It's too late for us.

Fel's soft voice echoed in her ears. Too late.

Yes, seeing her dragon was a dream come true—if it didn't mean she could be losing human Fel. Leah rested her face on his scales, their pleasant, warm softness a caress on her cheek, as she breathed in his scent mixed with the salty air of the ocean. It was still him. But if he couldn't turn back, then there was no way they could ever be together again. No. They *were* together. His warmth, his presence, they were enough to soothe her. And if he was her dragon, it meant their bond was much deeper than she had ever imagined.

And yet. With no idea exactly where they were going, leaving so much behind, fearing her connection with whatever she had called from the hollow, everything was confusing and strange.

A loud boom startled her. Thunder. Leah raised her eyes and saw dark clouds covering the horizon and moving towards them. Odd. The sky had been clear not long before. This... There was something unnatural about it.

"Fel?" Her voice was shaky, revealing the fear that she hadn't dared acknowledge yet.

Underneath her, he emitted a low, guttural cry, as if letting her know that he could hear her, understand her.

A bolt of lightning cleared the sky, followed by a loud roar, and it was as if a monster was awakening, a darkness that had been hidden and was about to be unleashed. Leah sensed something evil in it, something lurking, waiting. Unless it was her own mind, her own memories and fears playing tricks on her.

Unlike in her dreams, dragon Fel had wings. Large, brilliant wings, and they were now beating frantically as he turned sideways and flew parallel to the direction of the coming dark clouds. He wasn't running from the storm. What was he doing? A tiny speck of brown ahead of them was her answer: he was looking for shelter. There was an island there. The issue was whether they'd make it in time.

Heavy wind hit her face and hair. Leah leaned closer, afraid of being blown off his back. Another low growl under her calmed her down. Her silver dragon was here. She should be safe, except for that strange feeling, that eerie sensation that there was something out there, something evil. And then there was an odd premonition that something was wrong. Very wrong, much worse than all that was happening in Aluria.

As the tiny island got closer and closer, the wind got heavier and heavier, those magnificent wings struggling against its force. Leah tried to hold tight but didn't want to pinch or hurt him. What would be her odds if she fell in that ocean? Would she be able to swim to the island? Or would the tumultuous waves swallow her?

Droplets, then drops of rain hit her face, right as they were approaching that small piece of land. Not even a hint of green in it, just a big chunk of rocks together. She had no idea how Fel had seen it.

Then, something hard hit her head. A pebble. No. Hail. Leah buried her face on his back and wished she could protect *his* face from the incoming pellets. The island was so close... But it had only rocks with rough, jagged edges. A crash landing could hurt him—a lot. And here she was, helpless, hoping and wishing it would be all right. And yet, this would not shelter them from the rain and storm, which was getting harder and harder, hitting her back with increasing force, feeling like wooden sticks beating her.

Fel landed with a thud on what was likely the only flat surface in that spiky, oversized rock. Leah tried to jump to the ground, but a wing caught her, softening her landing, then pushed her until she found herself underneath him, his body above her, protecting her.

His wings spread around them, forming a cocoon, and even though the ground was cold and wet, his heat warmed her. Leah ran her hand over his belly, which was covered with large, almost white scales, softer than the ones on his back. If she basked in his soothing presence, she could perhaps forget her dreadful memories, quell her lingering fears, ignore that strange storm. They were together, and for now, it was all that mattered.

A loud thunder disturbed Leah's serenity, bringing with it a cold prickle that ran down her neck. Cold, cold, a dreadful cold that chilled her to the bone.

And then a voice sounded in her head. Raspy and old, it made her hair stand on end. "The iron dragon. We found him."

Oh, no. No, no, no. There was something after Fel.

As much as she had access to power, she felt that it was exactly that power that had allowed that strange voice to find the *iron dragon.*

Years and years hearing her father's instructions about what to do in case of war hadn't prepared Naia to see its reality, hadn't prepared her to believe that this could happen in Umbraar.

All around the Royal Fort, bodies were being burned, some of them strange and inhuman. This hadn't been a full-scale invasion, but a targeted attack, an attempt to kill her brother and father—which meant Ironhold knew they had been here.

River had an arm around Naia, and she pushed it, then stepped away from him. He'd known about this attack—and had done nothing to warn her. Nothing. She glanced at him, or rather, glared. He looked different, not only because he had no horns, but also because his eyes were blue and his hair was a deep, dark brown, almost black.

As if sensing her surprise, he whispered, "There can always be spies..."

"Sure." She then turned to Arry, who was still standing in front of her. "Let's go to my father's office, then you can tell me everything."

Perhaps Arry was no longer such a good friend to her, but he was still close to Fel, and seemed to know what had happened, so he was the right person to talk to.

She looked at River. "Stay here." Yes, that had been an order, and he had better obey it.

Naia had to stop swooning for the handsome fae and keep her wits about her. If neither her brother nor father were here, she was the one in charge, and had to honor her position and her kingdom. Taking the lead, she climbed the stairs to the second floor in brisk steps, trying to smother her anger, calm down her fury—as if it was possible.

All her time spent with River had done nothing to protect her kingdom, her family. All his sweet words to her had never meant he was her ally. The worst was that she should have known it. She should have known it all, and yet she'd been fooled like a silly girl in love—an appropriate and utterly embarrassing description of her.

Ugh. For someone who had always wanted to do something that mattered, she'd proven her incompetence in the first test. Silly, silly, Naia. Her father's admonitions against stupid love were starting to make sense.

At least River had listened to her and remained behind. Naia turned to Arry once they reached the second floor. "Has the rest of the kingdom been warned?"

"They've been put on high alert, but there's no sign of any other attack." He sighed. "Yet."

Yet. That was the right word. Scary, right word.

The young man continued, "The wounded are being treated, and we have sentries looking for more intruders. Your brother set it up well before he... he left."

It was so unlike Fel. And her father, gone? Again, so strange.

They arrived in front of the thick wooden door leading to her father's office. It had a combination lock, made so that it would always be accessible to Fel and Naia if the need came, as this was another place from where the king oversaw Umbraar and connected with potential allies. It was the first time she was turning this lock in more than a year, as she hadn't been here recently. More and more her father had discouraged her from coming to the fort. Even Fel, who once had been obsessed with weapons, lately had been more interested in staying home and practicing his magic around the manor.

But now she was back—and had to do her best to defend her kingdom.

Naia got in, took her place at her father's desk, then pointed to a chair, where Arry sat.

When she rested her hands on the table, she realized they were shaking. Fear, anger, horror, so many mixed emotions. Most of all, she had to know where her brother and father were. "What happened to Fel?"

"Uh..." Arry sucked in a breath. "It's a little complicated."

"No, it's not." She hated to be harsh with someone she used to consider a friend, but she wasn't going to sit here waiting to hear a long story while worry gnawed on her insides. "Is he dead?" Her voice almost cracked with that dreadful thought, that dreadful question. Arry had told her Fel was alive, but she wanted to be sure. "Hurt?"

"He's alive and not hurt, but..."

As she exhaled in relief, a figure appeared on the corner of the office, behind her brother's friend. River, of course, standing there, unglamoured, his eyes their usual reddish-brown, his horns showing. Naia grabbed a small book and threw it in his direction, but he dodged it. Prick. He should have been thankful she hadn't thrown a paperweight or a blast of fire.

Arry turned to check what she was staring at, then faced her, a puzzled expression on his face. "Something wrong?" So he hadn't seen anything.

Naia had no idea River could turn invisible, which only added to the list of many things she didn't know.

"A lot," she replied. "People are told to stay away and they don't."

Arry got up. "I apologize."

"Not you," Naia said quickly. "Sit. Tell me everything."

He sat down, his eyes wide. Naia schooled her expression not to appear so angry, as Arry was clearly misunderstanding her. River was no longer across the room and Naia exhaled, but then she felt someone touching her shoulder.

"No secrets," River whispered in her ear. What a hypocrite.

If she weren't in such dire need to hear Arry's explanation, she would do anything she could to send River away, but she didn't have time for that now.

Arry narrowed his eyes and glanced beside her. Could he see River? Or maybe it was because she had just glared in that direction.

The boy sighed. He had very light brown hair, almost gold, and a nice face. It was still odd to think that at some point in the past Naia had thought about him in a different way, not only like a family friend. That past didn't make any sense now.

He cleared his throat. "I'll start from the beginning, if you don't mind."

"I do, actually." She tried to sound calmer. "Start by telling me what happened to Fel." She then added, "Please."

Arry stared at her for a moment, then blurted, "He turned into a dragon and left."

"A... dragon?" She swallowed. "You mean a... big... animal?" He couldn't possibly mean that. This talk of dragons was bizarre enough if they were just these dragon lords whatever, but real dragons?

"With scales, claws, wings," Arry added.

It couldn't be. It made no sense. "How did you know it was my brother?"

"He sent me a thought, saying he was in his other form, and that he was leaving with the Frostlake princess."

Leandra? What was she even doing here? "And you believed what this thought said?"

"It was him, Naia. I know Fel."

Her heart was thumping in her chest. This still didn't make sense. Arry could be confused. "Did anyone else see this dragon?"

"Some people saw him burning the demons."

This was getting strange. "Demons?"

"They were attacking the, uh... reawakened dead ironbringer army."

More than strange. "The what now?"

Arry sat back. "Maybe I should start from the beginning."

"Fine. And what about my father? Where is he?" Perhaps it was true that he wasn't Naia's real father, but it didn't mean she didn't worry about him.

"He left last night, traveled somewhere. Fel didn't tell me where."

"Did my brother know where he went?"

"I think so, but I think it was a secret or something. Fel wasn't too worried about him, so maybe he wasn't expected to return yet."

Strange. Where had her father gone? And why? It meant that Ironhold had attacked Umbraar when he wasn't here. It could be that this had been a plan to keep him away from his kingdom, so that he wouldn't use his magic against his attackers. What was strange was her father not returning yet. Her chest tightened with worry. No, he had to be fine. Perhaps he had planned to be gone for a couple of days. Still, he should have a communication mirror. Oh, if only she could speak to her brother!

Arry then told her that Fel had raised an alarm at night, and it had been a good thing, as in the early morning, a large group of soldiers approached the Royal Fort, attacking it with some strange curving metal arrows, then melting the gate, meaning that they had ironbringers among them. Still, Fel defeated them. After the attackers were dead, though, they got up again, even if they had parts of their bodies missing.

Naia almost interrupted him, saying the dead couldn't be raised, but he sounded sincere, startled, and as surprised and shocked as anyone would be when facing the impossible. He continued telling her that Fel had remained outside the fort, by himself, and even if Arry tried to help him, it was hard to get close. Their men were trying their best to fight off the attacking dead bodies, but only fire could defeat them.

"Fire?" Naia breathed out.

She clenched her fists and turned to where River had been, wondering if he was still there, wondering if he was aware that her magic could have helped her brother and Umbraar's soldiers, except it hadn't because she hadn't been here. All because River had never bothered to warn her about the danger her brother had just faced.

"Yes," Arry said. "Then, after that, everything went dark. It was odd. Some... creatures came, and took care of the Ironhold soldiers, the ones who were already dead. They were helping us, I know, but there was some odd magic in the air, something old, eerie. It was otherworldly, and I know that a dead army reawakening is strange enough, but just remembering those creatures makes my hairs stand on end. Not that I'm a coward."

"What were they?"

"I'm not sure. I'm saying demons because that's what I think they were, but I have no idea where they came from or how they got here. Then there was darkness, and instead of Fel there was a dragon, and he burned them."

"Weren't they on our side?"

"In theory, yes, but I'm not sure if they would remain there. It's hard to explain. Then Fel flew away, with the princess."

Naia frowned. "What was she doing here?"

"She wasn't here when the battle was going on. She just... She appeared. With the creatures, I'd say, but that might be nonsense."

The Frostlake Princess' awful words to Fel still felt like nails grating on Naia's skin. "And you're sure he carried her away? Didn't eat her?"

Arry chuckled. "Your brother would never hurt his princess."

"His?"

He shrugged. "Your brother likes her."

"But is it the other way around?"

"There must have been a reason she came here. Either way, I don't know. You'll need to ask Fel."

Naia took a deep breath and rested her face on her hands. "How am I even going to talk to him?" Was it even him? Would he be able to talk? Would he ever be human again? Too many questions and worries in her mind.

"I don't have that answer." He sighed, then put a pouch on the table. When he opened it, the content surprised Naia. Fel's hands. His old ones. "I picked them up."

She frowned. "These were not the ones he used."

"Yes... I mean... The other ones got melted when the iron-bringer assassins tried to catch him." He must have noticed Naia's puzzled expression, as he added, "It was a few days before this attack, but Fel killed them. He then asked your father to announce he was dead. As a precaution."

Naia swallowed. Assassins sent to kill her brother? All this going on while she'd been kept away in that house with River, who had to know all this, and yet had never said a word. Not a single word. And now he was invisible, just to make her even angrier.

"Fel is fine," Arry said, as if sensing her worry.

"Is he? A dragon, you said." And then maybe it wasn't Fel at all, but something else. Maybe he was gone. So many dreadful maybes. "You didn't even see him transform."

"I don't think it was a transformation, but something else. He sounded fine. I know him, Irinaia. It was him. And we won the battle."

"And yet war might be upon us."

Arry took a deep breath, and didn't conceal the worry in his eyes. "It might."

"Thank you. For telling me everything. And getting my brother's hands. I... need a moment now. Alone. Not that I'm telling you to leave, but—"

"It's fine." Arry was already up and heading to the door. "I'll be around. If you need me."

Naia managed a smile as she watched the boy that had once been her dream walk out the door, meanwhile making a heroic effort to keep herself from setting the office on fire.

Once the door was closed, she growled, "River."

He appeared in front of her before she even finished saying his name. All of his playfulness and mischief were gone, replaced by a look that she'd call apologetic, if she thought he was capable of something like that.

"I did not know. I didn't, Naia." His voice was soft. "I thought they were sending just a normal army. I thought your father and your brother would defeat them easily. Well, your brother did defeat them. I—"

"They needed fire. Fire, River. Do you understand what it

means? My brother could have died and I wasn't here to help him, when I could have made all the difference. Do you have any idea what it feels like?"

His expression darkened. "No idea? You forget I lost a sister."

True. He had told her that, and yet she hadn't stopped to consider what it meant for him. It must have been horrible. "I'm truly sorry for your sister. I..." She looked down. "Don't know what to say."

"Some wounds never heal. That's just how it is." His voice was clipped, as if he wanted to end the subject. He then sighed and looked at her. "I understand what you're saying. Your power could have helped your brother and yet you couldn't do anything because you weren't here and you think it's my fault."

"I don't *think*. It *is* your fault." She wasn't as furious as before, but she knew that what he'd done to her was wrong.

River ran a hand over his hair. "You would have been in your house, Naia. You didn't even come here much, did you?"

She had no idea how he knew that. "I could have come here if I knew about this. You could have warned me. You could have warned my brother."

"Your brother was more than well prepared for Ironhold. He even knew they were going to have ironbringers. Umbraar had weapons without metal. Ironhold didn't know that, and didn't know he was alive. They still haven't grasped how powerful your brother is, not to mention that they don't realize the extent of your, uh, King Azir's power. Ironhold's pathetic attack would be stopped easily and I wasn't worried. Except I never knew it would come to this. I had no idea your father wouldn't be here. I had no idea a dead army could be raised. I never knew dragons, like real dragons, still existed. To my knowledge, 'dragons' were just a fancy name for magical humans. I didn't know demons or whatever would show up. I knew none of this."

"You still could have told me. Could have warned my brother. Could have warned him about the assassins, at least."

River sighed. "I *came* here. I spoke to Isofel."

"You did? And didn't tell me."

"I promised I'd keep him safe and I don't break my promises. I think it should be obvious I wouldn't allow your brother to be in danger."

"He almost died. He's a dragon now."

"I didn't know any of that." River threw his hands in the air. "I can't prevent what I don't know."

Naia scoffed. "Then what's the point of going to Ironhold? Of helping them? Because I know you're helping them. And yet they aren't telling you a thing. You're being used and played, River, which is ridiculous for a fae."

He scoffed. "Of course they think they're using and fooling me. That's obvious. That's how deals between enemies work: each side thinks they're tricking the other. And yet I found a way in. A way to figure out their magic, find their secrets."

"Certainly." She rolled her eyes. "You know everything about them, except their most bizarre magic or their battle secrets. Not that you'd share any of that, of course."

"I knew they had an ironbringer army, for example."

"Did you bother telling my brother that?"

River shrugged. "He was ready and didn't need any warning."

Naia took a deep breath. Getting angry wasn't going to help her find a solution. "What exactly have you been doing there, River? What you did just now? Listening while invisible?"

He sighed. "It's too risky. There's a high chance they could sense me. Then I'd be dead, and with me all my revenge plans."

Naia glared at him. "I see. Your revenge would be the only loss if you died. Nobody would miss you."

He looked down, then back at her. "I didn't mean that."

"Don't go back there. If they're withholding dangerous, unknown magic from you, you literally don't know what they're capable of, you don't know what their true plans are, you don't know anything. They're playing you. Don't get played."

"I know they have strange magic. That I know, even if I don't have the details. And I am always careful. Now, I need to find some proof they destroyed Formosa. I know it was them. And I think they have a dragon heart. I need to find it."

He'd mentioned the annihilated Umbraar city before, but Naia wasn't so sure it had been Ironhold. "The destruction of Formosa ruined the trade for all kingdoms in Aluria. Ironhold was the one that lost the most, since they traded gold with Fernick. Why would they destroy that city?"

"They probably thought they could control the way to Fernick instead of Umbraar, using their weapons."

"Except they don't. Also, I don't think they have a dragon heart. See, if it's true that my real father is a dragon, and that our hearts are special, Ironhold wouldn't have let me and Fel go, they wouldn't have given us to Umbraar."

"But they think King Azir is your father. They have no idea you're dragons."

"Yes, but... If they captured my father, let's say, then got his heart, they would have known what we are."

"Three dragons came from Fernick, Naia. They could have captured any one of them."

"They didn't, River. Think with me. You said the dragons came here after Formosa was destroyed. It means they have some way to know what goes on in Aluria, and some way to travel. If one of them or all of them had been murdered, wouldn't other dragons have come here to investigate?"

River shrugged. "Maybe not. I don't know."

"When your father captured me, he thought the dragons would sense my suffering and come. If that's true—"

"It might have been an assumption. He doesn't know much more than I do."

"He knew I was a dragon. I mean... If that's even true. But you didn't." There was still a part of her that resisted that thought, but she wasn't going to figure out anything if she denied the reality that had been presented to her.

River scoffed. "I didn't even realize you were an *ironbringer* when I first met you. There were too many feelings going on for me to sense your magic."

She caught a breath, but then recovered quickly. "You didn't know *my brother* was a dragon."

River paused. "True, but listen: only royal families in Aluria are supposed to have magic. It means that it doesn't pass on to the third generation. The dragons are the arbiters of magic in the world, so I think they are the ones keeping the human magic contained. Now, Ironhold is breeding third-generation iron-bringers, not from the royal family. To dodge such a law... they need something."

"And to raise the dead. Yes, something, for sure, but I don't think it's a dragon heart, River."

"I'll find out."

"You won't. Don't you dare go back there."

He shook his head. "It will be quick, and I'll be careful. First I'll take you home—"

"No. *This* is my home. I need to take care of Umbraar, don't you see?"

He sighed. "They might attack again."

"Then I'll be here and burn them all. Maybe you'll even bother to let me know about their plans in advance. In fact, what are they planning?"

"Not hard to guess, is it?"

"I know they want power. But how? How are they going to do it? Don't tell me you don't know anything."

River shrugged. "It's still pretty obvious. They are not that subtle."

"I know that they want to unite Aluria against the fae, or use the fae as an excuse to seize power. So what was the point of this weird magic here? Not even bothering to pretend it was the fae?" River was about to say something, when an idea hit her. "Wait. I know. They want us isolated. They want us ranting against Iron-hold while everyone is praising them for fighting the fae. That way they can attack us. And this magic..." An odd thought came to her. "It was a test. To see how much they could bend human magic."

He nodded. "That's a possibility." Then he sighed. "I have to go back before they notice I'm gone."

Naia got up and moved around the desk so that she wouldn't have it between her and River. "Don't go. I'm asking you."

She was definitely regretting having ended his promise of eternal devotion. Why hadn't she thought this through?

He set his reddish eyes on her. "I'm asking you not to stay here at this obvious target, but you're not listening either, are you?"

"I have to protect my people."

"So do I."

"River, what about the Ancient City? We need to do something. It's all dry. There's no way they'll survive long there."

"Dry," he repeated, thoughtful. "It wasn't like that before."

"Can you use the lapse stones again on the city?"

He closed his eyes, visibly distraught. "When I used them the first time, somehow my magic combined with the dragon magic isolating the city. That magic is broken now. And the stones are gone."

"But then the Ancient City should no longer be isolated."

He looked at her. "It doesn't look like they can get out."

"We need to find a solution."

"*I* need to find a solution. But I need to get back to Ironhold. We can discuss this later, Naia. Whatever happens, can you try to stay out of harm's way?"

"I'll be careful, but I won't cower or hide. That wouldn't be me."

He took a deep breath. "I'll be back soon."

Naia reached out and held his hand. "Don't go there. Tell me everything you've found out until now. We'll work with the information you already got. We'll figure out something. Together." She then added, "Please. Don't go."

He put his other hand over hers and caressed it. "We will find a solution. But I have to go."

She was still angry at him, angry that he hadn't told her any of that, and yet, at that moment, all she felt was a pang in her chest, a fear of never seeing him again, a horrible dread taking over her. She tiptoed and kissed his lips softly, then said, "Stay."

His arms wrapped around her and pulled her close, and then he kissed her, but this time there was nothing soft or hesitant about his movements. It was the deep, lasting kiss they hadn't had since he had forced her to sleep.

Oh, why had this memory intruded in this moment?

Naia pushed him. "I'm still upset at all the secrets you kept, and for enchanting me. But I know we'll fix this. Together. Stay."

He kissed her cheek and smiled. "I'll be right back. You doubled my motivation, Naia. Let me just figure out what's going on."

Naia wished *she* could make him sleep, wished she could keep him from risking his life, which was a horrible way to understand his dreadful actions. And yet, she watched quietly as he disappeared. She'd need to ask him how he did that, how he traveled so seamlessly to and from anywhere, without the need of faerie rings.

No, she'd need to find a way to convince him never to set foot in Ironhold again—before it was too late.

River slipped easily into the hollow, leaving Naia behind him, aware that he was able to contradict one of her direct requests for the first time—and hating it. Hating this entire situation. After all he had done to her, all he had hidden, she still asked for him to stay, despite all her anger.

He paused and shut his eyes tight. Of course he wanted to stay with Naia. Working with Ironhold was always a risk, and bound to get riskier the less that kingdom relied on his services. Aluria already believed in a new "white fae" invasion and while River's illusions could help keep up the charade, Ironhold could decide to use force just as well. What kept him somewhat assured was his deal with the king. Breaking a deal with an Ancient incurred a high price, and the humans still knew it.

The price would cause the destruction of Ironhold, and River could almost be happy about it, except that he had someone to come back to, a city to protect, and so much more to juggle than he had ever dreamed. And yet more than ever he had to find out what kind of magic they were using, how they were circumventing Aluria's laws. Not only that, they were also breaking magic rules and so far no dragon had come to see if anything was amiss, no dragon since Formosa had been destroyed.

It felt as if they had vanished—leaving his city isolated, forgotten. A lot of his anger towards the dragons had lessened once he realized Naia was one of them. It was still hard to believe it, hard to be sure, but if Isofel had turned into a dragon, it had to be true.

Still, that only opened questions: who was her father? Why had he left? Or had he been killed? But if that had been the case, shouldn't it have drawn the ire of the dragons? Unless something had happened to them. In this case, it was still possible that Ironhold had one or more dragon hearts. If not that, then the metal kingdom had something else—and he had to find it.

2

BACK TO IRONHOLD

The world was an explosion of smells and sounds. Fel had no idea he could feel and sense so much, but then he had no idea he had access to this other form, so strong that even the thunderous hail couldn't hurt him. Here he was, on this tiny island surrounded by a gray and furious ocean. Beneath him, Leah sat, suddenly scared, so tiny and human. Close and apart.

Her fear, though, that was something else, and it wasn't just the storm and all that they'd been through. He sent a thought to Leah, even if he wasn't sure she'd realize he was trying to communicate with her. "What's wrong?"

"Something's after you," she said, her voice low. "Don't tell anyone about your magic. Your human magic. I... I have to go. I'll find you. But I have to go."

Fel didn't even have the time to ask *why* or *where* before she disappeared. No time to try to ask her to stay, to tell her that they would solve it all together. Now he had no idea where she was, no idea how to keep her safe.

All he had was a hole in his heart as he lay down on the wet ground on that lonely island, away from his sister, his kingdom, his father. And yet, how much could he do when he had no control over his form, no idea about any of his dragon magic?

The rain quieted down and a path of clear sky appeared over the horizon, as if Leah had taken the storm with her. But where? They had taken so long to be together, only for her to disappear like that.

He stared at the clearing sky up ahead. Would he be able to make it to Fernick? Would he even find other dragons? Or should he come back, at least for now, and help his sister, his father, his kingdom? But how much could he do while in this form? There was only uncertainty and too many things that needed to be fixed, and yet he had no idea how to start.

RIVER WAS BACK IN FROSTLAKE. He'd spent so long trying to fool Ironhold, pretending he was their ally, and yet, right after they had taken a kingdom, in a decisive moment, he had left. Of course he would do it all over again—to save Naia. Hopefully King Harold hadn't noticed his absence.

That was foolish and nonsensical hope. Of course the king knew he'd been away, even if it hadn't been that long. Two hours at most, but still. The question was what the king was going to do with this information.

River approached his station, his hair tied back, his Ironhold uniform looking neat and tidy, glamour hiding the red in his eyes, his horns, and the shape of his ears. The general who'd been questioning castle workers was gone, and only two Ironhold soldiers remained. Like many of the invading forces, they were convinced that their kingdom was being heroic and saving Frostlake.

They both got up when they saw River.

"General Waters," one of them said, as a form of greeting. That was a stupid name, but since Ancients didn't do well with lies, at least it was close enough not to cause much discomfort.

"Is the questioning over?"

The soldiers looked at each other, then one of them said, "There's a message for you to see the king."

"Certainly."

River was about to go into the castle, when a soldier added, "Back in Ironhold."

"Understood."

This return to Ironhold surprised River. King Harold had been away for a while, traveling from kingdom to kingdom, gaining allies, or rather, weaving lies, sometimes with River's help. That king had no idea how poisoned this help was, how it was set to backfire in a few months. Of course, an ambitious man like that delighted in feeling invincible, strong, in thinking that the Ancients were cowering, hiding, and under Ironhold control.

King Harold's ultimate plan was the annihilation of River's people, but it didn't matter. River could pretend he was being played, being fooled. He was biding his time. The only issue was that now his city had awakened, and time was something he no longer had.

Ancients traveled from circle to circle, and so did River, except that he could create bigger circles and move within them. For Frostlake, it had been quite easy, as the dome around the city provided the material anchor for his magic.

The Iron Citadel was also quite easy, surrounded by a cliff, which also worked as a circle. Umbraar was harder, but he had an entry point near the manor and another near the Royal Fort, the places where the twins could be found, and managed to enlarge his circles. This wasn't something most Ancients could do, and it reminded him of his father's words about his *wasted potential*. He was trying to make it right now, even if any craving for his father's acceptance had been replaced by repulsion, loathing, and disgust. No, he couldn't let those ugly feelings take over his mind, and yet, the memory of Naia in pain, of what his father had tried to make River do, those images would never go away.

Still, here he was, trying to unravel Ironhold's secrets, trying to do what was within his reach, as the sole Ancient not confined to their city, probably the only Ancient immune to iron magic.

Despite being able to move within the Iron Citadel, River usually came to a small circle close to it, which had been reactivated for him. He didn't want them to know how much he could do, or it would ruin his plans. That was how he found himself crossing one of their bottomless bridges. It had railings on the sides, but it still had a view of the pit beneath it, something grotesque and unnatural, dug much deeper than anything should be dug. There was magic there. He'd always thought that his discomfort was because it was metal magic, but now he wasn't as sure, and felt his hairs rising as he wondered what was down below.

After the first gate, he moved to the entrance reserved for castle staff, a normal-sized bronze door. The bronze reminded him of his city, of his past long gone, and yet coming here always reminded him of his sister, always made him wonder if her departure from this world had been painful, and if it had been mixed with fear, horror, regret, or anything of the sort. Dying was certainly better than being taken captive, depending on the adversary, but it still hurt so much that she was gone. Gone for almost twenty years now, and he hadn't even had time to grieve. His father and siblings hadn't grieved either. Perhaps that should be a reason to try to understand his father, but no, he'd told him Naia was his life companion, and still King Spring insisted on hurting her. River no longer considered him his father.

River brushed all these thoughts away as he stepped into the king's antechamber. He had many rooms for meetings, audiences, and conferences. This was one of his most private ones, but it was where he usually spoke to River. It felt like yesterday that he'd first come here, with a faint hope, a half-formed plan, but also the certainty that the only way to defeat such a formidable enemy was by getting close enough to stab them from behind. His thoughts had been marred with bitterness and revenge, after so much loss and death, after his only spark of hope had ended in a poisoned kiss. A poisoned kiss that had made him stronger, insensitive to iron magic and iron, if not completely immune to them, a strength that had given him this insane idea, that had led him to this moment.

River stared as the door opened, and he stepped into King Harold's magic room. This was a huge, windowless chamber, surrounded by metal walls, the magic in them thrumming in the air. A polished black granite floor reflected the light from sconces on the walls, while some fifty white pedestals supported relics from Aluria and other places. River had never truly looked at what was in this magic chamber, as he didn't want to appear curious. There was no place to sit here, which was a good reminder that this was not a room for pleasant conversation, but a place where one should remain alert.

Two guards stood by the walls, wearing helmets covering their faces. River was glamoured, and found the king examining a mask.

When King Harold turned and noticed him, River bowed. "Your majesty."

The king looked at the mask again. "You're not curious why I'm back in Ironhold?"

As always, River kept his composure calm and his voice steady. "I don't believe it concerns me."

The king chuckled. One thing that River found odd was that he couldn't sense any bizarre magic in him. Sure, the man was evil, perhaps nefarious, but the only magic River sensed in him was metal, which wasn't unnatural in Ironhold, and certainly shouldn't make the dead rise again. There had been another magic at work in Umbraar, but he sensed no trace of it on this king.

"Any idea?"

There was likely a reason why the king was trying to probe him, but River didn't let it faze him. "Frostlake was a clear victory and you're satisfied with our work there, I assume?"

"What would you say about Umbraar?"

"Are you going to tell me about your victory?" Questions were open enough that there was a lot of room for hiding the truth, and that was one reason why River liked them so much.

The king narrowed his eyes. "Victory? So you don't know what happened?"

"I'm waiting for you to tell me."

He chuckled again. "So you can't lie, right? Tell me then, did we win or lose?"

"I can't guess things, your highness. What I can't do is contradict my thoughts, perceptions, and beliefs with my words, but I'm not omniscient. That said, I can notice that your highness is strangely uneasy—"

"Cut the crap, will you? Do you know anything about demons? Dragons?" His voice was partly mocking.

River's stomach sank, even if he showed no reaction. He hadn't considered that Ironhold must have had spies watching the battle from a distance, and hadn't considered what it could mean for Naia if they found out her brother was a dragon. If only River had thought better about it, he could have found Ironhold's informant, could have even changed their memories. Now it was too late. "Perhaps Your Majesty might want to get straight to the point?"

The king eyed River attentively. "Indeed. First of all, they were prepared. They had wooden weapons. Not only that, they were ready. They were ready for our attack hours before we got there."

"I see."

"You know what I see? Someone informed them. Someone who can move fast."

River pretended to ignore the implied accusation. "A person with a communication mirror could also be an informant, or else Umbraar predicted Ironhold's move."

"I think *you* informed them."

"I didn't. I couldn't even if I wanted to. Our bargain states that I can't share plans—"

"Perhaps you're lying about the bargain. Perhaps you broke it."

"Why would I inform Umbraar? What would I gain from that?"

The king shrugged. "Allies, territory, food. What do I know? Do you want to tell me?"

"I did not inform them of Ironhold's attack. I made a promise, and I can't break it."

"And yet, they were ready. They had wooden weapons and fire weapons, to counteract our... soldiers. They also had some strange animals, even a dragon. You know what that means?"

"Unusual magic?"

"Illusions, Mister Waters. Now, who here can create these illusions?"

River was so relieved at this bizarre theory that he almost showed his feelings by exhaling, but caught himself in time. "I can create illusions, but I was not in Umbraar during this battle."

"And yet you were not in Frostlake, like you should have been."

"I fulfilled my duty there. If there's anything that you believe should be done better—"

The king waved a hand. "It's a matter of trust, Waters. Perhaps we need to be sure that you won't go anywhere, that's all. As a way to solidify our pact."

"A deal with a fae works both ways, your majesty. I'm bound to it." This was a subtle reminder that the king was also bound by it. Perhaps he knew it to a certain extent, or he wouldn't feel so comfortable being alone with him, with guards that were way too far to react in time if River decided to do anything. Or perhaps he didn't know how fast an Ancient could move.

"True." The king had a smile that didn't reach his eyes. "But you break it a little, I break it a little, and we still keep our alliance intact. I'll have Aluria, and I'll leave Umbraar for the remaining of your people. Meanwhile, I want to make sure I know where one of my dearest allies is. As a matter of trust. Follow me."

The king moved to the end of the room, where he opened a door. There was a room inside, with a partition and a private area, as well as a jar with water, a glass, and some bread and fruit.

"We made it comfortable, and hope you appreciate our hospitality."

"My new quarters?" River hadn't been in his old ones for a long time, not since he'd left Isofel's girl there, but she had already escaped without his help. Now, this was an iron cage, meant to weaken a fae's magic and prevent them from using circles. Certainly not the worst punishment that could be inflicted on him, and quite predictable. "They look fine, but I hope your majesty understands it's a breach of our deal."

The king put his thumb and index finger together. "A small breach, Waters. Let's agree I'm being lenient. And you'll be comfortable here."

"Very well."

"Unless... Would you care to explain what happened in Umbraar?"

"I was not there during the battle."

"Fair, then. You might want to rest." The king gestured for him to walk in, which he did, then closed the door.

River was a prisoner, caught in Ironhold's clutches. As much as had known this day would come, he wasn't expecting it to be so early.

As angry as Naia was with River, it still hurt to see him leave, to watch him go somewhere so dangerous. The fear of losing him was overwhelming. Fear of losing him. It sent her a clear message on whether she wanted him or not. Ugh. Of course she wanted him, but she wanted to be sure she could trust him, she wanted to be sure he wouldn't hide things from her again, and maybe she wanted him to know she wasn't going to tolerate that crap again.

But with so much going on in Umbraar, this was not the time

to spare any more thoughts for River—at least for now. Her kingdom was in crisis, and with no sign of her brother or father anywhere, it was up to her to think about the next steps.

What was Ironhold expecting? They must have had a goal in attacking Umbraar. Would they have wanted to kill King Azir? Maybe. But they would have known he could have escaped. Kings often had special places to hide or some kind of procedure in case things went wrong in battle. Umbraar didn't do that, but Ironhold wouldn't know it. They wouldn't be sure that they would have killed the king. Had they wanted him dead, they would have sent assassins.

Assassins. They had sent them. For her brother! But why? Iron magic, of course. If they had ironbringers and wanted to count on the superiority of their magic, they couldn't have more people wielding it.

Naia sat and tapped her nails on the desk. What had been the point of the attack? Perhaps she would never know that answer. What would her father do?

That was the answer! Not the right answer, but it was what Ironhold would be expecting—something King Azir would do. Would he ask for help? Would he tell other kingdoms? She didn't think so. Umbraar was the only kingdom without an Ironhold delegation, the only kingdom who hadn't accepted their help.

There was no way to know if what Naia was about to do was right or wrong, but she'd always heard that kings sometimes had to act with their gut.

She got up and went to the communication mirror, which hung on a wall in her father's office, and pressed her palm on it, hoping it would still work, hoping her father hadn't removed her authorization when he had disowned her. Her stomach sank as the mirror showed only her own image, with no sign of magic. Perhaps she had been excluded from the royal family, and if that was the case, it was going to be a big problem.

And yet she kept watching the mirror, her hand stuck on it, hoping that it would work for her, hoping she wouldn't just sit here like a useless fool while important pieces were being moved in Aluria.

She took a better look. There was a faint blue glow by her hand. Relief washed over her as she saw the glow growing and growing, until she could no longer see any reflection, just a source of light. These mirrors were very old, and said to be made from dragon magic. Most of her life she suspected that maybe it was just some kind of forgotten magic, and they said it came from the dragons just to make it seem more special and mysterious, and to justify why they couldn't understand or replicate it. Now she wasn't sure. Perhaps there was dragon magic in that mirror, which only opened a dam of questions about her own power.

But what she had to do now was try to play the diplomat.

"Ironhold," she said. Yes, she was about to contact the kingdom who was their enemy, the kingdom River was spying on.

After many seconds, she repeated, "Ironhold," then added, "This is a request from Umbraar."

There was only silence answering her, which was normal. No king would spend all day in front of the mirror. That said, in this case, they should be watching it closely, which meant she should get a reply soon.

Meanwhile, she had to try another kingdom. She decided to try one of the non-magical ones. "Varana."

Instead of the blue light and silence, Naia was greeted by a man in his forties with a thin beard. The king.

He frowned. "Who are you?"

"Umbraar's princess, your majesty. My father, King Azir, is ill right now and I'm taking his place trying to alert Aluria."

"Were you attacked as well?"

As well? What did he mean? "You're the first king I'm speaking to. I don't know of any attacks other than here."

"Frostlake. I just received a message this morning. The fae were there, killed the king and queen."

Naia's heart was about to stop—or explode. Fae in Frostlake?

This had to be River's illusions. And in Frostlake? That didn't make any sense. They were allies.

The Varana king then said, "So you *were* attacked."

She nodded, trying to gather her thoughts and speak at the same time. "We think it might have been the fae, but this is why I'm contacting everyone and why it's so urgent; they were dressed in Ironhold garb." Naia almost choked on the stupid lie she was saying.

The king's frown had to be the longest lasting she had ever seen, but it got even deeper. "Why would they do that?"

"I'm not privy to their motivations, but if I were to venture a guess, I'd say they want to seed mistrust and conflict among us, they want to weaken us." There. She was anticipating what Ironhold could accuse Umbraar of doing, and making the first move.

"How do you know it was the white fae?"

"It's an assumption. Who else could it be?" She managed to make it sound natural, and not sarcastic. "It's an alert, too. If you see forces from Ironhold, or any other friendly kingdom, you need to pay attention."

"Who's friendly to us? Does anyone care about us?" he snapped.

Naia was surprised, even though she shouldn't be. She knew well that these kingdoms were always neglected in terms of diplomacy. Still, she pretended she didn't hear the accusation in the man's tone. "All human kingdoms are allies, isn't that right?"

The king burst into laughter. "Great allies. And what is it you want, girl?"

"Nothing. I just figured other kingdoms should be warned."

"Warned not to trust Ironhold? Hmmm." He then seemed concerned rather than annoyed. "How are you doing? Did you sustain any losses?"

"We managed to defeat them, at great cost for us, but they have been neutralized."

"Is your king alive?"

"He's sick." Naia had to clear her throat, an annoying itch bothering her.

"Sick, I see." The king was probably assuming he'd sustained injuries in the battle, which would have made a lot of sense. He then looked up, thinking. "How many fae attacked you?"

This was getting more complicated than she had expected. "I wasn't here, but I'm assuming some fifty, one hundred soldiers. They came to a fort. We had the advantage of height and walls."

"So you defeated fifty fae. Or one hundred. Who can even tell the difference?" He snapped his fingers. "Like that."

Was he doubting her? "With many losses, your majesty."

"I'll keep that in mind. You know, I hope to hear more from your kingdom."

"I have the same hope, except that next time we speak, I'd rather bring some good news. Now, if you don't mind, I need to warn other kingdoms."

"Understood. This contact can be severed."

The mirror returned to its blue glow. Interesting and shocking. Frostlake attacked. By "fae". Fae weren't attacking anyone. Those were River's illusions. Another thing he hadn't told her. The prick. And here she was, all worried about him. Perhaps he wasn't even going to Ironhold but to some other kingdom.

Why would Ironhold attack their allies? Unless... The Frostlake princess had come to Umbraar, and yet she was married to one of the Ironhold princes. It could be some sort of retaliation. Awful, unfair retaliation. Or else the idea was really to hide Ironhold's guilt. If they only attacked their enemies, it would be too obvious. They were planning something, and Naia had no idea what it was. No idea, even though she'd been literally living with someone working for Ironhold. Sometimes she really wanted to strangle River.

Regardless, Ironhold was making their move. If Naia's intuition was correct, they were looking for an excuse to call Umbraar traitors and retaliate against them—this time officially, perhaps even with the help of other kingdoms. Naia had to reach them first.

She tried Haven, Karsal, and Greenstone, and had no reply. When she tried Vastfield, a young man replied, one of the princes. They were a greenbringer kingdom, and bordered Umbraar on the north. Naia told the prince the story of the fae looking like Ironhold attacking Umbraar.

He listened to it stoically, then asked, "How can I know it's true?"

"I'm giving you my word."

The prince wasn't moved or convinced. "Perhaps you want to sow doubt and confusion in Aluria."

Great. He was calling her a liar now? "Of course not. If you have an Ironhold retinue, you know they're helping you. I mean in your borders or something, if you find people you don't know. They could be disguised fae."

He nodded. "I'll tell my father. Do you need any assistance?"

She knew that it was just a polite question.

"We are fine for now, but please be careful. They came from our Northern forests."

"Why wouldn't they dress as Vastfield soldiers, then, since they came from that direction?" His tone was mocking.

"Everyone knows Umbraar and Ironhold have had disagreements in the past, because of my father. It's more realistic."

He raised an eyebrow. "And the fae are privy to that information?"

"I don't know. If Ironhold had no reason to attack us like that, that leaves only one answer."

"Did you see them? Fae? Blond hair, pointy ears?"

"I wasn't here. The bodies were burned. They looked human."

"Well, then, there's another explanation."

No kidding. But Naia just blinked. "I don't follow."

"What if it was Ironhold?" the Vastfield prince suggested. Dangerous words.

Was this a test? "I already explained why it's unlikely."

"A lot is unlikely, princess, but I will pass on your information. Is that all?"

"Yes. The contact can be severed."

She managed to reach Wildspring, a wildbringing kingdom. It was an attendant who replied, and all he did was take note of what she said. Karsal then contacted her. Naia was still embarrassed that his brother had talked so much to their princess when he had never meant to propose. It was a reminder that even her sweet brother could be cruel. Well, she hadn't heard him making any promises. The Karsal king came to the mirror, and listened to her attentively, without interruption.

He was thoughtful. "Do you have proof that this happened? I'm not doubting you. It's a question."

"There are bodies here, and some burned uniforms."

He looked away. "And what's the proof it was the fae?"

Naia paused, trying to come up with some explanation, but nothing came to her. She sighed. "None. Other than logic, that is."

"Does your father think it was the fae?"

"He's ill."

"Yes, but did he say anything?" His question was phrased slowly.

Naia didn't want to put lies on her father's lips. "I haven't asked him. The soldiers who fought them were saying that the men looked like they were from Ironhold, but that it could be the fae." For some reason her throat hurt.

"Are you sure?"

"We can't be sure of anything, but I can tell you what I saw. I need to try to contact other kingdoms now."

"Of course. These are dark times, girl, and your kingdom is in a delicate position."

"I know. But I trust in the friendship among human kingdoms."

"Interesting trust. Do you need anything from us?"

"No."

"The connection can be severed."

Naia stared at the blue mirror. Great. She'd been trying to do exactly what her father would never do, as a way to surprise Ironhold, and it was backfiring. They could still say Umbraar was making baseless accusations, even if she tried to make it seem that she had no intention of implicating the iron kingdom. Perhaps her attempt had been stupid. Super stupid, with that ridiculous-sounding lie. Perhaps she hadn't been cut out to be queen after all.

As she was about to try Eaglehold, the mirror shone brighter, and a voice said, "Ironhold, Frostlake, Greenstone, and Wolfmark."

Five was the maximum in a communication mirror at the same time. And this was Ironhold. Not only Ironhold, but their biggest allies as well. *Now* she would see if she was fit to lead a kingdom. For the sake of Umbraar, she hoped so.

AZIR STARED at the waves crashing on this strange beach, in a strange world. Everything so different from what he had always imagined. He rested his face on his hands. Ursiana. Why? Why? After all this time, why would she choose to hurt him like that, staying back to die in his place? Perhaps that hadn't been love but hate. Perhaps she had known that she had hit him where it would hurt the most.

So much to do, so little he could control. Leandra—his daughter. In Ironhold clutches. Fel—in Umbraar. He should be safe—the question was for how long. Naia—it hurt so much to think about her, to remember those hateful last words. He shut his eyes tight. At least she was safe. Perhaps he didn't approve of the life she was leading, but at least she was away from any conflict, with the man she had chosen, and it was up to him to respect that.

That left Leandra and her mother. Ironhold had taken Frostlake. What a harsh, strange move to hit their closest allies and so soon. Perhaps they had done it because Leandra would give them legitimacy, whereas they wouldn't be able to take control of another kingdom as easily. Dirty move, but it made sense. The girl had said she was safe, and yet Azir should still rescue her. But then, Ursiana was in much more immediate danger. And her daughter could walk in the hollow. She could find Fel. Azir had to trust that she would do it.

That left Ursiana. He couldn't just walk blindly in the hollow. That would only get him killed, and he would not be able to help anyone if he was dead. There was, or rather, there had been a weapon—now buried under all the debris of a fallen city, under so many lost lives, so much pain. But it was his answer, and the only way to get back there and get both of them out of the hollow alive.

He'd sworn he'd never return to Formosa. Just the thought of seeing the ruins of the city he had once loved wrung his heart—but he had to do it. More than ever, he had to know what had been left of the castle.

He'd need to be fast—and make no mistakes.

RIVER FOUND himself alone in a room with a bed and a sofa, surrounded by walls lined with iron. Not only iron, there was metal magic throughout it, to increase its barrier, to increase its efficiency against an Ancient. River could sense layers and layers of metal magic in it, as if they had designed this place carefully, as if they'd planned to imprison him.

Hilarious—and predictable.

This cage was freedom, and this imprisonment was the moment he'd been expecting for days.

River was still physically unharmed, as King Harold was wise enough to understand the cost of breaching a deal with a fae, but deals were complex things. While it didn't state the consequences of taking away River's liberty, it meant that the king was no longer acting towards him in goodwill, which nullified most of their agreement.

It meant that River could disregard part of the deal as well, and he was now free to search anywhere in the castle, no longer bound by his word that he would neither seek nor reveal any of Ironhold's secrets.

Before, River had wandered through the castle, looking for the dragon heart, looking for some kind of Formosa evidence, but he had to keep his promise, and couldn't enter where he had been expressly forbidden, or any restricted place. He couldn't even tell anything if he ever found out, and it had been driving him insane. Naia's accusatory eyes demanding answers were always on the back of his mind. But then, so were her beautiful eyes filled with worry for him, pleading him to stay, but he had to do this, he had to figure out Ironhold's magic, had to understand what they were up to, or else there would be no way to fight them.

River was surprised at their idea of using iron against him, when they knew he was immune to it. He'd told the king it was because he was unique and partly human. Both true, of course, and yet not the reason he could stand iron. The reason was Naia. Naia and that wonderful, yet almost deadly kiss. And yet they were trying to use iron to lock him up? Iron magic. Perhaps they didn't really understand how he was also immune to it.

He stepped into the hollow for a brief moment, just to cross the wall, then found himself in that same large chamber, which had guards at the other end. It didn't matter, as River was under a glamour not to be seen. Freedom, freedom to go anywhere, was almost too much and he didn't even know where to start. The library had restricted sections, then there were floors and floors down below, dungeons with prisoners, and way too many floors with "nothing" in them, where there had to be something. No. River knew where to go.

As he was about to move, a sharp pain in his stomach almost

made him double over. He tried to recall what he'd eaten, but in fact he hadn't had anything for over a day. This wasn't hunger, though... this was... magic. Magic poisoning. Then his prison made more sense. The iron magic on its walls wasn't there to deter him, it was there to mask something else, something that made his insides curl. Even though he was weak, he slipped into the hollow again and found an empty room, as he could no longer hold his invisibility glamour—and had no idea what kind of magic was poisoning him.

3

THROUGH THE MIRROR

Darkness. That was a strange word. Had anyone ever truly seen it? True darkness, that couldn't be seen. No difference between eyes open and closed, so that a sense was gone.

Leah was far from Fel, bracing herself to face whatever had been looking for him, hoping it hadn't realized where he was, and yet she could still feel the eerie presence, still hear that eerie voice. And now she was nowhere, in the space between.

At least she had one sensation: cold. Cold as if she were stepping outside the Frostlake dome on a winter day—except she had no coat on. She would not last long here, and yet the only direction she could go was towards Fel, still pulling her as if they were tied together. But if something wanted him and they had somehow breached her mind, she had to keep her distance.

There was too much she couldn't understand, too much she could not see.

She had to leave this place. Now. A faint light behind her made her turn. Not a light, a spirit. Her father stood there. Her true father, the one who had raised her, loved her, not the king who had rejected and perhaps even humiliated her mother.

Leah's father was King Flavio, from Frostlake, and maybe Kasim as well, now that she thought about it.

She was about to hug him, but he stepped back.

"It does no good to touch this other world, Leah. What are you doing here?"

"I'm lost."

He tilted his head and smiled. "Are you?"

"I don't know where to go. I... There's something, and I don't know how to fight it."

He chuckled. "So you stay here and wait. It makes sense, it does. But is it a solution?"

"I can't fight something that I don't know, something so much more powerful—"

"Is it more powerful than you?"

Leah, who was already cold, felt a chill down her spine. "That's not even a question. Of course it is."

"Hmm. I'm sure you'll know where to go, if you dare follow your heart."

"My heart will take me to Fel. I know you said—"

"Humans, we're fallible. I made mistakes. We could say I did the best I could with the information I had, but it still wasn't right. You deserved the truth. At least you found it."

"So King Azir really is my..." She couldn't come to say it. "I'm a deathbringer?"

He sighed. "Indeed. You have his deathbringing and his blood. Looking back, hiding that magic from you sounds foolish and even irresponsible, but it's not fair to judge the past like that. Now, standing atop a mountain, seeing everything, the path we took is obviously wrong, but you can't see it when you are surrounded by woods." He had a light chuckle. "Or perhaps I'm making excuses. I planned to tell you one day."

"So you've always known it?"

He nodded. "Yes."

Leah shook her head. "I understand. I'm not upset. I just... How do I get out of this place?"

"Trust yourself."

"Trust myself that I won't put Fel in danger?"

"Is that what your heart is telling you? That you should return to him?"

She was going to say *yes*, but for some reason, it didn't feel that true. "No. I should... try to understand my magic."

"Then go where you can do that."

"And where is that?"

"You'll have that answer, not me. Regardless, you need to leave, Leah. This is a passage to places from where you can't return. If you stay here too long, you'll end up joining us. It's not your time yet."

She sighed. "I wish I could have helped you, I wish I hadn't..."

"Those are bigger destiny wheels than you can stir. What you have to do now is focus on your own. Your fear can be your signal. It keeps us away from danger, but it also keeps us away from change. Sometimes, instead of a warning to stay away, fear can show you the path you need to take."

Leah managed a laugh. "So... am I supposed to go where my heart tells me or where my fear warns me against?"

"Is there such a big difference? In many cases they are one and the same. That will be your hint."

Her father was getting translucent.

"Don't go."

"I can't stay, Leah, and neither can you. Get out of here, go somewhere else. Even if you're not sure it's the right choice, you have to move. You'll never be sure if you're picking the right path, and yet you need to keep going."

She recalled those dreadful creatures in Umbraar. "I'm afraid of dooming everyone, ruining everything."

"Then you have something in mind, something to fight against. Trust your strength."

His image disappeared, leaving only loneliness in its place. And cold. So much cold. Her heart only told her to go to Fel. If she wanted, she could—it would be easy. She could feel him pulling her, even if they were so far apart, except that she was afraid. But then, if her father was right, the fear could be an indication of where to go.

No. It wasn't as much fear as it was a feeling, a presentiment. She had to stay away from Fel to protect him. But that only left her in this darkness. Unless...

Darkness. She had once called its queen, who claimed she could teach her about her power. More than ever, Leah needed power. Again, the image of those dreadful creatures came to her mind, chilling her already cold bones. That voice had been different from the voice telling her to kill, and different from the voice recognizing "the iron dragon", but what if it was one and the same?

It was easy for her father to tell her to trust her own strength, except that she had no idea what it even was. All her life she had trained to be a necromancer, and for what?

Leah paused and mentally repeated her own words. All her life she had trained... magic. She wasn't an ignorant novice.

King Flavio had known she wasn't a true necromancer—and yet he had trained her. It couldn't have been all a game of pretend; he had to have hoped that something could be useful to her. Oh, if only she had asked him about it. But there had been such little time.

Instead of lamenting her nonexistent knowledge of deathbringing, she should turn to what she did know, and ask herself what a *necromancer* would do. She'd been hearing a voice for a while now, a voice telling her to kill, destroy. Then she had dreamed about a strange Queen of Darkness, offering her power. Leah had taken that offer, or at least assumed that was she was accepting, and opened the pathway for the creatures that helped save Umbraar at first, but that later were turning against them. It had to be all connected.

How would she explain it as a necromancer? It would be a spirit. It wasn't the case; there was no way to open up the land of the dead and get any help for a battle, no matter how unhelpful it turned out. Still, there were cases where a spirit would not want to go, where it would keep bothering the necromancer. It usually meant they wanted something, but sometimes they just didn't want to leave. Leah knew what could be done in such cases. She knew that the necromancers dealt with one place in the in-between, where it met the land of the dead. It was connected to the many realms in the hollow, which were like many levels. Deathbringers could connect with those levels and walk in some of them. Regardless, all it meant was that the techniques to banish a spirit could perhaps work to banish a living creature from one of the realms in the hollow.

The problem? There was only one place where she knew she could find the tools to do that, and right now, it would be brimming with Ironhold soldiers. She had to try, though.

What could she do to get there? Think about where she wanted to go? That had worked before, but it had been an accident and she had no idea how to replicate it. She then remembered walking with King Azir. It had been like moving through a thick, dark smoke, then floating over Ironhold.

She opened her eyes as much as she could, to check if she could distinguish anything, but saw nothing. Still only darkness, and yet she dared step forward, keeping her destination in mind. It couldn't be that simple, though. She had heard that death-bringers could get lost or trapped. All she could do was hope that it wouldn't be the case.

RIVER LEANED ON A WALL, pain and nausea tormenting him. What had that been? Something foul and strange. But what? Not metal or metal magic. It was some strange magic that Ironhold used to try to keep him contained.

He took a couple of slow, deep breaths, almost expecting guards to rush into the room and catch him while weakened, but there was only silence. River looked around. This was a small storage space, apparently abandoned, with shelves on one wall and clear, empty jars on it. Just one of the many spaces he hadn't yet touched. This castle was gigantic, with more than thirty floors connected by long stairways and a metal magic apparatus connecting it all.

While the Iron Citadel looked tall, it was also deep, very deep. The explanation for that depth was that it connected to a reserve of magnetite, which fed the castle's metal magic. If there had ever been an impenetrable fortress against the fae, it was this. His thoughts moved to his sister, gone so early, in such a foolish quest. She would have noticed that the magic had not been gone before getting even close to this castle. He'd never doubted the story that she and her friends had tried to infiltrate it, but she wouldn't have been *that* shortsighted. It was odd to recall Ciara, gone almost twenty years before, and yet, for him, it had been just months, months that had not been enough to ease the pain of her loss. An eternity wouldn't ease that pain.

Ironhold was going to pay. The only issue was that he didn't want it to affect Naia.

River took a deep breath. The nausea was subsiding, perhaps replaced by his worry, his anger. Or else those feelings were grounding him, giving him strength. Maybe that awful magic had not been meant as a barrier, maybe it was just that Ironhold's ironbringing was somehow corrupted.

As a fae, being attuned to magic was both a blessing and a curse, and to make matters worse, River was a rare case, even more aware of different types of magic than most Ancients. Of course, recently he'd been oblivious to dragon magic, but there was probably a decent explanation for that.

River stepped away from the wall and realized he could stand without help. It had been just a scare. The invisibility glamour took some more effort than usual, but he managed it—and left the room. This was his chance to explore the entrails of this heinous castle, his chance to find the missing key to defeat this dreadful kingdom.

His first instinct was to go to the literal depths of this building, but he was also curious about the king, about what had brought him back here. River knew that one of the princes had been killed, had felt the stench of death when trying to save Isofel's girl. Although he had no idea how she had escaped, he knew she was gone, last seen with Isofel.

The night River had saved her, he'd been magically tracking her, ready to sense any danger—as if there hadn't been enough things for him to worry about. It had been the cost to keep Naia's brother safe, the cost of having his word that he would announce he was dead.

What bothered River was how callous or at least unconcerned Ironhold was about Cassius' death. Unless it had been his impression and the prince was in fact alive. It still had been an attack within Ironhold's walls, and yet nothing in King Harold's demeanor suggested a concerned or affronted father.

River, still invisible, went to their dining room, where some of the family sometimes had meals together. The king and queen hadn't been there in weeks, as they'd been traveling across the land, visiting their "allies." He sat on the chairs one by one to try to sense any residual magic, any residual energy. There wasn't much that he could identify, until he took Lady Celia's seat. There was anger there, or rather, fury, and then the memory reached him.

"Didn't you say necromancers were harmless?" she asked someone.

"We thought so. But we'll find her."

"How?" she asked, her voice cracking with emotion. "If we keep it a secret, if we can't have a prize for her head, if not even our guards can know we're looking for this girl, how are we ever going to find her?"

"Everyone needs to believe she's still with us, still married to Venard. It will legitimize our grasp on Frostlake."

"Who cares for a kingdom of ice, far from Fernick, far from everyone? I'd rather see that necromancer slut dead. We should never have gotten a bride that didn't go through the trials. It's just not the same, just not the same."

"We'll find her, mother." So this was king Harold, his voice surprisingly pleasant. "She has nowhere to hide."

"I want to see it. When she yells in pain, when she begs for mercy, I want to see it. Make her suffer." The anger in her voice was chilling.

"I'll arrange that."

"What about Cassius? When can I see him?" Sadness now laced her voice.

"Soon. He's recovering."

"I have a right to see him. He'll recover much more quickly if he hears my voice."

"Soon. Sometimes waiting is worthwhile, and this is one of those times."

The woman's anger subsided, and so did River's grasp on the memory. This was fresh, from that morning. It meant that they hadn't told anyone that Princess Leandra had escaped and were probably using an impersonator to fool Frostlake. It also meant Cassius was alive, not dead, but there had to be something happening if they were not letting his grandmother see him. He couldn't be seriously ill or hurt, or his father would be more concerned. What was it?

PERHAPS NOW NAIA was going to finally find out what Ironhold was up to, after begging River for so long to tell her. She couldn't think about him now, or the annoyance would show on her face.

Four circles appeared in the mirror, through which she saw the kings of Ironhold, Greenstone, and Wolfmark, and an old man in military garb, wearing Ironhold's colors. That had to be someone speaking for Frostlake.

"Greetings, Umbraar," King Harold, from Ironhold, said. "Where's your king?"

"He's fallen ill—like my brother." Naia again felt something in her throat. If she had somehow acquired the inability to lie from River, she would be quite upset, and in deep trouble. No, this had to be nothing.

King Harold nodded. "And you tried to contact us?"

He probably wanted witnesses for their conversation. Naia was going to continue with her stupid lie. "I did. Something terrible has happened here. A fae attack."

The flicker of surprise in the Ironhold king's eyes was not subtle. "Fae? Like in Frostlake?"

"I heard it. I'm terribly sorry for that." She felt that he was going to say something, but she kept going, so as not to be interrupted. "The problem was that they looked like they were from Ironhold." She was getting tired of almost choking on lies, so she was trying to keep her words true. "Can you believe that?"

The Ironhold king managed to look incredulous. "Where did they attack?"

"A small fort, but it's where my family was. They must have known it. I wasn't here, I was in my house. But I saw some of the burned bodies, and they had Ironhold uniforms. We know this attack could not have come from a friendly kingdom, so that leaves us with only one explanation."

King Harold was rubbing his beard. "That's... quite unfortunate. Did you suffer many losses?"

"Many hurt. Some dead."

"Did you capture any prisoners?"

Right. He would want to know if Umbraar could question them. "I... don't know what happened. Something with fire. They all perished."

The Ironhold king was observing her attentively, likely trying to figure out how the battle had gone. "So you won?"

"We did, but it doesn't change the fact we were attacked, your majesty, which is troubling."

King Harold nodded. "These are dark times for Aluria. You may have noticed that my dear friend King Flavio is not here. In his place, I have General Faulum, from Ironhold, representing Frostlake. He's supervising the security forces there. We tried to help them, but we were too late." He looked down and shook his head, managing to look sorry. "Still, as far as I know, that was the only big loss. My son and my daughter-in-law are going there soon, to assume the throne, but our forces will remain in that kingdom, just in case something happens."

Daughter-in-law... Leah? She wasn't there. But then, nobody knew that, so they could just lie and send someone else, especially when they had control of the military forces and perhaps even the government in Frostlake.

The Ironhold King continued, "I brought here my dear friends Greenstone and Wolfmark to go over the next steps. This will be discussed with more kingdoms, of course, but we had to know what was going on in Umbraar. As you can all see, the fae are back, and they are not joking this time. They likely had been waiting all these years, perfecting their battle tactics, planning, getting ready to catch us unaware, unprepared. They've dealt a blow to Aluria. More than one blow, it seems, but they are going to pay."

All that talk about the white fae with so much hatred was something that bothered Naia. How did River think they could come back from that?

"We need a strong, united Aluria," King Harold continued. "Your father was not in favor of that. I assume he changed his mind?"

Naia sighed. "He's... not in a position to make decisions right now, but I have interim queen power, and my word is final."

"Hmmm. This is not the time for squabbles, niece."

That word startled her. She rarely remembered that she was related to that dreadful kingdom by blood, and she had never been addressed by that king as part of the family.

Naia just nodded. "I know."

King Harold continued, "Our land needs one army, one government, one power, if we hope to stand a chance against the fae. This is why I'm contacting you, and it's something that has been discussed with Wolfmark and Greenstone."

The two kings were both somber, and obviously hadn't really had a voice in the discussion. Probably haven't had a choice either.

"From now on," King Harold said, "Aluria will be the Ironhold Empire. My question, dear niece, is if you will stand with us."

Pretend to be dumb. The thought came to her in a flash. She smiled. "That sounds wonderful. A strong, united Aluria. We'll be happy to support you."

King Harold's eyebrows rose in surprise, but then he resumed his serious stance. "That means you'll grant passage to our forces, and allow representatives from our government—"

"No." It was bold to interrupt him, but she had to do it. "Didn't you hear me? Our attackers. They looked like they were from Ironhold. How are we going to know the difference?"

"That's a good question," The Greenstone King said.

King Harold grimaced. "You'll know because you'll have documents from our kingdom saying we sent them."

"What if they forge documents?" Naia asked. "We need a foolproof system." A bizarre idea came to her mind. "I know. We need an emergency gathering to decide all the details and come up with the best way to make sure this empire will make us strong, not vulnerable."

King Harold rolled his eyes and shook his head. "A gathering will be the opportunity for them to strike all of us at once. Don't you remember what happened in Frostlake?"

Naia did—and knew it had been drivel, a stupid lie. Another idea, again almost nonsensical, came to her mind. "That was in Frostlake, but we won't return there. This gathering could be in the one kingdom, the one castle, where the fae can't enter. It could be in the most powerful kingdom in Aluria, the one with the power to protect us. Of course it will be safe."

There. He couldn't refuse it now. The Wolfmark King's expression relaxed. "It makes sense."

"And an emperor needs a coronation, right?" Naia suggested. She hated that idea, but had to find a way to convince him.

King Harold chuckled. "You flatter me, but as I said, these are dark and urgent times. We have no time to plan a gathering, and having all the kings in one place would be too dangerous."

Naia pretended to be disappointed. "Oh. Your majesty really thinks Ironhold can't protect us?"

It was a matter of pride now. He had to accept the idea. Even Naia was not sure why she was suggesting this. Perhaps it was a way to gain time, a way to postpone whatever Ironhold wanted to do, maybe even a way to get into that dreadful iron castle.

The Ironhold King glared at the mirror. "The Iron Citadel is the safest place not only in Aluria, but in the world. Still, I wouldn't want to leave the kingdoms unprotected at a time like this."

So no gathering then. Great. Now Naia had to find another way to postpone whatever they were going to do.

"I believe the princess is right," The Wolfmark King said. "We need to sign a treaty about something as serious as that, and come up with strategies to avoid impostors. And we'll be only sending our kings, not our armies. The kingdoms will still be protected."

"I wouldn't mind leaving Greenstone for a short while," the other king said. "I agree that this matter must be thoroughly discussed and signed."

Were they also trying to postpone Ironhold's decision? Did they even believe in those fae attacks? Naia wasn't sure, but she was grateful.

King Harold sighed. "I'll consult the other kings. If they agree, and if there's a gathering, I'll want it in three days, but there won't be time for balls, and no place for families."

"That's reasonable", the Greenstone king said, while the other nodded.

King Harold took a deep breath. "Now that it's been decided, I'd like to inform you of the immediate measures—"

"But we can wait," Naia interrupted him. "Aren't we going to decide it all in the gathering?"

"A few days won't kill us," the Greenstone King added.

"It very well could," King Harold snapped. "Flavio was killed in one night."

The Greenstone King exhaled, seeming annoyed. "Very well. What do you suggest as provisional measures?"

"I'm sending my forces to all the kingdoms in Aluria."

No. No. This was exactly what Naia wanted to avoid. "We appreciate the support." She smiled. "But after what happened here, we want safeguards so we know we are dealing with friendly forces. We don't believe the fae will attack soon, so Umbraar could wait three days."

King Harold frowned. "Perhaps you are *collaborating* with the fae?" Finally he was getting where he had probably wanted to take this conversation all along.

"We were attacked," Naia said. "Each kingdom could send one emissary here to see. We'll show you. I don't expect anyone to take me at my word."

It would be very interesting if representatives from other kingdoms came and saw those bodies. At the same time, they would think Umbraar soldiers were savages, mercilessly killing them all.

"But you won?" Wolfmark asked.

"Yes, we defeated them," Naia said.

"Seems to me that with the exception of Frostlake, everything is under control," the Wolfmark king said. "At least for three days. We'll all remain alert, and then decide it all during the emergency gathering."

"So be it," King Harold said. "We'll communicate again confirming the date and providing you with further instructions."

The mirror turned blue all of a sudden.

So rude. He didn't even ask if Umbraar needed anything, and didn't even inform her that he was severing the connection.

Naia had three days to find a way to prevent Umbraar from

falling under Ironhold's clutches. What could be done in so little time?

She wondered if her father would be furious with her. He wouldn't have agreed with something like that. But then, it was obvious that King Harold wanted an excuse to further isolate Umbraar, maybe even to accuse them of working with the fae, maybe to invade them with the help of more kingdoms. By appearing willing to bend to Ironhold, Naia prevented its king from making any of those absurd claims. It was a win, not a great one, but the best she could do for now.

Something that nagged her was the other kingdoms' willingness to have a gathering, as if they also wanted to better discuss it or maybe even postpone the *Ironhold Empire*. And they didn't seem excited about that prospect.

Why was her father so stubborn? There could be some allies among the other kingdoms. With allies, they could find a solution, find a way to push back Ironhold. Perhaps meeting them in person would give them this chance. The issue was that they would be right under the enemy's roof, an enemy who had tried to kill Fel and had just attacked Umbraar. Naia had no doubt Ironhold was the enemy. The question was: what could she do about it?

4

FLYING FORWARD

Fly forward, into the unknown. It was the only thought that made sense.

Flying.

Fel was flying, and it wasn't just a trick of using iron rings stitched to a vest, it was the power of his wings beating, those huge, powerful wings that felt strange and familiar at the same time. Those wings that made him float in the air as if it was water, and yet without resistance preventing him from moving forward, he gained speed quickly. The ocean below passed by in a dash, a blur. Speed, power, and freedom. Everything so new, exhilarating, while scary at the same time.

Despite all his fascination with stories and myths, he hadn't paid that much attention to dragons. And then, perhaps even if he had read all he could, it would still not compare to the experience of being one, the experience of flying. He didn't know how to make sense of any of this, didn't know if he would be able to turn back to his human form, didn't know how to use his powers. As a dragon, he couldn't even sense the traces of metal on earth, which was like losing a sense of smell, losing part of who he was.

His heart felt the same as his human heart, pulsing inside him, even if it was probably some ten times bigger now. It tightened as he thought about his sister, his father, his kingdom, everything happening back in Aluria. And yet, more than ever, he felt he needed help if he was to defeat whatever evil had taken hold of his homeland. And amidst his worries, the most painful of all: Leah. Leah who had disappeared, gone who knows where.

Fel had no way to reach her, to find her, and perhaps that was also why he kept going: he had no clear path back. He couldn't simply return to Umbraar and take his place as a prince. He wouldn't fit in an advisory room and would definitely not be able to show up in a gathering. He wouldn't even fit in his bedroom, and had no way to enter his house. A chuckle escaped him, which was in fact a loud roar, at the ridiculous images he had just conjured. But it was true, he had to find a way to become human again, and then, only then, would he be able to help his kingdom achieve victory.

The sun was high up in the sky, all signs of that dreadful storm gone. Ahead of him, still at some distance, stood the mysterious Fernick continent. In a couple of hours, he would approach a place that had been lost to Aluria, that had been out of reach throughout all his life. Even when there had been boats going there, they took more than two days. Fel would breach that distance in a few hours. It wasn't tiring. If anything, being in this form felt invigorating.

A group of islands dotted the ocean ahead of him, like a sign that he was approaching firm land, that he was arriving. Fel decided to fly lower. Even though he was not tired yet, perhaps it would be wise to get some rest, and then wait for nightfall so that he would approach Fernick under its cover. Would the night even conceal his brilliant scales? Perhaps his body would reflect the moonlight and be even more visible than during the day—but perhaps he could fly really high.

As these thoughts crossed his mind, he relaxed his wings, soaring into the air. No movement, just floating in a slightly downward motion. The ocean and the islands got closer and closer. They were somewhat larger than the island he had landed with

Leah, but the biggest difference was the greenery. Even small as they were, the islands were covered by patches of trees. Tiny forests in the middle of the ocean. Fel wondered if maybe they would have fresh water, even if he wasn't feeling thirsty—which was incredible and a testament to his new strength and resilience.

As he flew low enough to distinguish individual trees, a sight surprised him. At first he thought it was a large, yellow bird approaching the island. Not just one bird; three, two of them yellow and one of them red. But there was a different energy coming from them, something...

Something chilled him, despite the heat and fire inside him. They were dragons.

Dragons.

That was the reason he was coming to Fernick, that was what he was after, and yet, instead of joy or excitement, all he felt was dread. Perhaps he hadn't considered what would happen when he finally met others like him. Perhaps he hadn't really thought he would find them. He wasn't sure what was wrong, but he couldn't shake that uncomfortable feeling.

They were beautiful. One of the yellow dragons was brilliant like him, making him look almost golden when reflecting the sun. The other yellow dragon had dim scales, which made him look very yellow, as if the color had been painted on it. The red dragon was gorgeous, with slightly brilliant scales, which were darker near his belly and face. Their wings were bat-like.

From a distance, Fel wasn't sure how big they would be, but they had to be at least the same size as him. Dragons. Real dragons. Creatures he had once believed were only legends. A lot of his beliefs had changed recently, when he'd seen the impossible become possible, the nonexistent brought to life, the dead reawakened. Then he himself had become a dragon. That was the easiest part to accept; he felt like himself. But now he was dreading this meeting.

"Who are you?" He tried to send the thought in the same way

he had done with Leah and Arry, but wasn't sure he would be able to reach them. "I come in peace," he said. "And wish no harm." Not that he thought they would be afraid of him, outnumbered as he was, but still.

And yet, he felt a threat of violence hanging in the air, something about to break out. The fire in him was begging to be released, that strange magical furnace inside him burning hot. And yet would fire even harm other dragons? Not that he wanted to harm anyone. And not that he stood a chance.

Fel was about to try to send a thought again, when a blast of fire came in his direction, from the dim yellow dragon. He managed to dodge it, but another blast came from one of the other dragons, and Fel eventually found himself facing a third blast, expertly sent to where he had last dodged. He was engulfed in fire for a brief moment. His first feeling was relief when he felt no burning sensation, no stinging, and yet if the blast did nothing, why were they sending it towards him? No, it did something. For a moment he felt difficulty beating his wings, but he spread them and was able to glide.

"I come in peace," he tried to send them this thought again, now wondering if their thoughts were language-based. He should try to say something in Fernian, except that he was terrible at that language in normal circumstances, and unlikely to be able to string a single sentence when in dragon form and under this strange attack. Unless it wasn't an attack and it was a way of greeting.

That was not what he felt like, and one thing Fel had learned to trust was his gut. He wasn't used to flying and much less to maneuvering, but he dove fast towards the ocean, figuring that being near the water could perhaps help him. He sensed rather than saw blasts of fire coming in his direction. Shrinking his wings, he breached the surface of the water and got immersed in it. It was much like diving in human form, in which he had to hold his breath. The water on his skin felt cold and strange. He turned, still under water, gathered his fire, then re-emerged and sent a blast towards the red dragon.

Fel only had time to see it retreating, unburned, and then dove again. He had to have lungs, which were running out of air, much like it would feel in human form. When he couldn't hold it any longer, he re-emerged and sent a blast of fire that missed one dragon, but then two blasts hit him at the same time. Still no burn, no pain. At that moment, another blast hit him, and suddenly he couldn't move his wings. The fall was short, since he'd been so close to the water.

Fel opened his wings and realized they could help him float in those turbulent waves. He was convinced that these dragons were not friendly, but was unsure what to do, unsure how to counter their incoming blasts. Even if he shot back, they had the numbers, especially now that the first dragon was returning for the fight. He was unsure what those blasts could do, but decided to take a deep breath and dive again, just to give him some time, just so he could recollect his thoughts and figure out what to do.

A movement underwater caught his eye. One of the dragons? No, it was still far away, and the skin was blue. Right. Fel had forgotten about the sea-serpents.

STRANGE. Seeing this place didn't hurt half as much as Azir had imagined. That fallen castle felt like a different world, something belonging to another reality. In a way, it did—it belonged to a past long gone.

He was in the safe, with strong reinforced walls which had indeed survived the disaster. Strange to see anything standing in a place where death still felt so fresh, so near, where the echo of thousands of screams still laced the air with horror.

And yet this was a treasure; magical objects and books about deathbringing. For now, all he took was a small object—a lamp that didn't need fire. It was just a clear stone, still with rough edges, and had a short, thin copper wand with a sort of claw holding it. Lightshield it was called, and said to be as old as time, wrought by the ancient dragon mages. Azir didn't really care who had made it. All he cared was whether this object would allow him to walk in the hollow unharmed. More specifically, he hoped it would keep the deatheyes away.

He let the darkness consume him, allowed his body to cross that thick veil, and tried to find that exact place he'd been with Ursiana.

Deathbringers usually moved safely in the hollow, unless in particular circumstances. There were too many traps—not only deatheyes, but other types of prisons. Some of them were obvious physical traps, but some of them could catch someone's mind. Azir had to be aware and careful not to get caught. Strange. He'd been so sure this had been where he and Ursiana had been caught. Unless... That thought was like driving a knife in his gut. Unless... He'd known it was a possibility, known surviving was unlikely, and still had dared believe that she would somehow escape.

For a moment, he felt dizzy. If the worst had happened, he had to at least find her body. If he didn't, he would always be consumed with doubt. No, she could still be alive. Hopeful, naive thoughts.

"Azir!"

He perked up. The yell was coming from one of the hallways. That led to a dangerous realm. It could be a trap. It could be so many things, but his thoughts didn't matter anymore. All that mattered was that he was running in that direction—and then falling. Falling, falling, falling. Falling to what could be his end.

No, he wasn't falling, he was standing at a ledge, outside a party, hating everything. He couldn't be there, it made no sense. Where else could he be? Here he was.

THIS WAS the moment River had been waiting for, his opportunity to find the secrets in the Iron Citadel, and yet, the enormity of that place and the size of his task were more overwhelming than ever, now that he could go just about anywhere in this dreadful castle. So many choices, so little time. Soon the king would again check River's quarters, or rather, prison, and he'd better be there if he wanted to keep playing this game.

Downstairs, in the several secret levels, there were probably many things he could find, or else he could check the royal vaults, or some of the restricted sections in the art collection. Perhaps instead of trying everything at once, he could opt for the simpler route: the king himself. Following him would allow River to see what he was doing. So much evil magic was loose now, and the king was a clear path and a clear lead on how to find out more about that.

First, River went back to the large room where his prison had been located, setting up an invisible barrier around the door. If anyone breached it, he would know it and return to his place. This was old Ancient magic, an enchantment few were capable of. More of River's "wasted potential". At least he was using some of it now, even if it wasn't in the way his father would have liked.

In the same way he could feel memories of a place, especially if they had high emotions, he could sense its tranquility, mix his essence with that place in such a way that he would notice if it was disturbed. This would allow him to explore the Iron Citadel at leisure.

River had magically tagged the king, but for some reason couldn't sense him. Had he left the kingdom again? River closed his eyes and focused, then felt a faint trace of him deep underground.

After a moment in the darkness, River found himself behind the king, in a gigantic dark chamber that looked more like a cave, with rough rock walls and ceiling. Strange how the lower parts of the castle weren't as well finished as the higher floors. This was not any rock, but magnetite, and the scent of iron magic was heavy in the air. River no longer thought it stunk, now that he realized Naia had some of that scent, except that hers was slightly different—and marvelous instead of atrocious. River had better not think about Naia and her scent or he would be unable to do anything useful or keep his glamour.

The king stood by his wife by a rectangular platform made of onyx, its black sides reflecting the faint lights of torches along the walls and on the floor. Something big was about to happen, but maybe not anything secret, as there were some forty guards standing by one wall of the room, in two lines, partly concealed by the darkness of that strange chamber. Why so many guards?

River approached the platform and realized it was hollow. In it, he found his answer. Cassius was there. There was no life in him, but he didn't look like someone who had been dead for almost a day. He was pale, but looked like someone asleep. River didn't quite know how to even explain what he was sensing from that body.

Unlike the king, the queen looked fragile and scared, holding her husband's hand and trembling. River thought that she was crying, but her eyes were dry, even if they were wide as they looked at her son, a strange emotion in them almost like hope, but not quite. Perhaps Cassius was sick. Or maybe this was some kind of mortuary ritual, but it was odd that none of the family was there, and then, the number of guards was extremely bizarre.

Queen Kara turned to her husband. "The fae. Are you sure he's been secured?"

"He won't leave his quarters. You don't have anything to fear from him, my love." His voice was soft, and River felt almost nauseous that someone so horrible could think he loved anyone. The king then smirked. "I know he disturbs you, but I've always had him under control."

"He makes me nervous." Her voice was shaky. Afraid of River. At least one person in Ironhold was sensible and showed some sign of intelligence.

The king kissed her cheek. "I'm here. You'll never have to fear anything, not even death."

The queen nodded and looked down.

What were they doing? Why was there nobody else in the room? If this was some secret magic ritual, why so many witnesses? There was something that felt unequivocally wrong about this place and whatever ceremony they were about to conduct. And it wasn't a coincidence that River had been locked up right before it; the queen feared him for some reason, as if she feared he would get in their way or find out what they were about to do. Whatever was about to happen wasn't for River's eyes, and it was ironic that their effort to keep him away had allowed him to come here, to unravel their secrets.

River was still invisible and unnoticed. He knew how to walk and move silently, and wasn't worried that anyone would hear him, but everything about this was uncomfortable. Even the air felt heavy.

The king squeezed the queen's hand. "Ready?"

She gave him a shy nod. The king then turned around and faced the guards. "Swords out."

All the guards unsheathed their weapons. River couldn't imagine what they were about to do. There was nobody else in this chamber. Then, he had heard about rituals with swords, and perhaps this was one of them.

The king then raised one of his arms, and, in a swift motion, closed his fist.

River heard a few grunts and noticed movement from the guards, but it took him a moment to comprehend what was happening. The men had been standing in two lines, and when the king made the sign, the ones standing behind the others stuck their swords on their backs. A few guards were fast enough to notice what was happening and turn to try to defend themselves, but were outnumbered. Two men tried to run, but were prevented from doing so by the guards who had been standing in the back. As much as River could appreciate military prowess, this was nothing but a senseless massacre, a disturbing bloody spectacle.

How could Ironhold hurt their own people? How could anyone be so callous? River felt nauseous again, and he wasn't sure if it was the gruesome scene or still some effect from the dark magic he had crossed earlier. He focused on his glamor, which wasn't something he usually had to do, but he wanted to ensure it was holding up. Sometimes he agreed with his father that humans could be atrocious. But then, so could Ancients, which wasn't something he wanted to dwell on.

Some twenty dead or severely hurt men lay on the blood-covered floor. The king didn't smile or frown or anything, while the queen kept her eyes on her son, undisturbed by the murders around her. Well, ignoring other people's suffering was something royals were very good at. For all her apparent fragility, Queen Kara was certainly unfazed by senseless death, violence, and blood.

The guards who had just murdered their colleagues stood tall and proud. In a time like this, anyone with half a brain should consider that they shouldn't obey such a gruesome order, should consider that it could just as well have been them standing in the front, but no. They were busy either being relieved they hadn't been chosen to die or proud that they were among the winning group of guards, unable to see that all it meant was that the king saw his men as expendable and worthless. They were probably under the illusion that their position as killers meant they were considered worthy. And that was how atrocities were carried.

The king turned around and faced the men. "Your sacrifice will be noted. For blood and sacrifice are the nourishment for a strong kingdom, are the essence of magic. You honor Ironhold with your bravery, and we won't forget your blood."

Blood? They hadn't shed any—yet. Oh, had they been smart, they would be running away as fast as possible, instead of taking these venomous words as a compliment. The king reached out to a staff leaning by the box. Not a staff, a lever.

Once he pulled it, part of the floor moved. It was actually a huge trapdoor that had been camouflaged by the dirt covering it. All the guards, regardless of whether they'd been dead, hurt, or standing, fell a compartment with long, sharp iron spikes. They were impaled instantly.

River wanted to retch. He understood dying in battle, dying to protect someone, and even understood that kings sometimes had to see their armies facing losses, but this was pointless. Pointless death, which was a reminder that for King Harold, these guards meant nothing, life meant nothing.

From his vantage point, River looked at the spikes and remembered the interrogation room in the Ancient City, except that those spikes had been made of wood, for ironbringers. Funny that Naia had been its first prisoner. King Spring, king of the Ancients, didn't value life either.

But there was a reason why they were killing so many men here—it was probably a magic ritual or something of the sort. Whatever power they were kindling, it had to be something so dark and heinous that had never been mentioned in any Ancient book. A chill ran down River's spine as he watched and waited.

King Harold took a black dagger from his pocket and moved it towards his son's face. To kill him? It wouldn't be sad to see Cassius dead, but it was still odd to see a father doing that to his son. But all the king did was touch the young man's forehead with the dagger. River felt strangely relieved not to witness any more gruesomeness.

Harold's voice echoed in the hall. "Sacrifice. For death shall bring life. From their blood your blood will run."

Queen Kara looked at her son with a calm expression, without any of the hope, anxiety, or fear one would expect a mother to have in that situation. A few long seconds passed, then the king pulled back the dagger.

At first nothing happened, then something caught River's eye. The queen had a necklace with a large red stone—a ruby or a garnet. A light in it pulsed, as if it were coming to life. That had to be a magical object, but of which kind, River wasn't sure, except that if it was bright when surrounded by senseless death, it couldn't be anything good.

The king moved the dagger, as if to put it on Cassius' forehead again, but the queen stopped him. "Wait. We need to follow the rules and wait." Her voice wasn't strained or worried. There was something about her that River couldn't quite understand. Perhaps it was just that he expected more feeling, more emotion. That and the creepy necklace was signaling to something strange.

The king cleared his throat. "I know what I'm doing."

"Let's just wait," she whispered in a gentler tone.

Cassius's face was pale and he wasn't moving, not even breathing. His parents watched him in silence, the queen composed, while the king was fidgety. After a while, the woman's necklace shone brighter.

At that moment, the prince exhaled, coughed, then sat up, his eyes wide.

The voice that came from his body was coarse, strange. "Where is she? Where is she?"

"Hush," his mother cooed. "It's all right. You'll be fine."

He glanced at his parents, then looked around. "Where am I?"

The king replied, "We're in the Iron Citadel, son, down below, and you can return to your room."

Cassius's eyes were still scanning the chamber, almost as if he were searching for something, perhaps trying to find the girl who had killed him.

King Harold extended his hand to his son and helped him climb out of the box, then they headed to the door, which the king opened with his iron magic. At no point did they spare a single glance at the guards' bodies.

They walked towards the metallic box that moved up and down throughout the castle. River was able to enter it with them. When they were in the upper levels of the castle, the queen turned to her husband. "I'll be right with you. I'm tired and I need to rest."

The king kissed her cheek. "It's been an ordeal."

She left the box and smirked once the king was no longer looking. River was sure she was planning something. The question was whether he should follow the king and see what kind of resurrection had been done on the prince, or follow the queen and see what that mysterious necklace was. As if to answer him, the red stone pulsed again.

A sign. Something was amiss, and this queen wasn't as innocent as she looked. As she retreated to her room, River followed her. He was going to figure out what was happening.

5

THE BOUNDLESS

Arry had brought Naia a plate of food and good news, telling her that most of their wounded men were healing. The casualties had been almost none, but it still hurt. One dead soldier was too many.

He left her alone, though, which was good, as she needed time to process everything, time to organize her thoughts. And yet, she couldn't even touch the food or think straight. All she kept thinking was about River. River with the enemy, River hurt, River captured. Dreadful images came to her mind and she couldn't shut them down.

Stupid worry. Wasn't she planning on going to the Iron Citadel in a few days? And River had powerful magic. He was also faster and stronger than any human. She had to remember that, and then remember how much he had hidden from her, and shut down her worrying heart. Her heart! All River's. After everything. No wonder her father kept saying that hearts were foolish.

At least she managed to speak to more kingdoms. Haven and Eaglehold already knew about the upcoming gathering and about the attack on Umbraar. Naia told them that the attackers were wearing Ironhold's uniforms and looked human. The Eaglehold King didn't seem to believe her.

Haven listened to her carefully. "We'd like to see that, if you don't mind."

Naia agreed to have them send three messengers the following day. It was an opportunity for an alliance.

Her head was buzzing, still with that silly worry for River, when the mirror turned blue again.

There was a way to know who was on the other side, but Naia wasn't good at using this magical object, so she just said, "Open the connection."

It was the Wolfmark King. "Princess Irinaia, will you grant me the honor of an audience?"

Honor? She wasn't sure if he was being sarcastic. "Of course."

"I would like to thank you for the suggestion of having an emergency gathering. It is indeed the wisest course of action."

"Nothing to thank me for. The suggestion emerged from the discussion, from all of us." It wasn't really true, but she wanted him to think she was giving him credit for it. Indeed, she wouldn't want other kings to think that the idea of the emergency gathering had come from her.

"Your words were wise and well measured, princess."

"I'm glad you think so."

He sighed. "I have some questions. You're saying you were attacked by a group of fae, but that they had Ironhold uniforms?"

"Yes." Naia needed to be careful here, as this could well be some kind of test, and she had no intention of crossing Ironhold —yet.

He frowned. "Some of the kingdoms don't believe it."

"I understand they won't take my word for it."

He took a deep breath. "That's not necessarily the case. It could be... a mistake. Maybe someone in your kingdom is mistaken, perhaps?"

"Mistakes can happen, for sure." She gave him a polite smile. "It would be quite pretentious to assume we're above that."

"Pretentiousness is a fault I don't believe your highness has. Still, what I mean is... your account is strange."

Of course it was strange. Her account was ridiculous, but she wasn't going to say that. "Aren't these strange, dark times?"

"Even in the most horrible of times, there's always some kind of logic, princess."

"What would be the logic of Ironhold attacking us?" To be fair, she hadn't truly understood it.

"Dangerous words. I didn't imply that."

"I don't know what your highness implied, then."

He smiled. "There are only questions from my part. No answers. And that is why I'd like to personally visit the fort where this attack happened."

Another kingdom coming to see the bloodshed. That could be good, but she didn't trust Wolfmark, and knew her father loathed King Sebastian. But the real problem would be if by any chance something happened to the king on his way. "Your highness. These are dangerous times. Umbraar is not in a position to assure your safety, and if someone assaults you—"

He waved a hand. "With all due respect, I can vouch for my own safety. Are you denying a peaceful visit? It's within your rights, of course."

"I would never deny an opportunity to establish close ties between our kingdoms. I'm just saying we cannot guarantee your safety on the way here."

"That's a warning, not a threat, right?"

"Of course."

"And you'll receive me. At your... Royal Fort."

"We have simple accommodations, not even a meeting room fit for a king, and we're all busy—"

He raised an eyebrow. "Am I allowed to come?"

"Of course. If you don't mind no special security, and no luxury."

"I care not for these things. All I care about is my kingdom, my people, and all the people in Aluria. This is a serious matter. I'll reach the portal hub later today, before the sun sets. Hopefully my passage will be authorized."

"It will."

He nodded. "See you later, then, Princess Irinaia."

"Yes. I'll sever the connection for now."

Naia got up. Great. One more thing to worry about. Now she needed to send a messenger to the portal hub in Umbraar to allow the Wolfmark king's passage. She had been honest claiming that she couldn't send a retinue, and she wasn't going to send it and weaken her defenses.

On the other hand, this was an opportunity to discuss things that could not be said through a communication mirror. Didn't Naia need allies? She should be happy. Her father would definitely want to strangle her now, being friendly with King Sebastian. At least she had already been disowned, so he wouldn't be able to do that again. Her father, perhaps not real father, but it didn't matter. Even if he was angry at her, she wished he were here, wished she could be sure he was alive. Hopefully he would come home soon. So much worry in her heart. If it kept like that, it would explode.

How long could Fel stay underwater? Not long. Was that sea serpent going to attack him? Strangely, he didn't think so, didn't fear it.

There were three dragons flying above him, while he was only one. It wasn't that huge of a numeric advantage, but it was a gigantic advantage when Fel didn't understand his body, his magic, or even how to fly and dodge properly. He didn't even know exactly what a blast of fire could do to another dragon, only felt that it wasn't anything good.

His lungs were demanding air. He had to emerge—but he had to do it right this time. Fel poked his head out of the water. Immediately, two of the dragons prepared to blast him. He timed it, then dove again. The fire hit the water, and Fel came out right away to blast both dragons.

They fell back, but then Fel was hit with a blast of fire from the third dragon. He submerged again, trying to think. In the distance, he saw a dark blue body under water. Another sea serpent. He didn't feel any malice or threat coming from it, but rather a kinship with the gigantic animal. When he had to get some air again, he emerged, then flew up as fast as he could, dodging one blast of fire and still receiving two. He blasted two of the dragons but missed one, then felt his wings getting weak and went underwater again. This time, he was going down, unsure even if he was going to be able to get out. Why were these dragons doing this? Who were they? He wasn't going to last long like this, and perhaps his underwater incursions would make him drown, which was a terrible idea, but he was unable to come to the surface, his body feeling numb and useless.

A sea serpent approached him, swimming under Fel, then raising him. Its force helped him meet the surface. He was able to breathe, but unable to take flight. The dragons had disappeared, though, which was a welcome respite. Perhaps he would need to land on one of the islands and rest, recover his forces—if only he could move. Of course his rest didn't take long. Soon he saw those three dragons coming from an island.

"I mean no harm," he tried to send that thought to them, unsure if they would hear or understand him.

All he felt was rage coming from them. And some mockery, maybe. Fel could hardly move, but he had to try something. With difficulty, he took flight and watched as the dragons approached. Perhaps he was only one, perhaps he didn't even know what being a dragon was like, but he wasn't going down without a fight.

As much as his wings were beating slowly, he tried to feel his heat burning, and sent the largest blast of fire he could manage, targeting two of the dragons, which were flying close together. The shiny yellow dragon, which was far away, hushed towards him, sending a huge blast of fire, which Fel met with his own. His wings lost force and Fel dropped into the ocean again. He had no option but to dive. These dragons hadn't targeted him underwater yet, and that was the only way for him to find some safety. Perhaps another sea serpent would be kind enough to help him.

Like that, he let himself fall, fall, fall, deep underwater. Soon he would need to breathe, but not yet. He took the time to rest, to try to regain his strength, regain his movements. When he couldn't take it anymore, he emerged.

To his surprise, the dragons weren't waiting for him, but flying in a different direction.

It wasn't good news, though.

Two more dragons were coming. Now he was definitely regretting having flown to Fernick on his own. At least Leah had gone away. Leah. He couldn't die and leave her. Fel thought of his sister, his father, his kingdom. He couldn't simply die because of such a stupid decision. The question was how to survive against five dragons.

Perhaps he could use the distraction to fly away—that if his wings worked properly. He had no idea what those blasts of fire did, but felt that they impacted his movements, perhaps even his reflexes.

Even then, slowly, Fel took flight.

He was going to turn around and try to find cover on one of the islands, when a sight made him change his mind.

The newcomers, a black and a gray dragon, were fighting the dragons who had been attacking Fel. They were on his side! Or maybe not. Maybe it was a squabble that had nothing to do with him.

Then he heard a female voice resonating in his head. "Fly away while we distract them."

That was the gray dragon. She was on his side, and Fel wasn't going to let her and her companion face his enemies on their own. They were dodging blasts of fire, when Fel approached the colorful dragons and blasted the shiny yellow one, while the two new dragons blasted the others.

The colorful dragons fell into the ocean. Fel thought that this was the end, but then the newcomers flew towards the colorful dragons, who were now unconscious or very slow. The gray dragon bit the red dragon's neck. Dark red blood mixed with the water, making it pink. The other dragon bit the two others. It was a bloody and gruesome spectacle, as the dragons who had attacked Fel plunged into the blody waters.

"Come. Follow us," the female dragon said.

"Are they dead?" Fel asked, unsure if he was relieved or horrified, unsure if he could believe that legendary creatures could die like that.

"Let's go before more of them come," she said. "Keep your thoughts to yourself. This place is not safe."

Fel was unsure who these new dragons were, but one thing he knew: he wasn't going to survive long here alone. He also knew that they could kill without remorse. Either way, he'd made this journey to find more dragons, and wasn't going to turn away or cower now that he was about to find his answers.

THE QUEEN WAS INDEED GOING to her quarters, but River still followed her from up close, moved by a nagging sensation that he was about to find out something. Odd how he had never looked much into her or suspected her of anything. Perhaps because he assumed she was just her husband's pawn, or because women didn't have a voice in Ironhold, at least not when they were young. But even the people who had no voice could do things, and do things while hidden, while ignored, taking advantage of how unimportant and unnoticed they were. Perhaps that was Kara's case.

Once in her room, the queen looked behind her, as if to check if she was alone, then entered her closet, pulled a drawer, and a secret passage opened. River followed her and found himself in another room, with yellow walls, illuminated by torches on cornices. There was a low table in the middle, where a small granite statue stood, but no other piece of furniture. Thick rugs with geometrical patterns lined the floor, and the air had an odd smell, like some tea or other kind of herb. Indeed there were some small, dried leaves spread over the rugs. They didn't smell like magic, though, and River couldn't sense any ironbringing in the room.

The woman kneeled by the statue. "The final sacrifice has been done, my lord. And the rest has been achieved."

A raspy, strange voice came from the statue. "So you secured the vessel."

River faced her and noticed that her necklace was bright. She had a satisfied smirk. "It's ready for you."

"Oh, I see." The sound of a light chuckle came from the statue.

"I told you I never fail." Her eyes then moved to where River was, that stupid smirk still plastered on her face. "Enjoying the view? There's no reason to hide, you know? We could be allies."

There was no question that she had addressed him, looking in his direction, which meant he'd been caught, even if he sensed that his glamour was still holding. He wanted to understand what was happening, but decided it would be too risky, and stepped into the hollow to get away from that room and that woman. Or rather, he *tried* to step into the hollow. Something was holding him back. Perhaps holding that invisibility glamour for so long had weakened his magic. Odd. It had never happened before. But he wasn't going to let it faze him.

River let go of his glamour and appeared in front of the queen. She knew he was a fae, so there wasn't even any point in disguising his horns or eyes. "Aren't we supposed to be allies already? Haven't I been helping your husband?" He wanted information, but more than that, he wanted to regain his strength and get out of this room. For that, he needed time.

She chuckled. "And you assume what? That I'm a piece of my husband? Or maybe his property?"

"No such thing, your highness." And it was true. As much as

River had to honor the verbal agreement with King Harold, he had no such deal with the queen.

Her head tilted and her eyes narrowed. "Is spying me part of your agreement?"

It wasn't. But he didn't want to give her any explanation. "You're saying I have no need to hide, that we can be allies. I assume you want something, right?"

She chuckled. "I... No. What would the meek, humble, Ironhold queen want? Isn't that what you think? That I'm a nobody, just my husband's appendix?"

River had to gain time and try to get some information. "Does it make a difference to you what I think?"

"Of course not, I should say. Isn't that what everyone pretends? And yet we care. We look at the lowest servant and care about what they think. Aren't we funny creatures?"

"Absolutely." She had to be going somewhere with all this. "Should I assume you have something funny to tell me?"

She leaned her face on her hand. "Funny? Maybe. Or perhaps tragic."

River decided to go straight to the point. He knew that even though humans could lie, their reaction when confronted with direct questions could sometimes be enlightening. "So," he pointed to the statue, "who's your friend? Care to introduce me?"

She pretended to ignore the question and stared into River's eyes. Her red necklace was bright. "Do you know why you're here?"

He smiled. "I'll be delighted to hear your explanation." Time, time, time, all he needed was time.

"Men—or fae. Male fae, I guess. You all think you're so smart. You think you pull all the strings. I'm pretty sure you think it was your idea to come to Ironhold." She made a mocking voice. "Oh, I'll trick them all." She chuckled and then her voice returned to normal. "Isn't that what you thought?"

"Many thoughts cross my mind. Collaboration between former enemies is always a delicate topic."

She waved a hand. "Spare me. Spare me your non-answers. My pitiful husband doesn't even notice that you never reply to most of the questions he asks. But I'm not him. I'll tell you a story, fae."

River wondered why the woman was stalling. For a human, she was being quite vague, but he wanted to hear what she had to say.

The queen took a deep breath. "There was once a hopeful girl. So hopeful, and yet so hungry. Do you know what it's like to have only one loaf of bread to share with your sick mother and four siblings?"

"I cannot assume to know."

"It was relief, joy. It meant we had something to eat." She frowned. "Hope when you have so little is tragic, you know? People fight for scraps and crumbles and it's sad, so sad. Such a dreadful, meaningless existence. But the girl with hope had a chance, had a chance to change her life—and she embraced it. Ironhold always has a competition to find the brides for their princes. It's meant to see who's resilient enough, who has the qualities of a future queen or princess. Only the most focused and ruthless get to the end, I'll tell you. You need to want it more than anything else. And this girl wanted it. Perhaps she had to poison some rivals, perhaps she had to sabotage others. It doesn't matter, does it? All that matters is winning, and so she did."

The queen looked away, a shadow crossing her face for a brief second, but then it was gone.

"The girl told herself she did it for her family, but I don't know how much of it is true." She turned to River. "Once she won, the king told her that her family would never starve again." She laughed. "The silly girl had tears of joy, tears of relief, she even told herself that any murders she had committed had been for a worthy cause. Very worthy, as her youngest sister was only seven, so thin and small that she looked like she was five. Her youngest brother was ten, always trying to look braver than he actually was, and yet also so thin, especially when he always gave his portions to his siblings. He just had to share, he just had to give. What mattered was that her sweet, generous brother would never starve again. Wasn't it worth it? Wasn't it a noble goal, a noble pursuit? The girl didn't even think she was doing it for herself."

River knew that the queen was talking about herself, and wondered where she was going with this. He would do anything for his sister, or rather, would have done, if he could.

The queen smirked. "It was a lovely day when they were brought to the Iron Citadel. The girl was there, and she was thrilled to see her family so joyous and excited. Her mother was so proud. It was a day of joy and happiness as they were brought in. None of them had any luggage, as they were told that they wouldn't need it. They made an exception for the little sister, who still clutched her favorite doll. And so they came. They were brought to a room down in the low levels of the Iron Citadel, and the silly girl still didn't realize there was anything wrong. When ten guards surrounded them, she still didn't realize there was anything wrong, or perhaps she didn't want to believe there was anything wrong.

"It was a dream, right? There were four more people with her then, the old king Stevan, who was still alive, and his wife, Lady Celia. They told the girl that this was the final test, a test to see if she would be loyal to Ironhold and Ironhold only, a test to see if she had an iron heart."

A chill ran down River's spine and he almost told her that there was no need to continue, that he didn't want to hear it, but perhaps this was a good opportunity to understand the woman. Maybe she could be an ally, even if he had serious doubts about her moral standards.

She continued, "The girl was told she had a choice: Ironhold or her family. And she had to watch—it was part of the test. The girl told herself that if she refused, they would all die, so the choice was only whether she died with them or not. It was obvi-ous, right? They wouldn't simply let her and her family walk away with no consequences. She wasn't ready to die. There was so much more she could do, she could achieve. The only way to do that was to say the word, to choose Ironhold. The girl was a coward, so while she kept her eyes open, they were unfocused. Her mind was elsewhere while those sad people screamed in front of her. But in a way, the silly girl also died that day. In her place emerged a future queen with an iron heart, and she understood that they had kept their promise: her family would never starve again. Isn't it wonderful?"

The woman stared at River, as if waiting for a reply.

He cleared his throat. "It depends on your idea of wonderful. I guess the iron-hearted woman is happy now?"

"*Happy* is a silly word. If people can be *happy* with a loaf of bread to share among five, you can see how that word is meaningless. *Powerful*, now that's a different thing. There are only two kinds of people in the world: the powerful and the powerless. You want to survive, stick with the powerful."

"I appreciate the advice." River didn't know what to say. The woman, despite her tragic story, or maybe because of it, was cuckoo. He wanted to understand what her necklace meant, and also figure out that voice and the statue. Well, she had given him the answer. *Stick with the powerful.* It meant that she had sought someone more powerful than the king. The question was who. "And I'm wondering if there's any deal your majesty would like to make with me?"

She laughed. "Of course, of course. It's always the *deal* with you fae. Let's make a deal, shall we? You tell me how you became immune to iron and I let you go."

"I'm a unique fae."

"Oh, not that." She waved a hand. "I want to know exactly how, when and where you became immune, with details. You know exactly what I'm asking for, don't you?"

A kiss flashed through his mind like lightning, but he tried to focus on something else, afraid that even his thoughts would escape him. If he told the story in detail, she would know about Naia, know where to hurt him, know how to threaten him.

"We don't always know details about magic, your highness."

She narrowed her eyes. "You, white fae, or Ancients, as you so presumptuously call yourselves, don't know everything. Do you have any idea what is it on the floor? What plant?"

River looked down at the small leaves. "I'm not a specialist in plants, you know? I'm pretty sure most humans can't name it either."

"Humans in Aluria obviously can't. Because it doesn't grow on this continent. It's sepialy, a silly little plant. Oh, I guess you *do* know it, except that you have a different name. Does *death grass* ring a bell?"

That was something from quite old texts, a plant that could impact an Ancient's magic, but it was considered extinct. No plants rang bells, though.

"No," River said.

At this point, he had definitely heard enough and should focus on getting out of that room as quickly as possible. He tried to slip into the hollow, but couldn't.

The queen laughed. "No, no. You won't escape. You're trapped."

With an open door right behind her? No.

River was about to walk past her, when the necklace emitted such bright light that it dazzled him, and he fell back.

"Oooh, not so strong now, are you?" The queen laughed again. "Tell me, how did you become immune to iron?"

"What makes you think I know?"

"Your non-answer, for once."

"Harm me, and you'll be breaking a deal with a fae. It has consequences."

"Don't be dim. I never made any deal with you, stupid fae. Now give me your answer or you'll die by the end of the day. Not a great loss, for sure, but I assume you are under the illusion that your life is, oh, so valuable."

He would never mention Naia, he would never give them this weapon to wield against him. He still doubted that this silly herb would contain his magic for long. "Ask something else. I'm sure there are other things you want."

"There are tons. But for now this is all I'm asking. Well, I'll let you ruminate on your choices."

As the queen headed to the door, River decided to try his last shot.

Mindmelding magic came easily to him. Perhaps he didn't like its cost, but this was a time where it could make her free him, and the fact that she was threatening him justified its use.

At the first contact with her mind, he saw himself in her thoughts. It wasn't River as he was now, but River as soon as he'd come back from his second time in the hollow. *He's the key*, the strange, raspy voice said. *I think I know what to do*, she replied. It didn't make sense. Had this woman been targeting him from before the time he had come to Ironhold?

The image dissolved in a sea of red, as her necklace flashed again. "Get out of my mind, worm. And yes, you're important. Yes, you are here because I wanted you to be, you are here because you are my weapon. You think you make the choices. Oh, no, you don't. You and king Harold are mere puppets in my play." She laughed. "But all I want for now is your answer, then I'll let you go."

River wanted to cause her pain, wanted to get into her mind again, but he couldn't feel his magic, couldn't connect to it.

"I cannot give you that answer."

"Then I'll have to give you time to think."

With that, she walked out, locking the door behind her.

River couldn't believe he'd fallen for such a silly trick, couldn't believe this queen was the one trying to hurt or kill him. He took a deep breath. There had to be a way out. There was always a way out. And he was going to find it.

6

A VISITOR

Being a deathbringer should be about controlling darkness—and yet Leah felt that it was about to engulf her, suffocate her. This was only a passage, though. She brought to her mind the memory of the moment she had traveled there, unwittingly, how she had awoken on the floor of her room, and kept that memory alive in her mind, with as many details as she could recall.

It wasn't exactly like what had happened with King Azir, but she saw an opening in that strange black fog, like a slit. It didn't lead to her old bedroom, but to a place above the Frostlake castle, except that she was outside the dome. Interesting. So this dome had more uses than just keeping the cold out. That said, she had breached it once, she should be able to do it again.

In a second, she was falling, and felt hard floor beneath her. Yes! She'd done it! No idea how, but she was where she wanted: King Flavio's study room, a place where she had spent many hours of her childhood, fascinated with everything related to magic. Light came from the round windows on top of the high walls.

Before she could rejoice, a woman's scream startled her. Leah got up quickly, and saw Falina, one of the castle's lead chamber-maids, with wide eyes.

"Princess." She bowed. "I... where did you come..."

There was no point in trying to hide her identity. Leah put a finger over her mouth. "I was hiding. It's... a surprise." Then she looked around her and her stomach knotted. All the counters and tables were covered with a dark green cloth, and the objects had been placed in burlap bags.

"What's happening here?"

"Why, miss? Your orders. This room is being cleaned for you."

Leah wanted to scream. How could anyone think she would want her father's office dismantled? "It must have been a misunderstanding." Or more likely, one of Ironhold's lies.

"Oh. I can try to—"

"No, no." Leah extended a hand. On second thought, it was better not to do anything that could draw attention. "Leave it."

"But princess, I can see now that this is a mistake. To be fair, I thought the order was strange, and now I think it's my fault. I kept thinking it was wrong, it didn't make sense, and yet I said nothing."

Leah shook her head. "Really, it's fine. I'm sure they're just... relocating my father's things."

The woman nodded. "I thought you were still in Ironhold. I'm so sorry for your parents."

Parents? It couldn't be. Unless she meant her mother was still missing. Leah decided to get more information. "No news of my mother?"

"Oh." The woman put a hand over her heart. "Princess. I thought someone had told—"

"What happened?" Leah swallowed.

"She... perished. Fell from the high tower."

Leah had a lump in her throat now. This was it. She was alone, the only person who could save her kingdom. Her mother... There were so many words Leah wanted to have with her. Many of them angry, but also sweet, loving words, and now she'd need to swallow them forever. At least she'd seen her father one last time, but her mother...

"I..." Leah looked down. "It's life, right? Never eternal or unchanged."

"I'm really sorry, princess. No, it's your majesty."

Leah was holding back tears, but this was not the moment to be sad, to get dragged by her emotions. She had come here for a solution, not to become a mushy mess incapable of action.

"Falina." She looked straight at the woman. "My father—and mother—appreciated your service very much. I'll continue to do so, but I need a favor now." How could she say it? "I..." She was going to mention a surprise, but that would be too callous. "I know you heard I wanted everything thrown away, but that was me, trying to prove to my husband and my people that I could move on, that I wasn't hurt by my father's death."

"Oh, miss. Nobody would expect you to."

"I know. But I wanted to prove it, right? I came here... to take a last look at this place. My husband doesn't know. Nobody knows. Can you keep it a secret?"

The woman frowned, which was unexpected. "The Ironhold generals say the fae might be pretending to be us, that we must inform—"

"Falina, it's me. I know your name. If I were a fae, I wouldn't be able to lie, so if I'm saying I'm princess Leah, I'm princess Leah. Or rather, I'm a sea serpent. A castle mouse. I can lie. I'm human, not fae."

The chambermaid raised an eyebrow, thoughtful. Why did she have to be so obedient?

Leah insisted, "Just give me ten minutes alone. Please. I need to mourn."

The woman nodded. "Yes, of course. But the men are coming to take it all away. They'll be here any second now."

This was so wrong. Who had given Ironhold the right to defile her father's lifetime of work and research? And why would they do that? What was their motivation to get rid of his magic study?

Unless... Unless they were not really going to destroy it, but take it to their kingdom. But what was the point? They already controlled Frostlake, and if they wanted to find anything, it would be much easier to do it here, with everything still organized. Well, Leah definitely didn't understand Ironhold and this was not the time to try to do it. What mattered was that maybe not everything would be lost, maybe she could eventually recover her father's work. For now, all she needed was to find what she was looking for.

Leah gave the woman a reassuring smile. "No problem. I'll be quick."

The servant still eyed her with suspicion, but walked out nonetheless. Hopefully she wasn't going to return with guards to test if Leah was some shape-shifting fae. Lying should be proof enough. Regardless, it was better to be fast.

How was she going to find anything in this mess? There were two objects she needed, meant to scare away clinging spirits. One was a small bell, the other, a necklace. She was not sure if any of that was going to work, but she had to try.

Her heart was still tight looking at that office, knowing that these usurpers were destroying it. How much more would they destroy before she could stop them? Stop them—that was a wishful thought. Leah had been barely scraping by. For now, all she could do was get rid of the creepy voice in her head—if her idea worked.

The bell had been on one of the shelves, now empty. Leah opened the burlap bags quickly, trying to find other objects that were from those same shelves, until she found a compass. That had to be it. Indeed the small, copper bell was at the bottom.

She took it and rang it. No sound—which was how it should be. It wasn't for human, living ears.

The other thing she needed was the necklace with dried krystal leaves. It would be better to have some and burn them, but she wasn't going to look in the garden now, and didn't know where they grew elsewhere in Aluria or wherever she was going, so the necklace should have to do for now.

Leah was moving to another bag, when a shrill sound made her tremble. It was inside her head, loud and disturbing.

And then, that voice came back. "Trying to get rid of me?"

Oh, yes, that was exactly what she was doing. Leah rang the bell again. And again. Meanwhile, she searched for the necklace, even if an odd sound still echoed in her mind, making her dizzy.

On top of another bag, she found the necklace, and put it on. Immediately the sound stopped, and there was no more voice saying anything. Yes!

Was it too early to return to Fel? It was the only direction that made sense. Before she thought a second more, the doors burst open.

Falina was back, with two Frostlake guards. Leah knew the oldest of them, which used to work near the royal chambers.

He turned to the old woman. "*That* was what you were hiding?"

"She wanted some time," the woman replied, and then, in a whisper, added, "And doesn't want *them* to know she's here."

Leah stared at them. "Can you keep this secret? And leave me here one more minute? That's all I need." She wasn't going to disappear in front of them, and, in any case, didn't even think she would be able to do it while surrounded by so many people.

The other guard bowed. "Sure, your majesty."

That title made her stomach churn.

"One minute, miss," Falina added. "They want this room empty"

Leah nodded and watched as they walked away. This was a problem. Walking in the hollow was hard enough when Leah was not in a hurry. Now? It would be insanity. And she didn't know about any secret passages in this room. Leah closed her eyes, trying to feel the darkness around her, trying to pull it towards her. Only two directions came to her clearly. One was Fel, and the other was that strange, desolate place among mountains. With no time to think, she picked the second choice.

With eyes open, she could see paths in the darkness. They were faint, blurry, as if her vision had lost some of her sharpness. Leah touched her necklace, wondering if it was the object's fault. Regardless, she had to protect herself and knew of no other way.

As the darkness around her subsided, she found herself in those mountains, in that same place where she'd been once, where a spirit named Ticiane had saved her. This was also the place where she had dreamed about that queen of darkness. Returning here was foolish, but it hadn't really been a choice. Perhaps she just had to regain her bearings and then go somewhere else.

As she considered what to do, watching out for any creatures that looked like children but had super sharp teeth, something pushed her down. Leah barely had time to soften the fall with her hands, so that she wouldn't hit her face. Before she could react, a knee pushed her down, trapping her against the ground, then two hands pulled her arms and shackled them. Considering where she was, being caught couldn't mean anything good.

"Don't even try to run." It was a woman's voice, one Leah didn't think she'd heard before, and it was gentle. "You won't be able to get rid of the cuffs, and I'm sure you don't want to get around like that. Plus, I'm not going to hurt you."

Leah's heart was speeding up, fearing she'd fallen right into the creepy voice's lair, and about to be punished for ringing that bell. Perhaps she could try to slip into the hollow and escape the cuffs, but then, considering she had trouble doing it normally, the odds of achieving that with someone pressing down her back were none. Her best bet was to try to gain time and come up with another solution. With some effort not to show any fear, Leah asked, "What do you want?"

"That's the right question. I want many things." The woman's voice was melodious and pleasant, but that didn't mean anything, considering she probably had long, sharp teeth and perhaps enjoyed eating people. Still, if she wanted something, it meant Leah wasn't in mortal danger—at least not yet. "But for now," the woman continued, "I just want you to listen to me, listen to me until the sun sets."

The place was dark and gloomy, and all Leah could see was some kind of dark fog. "How will I know when the sun sets?"

"It will get even darker."

Dangerous spirits were more active at night, and perhaps this was why this strange woman wanted Leah to wait. That said, it wasn't as if she was in a position to negotiate, and it didn't matter. For now, she could agree with whatever this woman wanted, at least to get out of that position.

"I'll listen to you," Leah said.

"You'll listen to me until night sets?"

"Yes. Hopefully in a more comfortable place."

The woman chucked. "Of course."

To Leah's surprise, her manacles clicked open. That had been fast. Leah got up and faced her captor—and couldn't believe her eyes.

FEL HAD NEVER THOUGHT he would find dragons so easily and quickly. Or rather, he hadn't imagined that he would be found like that. He was following two dragons, one black and one gray, and didn't think they had any evil intent towards him. If anything, he'd probably be dead if they hadn't shown up.

They were flying above the ocean, away from those islands. The sun was high up in the sky and he wondered if they were going to get to the continent like that, visible in plain daylight. He would never have guessed that dragons roamed Fernick without fear of being seen. Strange how this truth had been kept from Aluria.

The gray dragon, ahead of him, turned her head to look beside them. Fel followed her line of sight and saw six forms flying in the sky, against the sun, coming from the east, so he couldn't see them well. He would have guessed them to be birds if he didn't know better.

"Fly as fast as you can," the female dragon said, or rather, sent those words as a thought, then changed direction so that they were flying away from the approaching dragons.

"Are they dangerous?" Fel tried to ask, still unsure if his thought would reach her.

"Very," she replied, then added, "Keep flying as fast as you can. Just a little longer."

Little? All he saw was ocean below him, no land ahead. How far would he have to out-fly those dragons? His wings were still not in the greatest shape, not to mention that he was anything but an expert at flying.

"Now," the woman said, or rather, commanded. "Fast. Into the circle."

There was no... Oh. Both dragons sent blasts of fire, which formed a fire ring floating in the sky. They waited for Fel beside it. This could be a trap, but then, at least they were only two, instead of the six others, and for some reason he felt he could trust the female dragon.

Fel flew into the ring. Suddenly, there was no more ocean beneath him, but a large forest with tall coniferous trees, some-what similar to what he had seen in Frostlake. A large mountain range stood ahead of him. The two dragons were beside him in a few seconds, then made another of those fire rings.

"In. Again," she said.

Fel crossed the ring, and found himself over another forest, similar to the first one, except that now the mountain range was to his left, and the sun on his right. He wasn't sure if they were the same mountains, but realized he had changed direction. It was as if these fire rings were like faerie rings, transporting them through long distances. Hopefully away from the other dragons, if they were indeed dangerous. They had to be. The female dragon was too frantic and hurried for someone who wasn't afraid.

"We lost them," she said. "You can relax now. And send thoughts freely."

Fel's wings were feeling sluggish and heavy. "Can we land?"

"Up ahead. Just a little more. Then we'll be safe."

Perhaps the travel had caught up with Fel, or maybe it had been all the diving and trying to fight three dragons. Then there were the blasts of fire, which certainly had impaired him. Regardless, flying took a lot of effort, when all he wanted was to land and perhaps sleep. If dragons even slept.

They were approaching a plateau by the mountains, flying over a silvery river reflecting the sun, fed by a large waterfall.

"Follow us, and don't hesitate," the female dragon said. "Shrink your wings when it's time to enter the lair."

Lair? Where? They were heading to the waterfall. Perhaps there was a passage there. Indeed the black dragon crossed the water, then the gray dragon. Fel, who was following up close, made sure to enter at the exact same spot and shrink his wings as well as he could manage. Indeed, after a tight entrance, he found himself in a huge cave, illuminated with some fluorescent algae or something similar along the walls. Stalagmites adorned the ceiling, but the ground was smooth. Fel couldn't hold it any longer and collapsed, landing so abruptly that he hurt his front claws.

The two dragons landed by him in no time.

"Thank you," Fel said. In reality, he sent this as a thought, but he was realizing that was the way dragons communicated with each other, so it made more sense to think that he was talking, rather than trying to explain something so new with words that couldn't convey it well. *Saying* and *talking* didn't convey it well either, but they felt more appropriate.

None of the dragons replied. Instead, dark smoke surrounded them, and then they disappeared, leaving nothing behind. Fel was stunned. It felt strange to be alone again, and alone so far from everything he knew, in a strange, distant place. This feeling didn't last, though. A second later, a woman and a man replaced the dragons. The woman had short blond hair, light skin, and blue eyes, and stood where the gray dragon had been. The man, who had been the black dragon, had brown skin, wavy, short, dark brown hair, and brown eyes.

"Welcome to Fernick," the man said. "My name's Risomu."

"I'm Tzaria," the blond woman said. She'd been the one speaking to him in dragon form. Her human voice sounded the same, except that it felt more real, sounding like a normal person speaking rather than a voice reverberating in his head.

"My name's Isofel. I'm from Aluria. I... don't know how to get back to my human form. I'll need help for that." He wasn't sure if they would be able to hear his thoughts, but figured it was worth a try.

"For sure." Risomu seemed to have heard him, then stared at him for a moment. "Where are you from in Aluria?"

"Umbraar, but—" He was going to say he'd been born in Iron-hold, but then Leah's words, telling him not to reveal his human magic, came to him. "I was born elsewhere. Not sure where."

The man turned to Tzaria and said something in Fernian. To Fel's greatest dismay, he didn't understand a word.

The woman shook her head. "Let's speak Alurian. No need for secrets. We know who he is. Isn't it obvious?"

Risomu stared at Fel, as if examining him. "It should, but... We know these are dark times."

Tzaria clicked her tongue. "The boundless were *attacking* him, in case you didn't notice."

The man sighed. "And the dragon order seemed interested in him."

Fel had to interrupt their conversation, as he had so many questions. "Who are these people, I mean, dragons? Why were they attacking me?"

Tzaria turned to her companion. "I trust him. What do you say?"

Risomu chuckled and shrugged. "It's not as if things can get much worse. Go ahead."

She turned to Fel. "The dragons are at war. Not war per se, but we're having conflicts. The group who attacked you, they're the Boundless, bound to no magical rules, determined to destroy any dragon standing in their way."

"So they just attack any random dragon they see?"

The woman nodded. "If they don't know them, yes."

"What about those other dragons, the second group?"

"They are connected with the dragon order." Her voice was calm, but there was an edge of contained anger beneath those words.

"I assume it's also bad news?"

Tzaria exhaled. "It's all very complicated. They are not..." She looked away, then back at Fel. "Bad. They've been fighting a difficult war. You can't fault them for being suspicious. At the same time, we'd rather keep you hidden."

"Why?"

The woman looked down, a cloud covering her eyes. "I knew your father. We both did."

Father? Fel's enormous heart beat faster. "Who's my father?"

Tzaria stared at him. "Ircantari. He was the most powerful living dragon mage, a dear friend, and greatly missed—especially in a time like this." She then looked down.

There were so many questions circling Fel's mind that he didn't even know how to start. "Can you tell me more about him?"

She nodded. "For sure. But first, let's get settled. Try to drink some water from the entrance, the waterfall. You shouldn't feel thirsty in this form, but that doesn't mean you don't have to drink."

"Do I also eat?"

"Yes, but not very often. That said, you had a rough time with the Boundless back there. I'll try to get something for you." She turned to Risomu. "Can you watch him while I go and bring Saik? And some dinner?"

Risomu narrowed his eyes. "Perhaps we should wait and stay put. Make sure nobody else learns about him."

She shrugged. "The Order saw him."

"They still don't know who he is," Risomu said. "And I'd rather be extra cautious than under cautious. Let's do it differently then: I'll go and tell him we aren't coming back tonight, without any details, and I'll bring an early dinner for us."

"That's fair." Tzaria nodded.

Risomu traced a circle on the ground by pointing at it with his index finger, then disappeared in it, as Fel watched it, fascinated.

Fel turned to Tzaria. "You can move like the fae."

"Huh. Maybe. But they don't have a tenth of the magic we do. Go. Get some water, and then I'll tell you about your father."

All about his father. This was better than he had expected.

NAIA SPENT hours in front of the communication mirror, waiting to see if more kingdoms would contact them, wondering if they would accuse her of lying or something. All she got was silence. Perhaps everyone was waiting for the gathering, when they would all see each other in person again, when lies would be harder to conceal, and when looks would tell so much more than through the mirror.

Naia got up and walked outside. Arry was sitting on the floor in the hallway. She had already told him that there was no need to guard her, and wasn't going to repeat herself, so she just asked, "How's the infirmary?"

"Better. Fel... He saved us, Naia."

"Had *I* been here, perhaps we could have saved even more people." This was one of the things that hurt her, that made her angry at River. Only one person had died from Umbraar, but maybe it could have been different if she'd been there, with her iron magic and fire.

"Regretting does no good, Naia."

He stared at her in that way that would make her face warm not long before. She wished he wouldn't look at her like that because he was a good friend and she didn't want to hurt his feelings. The funny thing was that when she had been a silly teen with a crush on him, she had never imagined he would be interested in her. Now that her crush was over, his actions were blatantly obvious. It was so odd how her feelings had blinded her.

"It's not regretting," she said. "It's looking back and accessing what could have been done differently. That's how we learn."

"True. We sent the messenger to the portal hub."

"Thank you."

He stared at her. "The Wolfmark king is coming? I don't think your father will like it."

Naia knew that, but what was she going to do? "When he comes back, he can dislike it as much as he wants. I wasn't going to forbid a king from visiting." He was making her nervous here, reminding her of her father's wishes, reminding her that this was no longer her place. "Also, I wish you didn't try to meddle in royal matters."

"Sorry, your highness, I guess I forgot my place." He turned around and rushed down the stairs.

She hadn't meant to hurt him and regretted her words, but on the other hand, at least he wouldn't keep sitting outside her door. She went to the balcony and looked down at the court and the new temporary wooden gate. Beside it, some workers were preparing a new, better gate, also in wood. She'd suggested having two gates, both wood and metal, but it wasn't as if they could build a huge gate just like that. And as much as Naia could manipulate iron, she couldn't make a gate with it. She didn't think even her brother could do that.

As she observed the construction, a sound caught her attention: howls. Umbraar didn't have dogs in their army, and as far as she knew, there were no wolves in the area. She descended the stairs and saw Umbraar guards escorting a man on a horse.

Beside him, there were two white creatures. At first she thought they were ponies or some small horses, but then, when she looked better, she realized they were wolves. Right. Wolfmark; wolves. That was King Sebastian.

Naia was wearing just a linen dress and hadn't even done anything to her hair. Well, she had warned him he would find no finery here. She descended the stairs quickly and approached the king as he dismounted the horse. The two wolves sitting by him made her nervous, but she curtsied.

"Your majesty. What an honor."

He kissed her hand. "The honor is mine."

Naia resisted the urge to wipe her hand on her dress. At least the kiss hadn't been wet. The issue was that she wasn't used to being visited by other royals. She looked at the wolves instead, both sitting down. It was almost like he traveled with them to show off, to show that he had power over such wild and magnificent creatures. It was cruel—and dangerous.

Naia was about to make a request that could perhaps ruin this alliance.

"Your wolves, they'll need to be contained."

He smiled. "They are under control."

"Your control, and this is Umbraar territory. If you wish to stay, the wolves will need to remain in a cell. We'll give them water and food, but they'll need to be locked up."

King Sebastian ran his hand over one of the wolves. "They're tame. You aren't scared, are you?"

Naia approached and patted the wolf's head, even though she was a little afraid, then whispered, "My men, they're nervous. Please. I'll feel much more at ease if the wolves are away."

He smirked. "I'll accept that, but not for your men, for you, and you only."

Naia stepped back. "Thank you."

She then turned around and ordered two soldiers to lead the king and his wolves to a large cell in the underground. The sky was already darkening, so it wasn't as if the creatures would miss sunlight. To say that they would miss freedom was absurd, considering the king had been controlling them.

When King Sebastian returned, without his companions, he said, "Will you show me the signs of battle?"

"Of course." She pointed to the gate. "It was melted. They had..." She was going to say ironbringers, but that would make it too obvious which kingdom had attacked. "Some kind of metal magic." It wasn't that better.

"Your brother was here. He has metal magic, doesn't he?"

"He didn't melt his own gate, if that's what you're suggesting."

"I'm not suggesting anything, princess, I'm asking. What else can you show me?"

Naia led him outside, two Umbraar guards trailing them. The strange creatures had been completely burned, and most of the Ironhold bodies. She pointed to a large bonfire, now almost out, but the smell still remained. A couple of bodies had been left intact, so that visitors could see which uniform they were wearing.

"They don't look fae to me," the king said.

"Exactly. That's what makes them so dangerous."

"I'd like to speak with your highness." He eyed the guards. "In private."

"Of course. We'll go to one of my father's offices."

Naia led him inside, not to the office with his father's things and the communication mirror, but to a room beside it, which had just tables and chairs, no magical objects.

She sat behind a desk. Instead of taking the seat across from her, King Sebastian pulled a chair beside her and leaned over. "If more people see this, it will cause many questions."

"Only you and some emissaries from Haven are coming."

"You know that Ironhold could accuse you of staging a farce to blame them."

"Aren't they our friends?" She smiled. "Why would they do that?"

He laughed. "I like your sense of humor."

"It's not funny, actually."

"No. Ironhold is thirsty for a war, and they would love to crush your kingdom. You know that, don't you?"

She wasn't going to spell things that clearly, at least not yet. "Isn't there a war against the fae coming up? Why would they want more conflict?"

"The fae... I don't know. There's no doubt they are here, but I have my questions. It's all too convenient for Ironhold."

That king was so close to the truth... But she wasn't going to confirm his theories. "And yet nobody is saying anything."

"We will have to say something at the gathering. Find a solution. King Harold didn't tell you his request, but his idea was that all the kingdoms would fund his army, sending gold, food, whatever riches they have. In turn, they would offer everyone *protection*."

"I don't understand." She decided to make a bold suggestion. "You have a strong army—and strong magic. Can't you say you don't need their help?"

"We can't say it for the same reason you can't say Ironhold attacked you." That was quite bold. "We'd be branded traitors. The only way to do it is if we all unite. Perhaps even... turn against them." He was going there? That was fast, and good—but not that simple.

"The kingdoms are too afraid of the fae to do that. Some of them, the ones with fewer resources, might believe they need Ironhold."

"Few resources, Princess Irinaia. It means they won't be happy to pay for help they don't need. They saw what happened to Frostlake. Ironhold was there, supposed to protect them, and yet the king and queen were killed. What kind of protection is that? Kingdoms have questions, questions they won't dare voice through a communication mirror."

"We'll be in the Iron Citadel. It will be almost impossible to conspire."

"Almost, but not impossible. And maybe we can hurt them

from the inside. Their castle is all made of metal, isn't it? And your brother is alive."

"This suggestion borders on treason."

"More like mutiny. We'll need to get rid of the kingdom who wants to crush us. The fae... We'll deal with them like we always dealt."

Hopefully this wasn't some kind of test. "I just want to see peace in Aluria."

"Same. And I'm glad to know I can count on you. But what about your father?"

"He is quiet and reserved, but he also wants the best for Aluria and Umbraar."

"Good." He looked around. "Are you happy here?"

"I... don't actually live in this fort, if that's what you are asking."

"I mean, this is a simple room. Your clothes are simple. You didn't even attend the gathering, why was that?"

That wasn't true. "I went to the gathering."

"I'm absolutely sure I would have seen you, princess Irinaia. I'm assuming you weren't at the ball or dinner."

He hadn't *seen* her? Big purple sleeves and all? River. He had made her unnoticeable indeed. She did want to strangle him. "I was in a corner."

The king took a deep breath. "We need strength, alliances. I saw you earlier today, and I was impressed. Never in my life would I imagine I would meet an intelligent woman."

If that was the case, it could only mean he had never bothered talking to any of them, but Naia bit her tongue. It would do no good to cross a potential ally. She forced a smile. "You exaggerate."

"Not at all. Now here, I'm looking at you and thinking you should be covered in jewels, expensive silk, gold, diamonds. I'm thinking you should have servants and servants trailing you. Wouldn't you like that?"

She almost told him how Umbraar didn't delve in pointless

ostentation, but she didn't want to offend him. "I'm happy the way I am."

"Perhaps because you haven't seen more, haven't tasted more. I came to a conclusion. You should come to Wolfmark—for a marriage alliance. You'd make a great queen."

Uh, what? Had she heard right? Of course the answer was no. The only person she wanted was River. River, River, River, thinking about him knotted her heart with worry.

But then, Wolfmark was a potential ally, so it would be stupid to deny his proposal like that. As far as she recalled, he had two sons, still unmarried, so the king was suggesting marrying the crown prince, but she didn't even remember his name or what he looked like.

"I... It's an honor, your majesty." She tried to measure her words carefully. "I'll be honest that my dream is still to marry for love, and I'm sure your son wishes the same. What I can promise is to meet him and consider your honorable proposal."

He chuckled. "Son. Princess Irinaia, in all my life, I've never seen a woman as beautiful, gracious, and intelligent as you, and I've never seen a princess so overlooked. Your true place is as the queen of the most powerful kingdom in Aluria, and I can give you that."

She frowned. "Queen of Ironhold?"

"Wolfmark. Ironhold will no longer be."

"Oh. It's an honor. I will be happy to meet your son and consider it."

He leaned forward. "Why wait, princess? You could be queen now. With you by my side, I have no doubt we'll crush your enemies."

By *his* side? Wasn't he interested in marrying her to his son? "Of course." She wanted to sever the connection and wished this meeting were not in person. She also realized she was alone with a man in a room, which was looked down upon. Her idea had been that she was acting as interim queen, and kings had private meetings. "Like I said, I will consider your proposal. I think we've discussed enough for today."

"No. We just started. There are many points about this alliance we need to discuss."

"I think we can discuss them later."

He ran a hand through her hair. "I want to teach you to be queen. You need a strong hand, a strong, experienced man to guide you. Aren't you curious to know what it feels like?"

At this point, she was sure that the proposal was to marry him, not his son—which made no sense. "Don't you have a queen already?"

He leaned back. "Oh. That. My beloved wife passed away over a year ago. We haven't told anyone. I've been lonely, sad."

"I can see that you look devastated."

He looked down. "Kings have no luxury of showing their feelings. And it had never been a marriage for love, but a marriage for duty. Now I'd like to marry for love."

Naia got up and walked to the door. "I'm sure you'll find someone."

"I already found my queen." He stared at her. "And I'll stop at nothing from having her. Nothing."

Naia opened the door and yelled, "Guards!" Two men came running. "The king is leaving. Please escort him to his horse."

"It's almost night," one of the men said.

She was about to yell *so what*, when King Sebastian said, "I'm staying. She meant to escort me to my rooms."

How dare he talk over her in her own kingdom?

He turned to Naia. "I'm sure you wouldn't want me to break my neck from a fall because I'm galloping at night."

She wouldn't mind that at all. Still, she smiled. "Apologies. This is a soldier outpost, and I hope you don't mind a soldier's room."

"Your hospitality is much appreciated."

"Please provide him accommodations," she ordered the guards. When they were gone, she slammed and locked the door.

What a creepy king! At this point, she was about to faint from worry about River. As much as she thought it was ridiculous, she had never felt like that. When they were at the house by the ancient city, he would spend his days in Ironhold, and she had never felt so much worry. What was happening?

7

CONVERSATIONS

F el was drinking straight from a waterfall, only now realizing that he had been thirsty. Drinking water was unlike drinking as a human. It was rather a soft, soothing sensation, as if he was putting a salve over a minor burn, one he hadn't noticed yet—not that he was burning anywhere. In fact, he had no idea where his fire came from, how he had become a dragon, and how any of this worked. Still, for now, what he most wanted was to learn more about his father.

He came back in to find Tzaria waking back and forth in the cave, as if apprehensive. She stopped when she saw him, and sat on a rock.

This cave had no comfortable place for a human. "Is this your..." He was going to say lair, but then thought it could be offensive. "Where you live?"

"No." She chuckled. "This is where we hide when we have to."

"You're hiding me."

She raised an eyebrow. "Perceptive."

"Why?"

"To make sure you remain safe."

"From what?"

She stared at him for a moment, then sighed. "We stayed as

far away from Aluria as we could, and made sure all the dragons did so. That was how we protected you."

Fel tried to understand what she was saying, but it was hard to try to piece together half-formed ideas. "Are you going to explain it?"

She closed her eyes, then took a deep breath. "I was thinking maybe me and Risomu would tell you everything together. He was there too. But I can start. Your father was part of the dragon order. So was I, in fact, and Risomu as well. Most dragons are part of that group, unless they are rogue dragons or have joined the Boundless."

She stared at Isofel, perhaps sensing his question. "I know, lots of information. I'll explain it all. Ircantari, your father, was the Seventh Dragon Mage. Few dragons achieve that level of magic, as it takes a lot of dedication and study to control that much power. And talent as well. There's only one living mage right now, and she isn't..." Tzaria shook her head. "No matter. Your father, he was concerned with a seed of evil that he believed was about to sprout. He was right, of course, but at the time, very few dragons realized that great evil was looming."

"What was it?"

"Not was—is—or will become. About a thousand years ago, darkness rose among the dragons. One of our own, the Second Dragon Mage, carved a path of pain and destruction. You never heard anything about it, have you?"

Fel was rather wondering when she would tell him how his father had died, or why he'd gone to Aluria, but he decided to answer her question and see where she was going with this. "I studied some Fernian history, but not much about dragons."

She shook her head. "You wouldn't have learned about it anyway. Some things are not written. But I can tell you about it. War, with all its horrors, ensued. Everyone joined in; the magical peoples, humans... There was no escaping it. In the end, we achieved victory—at great cost, but we did. The Second Dragon Mage was imprisoned, and the dragons took all the measures they could to make sure something like this would never be repeated. That was when the Noxious Fae, I mean, white fae, were sent to Aluria, along with some humans. The Dragon Council struck that dragon mage from our books, struck that war from our records."

Fel was stunned. "That makes no sense. How can you learn from the past if you don't talk about it?"

"True—most of the time. But this is a unique case. The Second Dragon Mage cannot be killed, so he was imprisoned. If his story was buried, it was to make sure nobody would seek him, it was to make sure nobody would try to find him and gain power."

"I'm guessing the strategy didn't work?"

She tilted her head. "It did—for a while—but some things find a way to return."

"So he's back?"

"Not yet. But something's awakening. His followers are amassing. They are the Boundless, like the ones who attacked you."

"Because of my father?"

She shook her head. "I do not think so. They likely don't know who you are, maybe don't even know you're from Aluria. All they know is that you're a dragon, so you're their enemy."

"And why... what does it all have to do with me? With my father?"

"I'm getting there. Part of your father's plan was to set up a trap, set up a powerful, destructive magical object that would attract the Second Mage's followers like light attracts a bug. It wasn't the original object, but a replica—or at least he thought so. We'll never know how, but someone switched the objects, so that the real one was in the trap. Not only that, someone stole the death staff and escaped, even though it should have been impossible. Only Ircantari himself could have undone it. We lost track of the staff—until we heard about an accident. An entire city destroyed."

"Formosa. It was my father's city. I mean, adoptive father."

She raised an eyebrow. "So you were truly raised in Umbraar?"

"Yes. By the king."

"I'm glad to hear that, you have no idea how much." Her expression was thoughtful. "It's as if... sometimes destiny takes care of things."

"Sometimes it doesn't."

"Indeed. I still can't quite grasp what happened..." She shut her eyes. "Anyway, that staff was what brought us to Aluria, and that accident. Your father traveled with me and Risomu, and that's why we know... so much." She sighed. "And it turned out that it had been the noxious fae who'd stolen the staff, which, for us, was quite unbelievable. None of them should have been able to reach Fernick."

"So that's how they destroyed Formosa?" Fel had never been there, but he'd grown up seeing the pain in his adoptive father's eyes at the briefest mention of that city. Just that thought made him hate the white fae, hate even River.

"Maybe. Maybe not. They claimed they didn't do it."

Fel would probably have rolled his eyes if he was in human form. He wasn't sure what he did now. "Obviously."

Tzaria's eyes were distant, as if reliving past memories. "But they can't lie—as far as we know. Of course, we could be wrong. Either way, we decided to listen to their word, and that took us to Ironhold."

If Fel were still human, he would straighten his back at that mention. As he was, he tucked in his wings. "Where he met my mother."

"Yes. We went there to speak to their king, but they did not know who we were, and sent us to see some mere lower advisors, as if we were commoners. But princess Ticiane was there, behind a curtain. Even then, Ircantari saw her. The thing with dragons is that they can see glimpses of their future, and sometimes they know who their partner is. He *recognized* her, and knew she was the one he was going to spend the rest of his life with." She sighed. "Of course, he had no idea how short it was going to be. The princess was trying to run away from her kingdom, her family, and she came to us in Cinaria, the city by their castle."

Tzaria chuckled, her face amused. "Ircantari was thrilled, of course, except that he almost scared her away. He had never flirted with a human. In fact, I don't think he had ever mated in human form. He had no grace, no manners..." She laughed again, a happy memory like a glimmer in the dark.

"What was she like? My mother?"

"In the beginning, she avoided Ircantari, which, to be frank, was totally understandable. I was trained as an ambassador, and as such I was able to gain her trust, also because I'm a woman too. I told her we could bring her to Fernick with us—even if she never spoke to Ircantari. She wanted to run away from her kingdom, so it was a good proposal."

"Why was she running?"

"They wanted to force her to marry someone. Ircantari was furious. It's against all magical laws to force someone to marry. Had it depended on him, he would have executed her parents or at least taken away their magic."

"He could do that?"

"And more. She begged him not to harm her family, though, and he relented. To be fair, we hadn't come to Aluria to interfere with human traditions, even if they were horrific. Ircantari and your mother ended up getting along, and were happy—for a few days. Your mother was shy at first—and sad—but once you cracked that shell, she was funny and very kind. She was also curious, and could hear the most boring magic theory, stuff only your father could care about, with bright, attentive eyes. He adored her, even if it was short."

Fel's heart warmed at hearing about his mother for the first time, learning that she had been loved. And yet, the shadow of tragedy darkened Tzaria's words. Dreading what he was going to hear, and still wanting to know more about it, he asked, "What happened?"

"Her family was searching for her, probably thinking she'd been kidnapped. By that time, we were in Umbraar, to check the ruins of the fallen city. Ircantari was anxious, though, and determined to bring Ticiane back even if we didn't find much, but before he could do anything—"

She turned around, startled.

Risomu appeared in his human form, a bleeding gash on his forehead. "Run."

Tzaria turned to Fel. "Fly away and hide."

He was turning to leave the cave, but then she sent him a thought, "No. Wait. Listen carefully to my instructions and don't be afraid."

"Who's coming?"

"The order."

AZIR FELT himself transported to another place, another time, to that strange celebration that he felt no reason to take no part in.

It was in the Wolfmark castle, and no amount of scowling kept the princesses or their parents away from him. He'd been feeling like a piece of meat surrounded by flies and at some point could no longer stand it. That was when he walked to the outside balcony, then climbed to the parapet above it, from where he could see the Aluria Mountains and the stars, and try to forget everything going on in his mind.

King. He was king and duty demanded that he return to that wretched ballroom to represent Umbraar, but for now, he could no longer take it.

His peace was short-lived, as soon he heard someone climbing the balcony. It was a young woman, who was now also standing on the parapet. How she had done it with a dress, he had no idea, but it was just proof of the lengths they would go to catch him.

Being the sole heir was terrible in too many ways to count,

and then there were all the princesses throwing themselves at him, looking at him with hungry, ambitious eyes. The young woman who had just climbed was petite in frame, dark skinned and dark haired, and wasn't someone he had seen in the ball.

Before he had the chance to tell her to disappear, she extended her arms. "Please don't. I know you're suffering, but you have to believe that there's still something for you, that you can do good in this world, that there's joy and laughter somewhere ahead."

Her words made no sense. "I..." He paused, then realized where he was standing, and the great height below him. Did she really think he was going to jump? At least that made him chuckle. "It's none of that. I'm just taking some air."

She frowned. "Up here?"

He sighed. "Where foolish me thought I could be left alone."

Her eyes were set on him for a long moment. "Are you sure you're fine? Would you like to talk?"

"I'd much rather be alone, thank you. And no, I'm not interested in marrying you."

Instead of taking the hint and leaving, she looked at him with concern. "Oh. You think..."

She made a sound as if trying to stifle a laugh, then took a deep breath and got back to that weird, serious tone, as if she were his mother or something. "I understand this gathering is hard for you, when you're still mourning, when you lost so much, and I can see that nobody is showing you any compassion or sympathy—"

That irked him. "I don't need compassion."

"I see. You just need space. I can certainly understand that." She crouched and was about to climb down.

At that moment he regretted his words. Perhaps all she wanted was his kingdom, but she had been the first person not to speak with him as if he were a crown or a throne. "Wait. I was rude."

She shrugged. "You're hurting."

"I'm not—" He sighed. "Maybe I am. But that doesn't excuse my words to you. What's your name?"

"Ursiana. From Greenstone."

"How come I didn't see you before?"

She had a sly smile and pointed to her dress. "Cream. It blends with the walls. Genius, right?" Even in the dark, he could see the sparkle in her eyes.

Azir wasn't sure if she was serious or making fun of the fact he hadn't noticed her, so he just said, "Indeed."

She stared at the dark scenery below her. "I'll have to say, coming here is a better idea than trying to blend in with the walls. Look at the vastness of the land beyond us and the sky above us. There's so much, so much more. That ballroom is nothing but a speck of dust." She smiled, admiring the view, while the breeze blew her hair, but then her smile faded.

"Something wrong?"

Ursiana shook her head. "I have to go back. My family wants me to help them make alliances." She chuckled. "Of course, they still haven't noticed my wall concealment trick, but they'll want me to be there. Enjoy the view—and the peace."

She then climbed down before he had a chance to reply. Azir wished she had stayed. Perhaps she was just like the other princesses, who were hungry for a chance to be queen, but at least she was more pleasant than most. Silly thought. She was just more efficient at trying to snare him, and now *he* was the fly getting stuck in her web. No, he wasn't getting stuck on anything; he was just appreciating mildly decent company.

Without that company, the parapet felt lonely. Perhaps it had been foolish to come to a place where nothing could distract him from his own thoughts.

He decided to get back to the ballroom, and this time he was going to pay a lot of attention to the walls to see if he could spot the Greenstone princess in her cream dress. But as soon as he walked in, realized it wasn't necessary.

Ursiana was in the middle of the room, dancing with one of

the Wolfmark princes. The first thing he noticed was that she was beautiful. Perhaps not the most beautiful girl in that ball, but she must have indeed been hiding very well to have been ignored for so long. He hadn't looked much at her while on the parapet, as it had been dark. Swirling on the bright dance floor, she was enchanting. And yet, there was something about her posture, her tight shoulders, her head down. She was clearly disliking her dance. The song took forever and ever to end. When it did, he approached her.

She had a hint of a smile. "Changed your mind about the ball?"

"No. But you don't like this either, do you?"

"I like the music. And I enjoy dancing, but..." She looked down for a moment, then back at him with a forced smile.

"You don't want to dance with the Wolfmark prince?"

Ursiana looked down again and shook her head.

Azir sighed. "Can't you say no?"

She swallowed. "My family would be upset. I'm supposed to be encouraging prospective husbands."

"But you don't want them."

"No."

Her sadness contrasted so much with her bright eyes from a few minutes before, when she had stared at the scenery below. "What if your family thought I was a prospective husband?"

Her chuckle was bitter. "They'd obviously be thrilled."

"Dance with me then. All night. And the next. Your suitors will leave you alone. The princesses will leave me alone. I'm in no mind to look for a wife and we'd do this as friends, if you agree. I have no interest..."

"I know. If you keep reminding me of that, this is going to get quite awkward. I'm seventeen, Azir. I don't want to belong to anyone, and even if I did, I'd like to live my life a little before becoming someone's personal slave, thank you."

"*Slave?*"

She rolled her eyes. "What do you think marriage is about, for a woman?"

"No idea. You're all so interested in it, I'd think—"

"We're conditioned, can't we see? If marriage were so great, we wouldn't need to be teaching girls to want it, we wouldn't need to be making up stories as if marriage was the greatest thing. Nobody teaches kids to like cake. You don't have to."

Azir frowned. "I guess."

His thoughts then turned to his sister, his sister who had left her home to a different kingdom, her eyes filled with fear. His sister whom he'd seen only once after that, her eyes hollow, her face pale, as if her light had been quenched. His sister who had died from pneumonia, which he still believed might have been sadness. And that had been before the war.

For the first time, he had the courage to tell anyone about it, tell what he'd seen his sister go through, tell a stranger that he believed the Eaglehold prince—or their family—had killed his sister.

It was like opening a dam, and then all his memories flowed through, as he was speaking to someone who listened, who perhaps even cared. So many words, so many feelings that had been buried. The ball passed in a flash, as their words flowed and flowed while they danced.

She told him about her plans to travel across the continent, get to know more of the world, and even how she had dreamed about visiting Fernick as a child. She knew it was an impossible dream now, but she still yearned for freedom, and that was why she truly did not want to get married.

He found himself sneaking into her bedroom. The ball hadn't been enough for what they had to say to each other. Then, for the first time, he realized the pain he was still feeling, the loss, the horror. His city, his family, his castle, everything gone. Even little things hurt, like the books from the castle library, most of his personal belongings—little, stupid things that shouldn't hurt and yet they did. They did.

What hurt more were the angry words, the last words he'd

told his brother. His brother who had blamed him for a silly prank in the kitchen. Azir had been grounded, sent to the Royal Manor, away from the castle, even if a war was raging on the continent. And that was how he'd found himself alone, the sole royal survivor when his city had been destroyed. Only rubble in the place where he'd grown up. So many swallowed tears whose bitter taste had never left his mouth. But the tears were falling now, falling as Ursiana hugged him and caressed his hair. He'd been king for six months, trying to hold everything together, having to remain strong despite all the tragedy, without any chance to feel his pain.

Azir was strong, but he also wanted a shoulder to cry on, someone to console him, someone to love him. The hug turned into a kiss, followed by more and more kisses. He'd found his queen, his love, his life. He'd travel with her, he'd give her all the freedom she wanted. Perhaps she'd been wrong that he'd have jumped from that parapet, but she'd been right that there hadn't been much will to live in him.

Up until now.

After they had told each other everything, even those dark, shameful parts they perhaps wouldn't have dared even admit to themselves, after they had peered into each other's souls, there could be nothing indecent or improper in getting rid of the clothes between them, in breaching the distance between them. Ursiana was and would always be his one and only love, the only person who understood him.

He buried his pain, his despair, his fears as he buried part of him inside her. Over and over and over, their bodies said what words couldn't.

The sun was already up when he left her room, dreading spending any second apart from her.

Despite not having slept, he felt more energized than ever, more alive than he'd ever felt. In a way it was a good thing that he had some time alone, as he asked the palace attendant for a jeweler. An old man came half an hour later, bringing a few examples of interconnected rings. Azir didn't want to commission brand new pieces, he didn't want to wait, so he bought one of the samples: two silver adjustable rings, with no decoration. They were in the Umbraar tradition, and therefore could connect and form one ring, which he put on, then wondered if she would like it. Well, they could change it for something different later. What mattered was what the rings represented; the two of them completing each other, together forever.

He was about to leave and request an audience with Ursiana's parents, when someone knocked on his door; a woman with a hooded cloak. At first he thought it was a servant, but when she lowered it he saw it was princess Katia, from Wolfmark.

"What do you want?" He didn't bother hiding the annoyance in his voice.

"I have something to show you." She tilted her head and batted her eyelashes, obviously unaware of how ridiculous she looked. "Because I'm your friend."

He didn't want to be rude and cause a commotion, but then he realized she had no guards or servants with her. "Are you alone?"

She lowered her head. "Don't tell anyone. I know it's inappropriate, but my motives are honorable. I just couldn't bear the thought that you would—"

"What is it?"

She put the hood back on. "Follow me."

"I'm not interested, thank you." Again, he made no effort in hiding his displeasure.

He was closing the door, but she pushed it open. "It's about Princess Ursiana."

IN THIS STRANGE IN-BETWEEN PLACE, where Leah had been attacked once, she was now staring at a creature right from history books—a white fae.

Yes, Leah had seen a fae once, but it had been a brown-haired young man. This woman had red eyes, long silvery white hair, and white horns. It was exactly like her kind had been depicted in books, and somehow Leah had always thought it was an exaggeration, that nobody could look like that. She had been wrong.

Unless it was a shapeshifter. Hopefully it was, otherwise Leah had just agreed to a deal with a white fae, meaning she would have to do what she had promised and listen to her until night. What if time ran differently here and it took days, months, years? Well, Leah should have considered it before agreeing with anything.

Beside the fae stood what looked like two human children or young teenagers, but Leah knew that their looks were deceiving.

"Come," the fae said. "This place is dangerous."

Well, of course. But if this fae lived here, why would she say that? "Even for you?"

"We'll talk later." The voice was still gentle, but there was a hint of tension in it. "Follow me."

This was getting similar to her dream, except that in the dream, the creatures had been the ones leading Leah to a cave. Well, no, this was getting different. The fae went to the edge of the mountain, and then descended narrow stairs carved on a rock wall, followed by the strange creatures from this place. Leah was having trouble keeping the pace while still making sure that she didn't break her neck in the precipice below. Technically, she could refuse to do this, since it wasn't what she had agreed, but the fae seemed to be in a hurry, and the "children" seemed frantic, perhaps anxious. If *they* were afraid, then Leah had even more reason to fear.

There was a rocky valley below and more pointy, rocky mountains surrounding the area, and they kept descending, descending, descending those strange stairs. The air was stuffy and humid, and drips of sweat ran down Leah's neck. Only then she remembered to try to cross her hands, and they touched. This was no dream.

Then she moved her hand to her chest, and found the necklace with krystal leaves, which gave her some comfort, even if she wasn't completely sure it would offer her any protection in this place. The creatures she was dealing with were pretty much alive, after all.

The fae was very gracious and was dressed in a long, white tunic. How she could keep anything white in this place was anyone's guess. The "children" had gray or perhaps dirty, simple tunics, and Leah couldn't recall if they were the same or different from what she'd seen them wearing before.

They came to a narrow ledge and the fae walked sideways, grabbing onto rocks.

"Careful here," she told Leah.

Right. As if she was going to run there or something. For a moment, Leah hesitated. A fall from that height would be deadly, and, again, she had only agreed to listen. Still, the fae and one of the creatures were going, and Leah was taken by a sudden fear of being left alone or with the creature behind her, and she followed, taking care to step well in places where there was room for her feet.

They came to a slit on the rock, and the fae jumped in it. The creatures didn't follow the fae, and instead, waited outside.

"Come," the fae said.

Leah had to enter it sideways, but soon she found herself in a cave with stairs going down to a valley, where they came up to a cave lit by an odd orange glow. Actually, it was some sort of fireplace, except that it wasn't a fireplace per se, but a hole in the rocky wall. It probably had an opening somewhere, as there wasn't much smell of smoke inside. Other than that, there was a sort of bed by one of the walls, made of dried leaves, and a table made of a flat rock. This was a house. The fae's house?

"This is not great, but it's more comfortable, isn't it?" She moved near the fire and took what looked like a wooden bowl. "Want something to drink?"

Accepting something from a fae was usually a bad idea, and

accepting something in this strange place was even worse. Leah smiled. "I'm fine, thanks."

The fae sighed. "I understand you don't trust me. We're at war, after all."

"No." Leah almost corrected her, saying the war had ended years before, but then realized information was valuable, was something she could use to bargain, so she decided not to mention what she knew. It still struck her as strange that this fae wouldn't know about that. She wasn't that old. Twenty-five at most, perhaps thirty if she was really youthful—unless fae aged more slowly. Or unless she was no fae. "I wouldn't trust anyone in this place, that's all."

"Fair. And wise." She stared at Leah. "You're a deathbringer. I thought your kind had all been killed. I'm truly sorry for your tragedy."

Tragedy? She meant Formosa, the city the white fae had destroyed. The woman probably thought Leah was part of the Umbraar royal family. But Leah had another question. "The tragedy your people caused? You're sorry for that?"

"I don't know how Formosa was destroyed, but yes, I'm sorry. Tragedy and loss are tragedy and loss no matter where you come from." There was longing and sadness in her voice. Perhaps she was trying to make Leah pity her. No chance.

"And what did you want to talk about?"

"Tragedy and loss. Or rather, how to avoid them."

Leah was still suspicious. "What would you know about that?"

"I spent years here and survived. That has to count for something, doesn't it?'

"It means you have some questionable allies. I mean, the toothy girls didn't bite you. There has to be a reason."

The fae nodded. "Allies. You're right. As to questionable, who knows? You can call me Iona."

"Are you really a fae?" Leah was half expecting the woman to try to bite her at any moment. Of course asking wouldn't solve anything. If she was a shapeshifter, she could lie.

"I'm an Ancient. Humans from Aluria call us white fae. I'm not from here, no." She looked at Leah. "You don't believe me, but it doesn't matter. And you, deathbringer, do you have a name?"

It wasn't as if this would make any difference, so she decided to be honest. "It's Leah."

"Incredible. I'm truly glad some of you survived. Your power... it can change everything. It's the key, Leah. I had smelled your magic once, some time ago, but then it was lost. This time I was ready, alert, and I found you. Things like these, they almost make me believe in destiny, except... It's hard to think that awful things were meant to happen, so I don't know anymore. Or maybe some good things just find a way to show up in our path." She pointed at the bed. "Sit. We have a lot to discuss."

This was too calm. What if this nice lady was setting her up for the creepy voice? What if she was the creepy voice? Asking was stupid, but Leah couldn't help herself. "Is this a trap?"

The fae stared at Leah, almost as if looking through her. "Are you afraid of the shapeshifters? The creatures from here? Or something else?"

"Who are you?"

"An Ancient, from Aluria. I came here by accident." She raised an eyebrow. "The shapers, short for shapeshifters, are harmless, once you understand what they want. Now... there's something else, isn't it?"

Leah touched the krystal leaves in her necklace, knowing they wouldn't bring her any solace or help. "What if there is?"

"Then it means you already know part of what I want to tell you. As much as what happened between our peoples has been horrible, there are more horrible things out there. These are the things we need to fight. As a deathbringer, you can do much more than just open a window to other realms, you can actually open doors."

"You want something with my magic." The dreadful image of

those creatures attacking Umbraar came to Leah's mind. It had to be something of that sort that this woman wanted.

Her strange, dark-red eyes were set on Leah. "It's not me you have to be afraid of. I'm not this horrible thing, Leah. I want to fight it."

"You want my magic to help you."

"Yes." The woman had a small smile, almost a little condescending. "I can see that you still don't believe me."

"Would you expect me to?"

"No. But listen, as a deathbringer, I assume you studied about the eleven realms, right?"

Leah wasn't sure how to reply. If she confessed she knew nothing about deathbringing, would this fae hurt her? Kill her? She decided to take a guess. "You mean the levels in the hollow, right? Like this one?"

"Yes. Do you know what the eleventh realm is for?"

Leah swallowed. "I agreed to listen to you, not answer questions."

The fae inhaled a sharp breath. "You don't know then, I see."

"No, I—"

"It's fine." She stared at Leah again, and it made her quite uncomfortable. "Did you study any deathbringing?"

"What difference does it make?"

Iona took a deep breath and closed her eyes, then stared at Leah. "If you can't use your magic, then you'll need to learn it, otherwise you won't even be able to help yourself. If you don't know anything about traveling in the hollow, much of what I was going to say won't make sense. If you try to fool me and pretend you know magic you don't, I'll figure it out, Leah. And we'll waste time we don't have. I suggest making it fast. How much do you know?"

Leah sucked in a breath. How much was safe to tell this woman?

8

THE FAE

Fel didn't understand much about this conflict with dragons, but he noticed that Tzaria and Risomu considered the dragon order a threat. Perhaps he should have asked why, which only added to the infinite list of questions hanging in his mind.

Soon seven people appeared inside the cave: four women and three men. One of the women, dressed in dark red leathers, was saying something in Fernian, and seemed quite angry. She was in her forties and had black hair tied in a tight braid, with unnatural bright blue eyes.

Tzaria replied, still speaking in Fernian, then started sending thoughts directly to Fel's mind. "They fear you might be with the Boundless because they don't know you. We're telling them you're from Aluria, but you must not let them know your mother was from Ironhold. It's very important. They'll question you, and if I'm correct, they'll put you in a cage that prevents you from lying. It does not prevent you from skirting questions or giving misleading answers, though."

He was almost asking her why, when she added, "Don't send me thoughts. You don't know how to block them from being overheard. Be careful, but don't be afraid. We're coming for you."

These thoughts came to him quite fast, in only a couple seconds in which these words wouldn't normally fit, as if they had been his own thoughts crossing his mind in a flash.

Tzaria then turned to that woman who was staring at her. "He speaks only Alurian. And he's not some random rogue dragon. He's Ircantari's son."

Most of the newcomers took a sharp breath, likely stunned by the information. So this wasn't the reason Tzaria and Risomu had been hiding him, or at least not the full reason.

The woman in dark red looked at Fel, then back to Tzaria, and spoke in Alurian, "Then you have no right to try to claim him. You, of all dragons." She looked again at Fel and narrowed her eyes. "A halfling. And yet somehow he managed to swap forms without any training, out of his own volition."

"I did." Fel tried to send these words to them, unsure if he was being successful.

Tzaria then said, "Question him if you're worried he's lying, but don't hurt him."

The woman in red sneered. "I hardly think it's *us* he has to be afraid of." She then turned to Fel. "Come." Her tone was friendly.

"I... can't swap forms," Fel tried to communicate to them.

The woman smiled. "We'll fly, then. I'm Relia, one of the Dragon Eyes. You'll be safe with us." She turned to the group that had come with her and said something in Fernian, then turned to Tzaria and frowned. "Do not interfere with us. Or there will be consequences." There was so much anger in her voice, even if it sounded that she was trying to contain it.

For a moment Relia and a young man disappeared, soon to be replaced by dragons. The woman had become a dark red dragon, like the colors she'd been wearing, and the man was a green dragon.

"Follow us," Relia sent these words as a thought.

Fel glanced at Tzaria, who nodded as if encouraging him.

Relia flew out of the cave, then Fel followed. At least his wings were feeling better now. Behind them came the green dragon.

Two more dragons joined them, then made a fire circle, through which they all flew. On the other side was another forest, but farther from the mountain range—if it was even the same one. It was like crossing the kingdom portals in Aluria, except that these were not stone buildings, but ephemeral fire rings.

Down below, a river cut the forest in two. Fel didn't know if it was the same river he'd seen. So much portalling was making him disoriented.

Relia descended, then she landed on a tight clearing, part of it covered with the canopy of the surrounding trees. Fel had to be careful not to get scratched while reaching the ground. It was still strange for him to use this form, but he was thankful that flying came naturally to him, as if he'd always known it. Perhaps a part of him had indeed known how to fly all his life.

The green dragon was the last to land, and the two other dragons hadn't followed them. It meant they weren't afraid of Fel, if all they had sent with him were two escorts, including a woman who seemed important. They probably didn't see him as the enemy, which was good. But then why had Tzaria and Risomu been running from them?

The green and red dragons swapped their forms to human. It took them less than two seconds, as if it required no effort at all. Hopefully Fel would learn how to do that trick too. He enjoyed the freedom of flying, the power of his fire, but didn't want to remain a dragon forever. Seeing them swapping so easily gave him hope.

The woman traced a large circle on the ground by pointing her finger at it. Despite the distance, it created a faint line on the earth. Soon it felt cold and dark around him, but just for a moment.

When he looked around again, he was in a valley surrounded by a tall, steep gorge on one side, and steep mountains on the other, as if the valley had been carved out in a hole in the rocks.

Somewhat far from the ring, stood a city with about a hundred houses made of compact earth, with round ceilings.

Many of them had huge doors. A few people and dragons walked on cobble-paved streets. A larger square building stood at the edge, near one of the rock walls. Made of white marble, it stood out among the darker houses. This was a peaceful city, where dragons lived, and all he could sense was tranquility and calm. A lovely place, really.

Fel, Relia, and that green dragon, now in human form, were standing in a circle surrounded by some small rocks, at some distance from the houses.

"This is our sanctuary," Relia said, standing quite close to Fel. "We need to protect this place at all costs." She then moved in front of him, so as to look into his eyes. "We'll need to ask you some questions, but it's just a matter of precaution. These are hard times, that's all."

"I understand." Fel sent this as a thought and she nodded, meaning that she could hear him.

"Follow me, but not flying, walking."

Walking felt strange and slow, but he did as he was told, and noticed three dragons flying in circles above them, as if to watch him. The woman led him in the direction opposite of the houses and came to an isolated building, also made from packed earth.

It was much larger than it had seemed from a distance. The front door was huge, and he could enter it without difficulty, as long as his wings were not spread out.

Inside, there were no interior divisions. This was all one huge room, illuminated by sunlight coming from the center of the domed ceiling. A huge metal cage made of bronze stood in the middle of the room. The fact that Fel could sense the metal so quickly meant not all of his ironbringing was gone—it was just weaker, as if it were a dim and blurry vision. It still felt good to know that he had access to some of his magic even as a dragon. Of course, ironbringing was the part he wasn't supposed to let anyone know about, even if he had no idea why.

The male dragon, in human form, opened a huge door leading to the cage.

"This is not a prison," Relia said. "It's a tool we use for interrogation, and shouldn't harm or hurt you—as long as you speak the truth."

Fel had no choice. Even if by some miracle he could fight his way out of that building, he had no chance of leaving the valley. And then, Tzaria had warned him this would happen and had told him not to worry. But then again, why was she afraid of these dragons? Running away from them?

There was no point ruminating on these questions. Even if they had been asking him to step into a torture chamber, he would need to obey. Fel mustered all his dignity and walked into that cage, then heard its door being closed behind him. The bottom of the cage was also made of bronze. It had to have some magical meaning, but it wasn't something he could identify. Then again, his magical senses had been terrible since he'd swapped forms.

They stood in silence for a few moments, then some ten guards entered the room. They were either human or dragons in human form, and wore some kind of white shiny metal armor. It was funny and ridiculous. Had he been in control of his iron-bringing, he could incapacitate the entire group in less than a second. Of course, if they were wearing that, it only meant they indeed had no inkling about his magic, which was good.

A few more minutes passed, then three people entered, wearing shiny armor like the guards, but theirs was dark blue. Perhaps it was some kind of ceremonial attire. Again, all Fel thought was that if he had control of his magic, none of these dragons would stand a chance against him. It was odd to be so powerful and powerless at the same time.

A man wearing blue armor said, "Stranger, can you use your human form?"

"I can't." Fel tried to send the thought to him, wondering if the others would hear it. To his surprise, his words resonated in the room, as if being reflected by the walls. Strange magic indeed—but helpful.

"It's fine," Relia said, her tone gentle. She turned to the man. "He's a halfling." The woman then smiled and turned to him. "Half dragons rarely transform, unless they get a lot of training." Her tone then changed to formal. "Let's start. Can you state your name and where you're from?"

"I'm Isofel Umbraar, from Aluria. More specifically, the kingdom of Umbraar."

Relia narrowed her eyes. "And who's your mother?"

Fel couldn't say it, but he figured he could get around the question. "I never met her. I was raised by the Umbraar king, and always thought he was my father. He never talked about my mother." It was a faint hope, but maybe they wouldn't ask much more.

"Have you ever heard about Ircantari, the Seventh Dragon Mage?"

Relief washed through him as he realized the questions about his mother were over, and now he could simply tell the truth. "Tzaria mentioned him. She seems to think he's my father."

"Huh." Relia laughed. "Quite a strange assumption. As if Ircantari would—"

"No." One of the newcomers interrupted her. "Can't you see it? Can't you sense it? He *is* his son."

Relia's expression soured. "I guess."

The man stepped forward and removed his helmet. He was about thirty or forty, and had dark brown hair, medium brown skin, and yellow eyes. "I'm Ekateni. Your uncle."

Fel exhaled, and was so surprised that he released a soft blast of fire by accident. None of the people around him seemed to find it strange or threatening, though. Uncle? It meant he had family here?

"Promise you won't hurt me," Leah said.

Iona sighed. "I already told you I have no intention to do so."

"But I want a promise. Then I'll tell you how much magic I know."

The woman stared at her. "I will not commit any action or say any words with the intention of causing you physical or mental harm. Happy?"

Leah couldn't find any trick in the words, and in any case, she was curious to hear what the fae had to say. She took a deep breath. "I didn't know I was a deathbringer, so I don't know much about that magic." The fae didn't seem disappointed. If anything, her eyes had a spark of curiosity, relief, something. Leah then added, "But I was... uh... interested in necromancy, and learned that type of magic, so... I know a little."

"You know about the passages of the dead." She glanced at Leah's necklace. "So this is for something..."

"Scares evil spirits."

The fae nodded. "I see. I'm no deathbringer either, so we might be in trouble. How did you even get here?"

"Accident. I can walk in the hollow, but I can't control it very well."

"I see. Well, there are eleven realms, or eleven levels connected to our world. They are all different, or at least should be. Fae and deathbringers usually walk through the third realm. We don't see much of it. All we can do is go from point to point, or circle to circle. As if... Imagine fae can't see, and all we do is walk through these pre-made paths, or hold on to these ropes leading us from one place to another. If we lose them, we'll get lost. Deathbringers, for some reason, walk in the hollow and can go wherever they wish. That's not completely safe either. If they don't pay attention to where they are going, they could end up somewhere dangerous. We tend to use the third realm because it's the safest. There are no large creatures living there, and that's probably from where the idea that it's hollow, or has nothing, comes from."

"What's in the third realm?"

"Not much. A dead land, and a warning, a warning for something that should not be repeated."

"It had life once?"

The fae nodded. "All gone now."

"And how do you know that?"

"The shapers speak, and some of them are very old and can see through windows into other worlds. Do you know about that?"

Leah shook her head.

"Well, one reason deathbringers can be so dangerous is that they can open glimpses of these other worlds. Imagine you could open a door, and on the other side there were horrifying monsters. There are bars, though, all you're doing is allowing a glimpse of it, and yet it can be terrifying enough to scare animals. That's one thing deathbringers do."

"What if we were to open those bars?"

"What if... I'm sure you can picture it."

Leah almost told her about those creatures helping her with the battle in Umbraar, but decided to listen more and see how much she was willing to trust the fae.

"Of course," Leah said. But she had one question. "How can deathbringers kill with a stare?"

Another smile. "And here you are, afraid of me. You open that passage a little more. It's usually to the fifth realm, where they survive by sucking life force. So you aren't opening the door wide enough for creatures to come in, but it's a slit wide enough for them to pull someone's life."

Leah swallowed. "That's... dangerous."

"Indeed, but I believe deathbringers spend a lot of time learning to control their magic, so that it's somewhat contained. You, on the other hand, don't have that control. There's danger in it, but it can also be an advantage. Anyway, as I was saying, there are eleven realms, with varying degrees of danger. The one you need to worry about is the eleventh. Have you ever heard of it?"

Leah shook her head.

"It's a prison. A prison for things, creatures, beings that can't be killed. Now, imagine how strong someone must be to become immortal."

"Souls are immortal. Why take the trouble to stick to your physical form?"

"Who knows? Perhaps they are souls, like your dangerous spirits." She pointed to Leah's necklace. "But if they are, they haven't crossed over to the land of the dead, they haven't re-entered the life cycle. I don't know why. All I know is that there are powerful creatures in the Eleventh realm. Now, can you imagine what all these creatures could do once together?"

"Fight each other?" She didn't think they would just sit around nicely.

"Probably. Until one day someone shows up and unites them. What do you think happens if they do that?"

"They try to escape."

"*Try* is not the right word. Realm after realm, they've been getting through. They have a leader. In the language here, they call him the *sy laa on*, or chain-breaker. We call him Breaker in the Ancient language. He promises freedom and power."

"Power?" Leah's stomach was cold all of a sudden, remembering how she had felt when that voice had made her kill.

Iona narrowed her eyes, as if reading into Leah's reaction, but then just said, "Yes, power. That's why he is celebrated as this chain breaker."

"I assume he's trying to get into our world."

"Indeed. Actually, he is from there. I can't say whether he's already back or if he's getting there. He can't move out of his own will, but he can do what a deathbringer can, which is to open these windows. Through them, he can communicate with magic wielders or even normal people, and, if he finds someone willing and capable, they will let him through. Even if he's not there, he's strong enough to influence someone and can cause pain and destruction. I've been considering all this, and you might think it's an excuse, but Ancients and humans had lived in peace for generations in Aluria. Generations. We speak the same language. Then all of a sudden we're killing each other?"

"Is that why you think this... uh... Breaker is returning?"

"No. That's just a theory. And might be wrong, for all I know. But the thing is, we're in the sixth realm, and he can come here."

Leah got up. "Can't he listen to us?"

"The tree roots protect us. We're under a very old tree."

Tree? In fact, beyond some rocks, Leah noticed some old bark. Still, that sounded like some silly superstition.

Leah touched the necklace. Who was she to distrust the fae's protection? But she still had some questions. "Wouldn't it have found you by now?"

"There are many realms and many creatures. He can't be paying attention to each of them. In any case, for him I might be just a lost fae, minding my own business."

"Wouldn't he try to control you?"

"Maybe. But he has no reason to insist on it. There are thousands of creatures here, many of them happy to listen to him. He's not going to spend his time going after the unwilling. And by myself, I'm no danger to him. Still, my guess is that he hasn't sensed me. I can disguise my magic and cloak my scent. This is something I can help you with, as you'll need it."

"How come... how come he hasn't found *me* yet?"

"I'm protecting you. Maybe your necklace is doing something."

Leah took the little bell from her pocket and rang it.

The fae had no reaction other than asking, "What's this?"

"It's also against evil spirits."

"How do necromancers define evil?"

"Evil might not be the right word. Spirits usually mind their own business. If a spirit keeps trying to contact you or bother you even after you said no, then they are usually up to no good."

Iona shrugged. "They could just have a message."

"Maybe. It's why we shouldn't be ringing this all the time."

Leah's father had always told her to be careful not to scare away the spirits who needed help.

"And you think this can scare the Breaker?"

"I don't know, but trying can't hurt."

"See? Now that's a funny thing. You came here with this necklace and this bell, afraid of some evil spirit. You know something, don't you?"

Of course Leah did, and she was starting to like the fae, but she also wanted to be cautious. "Wasn't I just supposed to listen?"

"Right." Iona snorted.

"Let me trust you first."

"There isn't much I can do other than let you see things for your own eyes and understand the danger you're in. The shapers say that he hasn't breached the second realm yet, so that has to be true. It doesn't mean it isn't using its intermediaries there."

"Second realm? So it's just one more until they get to us?"

"No. Aluria is in the Second Realm. We're next."

"What's the first realm?"

"I don't know. Some say it's the land of the dead, but it doesn't make sense, as it cuts across all realms. But that's not the issue. The issue is that the Breaker will soon reach your land, your home."

"It's been years, though. It could take years again." Leah knew it was just wishful thinking, but there could be some truth in it.

"He reached *this* realm recently."

"And what did he do?"

"Do you see any life here?"

"The shapers."

"This realm is dying. Not everyone wants to serve the Breaker, not everyone wants to see so much death. Some are willing to fight, but there's no point trying to fight the Breaker here. He's from the second realm, and can only be killed there."

"I was thinking we should prevent him from coming to our world."

"It's unpreventable, Leah, and too late already. We'll need to fight. You're right. It could take years. Let's hope it's the case, so we can prepare. How many: Two? Ten? Fifteen? Whenever it happens, something will need to be done."

"Something... that I assume involves me?"

"Or maybe another deathbringer, not that I think another one will come strolling by any time soon."

"And what is it you want me to do?"

"I don't want anything. I'm trying to save the people I love, that's all, save my people."

Leah felt a knot in her stomach, knowing that the white fae hadn't been seen in almost twenty years, fearing that perhaps most of them had perished.

"What?" Iona asked.

"You heard of the fall of Formosa, and yet you didn't know a deathbringer had survived." It meant Leah could pinpoint the approximate period when this fae had come to this realm, which must have been right after the Umbraar tragedy, and before Azir had been appointed king.

"You must have been a young teenager. I didn't know all the royal families in detail."

The fae was way off in terms of time, thinking it had been some five years or so. "I have... some things to tell you, but you need to promise..."

"I already told you twice I won't harm you."

"Promise to tell me all you know."

The fae rolled her eyes. "What does it look like I've been doing?"

"I mean... don't conceal anything."

"You're the one to talk. I've been nothing but honest, while you're keeping huge, dangerous secrets. I'll help you much more easily if you tell me what you know. And yes, I'll tell you what I do know, in case there's anything I forgot."

Leah took a deep breath, hoping this was really a fae and that her promise not to harm her would stand. If that was not the case, Leah could be in huge trouble.

GREAT. After being careful for so long, making sure he didn't get caught, River ended up in a room like this.

No, he shouldn't waste his time berating himself. Instead, he had to think. What was this stupid herb? Truly, it looked just like regular salatia, which grew even in the underworld, in the Ancient City, but if his magic was being impaired, then it obviously had some effect on him.

Then he sat as far away from those leaves as he could and tried to relax and regain his strength. All he had to do was get away, step into the hollow, and then he would find freedom—and his way back to Naia with a bunch of new information. Yes, because whatever this queen was dealing with, it was something big, dangerous, and that had to be stopped.

He glanced at that little statue and the table. Right. He could use them as tools to try to break the door—or he could smarten up once and not fall into a trap. Right? Not suspicious at all that he was left here alone with an evil statue. Perhaps the whole point in keeping him here was for him to touch it. When there was talk about the key and the vessel, he wasn't going to fall for such a simple trick. If anything, that queen wanted something from him, so she would return. Then, if neither deals nor magic worked with her, he wouldn't have much of a choice.

River sat by the door, then pushed that herb as far away from him as he could. The one thing he could do now was keep his strength and his wits, and wait for the right moment to strike.

Long hours went by and still he couldn't manage to slip away. He wondered if the statue would talk to him, but apparently it wasn't in a chatty mood.

When soft steps sounded beyond the door, he stood up, alert. This could be quick. The door opened, then, in less than a second, he had the queen pinned to the floor. No, not the queen. The youngest prince, Venard. River released his hands only enough to let him speak.

"I'm here to help," the prince croaked. "Don't kill me. I can't help you if I'm dead."

River had never spoken much to any of the princes, and never thought he had been missing much, but even if he'd been quite friendly with the brothers, this visit would never be anything but baffling.

The door of the room was already closed, and River decided to hear what the prince had to say, so he let go of him, then asked, "Explain."

The prince put a hand on his neck. "What's wrong with you? Do you alway try to kill people who want to save you?" Was Venard expecting him to apologize? He truly didn't know fae well.

River smiled as he got up. "An unfortunate habit, I know... How do you propose to help me?"

"I want a deal," the prince said, still lying on the floor.

"Aren't you in luck? They are my specialty." River had no clue what that prince could want, and didn't understand why he was here, but made an effort not to show any mistrust or bewilderment.

Venard got up slowly. "I'll get you out of the castle,but—"

"Out of the room is enough."

"No." He shook his head. "Your magic has been compromised, fae."

"Would you have any idea why?"

"I only know what my mother said. She says even if you manage to break out of the room, you can't leave the castle by disappearing."

River raised an eyebrow. "She told you that?"

The prince looked down. "I overheard it. Much better."

That could be true or not, and they could both be manipulating River, maybe even working together. And then there was the deal with the king—a deal that was practically worthless by now. There wasn't much point in continuing in The Iron Citadel without his magic—it would be too risky. River had already gotten a lot of useful information and could try to return once he was sharp again.

"Great. Get me out of the castle, then." River smiled. "What's your price?"

The prince swallowed, seeming nervous. "I want to learn about that magic. The magic that made my brother alive again. I want to learn it."

River was almost reminding the prince that he was a fae, not a necromancer, but it was better not to confess he couldn't help him much in case that was the only thing he wanted. Instead, he said, "I could offer you better things, prince—"

"No. I want to know what that magic is. I know you don't know how it's done, but you can sneak around. You can figure it out."

River considered his words, then said, "That's a fair deal. You let me escape, and in turn, I'll tell you everything I learn about this magic." This was a crappy offer, because by *everything he learned*, he meant *nothing,* since there was no incentive for him to go looking for those answers. Still, it was always a good idea to start negotiations with the bare minimum. Anyone with a wisp of sense would see that, but River had to figure out the prince's baseline of negotiation.

Venard nodded. "Good. Thank you."

Really? Like that? River should feel happy the prince had agreed so easily, and even thanked him, which meant an open debt. Instead, he felt underwhelmed that he didn't get to twist some truths and entangle the prince with verbal traps. But then, River had to escape, not practice his deal-making skills. Keeping his face neutral, he said, "I guess you'll show me the way?"

"Yes." The prince's voice was weak, hesitant. Then he repeated, as if making up his mind, "Yes." He turned back to River. "We need to be fast, and once out of this room, silent."

River nodded. It was highly unlikely that a human would be faster or more silent than him, but this was not the time to argue that. Venard had a key to open the only door in the room, and then, from the queen's closet, he opened another secret door. From there they stepped into a narrow, dark hallway, lit only by a candle on the floor. After taking the candle, the prince whispered, "Emergency passages."

River knew the Iron Citadel was full of all kinds of concealed and secret corridors, but didn't know them well, since he had better, faster, and safer ways to move around the castle—when his magic worked, of course. In fact, this was a good time to check if it was true that he was weakened. He tried to slip away, but nothing happened.

The prince then added, "This is not soundproof."

Right. Silence. They kept walking and then the thin hallway got wider. Eventually they reached a place where there was a hole with a rope in its middle. If someone walked here without a light, they could easily plunge to their deaths, since there was no end in sight to it. The prince placed the candle on the floor, by the edge of the hole, then reached out his hands to the rope. Great. So they were indeed going down.

River watched the prince grab the rope and slide down. Perhaps he could find his own way. Maybe it was a better idea than following Venard. Who knew? *That* could be a trap. On the other hand, they had a deal. The prince had to know enough about fae to know better than to break it. So after a second of hesitation, River grabbed the rope and slid down, jumping away some six floors down, after Venard.

This floor had some distant light coming from sconces, and another candle on the floor, which the prince picked up. He then looked at River and nodded in approval. "Great reflexes, fae."

"Did you expect any different?"

"No. Had it been anyone else, I wouldn't have taken this passage. But this is the fastest and safest way. And I have to show you something."

"Our deal was that you'd get me out of the castle."

"I didn't say when."

Indeed. The prince could keep him prisoner for some twenty

years and still not break their deal. Silly River had not noticed that, surprised by the loose terms of the bargain. Loose for *both* of them. Regardless, the important thing was that he was out of that dreadful room, far from whatever thing that had been keeping his magic blocked, and could probably soon find his way out on his own.

They got to a narrow staircase and the prince started descending.

This couldn't be right. River stopped. "The bridges are upstairs, prince."

"Exactly. Where all the guards are. Frankly, I don't underestimate your intelligence that much to think you need help to find the main entrance." He smiled. "That said, maybe I overestimated it…"

"There's another way out of the castle?"

"Believe it or not, we are not standing on a bottomless pit."

True. But that would lead him straight to the magnetite deposit. Even immune to iron, River still dreaded the iron magic in this castle, and whatever was at its base. The thought of descending so far down gave him chills.

Venard then added, "It's safe. There are no monsters down there."

"You think I'm scared?"

He shrugged. "I'm just saying. And there's something else I have to show you."

This something didn't sound right either. "You do realize our deal implied that you'd help me leave the castle unharmed, right?"

Venard chuckled. "Afraid I'm leading you to a trap?"

"It's just a reminder."

"I need you to see something—to help me. Then I'm taking you to a secret exit. If by any chance you can do your fancy disappearing, go on, but please wait until you see what I have to show you."

That made River curious. *Please* was not a word Ancients

used, and by itself would only make him less interested in seeing whatever the prince wanted him to see, but his curiosity had been ignited.

Plus, if his magic didn't return soon, he would indeed need help to find that secret passage.

9

INTERROGATION

A lost uncle. A lost family. This was something Fel couldn't have imagined finding when he'd flown to Fernick.

"I..." Words were difficult. What was he meant to say? "... am glad to meet you. To meet you all."

His uncle Ekateni turned to the other dragon lords. "Let him out."

"No," Relia said. "We need to follow procedure. Just a couple of quick questions."

The man sighed. "Very well. But *I* will question him." He turned to Fel. "Don't lie or it will hurt, all right?" His voice was gentle. "Have you met other dragons before?"

There was no reason to try to evade the question—and no point, really. Fel related his encounter with the hostile dragons on the way, then Tzaria and Risomu saving him. He then added, "Before this morning, I didn't even know I was a dragon. In fact, I didn't know dragons, real dragons, still existed."

His uncle frowned. "How did you swap forms?"

"I'm a prince, and responsible for the people of Umbraar. There's some strange magic in Aluria. There were these things... Like dead bodies coming back to life. We couldn't save them. I couldn't save..." He was going to say Leah, but then realized they wouldn't know who she was. "Anyone." He decided not to mention his sister yet, at least for now. "I was desperate for fire. Somehow, I figured if I had that power, I could defeat them. And then I felt different, and I had fire, so we won. But it's not as if I can understand what I did or how I did it. We need help, that's another reason why I'm here."

"Dead bodies coming to life?" Relia sounded incredulous.

One of the men in armor shook his head. "That human magic, it's quite volatile, especially their necromancy. I never liked that magic running loose like that."

"It wasn't necromancy," Fel said. "Or deathbringing. I was raised in Umbraar, I know what those types of magic smell like." In truth, he didn't know how to sense necromancy. All he knew about it was what Leah had told him, but she was a deathbringer, not a necromancer. Leah. Thinking about her brought him so much agony, but he was doing what he could, and indeed had found other dragons, which was a great victory and could perhaps help his kingdom and hers.

"You can *smell* magic?" That same man sounded incredulous.

"Sense it. I don't know. It was something else. Aluria needs help. Urgently."

Ekateni nodded. "We'll try to send someone, but, as you noticed, we have our claws full." He didn't sound the least concerned about what he'd heard.

Fel had to insist. "What's happening there is quite serious, and if you regulate the magic in the world, you should see it."

"We'll talk about it," his uncle replied. "Come."

Ekateni was about to open the door, but then Relia stopped him. "A couple more questions."

"He's family."

"Family who could have been brainwashed," the woman replied. "Family who was with the filthy exiles. It won't take long."

"Fine."

She turned to Fel. "Just say yes or no, and it will be quick."

There was no anger in her voice. If anything, it was true that she was doing it just as a precaution, and didn't think Fel was a threat. "Do you have any connection with the boundless?"

"Not that I know of."

"Are you spying on us?"

That was an absurd question. "I wasn't even planning on coming here and had no idea this place existed."

"I need yes or no," she said. "Are you spying on us?"

"No."

"Have you ever heard of Cynon?"

"No."

"The Second Dragon Mage?"

Fel recalled some of what he'd heard a few minutes before. "He's... some evil old dragon, isn't he? Tzaria told me my father was... doing something against him."

"That's Cynon, by the way, the Second Dragon Mage's name. Are Tzaria and Risomu working with him?"

"She seems to think he's evil, so I don't think so. Tzaria was just telling me about him when you came, and then she didn't even get to finish her story." Didn't even get to tell him what had happened to his mother, but he didn't want to say any of that.

"Are *you* supporting Cynon?"

Fel was going to protest that he didn't even know who he was, but it was easier to answer the way they wanted. "No."

Relia sighed. "Are you here to gain power?"

"Maybe. I want to turn back to my human form. I want to help my kingdom and my land. I want to understand what it's like to be a dragon. In a way, all those wishes are related to power."

Ekateni approached the cage again and smiled. "You're home, Isofel, and we'll obviously help you connect with your power."

"Can you help me become human again?"

He paused and furrowed his eyebrows. "Maybe. But it won't be soon." He then smiled. "Come. I'm sure you need some rest." He turned to Relia. "Is the procedure over?"

"It is, but we need to understand how the exiles found him, and what they want with him."

Fel recalled Tzaria and Risomu fighting bravely against the enemy dragons, even if they'd been outnumbered. "I think they were trying to protect me."

Relia sneered. "They are so great at protecting."

Ekateni sighed. "I'll talk to him once he's rested, and once he's not in this cage."

The woman frowned and said something in Fernian to him.

Ekateni nodded, then led Fel outside. "Come. We'll fly, but please go slowly and carefully." They walked outside and he turned into a dragon in the blink of an eye. His scales were light blue and shiny. "Follow me."

No guards were following them, not even Relia. They were soon up in the air, moving towards the edge of the mountain. Of course they had to fly slowly here, as they passed over the city. If everyone flew at the same time, it could get confusing, not to mention possibly windy.

"What did she say?" Fel asked.

"She hates Tzaria and Risomu." Ekateni's voice sounded clear in his head. "Had it depended on her, they would have been executed."

"For what?"

There were a few odd seconds of silence, then he said, "Making mistakes."

"They saved me today."

"Maybe. Or maybe they were working with the Boundless to gain your trust."

That didn't seem likely. "They killed those dragons."

"It doesn't really work like that."

"You mean dead dragons don't remain dead?" Horrendous images of the battle around the Royal Fort came to his mind.

"Dragons can swap forms," his uncle said. "If you hurt one of them, their other form will still be intact, and if they swap fast, they'll survive."

"I see." It explained how those three dragons had disappeared. Fel had thought they had plunged into the waters, but perhaps it was just that they had taken their human forms and had been concealed by the blood around them. That image still disturbed him, but then, he wasn't sure if leaving these enemies alive was a great strategy either. "But their dragon form would be hurt, wouldn't it? Why would they do that just to gain my trust?"

"It's what we're trying to figure out."

"You think it's because of my father?"

"Most likely."

Ekateni flew towards a steep stone wall, edging the mountain around the valley. Fel didn't quite understand where he was going, as he had expected to land in the city. For a second, he wondered if he should trust this dragon, but he felt a sense of ease. When he had met the Boundless, he could sense their aggression, but there was none of that here.

When they approached the edge of the chasm, Fel realized there was an opening large enough for him to fly through, if he tucked his wings through the passage. The opening was rough and unfinished, and likely a natural rock formation, but after that there was a huge open door, through which Fel followed his uncle, and then he was in a large chamber with a floor made of polished wood and painted walls, with what looked like huge mattresses on the corners. There was another huge door, in wood, but it was closed, and a small one, which he figured led to human-sized living quarters.

"I hope you can feel at home," Ekateni said. "You can take the seat by the far wall, for a comfortable place to rest."

"Those are *dragon sofas*?" Fel was surprised.

Ekateni chuckled. "Feels unnecessary, I know. Perhaps an extravagance. Wait 'till you see the beds."

"I thought you would rather sleep in human form."

"No. Most of us spend as long as dragons as we can. The human form can perform better magic, and it's better for communication, but a dragon lives longer, some thousand years or even more. By sleeping in dragon form, we get to age more slowly."

"A thousand years? That's... An empire can rise and fall. So much can happen in a thousand years."

"Indeed. But remember we're also human, so most of us aren't living *that* long. Still, it means we remember things that would otherwise have been forgotten."

"Like the Second Dragon Mage."

"Yes."

Fel decided to lead the conversation where he wanted. "What about my father? What did you know about him?"

Ekateni disappeared for a second, then reappeared in his human form. He had a bitter chuckle. "So much. And yet perhaps so little. He was obsessed with studying, spent all his time trying to understand the nature of magic. See, most magical peoples *use* magic. They have access to it, and use it the way it is. Dragons can *mold* magic, change it, control it. It's an incredible power, and only the dragon mages can do all that. I don't think Ircantari did it for power, though. Maybe for the challenge, maybe because of a fascination with the theory of magic, with the nature of things. But it was also because he thought he could make a difference." His voice choked with emotion. "And why it hurts so much that he's gone."

"Do you know what happened?"

He sighed. "Negligence or malice, I do not know. Tzaria and Risomu killed him."

RIVER STILL COULDN'T BELIEVE his magic was failing him, couldn't believe he was following one of the Ironhold princes, and couldn't believe that prince was likely betraying his family in exchange for a vague promise to tell him about creepy magic. No, the worst part was feeling so powerless.

Yes, River could fight, and being an Ancient, would have a

natural advantage against a human or two, maybe three or even four, depending on their skills and strength. Still, he had always relied on his magic, and to feel it gone like that was troubling and strange, as if he were no longer fully himself, as if a part of him was missing. Well, it was.

He kept going, doing the only thing he could do for now, which was to follow that prince despite all his misgivings, dreading the idea that he was about to go to the bottom of the chasm where the Iron Citadel stood.

They weren't quite at the bottom when the prince led him to another set of slim passageways, so slim that they had to walk sideways. River felt the walls pressing against him, feeling suffocated and trapped in that tight passage in enemy territory, with no way to reach his magic.

The corridor ended in a door leading to a bedroom, with a large four-poster bed in its middle, a wardrobe, and a dressing table. The room was lit by sconces on the walls, had large oil paintings depicting fields and flowers, and a light pink carpet on the floor. For human standards, this would probably be a woman's room, except that there was something strange about it. Well, there was no door other than the small one through which they had entered, and no windows either, so it was more like a prison.

River turned quickly, to see if Venard was perhaps trying to block the door or lock him in, but no. His eyes were sad as he stared at the bed. There were no guards and no apparent threat. Even then, River was watchful. He looked at the bed again, and realized someone was lying there.

He turned to the prince. "Why are we here?"

"My reason. You have to understand my reason." He approached the bed. "Come. Look."

It couldn't be anything good. River took careful steps, shivers running down his spine, even though this was just a bed. When he got close enough, he looked away quickly before disgust took over his senses. No, it couldn't be. He looked again.

On the bed lay a dead young woman's body. She was dead, dead, dead, unlike Cassius, who didn't seem to be breathing, but wasn't completely devoid of color. There was no fetid smell, thank goodness, as the body had probably been embalmed, but it had been embalmed somewhat late, when the body had already started to decompose.

Venard choked a sob. "I miss her. I want her back."

From horror, River's thoughts turned to pity. "Prince Venard. You know that you'll meet her again. When the time is right."

Tears ran down the prince's eyes. "No, I won't. Do you think me and her, we're going to the same place? Do you? I'm pretty certain the answer is no. I have to say goodbye."

Humans from Ironhold and most of Aluria believed in an after-world of many levels, depending on how they lived their lives. It was bizarre that some of them believed in eternal punishment while at the same time acting as if all that existed was power and money. Ancients believed in a cycle of lives, but there was no point in trying to argue with the prince. At the end of the day, these were all conjectures anyway.

River still tried to console him. "You'll meet her. Eventually you will. What you have on the bed is an empty shell. It will do you no good to try to change that."

"There's a way." He turned to River. "Isn't there?"

"Not really." He then felt the force of the deal compelling him to tell him what he knew. "Cassius was re-awakened, yes, but before that, he didn't seem to be fully dead. I can't explain it, but it was different. And what I heard from Umbraar was that the fallen men who re-awakened were something else, not themselves."

Venard sighed. "I don't care if she's different."

"What about your wife?" River knew she had escaped and was with Naia's brother, but he wanted to understand Venard's point-of-view.

"I tried. I tried to be her friend. I tried to protect her. I even thought maybe... maybe I could come to like her. Nothing worked, and then my brother..." Venard sighed and looked away. "I betrayed her. I..." He shut his eyes. "I'm glad she escaped, but I wish she had killed him for good."

This was strange and surprising. So Venard would have liked to see his brother dead? And he was not angry at Princess Leandra. Interesting. But River was still moved by pity, and tried to make the prince see some reason. "There's no guarantee this new Cassius is your brother, no guarantee he's the same person."

Venard rolled his eyes. "I doubt he can be any worse."

"Things can always be worse."

"You think I'm crazy, don't you?"

River shook his head. "I think you're grieving. Grief takes many forms." He then tried to remind the prince of their deal. "I will tell you everything I find out about this strange magic, but I can't do much in here."

Venard turned to him slowly, as if reluctantly. "I know. Do you understand? Do you understand me now?"

Not at all. This room was morbid, and his idea of trying to re-awaken that dead body was gruesome and macabre, but River understood a little of what the prince was feeling. "I know what it's like to miss someone."

"Wouldn't you do the same?"

"We're different."

The prince stared at him, his expression blank. "Let's go, then. We have a lot of stairs."

That was no joke. They found a spiral staircase and after way too many turns to count, River was starting to get dizzy. "Once there, how do I go up?"

Venard's face looked eerie illuminated only by the candle he held. "There is a passage embedded in the rock, leading to some stairs. Far from the castle. But you might be well enough to do whatever you do that you just... Puff."

River paused. "How do you know my magic will be better?" It was odd that the prince had overheard so many details.

"I... I'm assuming. You're welcome to take the stairs. Or climb. Whatever you feel like."

River could sense some sign of deception and lies, but he couldn't quite identify what it was. And he had another question bugging him. "Won't they know it was you? Won't it be obvious?"

Venard swallowed. "I don't think so. How would they guess?"

Then why was he nervous? River pushed him. "And you're not afraid of betraying your family?"

"My mother. And—" He bit his lip. "Let's not pretend to be obtuse. Me and you, we are on opposite sides."

"I've been helping your father..."

The prince raised a hand. "No. Not even my father ever trusted you. I'm not sure exactly on which side you are, and how many sides we're dealing with, but I'm smart enough to know that there's a chance my family will lose. Ironhold will still need a king. If you're on the winning side, remember I can be your ally."

River frowned. This was not even a deal, but he couldn't let this request float unanswered, knowing he would likely never honor it. "I don't know if I'll ever be in a position to have any power over this kingdom's throne, prince."

"You don't know that you will *not* have that power, fae. I'd rather have allies than enemies."

Treacherous allies were worse than enemies, but River said nothing and they kept descending those infinite, dark steps. He wasn't even sure why that prince was helping him escape. His disturbing obsession with his beloved's corpse was not a good explanation, especially considering that the people who knew the magic he wanted were exactly the ones he was betraying. Wanting a possible ally didn't quite make sense either. The prince had no idea that River had ever belonged to the Ancient's royal family. Good will? No. Ironhold hated his people.

But then, River had better pay attention to his surroundings and to his own magic than waste his focus trying to figure out someone's bizarre decisions. If this was a trap, he couldn't afford to be entangled in his own thoughts.

It turned out that the staircase wasn't infinite, after all. They reached an open area that would look like an old deposit, except that it was empty and had a high ceiling.

"Lovely place," River murmured.

"I've never learned what's on these lower floors," Venard said. "And maybe the answer is simply *nothing*."

"If you haven't been here before, how do you know there's a door?"

"Scurry around and listen enough, and you'll hear a castle's secrets." He stared at River. "I mean, you obviously know that, don't you?"

River shrugged. "I guess. If only I hadn't been busy helping his majesty, maybe I would know all about secret doors."

The prince chuckled. "You wouldn't. Never thought you'd need them, did you?"

"There are way too many things one can never think, isn't it so?"

"You don't think I can be a useful ally either, do you?"

"I'm following you, aren't I?"

Venard nodded. "Once it's over, or *before* it's over, we might face each other on opposite sides, and I hope you remember this."

"I won't forget." That meant nothing, thankfully.

They walked into that huge empty room. It had rusty iron walls and stood over a deposit of magnetite. If River hadn't become immune to iron, he wasn't sure he would be able to even walk in this place. Perhaps this was a prison for Ancients, or some other kind of prison.

They came to a humongous door, a gate actually. What were they expecting to pass through that? Beside it, there was a normal-sized door, big enough for a human. A large lock kept the door tied to a bar on the wall. The prince pressed something on that bar, and it disconnected from the wall easily. The hinges squeaked, their sound echoing in that strange chamber, and then River was facing the bottom of a chasm, so dark that it looked like it belonged in the hollow. No lights from the stars or moon reached down here, and since it was already night, only blackness awaited him.

"Run and hide," the prince said. "There might be things hiding there. But you're out of the castle."

"You said there were no monsters."

"Monsters aren't the only things that can hurt you. And remember I'm not a fae." Meaning that he could lie.

River stepped outside, then looked back to see the door closing, shutting away the flicker of light coming from the prince's candle. He turned again, to face the darkness ahead of him. At least he was out of the dreadful Iron Citadel, and yet, within the deep pit surrounding it.

IO

GLIMPSES OF THE PAST

Fel listened, stunned, as his uncle told him that Ircantari had gone to Aluria and never returned.

Ekateni added, "We never really understood it. He was more powerful than both of them combined. They had traveled with him to Aluria, to punish the noxious fae. Then they claimed they had a training accident on the way back here, and wouldn't answer all the questions, saying they were too traumatized. We had no option but to exile them."

Fel's uncle then paused and took a deep breath. "I mean, they could have been executed, but I insisted they should be kept alive. I had to understand what happened, and that's why I had them watched closely, to see if I could find any sign of betrayal, any sign that they'd been planning something. To be honest, it didn't look like they were guilty of anything, and I was almost convinced my brother's death had been an unfortunate, inconceivable accident—until now. They knew how to find you."

"It doesn't mean they killed him."

"They did, Isofel. They confessed as much. The question is just whether it was on purpose or not."

"Didn't you say my father was more powerful than them? How do you think it happened?"

"It must have been some kind of betrayal, perhaps they caught him when he was asleep or somehow vulnerable. Even then, it would have been hard. Perhaps someone helped them. Now, assumptions are a roadblock to the path of truth. You get stuck on them, trying to see everything from that angle, and then can't identify the truth when it appears in front of you. I haven't tried to come up with any explanation. All I've done was watch the exiles as much as possible. I even went to Aluria, where indeed Ircantari punished the noxious fae."

"The white fae. Why do you call them *noxious*?'

"Their magic is corrupted, dangerous, and if they join Cynon again, then we are doomed. But there's no way they can do anything now, the way they are. I also sensed no dragons." He stared at Fel. "Not even *baby* dragons."

"But I come from Aluria."

"I don't know how I couldn't find you." He was thoughtful.

"I was raised in Umbraar, by a deathbringer. Maybe his magic concealed me?"

"It's a possibility. Indeed, human magic in Aluria has become more and more corrupted."

"Which is why you need to do something. We're having issues there. It's why I came."

"We will, we'll certainly do something—once we get rid of Cynon's shadow and the dreadful Boundless. Unfortunately, that's where our efforts need to focus now."

"People are dying, Ekateni."

"If we don't contain Cynon, a lot more people will die. Power over magic entails tough choices."

Fel understood that, to a certain extent. "My father—" He shook his head. "—adoptive father, always said that kings have to make difficult decisions, even sacrifices. But he always told me that I should never sacrifice my humanity, my compassion, or I would end up damaging my moral compass and then could no longer be trusted to make decisions."

Ekateni stared at him. "You were raised by a kind human, and

I'm happy for that. Still, I assure you that my compassion—and moral compass—are intact. It's just a matter of priorities. I will arrange for you to speak to the high council and request that a few dragons be sent to Aluria. We will do something, Isofel, I promise, but you'll have to be patient."

Fel thought that his uncle's tone was condescending, the way some adults speak to children, but then perhaps it was just that Ekateni didn't understand the gravity of the situation, caught up in his own problems with Cynon and the Boundless. Fel would need to find a way to convince the dragons and get the help Aluria needed so desperately. "I'll be happy to speak to your council, thanks." And there was something else he wanted desperately. "Can you help me turn back to my human form?"

Ekateni stared at him. "You'll live longer as a dragon, and if you stay, we'll get you appropriate lodgings."

"No. I need to come back, to help my kingdom. I can't do much like this."

His uncle shook his head. "Forget Aluria, forget your past. You're home now."

"No. I need to help them. And I..." He was thinking about Leah. "I'm betrothed." This wasn't really true but wasn't that much of a lie either.

"You'll forget about her, I promise you. You're a dragon now, and you'll find a dragon companion."

There was no point trying to argue. "I see you're in human form. Relia took human form, as well as the guards surrounding my interrogation. I'd like to be able to do that as well."

"Certainly. It might take a few years, but you'll get there."

"I don't have years."

"Of course you do." Ekateni chuckled. "You'll live much longer now, Isofel. Accept your power and who you are."

It took a lot of self control not to torch his uncle. Would fire burn dragons in human form, though? "And how am I going to learn about my power? Is there someone who can teach me?" Hopefully someone with more empathy.

"That's a good idea, in fact. I know the perfect dragon to mentor you.

"And who's that?

"You'll see."

AZIR FELT his heart beat faster as he stared at Princess Katia, from Wolfmark. "Is Ursiana hurt?"

"No. But you have to see what she's doing, you have to. You'll thank me."

"I have to follow you?" He sighed.

"Yes."

"Is this a trick?"

"Of course not. You'll see." She batted her eyelashes again.

Azir had no choice but to walk with that princess, consumed with worry and fear that perhaps Ursiana would be in danger. They walked down to the gardens of the castle then went to the part where there was a small maze and several greenhouses. A few guards had seen them passing by, but thankfully she still had her cloak on. If someone saw them together, he would face the wrath of the Wolfmark family. Perhaps that was her plan.

"Wait," he said. "Why are you bringing me here?"

"To see the Greenstone princess. You know that."

"Just so you know, if by any chance this is a plan, if you want to set me up, I will not, I will absolutely not marry you."

She shook her head. "This is no trap, Umbraar king. I'm rather *alerting* you to a trap, before you marry a slut."

Azir was about to slap her, but words rehearsed since childhood came to him. *Control your darkness.* Control, control, control, he had to control it. And yet, there was only so much he could take. "Say that word again about her, and you'll face grave consequences."

Princess Katia shrugged. "We're almost there. I'll let you make up your mind."

They were walking through a path covered with plants, when Katia tripped and fell. He should perhaps have held her, but he was still suspicious about this princess, and wondered if she'd tripped on purpose so he would hold her. Her yell was loud enough that could have alerted some guards, so he stepped as far away from her as he could, just in case someone came.

The princess got up and shook the dirt from her skirt. "Thanks for the help."

"You got up just fine, didn't you? Where are we going?"

"There." She pointed to a storage shed.

"I'm not going in there."

She rolled her eyes. "There's no need. There are gaps between the wooden panes on the wall. You can see from the outside."

"See what?"

Her laugh grated on his ears. "Oh, aren't you dying with curiosity?" Then she put a finger over her lips. "Silence now. Or they'll hear us."

"They who?"

She pointed to the shed, a smirk on her face. "Go. I'll wait."

It would be easier to do what she was asking than argue, so that was what he did. He heard a moan before he got close enough to look. Was Ursiana hurt? Was she...? It couldn't be.

He looked through a gap—and couldn't believe what he saw. There was a couple there—both naked. He was standing, kissing her neck, while she was sitting on a counter, her legs wrapped around him. The man was Sebastian, the oldest Wolfmark prince. And the woman. The woman... Azir wanted to look away, but he couldn't stop staring. That same dark, curly hair, that same skin, even a birthmark on her hip looked the same. But it couldn't be her. It couldn't.

Azir wanted to enter the shed and kill them both. *Control the darkness.* Why was that voice pestering him? He wanted to kill these two horrible people who were mocking him. The woman was obviously not Ursiana; this was a prank in poor taste. It had to be. But the birthmark...

The prince stopped kissing her, then said, "I'll miss you when you marry that stupid king."

The woman sighed. "The plan was yours." The voice was wrong. Too high.

He wrapped his arms tighter around her. "And I hate sharing. Did you really have to spend the night with him?"

"I had to be convincing." The voice was high, excessively sweet. "It was disgusting, though. He's so pathetic, spent some three hours crying." She sneered. "And he has no idea how to even do it... I don't know how I didn't laugh, frankly."

Azir stepped back. Only one person knew that he had cried. Only one person knew where he had spent the night.

And yet he couldn't kill her, couldn't hurt her. He turned around and walked back to the castle, promising himself that he would never make a fool of himself again. He would never fall in love again. He'd keep the rings as a reminder of the love that would never be.

"No." A different voice came to his mind. "This is not true. You can change it. Change it. Look again."

Azir went back and opened the door of the shed. The woman was getting dressed and had her back to him. The prince was also getting dressed, but looking at the door.

"Woman, turn around," Azir said.

The prince stared at him. "Get out."

"I want to see her."

The prince sneered. "You have no right."

"I do have a right. Aren't you putting on a show for me? You heard it when your sister yelled, you timed it so I could see you, hear you." Azir let some of the darkness escape. "Turn around or I'll kill you both."

The woman turned, trembling, tears in her eyes. "Please, it's not my fault."

Azir exhaled. The skin tone was the same as Ursiana's, but she didn't really look like her and was clearly older.

Azir pointed at the *birthmark*. "Can you rub that?"

The woman did so, and the mark got smeared. It was ink.

The Wolfmark prince raised his hands. "Hey, I was just having fun. It was a joke."

"How do you know what happened in Ursiana's room?"

"A bird told me."

He was a wildbringer, after all—but birds couldn't talk. Perhaps someone had been spying on Ursiana. A lot more likely, and yet it was chilling that someone could have seen or heard them.

Still, Azir's anger dissipated, now that he knew he could change the course of his life. Change. It meant it hadn't been like that. This was a memory. Just a memory.

He then was transported to another place. A girl, about five, was trying to hit a target with an arrow, but kept missing. A boy beside her chuckled.

"What's so funny?" the girl asked.

"Nothing." The boy crossed his arms. Just arms. He had no hands, but somehow it wasn't surprising or strange.

The girl then tried again, and the arrow this time turned around and landed at the girl's feet. She looked at the boy. "Did you do that?"

He just laughed.

Instead of getting upset, the girl smiled. "You have magic!" She turned to Azir. "Dad, he has iron magic!"

No. This memory couldn't exist. He was back in front of the shed, about to go back to the castle and propose to Ursiana, when an arrow came in his direction and stopped mid-air.

The girl came running. "I can do it too! I can do it!" She stared at him, this time serious. "You can do it. Get out. Get out. Snap out."

The girl ran away and disappeared, then a huge white dragon flew towards him, as the girl's voice resonated in his head.

"Get out. Get out. Get out."

He opened his eyes.

RIVER FELT DISORIENTED, without much of his magic, still unsure how Queen Kara had done it, thinking it strange that there was a plant that could block fae magic and yet he had never heard anything about it.

What he had to do now was find one of those stairs and climb out of this hole—unless his magic returned, then he could just disappear and go home. Home. It wasn't really home he wanted, but Naia. Naia who had warned him against coming to Ironhold. She had been right—this place was more dangerous than he had expected—but also wrong: he had found important information that would make a difference.

A sudden movement on his right caught his attention. He couldn't see anything, just felt the air shift, and there hadn't been any smell either. Before he could even try to figure out what it was, something large and hairy hit him across the abdomen, pushing him back. He fell, then rolled away. The ground shook beneath him. Whatever had pushed him had tried to impale him to the ground. River had no weapons and no magic. Now, that was foolish. An Ancient should always carry at least a dagger, ideally two or more.

Since the creature didn't move again, River moved his hand to touch whatever had been stuck to the ground and felt something thin and hairy. That had to be a giant spider. They should have been extinct. This wasn't the time to try to figure out what it was doing here, but to find a way to defeat it.

River ran and climbed the pincer until he found himself above what felt like a round, hairy ball. It had to be the back of the spider. That way, it could not reach him, at least for a while. He felt something slimy beneath him, and when he touched it, he realized it was his own blood. This was bad. There was also some kind of insect on his neck. River lay down, trying to save his forces. Even though the spider was jerking sideways, he held onto it. His only plan now was to try to remain there for as long as possible, until he could see anything or until his magic returned.

His magic. He felt a slight tingle, a different sense of smell. Now, if his magic were weak, he wouldn't be able to go far, and could get lost, but then, he had no choice. If he remained here any longer, it would be certain death. Possible death was a much nicer possibility.

NAIA WATCHED as Arry walked towards whatever room they had given King Sebastian. She wanted someone trustworthy watching the king, so that he wouldn't find out more information than he should. She didn't want any soldier telling him for sure that it had been Ironhold, or mentioning anything about the dragon. Arry would know how to keep their secrets and make sure their visitor didn't wander around the fort by himself.

Naia didn't trust the Wolfmark king, but then she didn't want to send him home in the middle of the night with a horse in unfamiliar terrain. Perhaps she should have suggested he use the wolves to guide him. Well, too late now, he was going to be their guest for the night. She hoped her father would arrive soon, and this time, she wouldn't mind if he were rude to a "potential ally." Naia wasn't interested in the disgusting alliance he had proposed. That said, the king wasn't interested in bending backwards to Ironhold, so he could still be an ally.

Naia then felt something. A call. A pull. It wasn't mysterious this time. She knew exactly what it was.

II
HEALING

Naia's feeling was unmistakable. How strange that it had seemed so mysterious a year before, when she had found River for the first time. For some reason, she could sense him—behind the fort, in the woods, and probably in danger—unless this last assumption was just her pointless worry. No, something was happening.

She passed through the guards by the gate and asked not to be followed. It would be terrible if anyone witnessed her rescuing a fae—unless River was glamoured. Being alone in the woods after such an attack was dangerous, but she paid attention to her metal magic, which could sense metal not belonging to the woods. Since most soldiers or assassins carried daggers or swords, she would be able to sense them.

But what overwhelmed her sensations was River. She found him lying down, but with eyes open.

Naia kneeled by him and held his hand. "River. What happened?"

He smiled. "Did you know I love you?"

The words chilled her, not because she didn't like to hear them, but because he had to be wounded and perhaps even dying to say that. She touched his stomach—and felt blood. "You're hurt."

"Um-hum." He was chuckling.

"I don't know why you find it funny. I almost died of worry." She realized she was crying.

"Me too, I almost died."

You should have listened to me was on the tip of her tongue, but it wasn't the time for that. All she wanted was to make sure he survived.

Naia placed a hand on his shoulder. "I'll need to get some large piece of metal to put you over it. I can't carry you, and I don't want anyone to see you."

As if it would help. They would have to cross the gate. She could perhaps put a sheet over him and pretend it was a soldier, perhaps even pretend it was her brother.

"No. I'll get up. Take me inside. Directly. I... no glamour."

Then people would see him. "The guards..."

He held her hand. "Help me get up. The hollow."

Naia wasn't sure if this was going to work, wasn't even sure if he could get up, but pulled his hand and supported his back as he got up. River was hurt and she wanted to cry and yell and scream. She was so angry that she was sure she could crush the Iron Citadel if she went there right now.

River leaned on Naia and wrapped an arm around her. Slowly, the woods got darker around them, darker and darker, that oppressive darkness that felt as if it would swallow her.

"You have to look," he whispered.

Naia opened her eyes and realized that there were some parts where it wasn't as dark, as if they were faint lights in the distance, blurred by some kind of fog.

"Take me inside," he added.

This was insanity. She took a step towards where she thought the fort was, and the lights shifted.

"See the place where you want to go."

Naia looked down, and suddenly it was as if she were floating above the fort, but it didn't feel real and three-dimensional, it was as if it were a small drawing on the ground, below a blurry glass. She moved to where Fel's room would be. While she used to have a room there, she didn't know if it was still unoccupied or if it was habitable. Fel's was on the end of the hall on the second floor, remote enough to give her some privacy, and should have a proper bed, covers, everything.

They were right above his room. "What do I do now?"

"Is this the right place?" he asked.

"Yes."

River held her close and now she felt the darkness pushing against her. Against them. She even feared making his wound worse, since she was touching it.

As that horrible feeling dissipated, she and River were in Fel's room. The bed was made, but other than that, it had books everywhere and even some clothes on chairs. Fel, Fel. She missed him so much.

River sat on the bed. "See? I'm back."

"Don't lie down. Let's get this shirt off." She undid the buttons as fast as she could and tore it.

The gash across his stomach was deep and red and bleeding. Abdomen wounds could lead to death. She got up, glad that the dresser was complete with a jar of water, a soap, and a basin, so she took it and proceeded to clean the wound.

"Can I lie down?" he asked.

"Yes." Her voice came out full of anger. Well, she *was* angry. He had ignored her pleads not to go to Ironhold, and here he was, with that awful wound. She got up. "You need stitching. I'll have to get someone." Who could she call that wouldn't tell anyone about River? Arry came to her mind, but she wasn't sure he'd know how to do that.

River held her hand. "No need. We heal faster."

"You better heal before you die. River, I want to scream at you. How am I going to do it if you're dead?"

He closed his eyes. "Just stay. Stay close, while I rest. Your magic will help me."

What magic? She didn't have any healing magic. Would this be enough? Perhaps what he needed was a real healer. Either way, she could leave him be for a few minutes. This was the second time she saw his chest, felt his skin, but all she felt now was panic that he could be dying. Naia got up to make sure the door was barred, but then got back and lay down beside him. Her own eyes closed.

FEL'S NIGHT was filled with strange dreams. He was in human form, walking through long, dark hallways. Leah was there, but hiding from him.

From a distance, her voice echoed in the walls. "Go away. I can't let them find you. Go away."

It wasn't that she was angry or afraid of Fel, but rather afraid *for* him, trying to protect him, and yet he knew that they would be stronger together, but there was no point in calling her. Her voice echoed on the walls, such smooth walls—metallic walls.

Fel shredded them to pieces, and then stood in an empty valley, only mist surrounding him. Dark, heavy mist, as if to conceal him.

He opened his eyes. "Leah?"

No voice came from him, just a thought sent out to nobody, an empty, pointless thought. He'd slept at his uncle's house, on one of those *dragon sofas*. There were dragon beds inside, in rooms that belonged to his two cousins, who weren't there, but even then, he didn't want to take anyone's bed. In fact, he didn't even think he needed a bed at all. One thing he had been in desperate need of was sleep, though.

It felt like an eternity from the previous evening, when he'd eaten some kind of raw meat his uncle had brought him. He hadn't asked where it had come from or what it was, and perhaps it was best not to think too much about those things.

Sunlight came from the door that led to the opening, so he'd probably slept through the night. Being in this form didn't feel strange—it felt good, in fact, but he couldn't wipe from his mind everything going on in Umbraar. He hoped his father—adoptive father—was all right, hoped his sister was safe. She should be. For some reason he didn't hate River as much as he hated the white fae, perhaps because of how much he seemed to care for Naia.

Fel had to find an answer, a solution for his kingdom. At the same time, he wanted to understand what had happened to his father, to his mother. The answer was in Tzaria and Risomu. The question was how to get to them, and whether they would tell him the truth. Then he also had to wonder what they wanted with him, and on which side they were. There was no doubt that the dragons in this city were peaceful and wished him no harm. He couldn't say the same about those two dragons, though.

"Hello?" He sent a thought throughout the house, and it went unanswered. Fel was alone in this dwelling in the mountain, realizing he was unsure where to go or what to do.

Could he fly down and find someone to teach him about dragon magic or how to swap into his human form again? Probably not. He wouldn't even know where to go or who he could speak to, and he didn't even speak Fernian. But waiting idly, alone with troublesome thoughts, was agonizing in its own way. When there was so much to be done, sitting in a dragon-sized room by himself was an enormous waste of time.

A bright circle then appeared on the floor, and Fel exhaled, relieved that his uncle was back.

But the person standing in the middle of the circle wasn't Ekateni—it was Tzaria. "Sorry I took so long." She was speaking quickly, in hushed tones. "We need to be fast. I'm going to open a large ring—"

"No. Why should I go with you? Why are you pretending this place isn't safe? This is a peaceful city. I'm at my uncle's house."

"Isofel. When you don't know where the enemy is, unfortunately, you have to hide from everyone. The Boundless have corrupted too many dragons. This city is not safe."

"Right. Says the dragon who didn't protect my father. Was that why you didn't tell me how he died?"

She sighed and shook her head. "Things are not as simple as they seem. I'll tell you everything, but we need to go."

"How can you even get in here? Isn't this city hidden, isolated?"

"Exactly. Makes you wonder, doesn't it? Isofel, I'm begging you. Come with me. I'll tell you all about your mother."

That was a low blow. Tzaria knew how much he wanted to know about her, and was using it to try to get him away from here, perhaps away from safety.

He tried to understand why she was doing that. "You think I'm in danger here. Truly? Perhaps my uncle is planning on murdering me in my sleep—except he didn't."

"No." She frowned. "You can trust Ekateni."

"Well, then, he's saying this city is safe, so I guess I'll trust him."

All she did was stare at Fel for a few seconds, then said, "Let's hope he's right." She disappeared in a cloud of smoke, and then there was no sign of her or the brilliant circle on the ground, as if it had never existed.

Fel then heard wings flapping outside. He perked up, hoping to see his uncle, but instead saw a light-green dragon with brilliant scales entering the room. The newcomer soon changed his form to human, and was a young man in his late teens or early twenties, with black hair, brown skin, and brown eyes.

The new dragon asked, "Can you understand me?" He had a strong Fernian accent.

"Yes. Can you hear me?" Fel still wasn't sure how this whole thought-sending thing worked, but tried it anyway.

The young man smiled. "I can! You're good at this."

"Is it supposed to be difficult?"

"It takes some training, I think, but then, taking your dragon form takes a whole lot more training, and apparently you didn't have any. Is that true?"

Fel reclined back, his belly feeling the cold floor of that strange stone house. "I didn't lie, if that's what you're suggesting."

"No, no." He shook his head. "I was just asking, and surprised you did it." He then smiled again. "My name's Siniari. I'm Ekateni's son—and your new mentor. Your cousin too, it seems."

"You don't believe it?"

Siniari shrugged. "Don't blame me for being stunned, but don't get me wrong; we're happy to have you here. What do you want to learn first?"

That was an easy question to answer. "How to swap into my human form again."

Siniari scratched the back of his head. "That's a complicated one. I can show you the village, though."

Fel straightened his neck. "It can't be that complicated. I've seen many of you doing it as if it were nothing at all."

His cousin bit his lip, as if thoughtful. "I'm sure you've seen people writing or reading without effort. It doesn't mean it can happen like that." He snapped his fingers. Lovely. He had just done something that was impossible for human Fel, which was an unwelcome reminder that not everyone could do everything.

The heat in Fel's chest felt like it wanted to come out. Instead, he sent a thought. "So let's start this learning."

Siniari stared at Fel for a moment. "I see you're in a hurry. Why don't we do this: I'll start by showing you the village, so that you at least feel more at home—"

"This isn't my home."

"I said *feel* at home, so you're not as lost." He shrugged. "But you're welcome to go back to the desolate continent now, if that's what you want."

"I need to learn how to turn back to human, and learn about my magic."

The young man sighed. "Hurry is not the solution."

"You don't understand."

Siniari sat at the edge of one of those dragon sofas. "Then explain. Explain what's happening. Tell me everything, and I'll see what I can do. There are always shortcuts—if you're not afraid of stepping in uncharted territory and getting scratched by thorns."

"I'm not afraid."

He stared at Fel for a moment. "Great. So let's fly. Follow me."

Siniari ran to the edge and jumped. Fell watched in horror as his cousin fell on the chasm. Before his body reached the ground, he swapped forms and then soared up in the sky.

Fel took flight after him. "I thought we were not supposed to fly fast here."

"We aren't." His thought did not sound clear, as if he had some difficulty communicating. Perhaps that was why dragons took human form to talk—perhaps it wasn't that natural or easy.

They flew up, away from the village, then landed on a ledge in the mountain surrounding it. From there, all Fel could see were rocky hills—no houses or any construction.

"Did it disappear?"

Siniari swapped into his human form, then said, "You can't see it. That's one of our protections. Not the only one." He chuckled. "In case you're an incredibly smart Boundless, don't get any ideas." He stared at Fel. "I don't think you're a traitor, though. Just a newbie dragon, which is awkward. I mean, it's not as if you haven't been a dragon since you were born, and yet you're new... at being you."

That was a funny way to put it. "I didn't know. I didn't even know dragons existed. I grew up thinking the Umbraar king was my father."

His cousin was thoughtful. "But if you were a king's son on that continent, you should have human magic, right?"

Fel *had* human magic, but he didn't want to tell his cousin about it, even though he was almost sure he was trustworthy. Perhaps he *should* tell everything. No, Leah's words were fresh in his mind, asking him to hide his ironbringing. And then Tzaria had also warned him against it, not that he cared that much for her word.

"I just figured I didn't have my father's magic. Never thought I could have... a different father."

Siniari nodded. "That's why you want to return? Because you're a prince there?"

Fel paused, thinking. The reality was that those words made sense. "I have a duty to my people, yes. That's one reason."

His cousin looked away, staring at the mountains and clouds. "We don't think much about Aluria, to be honest. It's as if it didn't exist for us. Forgotten. But if you have people you love there... I can see why you'd be attached." He turned to Fel. "But you're also a dragon, and there's a lot you can learn and do, and we might need you here as well. Your father—your true father—was quite powerful."

"I heard. And hopefully I can use that power to save the people of Aluria."

"Tell me about it. Tell me what's going on there. Magic is misbehaving, right? I think I heard my father saying something like that. What's happening?"

Perhaps it would be easier to convince his cousin, who was young, and hopefully not yet jaded like the older dragons. Fel decided to tell him everything, or rather, *almost* everything. He wasn't going to mention that he was an ironbringer or that he had a sister—just in case.

Fel started by telling his cousin about the odd water snake, then the strange fae attack inside the Frostlake castle. The story got all messy because he avoided mentioning Naia and then couldn't mention River. That said, he did tell him about the attacks in villages, Ironhold gaining power, and then attacking

Umbraar with ironbringers and an army that could be re-awakened.

His cousin, who had been listening attentively, asked, "Can't... necromancers do that?"

"No." How could he explain it? "I was... am... betrothed to a girl—"

Siniari pointed at him. "That's why you need to turn human!"

"Yes, that's one reason."

"You were saying something about necromancy?"

"Yes, my betrothed was raised in Frostlake, by the necromancer king, and knows all about that kind of magic. It has very specific, limited applications, and can't reawaken an army."

"But magic is alive. It changes, evolves, sometimes degenerates."

"True, but the attack came from Ironhold. Their magic is metal."

His cousin bit his lip and paused for a moment, then said, "You're right, absolutely right. We need to send some dragons to check that." He sighed and looked down. "It's just..."

"What is it?"

He took a deep breath. "We're hiding. We used to rule the magic in the world, and it's not that we miss the power, it's just... Controlling magic is our duty. The same way you say you have a responsibility, so do we. And yet here we are, hiding. Divided. We lost many dragons, enchanted and seduced with promises of something... I don't even understand what." He stared at Fel. "I lost friends."

"To Cynon? Why would they want to follow him?"

"They don't think they're following anyone. They end up believing that it's time for the dragons to re-awaken, to take their place in the world, to fly freely over all lands. They think they found a way to increase their power, a way to gain freedom."

"Can't you just let them be?"

Siniari shrugged. "We could—if they left us alone—and if they left anyone alone. I don't know what happens once they join them, but it corrupts the dragons. We've sent spies to infiltrate them, learn their secrets. We learned a little, yes, but we mostly lost friends—either to death or to the Boundless."

"If you lost friends, they would know where this city is, wouldn't they?"

He shook his head. "We only come through circles, and it's all sealed. You can't fly in or out. If you were to try to fly higher, you wouldn't be able to. That keeps us safe—for now."

Fel almost mentioned Tzaria, but then, for some reason decided not to.

"How do... Is this Cynon back and leading these Boundless? Recruiting them?"

"My father doesn't think so, but thinks he's crossing the threshold and communicating with us. He has a way to increase their magical power. It means you can fly faster, live longer, have more fire. It sounds good, right? But there's a price."

"You mean the boundless are more powerful than normal dragons?"

"Usually, yes."

"I fought against three of them, then Tzaria and Risomu defeated them."

He shrugged. "Tzaria and Risomu were part of the higher council, and were once among our best. I'm not surprised they'd defeat three sentries. How you lasted so long against three drag- ons, I'm not sure. Got your father's blood, I suppose."

Fel wasn't comfortable with the idea of simply inheriting magic, instead of practicing to hone it. "Or maybe I was lucky."

He chuckled. "You were definitely lucky, there's no question about it." He shrugged. "I mean, don't blame my mother for being suspicious."

"Your mother?"

"Relia."

Fel hadn't gotten the impression that she and Ekateni were a couple. "Why don't she and your father live together?"

"They are not married anymore."

"You can stop being married?"

Siniari paused for a moment. "Right. Some humans don't dissolve marriages. We do."

"That's sad."

"If you saw my mother and father together, you wouldn't say that." He sighed. "But they both liked Ircantari very much. Seeing you is like getting a part of him back."

"I'm not my father, though—and never met him."

Siniari chuckled. "I know. Nobody's expecting you to become a dragon mage—not that we'll be upset if you decide to become one."

"Don't I need my human form to study magic?"

"I'm sure you'll learn to swap eventually." He looked away, as if deep in thought.

There was something about his hesitation... Like something he wasn't sure about saying or not. It was odd that Fel thought he could sense some emotions, but he decided to trust his impression. "There's an easier way to swap, isn't there?"

Siniari's eyes widened. "I wouldn't call it easy. Potentially fast, maybe. Possibly deadly. Incredibly reckless."

"What is it?"

He chuckled and shook his head. "My parents are going to kill me if I tell you, cousin."

"And yet you're dying to tell me."

Siniari stared at him, immersed in a cloud of indecision, confusion and fear. He sighed. "Promise you'll pay a lot of attention to the risks, then."

"I do have big ears."

NAIA OPENED her eyes and didn't recognize where she was. Everything was dark, but a familiar smell lingered in the air, so familiar, soothing... River. He was lying beside her. Faint moonlight came from the window. She was in Fel's room in the Royal fort, and the only candle had gone out.

No, no, no. Sleep had taken over her and she hadn't checked on him. Touching his shoulder softly, she whispered, "River?"

"Naia?" He sounded surprised, but not hurt or in pain. "Where are we?"

"The fort." She got up and lit a candle, then moved back to the bed to examine his wound. She blinked, then touched his stomach. There was nothing there. Well, there were muscles, his lovely soft skin, but no wound other than what looked like an old, faded scar. Had she dreamed it? "I... you were hurt, weren't you?"

River pushed her hand away and closed his eyes. "I remember now. It was something silly. A giant spider."

"Silly? What happened to your wound?"

He looked down. "Healed."

"Does it hurt when I touch you?"

"No."

"You pushed away my hand."

"For other reasons, Naia. I like it too much."

She wanted to put her hand back there and torture him, see him lose control and drop that superior smirk, but he was looking at her with some vulnerability and fear, and perhaps he was about to open up for once.

Still, her anger hadn't subsided. "Why didn't you listen to me? I knew something was wrong. I felt it. All day I kept feeling it and telling myself I was imagining it."

He took her hands in his and kissed one after the other.

"I'm sorry, Naia. Listen, I had a deal with the Ironhold King. It bound me. I couldn't simply decide to walk away and no longer help them, I couldn't tell anyone what I was doing. And I had to find out their secrets."

"What happened?"

"Is this room safe?"

"If we don't speak too loud, nobody should hear us."

River kissed her cheek. "Through it all, the one thing that

made me worry the most was that I had to come back. What I most wanted was to come back to you, Naia. And it's not only that I missed you, I wanted you to know that I'm willing to do things the hard way. Work together, trust you, and open up."

Naia wanted to kiss his lips, but she also needed him to tell her what was happening, what was going on, and why he'd gotten hurt. "I'm glad you're ready, and I want to know every little detail."

"I offered to help the king a couple of months ago. It was my opportunity to infiltrate them, but I couldn't tell anyone about it."

"But you told me some of it."

River shook his head. "I didn't deny it when you guessed it correctly, and there's a difference. I wasn't the one telling you."

"But now you can talk about it?"

"I can—but I'm starving. Aren't you hungry?"

Great. Right when she thought he would tell everything, he found a way to change the subject. "You know, I fear that if I go down and bring something to eat, this helpful, truthful River won't be here anymore and then you'll start giving me vague and useless answers."

"Great point." He chuckled. "And you didn't even check if I'm an impostor."

Naia scrunched her face. "I know it's you. A different you, but still you." She got up. "I will bring something, though, as I'd hate to *starve* you."

In truth her stomach was growling as she descended the stairs and crossed the yard to reach the kitchen. Howls coming from the prisons reminded her of their unwelcome night guest.

The cook was already working, as the sky outside was turning purple. It was morning already.

"Princess," the man said. "It will be ready soon. I can call you, or ask someone to bring you your breakfast."

Naia smiled. "It's fine. I'll just grab a few things. Don't mind me."

She put some bread and jam in a basket, then hushed back upstairs.

When she got back to Fel's room, River was sitting at the table, wearing a white shirt. "I took it. Hope your brother won't mind."

"I thought fae were all natural and free and didn't mind being naked."

His face relaxed into a happy smile. "You want to see me naked?"

What if she did? What if she said yes? But she didn't want to encourage his smug smile. "Right now I want you to tell me what happened."

"Exactly. I don't want to distract you—or get distracted." He looked at the basket she had. "What did you bring?"

"Bread and jam. We don't have a lot of stuff here. Not yet, at least."

"It's great."

He took a piece of bread and stuffed it in his mouth, then put jam on another and ate it, almost all at once. Naia realized she'd been starving as well, so she also ate, hopefully with more grace than River. Well, he had gotten seriously hurt, so his lack of manners was understandable.

"So?" she asked once she thought he had filled at least part of his stomach.

His pretty reddish eyes were set on her, and then he finally started speaking. He told her how Ironhold had been planning to make Aluria fear the Ancients again, as a pretext to gain power. His words implied that they were still planning it, that it was something in the future, and Naia had to correct him.

"King Harold contacted the other kingdoms, including us. They just decreed that Aluria would become the Ironhold Empire."

River tensed. "What did you say?"

She chuckled. "I said sure, lovely idea! But let's wait a little."

"You're joking."

"I'm not. That's exactly what I said. Now it's all going to be decided in three days. Two, actually. An emergency gathering in the Iron Citadel."

He squeezed the piece of bread he was holding. "No, no, no. You're not getting anywhere near that dreadful castle, and nobody from your family should go there."

Naia tilted her head. "Oh. Really? It's annoying when someone you like goes to enemy territory, isn't it? You get worried."

He stared at her, his eyes like burning hot coals."It's worse. Much worse than any of us thought."

"Speak for yourself. I knew they were bad."

"You didn't, Naia. You don't know half of it."

"Well, tell me, then."

12

THE BREAKER

It was as if the light went out of Iona when Leah told her that the white fae had disappeared, not that she had been any kind of beacon before.

"But I saw a fae once," Leah added quickly. "So I'm sure your people are only hiding or something." She would never have imagined that she would be relieved to say that the white fae weren't all dead. The fact that humans in Aluria had been celebrating their demise felt sick now that she thought about it.

"Where did you see him?"

"In the Iron Citadel. He helped me for some reason, and made me walk in the hollow from one room to a different one, where I could hide."

The fae shook her head. "No ancient can walk in that castle. Too much iron magic. It must have been a spirit."

That didn't seem likely. "He was solid and held my arm—or hand."

"It couldn't have been a real fae. Not in the Ironhold castle."

Leah was pretty sure it had been a fae, but didn't want to argue. "Still, your people might be hiding, or maybe they moved. At least there's no more war."

The fae looked away and shook her head.

Leah was at a loss for words, so she just continued, "That was almost twenty years ago. I wasn't even born then. My... real father was the only survivor of the Umbraar family. I think he was a teenager then, but not too young." Not too young to disgrace and humiliate Leah's mother. "I... didn't know he was my father. I was raised by the Frostlake king, thinking I was a necromancer."

"How did it work?"

"I could... revive dead animals. For a few seconds. That was all my magic."

"It's like you were using your deathbringing backwards, like some people when they whistle by sucking in air."

"Can you even do that?"

"Apparently yes, if you're saying so."

Leah had meant the whistling, but it was something too foolish to discuss. The fae had her head down, covered with her hands.

"I guess... you won't need me anymore." Leah realized she might have made a mistake telling the truth to the fae. "Now that you think there's nobody to be saved."

The fae snorted. "Don't be ridiculous. There are still humans, for once. I'm part human. You might be right that the Ancients are hiding. And even if they aren't, if I was meant to survive, there's a reason."

"I'm really sorry."

"Nonsense. It is what it is. And it's true, maybe it was just a way to stop that war, to find peace. Maybe the Ancients are living happily somewhere. If the Breaker hasn't found them." She sighed. "What else do you want to tell me? You know more, don't you?"

Leah had to figure out what was going on, and this was her chance. "I think... This Breaker has been speaking in my mind. I... I killed people. Killed in self-defense, which was good, but also killed when I didn't have to. I felt a rush of power, excitement. Then... I had a dream. There was a woman, in this very realm, calling herself the Queen of Darkness, saying I could be much more, as if offering to give me more power, but it was a woman." Leah stared at the fae again, wondering if by any chance they were one and the same.

"The Breaker doesn't have a form. I can see you're wondering if you saw me. Maybe it was a farseeing dream that got somewhat contaminated. It's hard to explain."

"What if he's here, now?"

"Do you hear him?"

Leah shook her head. "Nothing after I put on this." She touched the necklace. "But there was more, before. You mentioned opening a door, and I did it. It was during a battle. Ironhold was attacking Umbraar."

"You're at war again?"

"It's recent. Anyway, they were attacking them, and I asked for help. Some strange creatures came from the sky. They helped me, but then they didn't. I think it might have had something to do with the Breaker."

"What did the creatures look like?"

"Some of them had wings, some didn't."

"Maybe you got some from the Fourth realm, but couldn't control them. They also suck life force. How did you defeat them?"

"Fire."

"Regular fire?" The woman was suspicious.

Leah wasn't ready to say anything about Fel, so she was going to say she wasn't sure, but then she felt something pricking her throat and felt difficulty breathing.

"Say it," Iona insisted. "It was your idea to make the deal, so it will hold you to that."

"Dragon fire." Leah took a large gulp of air. That had been horrible. "Please, don't make me explain how or why. I don't think it matters."

"Their magic is very powerful, Leah. If dragon lords have come to Aluria, maybe they're after something. Are they involved in your war?"

"No. They're not. The person who did it didn't know he was a dragon, but he was able to take his dragon form and then summon fire to defeat the creatures. I'm not sure how it happened, or even why he's a dragon. I really don't know."

"You need to be careful. If the Breaker knows about this dragon, he'll certainly spare no efforts trying to target or kill him."

"I know. I heard his voice in my head, and that's why I ran away, to stay away from him, to drive this voice away from the dragon."

"I can teach you some tricks to cloak your magic and your dragon, and to close your mind, so that the Breaker doesn't see you. Would you like that?"

Fae didn't offer anything for free. "What is the cost?"

"None. You can fight a common enemy. Why wouldn't I want you to be at your best?"

Leah shrugged. "Don't know. You could fear I could turn the knowledge against you?"

"None of that would affect Ancients. First, we don't try to get in anyone's mind." he looked down. "Not like that, at least. Second, we have other ways of sensing magic. Only masking your scent won't do much. I'm not offering you any advantage against the Ancients, but an advantage against our common enemy."

"You still haven't said what you want from me."

"First of all, I want you to know what's happening. It seems that's not a hard task, since you've felt it yourself, and you're in love with a dragon lord, who could be in danger."

"How do you know?"

"That he's in danger?"

Leah frowned. "That I'm in love."

"Your face is an open book. And to be honest, I'm glad there's a dragon lord around. Their magic is helpful."

Not any dragon, but Leah didn't want to think much about it, fearing the fae would pry the truth from her, and she wasn't willing to tell that much. "If dragons can help so much, shouldn't we go to Fernick and call them?"

"How would we even get there? I mean, I guess *you* can. They might know more about it and might be able to help, but then, they might already be getting ready for this fight."

"Can't they deal with it?"

"They might not be concerned with Aluria, and their magic might not be enough. Deathbringer magic is quite special, it's good that it evolved to be like that. Maybe the magic itself knew it would be needed."

Leah thought about Azir Umbraar. She still couldn't forgive him for what he'd done to her mother, even if he had been nice to Fel and Naia. "You'd assume all deathbringers are good people. Get one of us on the wrong side, and you could wreck countless destruction."

"True. But you seem nice. If you weren't, the Breaker would have gotten you already with his promises of power. He didn't. But you need to close your mind a little better, and learn to control it. Are you ready?"

"For what?"

"To learn it."

This had been a bit sudden. "Sure."

"Close your eyes then, and listen."

It took a lot of trust, but Leah obeyed. This better not be a trap, or she would be in trouble so deep, she had no idea she would be able to escape.

FEL WAS FLYING through his third circle in a row. His cousin Siniari was very good at doing them. "Don't you usually need two people?" Fel asked. "For these fire rings?"

"Usually. Not always." Siniari's voice was faint. Fel had forgotten his cousin wasn't good at communicating in dragon form.

They were now by a mountain chain and the sea, but it didn't look like the sea between Fernick and Aluria. Siniari flew towards an island which looked like a continuation of the mountain chain, but in the water. It had a high, sharp peak, and Siniari landed near the top, on a flat surface by a shallow cave, then immediately swapped into his human form. Fel landed beside him.

Siniari took a deep breath. "Are you sure about this?"

"You know I am."

He shook his head. "Did you pay attention when I said you could die?"

"Everything has risks. Of course I understand that. So do you, or you wouldn't have brought me here."

"I..." Siniari looked away. "I want to help, that's all. I know my father will never agree with this, but I know what it's like to want something, but..." He closed his eyes. "Please be careful."

"You said I could quit."

"I think so, but I've heard some people have died trying to speak to the First Dragon Mage. He's not evil, but he doesn't view things in the same way we do, and—"

"He could help me swap into my human form. That's what matters."

Siniari nodded and bit his lip. "You need to step into his cave—"

That would be a problem. "I don't fit."

"Just put the front claw, just face the opening. State your name and near family line, and ask to speak to the First Dragon Mage."

Fel was staring at that cave, but he turned to face his cousin, surprised at his words. "Dragon Mage? Like my father?'

"Not quite. The First Mage is thousands of years old."

Thousands. That was a lot. "How can anyone live that much?"

"He's a full dragon. Must eat healthy. Lives alone. I don't know. He will open a circle for you. Nobody really knows where he lives, and he doesn't take in anyone either. If he does take you, please—"

"Be careful, I know." Fel had heard it some fifty times.

"I hope you do. If you don't come back, I think my parents will kill me or maybe send me to a settlement in the far north isles, where it's almost always cold and dark."

"Why take the risk, then?"

The young man took a deep breath and stared into Fel's eyes. "I'm trusting you and trusting that you want to live. Trusting that you want to come back and save the kingdom you call yours, marry the girl you love so much. You have a goal, so don't lose sight of it. If things turn difficult, come back. It might take long, but you'll eventually learn to swap back into your human form. Do you understand me?"

"Perfectly." What Fel understood was that he was about to do something risky and difficult, but he was no fool and would make sure to come back alive. He was not interested in swapping forms to a corpse.

"Go on, then." Siniari gestured to the cave. "I'll fly close by, and I'll keep watch. If you come back and I'm not here, wait. I'll probably be right back."

Fel would have nodded if he were human. Well, he did move his head but he wasn't sure if the effect was the same. He was thankful to his cousin and happy to have found some of his family, but he had to turn human again or else things would be very difficult.

Since Siniari had explained that the First Mage himself would open a fire ring—if he wanted to—there was nothing Fel could do other than stare at the stone wall and state his name. Not only his name, his name in the dragon way, which his cousin had explained to him.

"First Mage, here I stand, humbly asking for an audience. I'm Isofel, son of Ircantari and Ticiane." It felt strange to state that long-forbidden name of the mother he had never met, not to mention his dragon-famous father, who he had no idea existed until recently. He continued, "Heartson of Azir." He would have said Azir Umbraar, but dragons didn't use last names. "Grandson of Ilaya and Kasiel." Those were strange names that he had just learned.

Fel then added, "And Celia and Stevan." Those were the names of the previous Ironhold queen and king, which felt strange on his lips as he pretended they had any relation to him, any meaning. He watched and waited, his heart speeding up in anticipation of this mysterious dragon, this great unknown, the possibility of finding his answer, despite whatever danger awaited him. Fel was ready. And yet, all he heard was the wind close by, the ocean down below, and a few birds chirping in the distance.

Then he heard a thud behind him. Fel turned around and saw that Siniari had landed, magnificent with his brilliant green scales. Like usual, he swapped to his human form right away. "What did you say?"

Fel was going to crack a joke, but wasn't sure if this was the place to do it. "I said what you told me to say, my name, my parents' names, grandparents' names, and that I'm requesting an audience."

His cousin paused, thinking. "Do you understand why you say your family's name?"

"So he knows who I am?"

Siniari stared at him for a second, then burst into laughter. "Cousin, cousin. Noob dragon indeed you are. You think the First Mage doesn't know you? He knows every single dragon that walks this earth."

"Why doesn't he defeat this Cynon, then?"

Siniari put a finger in front of his lips. "Dangerous words for this place. I told you he sees things differently—and takes no sides."

"So I could be a Boundless here, asking to become deadlier, and he would grant me an audience?"

"That is the question, isn't it? I'm not sure. Now, you're here for *your* audience. You don't state your ancestors just to list them.

There's no point. It's about praising your past first, then looking into the future."

"I don't know my grandparents." He was rather thinking about Ironhold, but it was true that he had never even heard about his dragon grandparents either.

"You don't need to know them to appreciate your life, your form, your dragon magic, even if you don't use it much. Your ability to fly. It's who you are, the blood in your veins, and you honor it. I mean, we do, so I believe that's how it should be done."

"I'll do that."

Siniari nodded, swapped forms, then flew away. So much freedom in that one change, so much possibility. The thought of having human magic, a human body, and his dragon form at his fingertips—or claw tips—filled his heart with hope. He had to do this right, and he was going to do it.

That said, the first step was already proving hard. How was he going to be thankful to Ironhold? Celia was still alive, but he hadn't even seen her, as she hadn't taken part in the balls. She had been in Leah's wedding, though, not that Fel could remember who was there, his mind blind with anger at that moment. Such stupid, foolish anger. He should have stopped that wedding and taken Leah with him. Funny how things in retrospect made so much sense, felt so clear.

A thought hit him: his love for his iron magic, his use of his metal hands, his ability to manipulate several pieces of metal at once, something that filled him with pride, joy, a sense of accomplishment. He had gotten that metal magic from the Ironhold family and it was part of who he was—at least part of who he was in his human form.

Fel closed his eyes, feeling grateful for the magic he had, and then stated again his name and his near ancestors, this time trying to put some appreciation and thankfulness in his words.

Again, silence was the only reply he got.

No, he could feel there was something about to happen, almost like a change in the air before a storm. His heart was thumping in his enormous chest when he saw a ring of fire appearing in the cave. Although it didn't seem to lead anywhere, Fel decided to trust it, and jumped into it, truly hoping it was a dragon ring, or else he would hit his head on the wall.

He found himself not flying, but falling. He tried to flap his wings—but had none.

NAIA LOOKED AT RIVER, stunned at his openness. He sounded sincere and spoke candidly about his role in the invasion of Frostlake, where he had cast some illusions and helped convince witnesses that it had been the fae attacking them.

Ironhold hadn't been careful. Instead, they had marched into the city and castle with their full forces, under the pretext that they were helping Frostlake fight the invaders. There had been many witnesses, but Ironhold was counting on creating fear and confusion. People generally tended to remain quiet rather than risking being deemed traitors.

Something still puzzled Naia. "Why Frostlake?"

"They had the princess, so they knew the kingdom would be theirs once they got rid of the king. It was an easy conquest."

That was true. Still, she couldn't quite believe he could have helped Ironhold do something so awful. "River, people died. The queen and king *died*. Couldn't you have warned them?"

"I had a deal with King Harold. And to be honest, they would have done the same with or without me, except that they would kill many more witnesses. If anything, I saved lives."

Did he really believe that? Or was that what he told himself?

"Really, Naia, there are other ways to create and perpetuate lies, and they are usually much worse than illusions."

"Then why were they working with you? They must be well aware you're their enemy. Why did they bother?"

"I can persuade people." He looked away and shrugged. "It's not something I like to do, but it's what I did."

"Was it worth it?"

He turned to her. "Being with Ironhold took me to Frostlake, where I saw you again."

Naia rolled her eyes. "Of course. How else could you find me, having no idea where I lived…"

"I thought you had tried to kill me. I was hurt, confused. And wrong." His voice was soft and she wanted to lean over, touch his hair, and kiss him, but she also needed to know what was happening.

"What happened yesterday?" she asked, still horrified at the image of River hurt.

"Long story." He sighed. "As you know, I left my post to go to the Ancient City last night. Well, King Harold thought I had warned Umbraar or betrayed him somehow, which, as you know, wasn't true." He stared at her. "My deal with him wouldn't have allowed me to do that. Still, he imprisoned me. That broke part of our agreement, which was actually good for me, meaning it also freed me. Plus, I was placed in a room with metal walls and metal magic, which obviously did not hold me. I escaped. For the first time, I was free to explore the castle and even enter areas where I had been forbidden before."

There was something ominous about his tone, and Naia was sure she wasn't going to like what he was saying.

He continued, "Deep down in the entrails of the Iron Citadel I found the king and queen, in a strange ritual. They were reviving their son, Cassius."

That was strange. "He died?"

"The Frostlake princess had killed him the previous night. Or maybe *almost* killed him."

"Leah?" Naia recalled the cute, sweet princess who'd broken Fel's heart. "She *killed* someone?"

"I think she's a deathbringer. Unless necromancy is similar to it. I don't know. She left Ironhold, in any case."

"I know. She's with my brother." Naia tried to stifle her worry about Fel.

River nodded. "What I do know is that yesterday I witnessed the most horrible ritual ever. They had some forty guards, Naia, forty young, healthy men. The king ordered half of them to kill the others."

That *was* horrific.

He frowned and had a bitter chuckle. "They obeyed. Obeyed it, Naia. But then the king opened a kind of hidden trapdoor, and they all fell to their deaths." With eyes shut tight, he took a deep breath, then looked at her. "Then the prince woke up again. I... don't know if he's himself or what he's like. I followed the queen, as there was something about her. She had this strange necklace, then went to this hidden chamber. There was this eerie, weird voice, and she spoke about the final sacrifice. I'm assuming it was the ritual, but I don't know what it was for. But then, she saw me, even though I should have been invisible. The room had this strange herb, she called it sepialy—it blocked my magic. Have you ever heard of it?"

"No."

"That's what I thought. I mean, if it had been common knowledge, the humans would have wiped us in the war. We do have stories about a plant called death grass, but it's not supposed to exist, it's not something real—or shouldn't be."

Naia considered his words. "But if Ironhold knew about it, why didn't *they* use it? During the war?"

"Maybe they don't all know it."

He proceeded to tell her about the queen, and the "test" she had to go through in order to marry into the family.

Naia couldn't believe it. "These people are sick."

"They are. The thing is, Queen Kara, she has no love for her husband. I'm not sure she has any love for anything anymore, and she's working with someone else, something else, this strange voice. She's not working for Ironhold, it's as if... she believes she is the one manipulating them. I also heard her saying that the *vessel* was ready. I'm assuming it's a vessel for this creature. And yet, I can't bring everything together."

"What do you think?" Naia asked. "Do you think she's the one pulling the strings? Somehow manipulating King Harold?"

River nodded. "I think it's very possible. There was a strange power, strange magic in that room. It's something much worse than just an ambitious and unscrupulous kingdom. And there's more." He sighed. "I... have something to tell you. Do you remember when you were in the Ancient City, those hooded Ancients trying to make me kill you?"

"That's not something one forgets."

"I know. They are called mindmelders. It's rare magic, most Ancients don't have it. It means... It's very unfae like, in the sense that you can compel a person, you can mess with their mind without their consent. Fae law determines that we respect free will. Even when we trick someone, they accept being tricked, they willingly enter a bargain. Mindmelders can... well, you saw it. You can even physically force someone to do something. And read minds, too, find memories. I..." He looked down. "Have that magic." He looked away, as if embarrassed. "Never wanted to use it, as it has a price, but not only that, it's... awful."

"What is the price?"

He stared at her. "You lose your individuality, your will, your sense of self. Eventually you become a hollow shell."

"Why would anyone want to use it, then?"

"It's considered a high honor among ancients. They'll live with royalty, have anything they want. They don't realize that in a few years they'll stop wanting anything. For a time, it's good. They also think it's their duty, since they were born with that magic. That was what my father told me."

"He wanted you to use it?"

River chuckled. "I chose to be a disappointment instead." He smirked. "Much more interesting. But yesterday... yesterday I used mindmelding magic at its full force. I used it to breach Kara's mind. I wouldn't be able to do it with King Harold. The deal would have prevented it, but with her, I was free. And what I saw..."

The look in River's eyes chilled Naia's bones. "What?"

He swallowed. "I saw her, in the past, looking at me, saying I was the key."

Naia felt as if her heart had stopped.

He bit his lip. "I... I don't understand why or for what, and before I saw anything else, she pushed me out. That would have been impressive, if my magic weren't so weak. I couldn't move, I couldn't slip into the hollow. It was horrible. She then said she would let me go if I told her how I became immune to iron, and she wanted specific details. I would need to tell her about you. I would never do that. I would never let them know how important you are to me, or even suspect it."

"River, you should have told her everything and escaped. They already tried to kill my brother, they attacked us. I don't think they can do any worse."

"I'm sure they can. And this wasn't Ironhold, but queen Kara and this weird something else. I didn't tell her anything, and she left me there. I..." He frowned, thoughtful. "Do you think my resistance to iron has anything to do with this? It sounds odd to me. I... don't know what she really wanted, if it was an excuse, but she left me alone. For the first time in my life, I couldn't feel my magic. It was as if I wasn't myself, Naia. It was horrible."

"How did you escape?"

"The prince. The youngest, not the one who died, he came and led me outside."

"That's..."

"Venard. The one married to the Frostlake princess. I guess not married anymore, I don't know. He wanted me to... This is quite weird, Naia. He had a lover who died, and had her preserved body. He wanted me to tell him how to revive her, like they had revived his brother. I told him it wasn't worth it, but he still insisted. I mean, I made a deal with him, but his words were so loosely woven that they're meaningless. He also asked me to remember he could be an ally. Then he led me to a door at the bottom of the castle, down in the precipice. It was dark, and I was attacked by a giant spider. I guess we know what kinds of creatures live there. That's how I got hurt."

Naia's heart was speeding up. This was all very strange and dangerous, but there was something else she needed to know. "How did you heal so fast?"

"You're not going to like it." He had a smile, though, so it couldn't be anything bad.

"Tell me or I'll make you demonstrate your healing ability again."

13

THE FIRST MAGE

Fel hit the ground with a thud. At least it was soft, with tall grass in what felt like a clearing by a hill. Thick fog prevented him from seeing much of his surroundings. He was himself, wearing the same clothes he'd been wearing when fighting the Ironhold invaders, in that odd, distant, past, but for some reason, it felt strange to be human again. In fact, something felt wrong.

His stomach sank and he realized he had no magic. He couldn't sense the traces of iron on the earth, couldn't feel whether there was any metal nearby, couldn't sense anything. Fel was literally being deprived of one of his senses, which was as important for him as sight or touch. Without magic, the world around him lost its sharpness, focus.

"Hello!" he called. Even using his voice again felt strange. He then tried something different, and sent that word as a thought, the same way he'd been doing as a dragon. It felt the same, but he had no way to know if it worked or if there was anyone around him.

All of a sudden, a strong gust of wind hit him, which cleared up some of the fog. He then realized that what he had thought was a hill was in fact a dragon, much bigger than he would have imagined. Great dragon indeed. Each of his claws was bigger than Fel in human form. His scales were dark brown, like old tree bark. Yes, Fel had heard them say that this dragon was thousands of years old, but now that he stood in his presence, he felt as if he was older than time, older than this world, older than all things for which there were stories, as if this dragon had lived before all that, in a time unknown.

"State your purpose," a thick, deep voice asked. The sound was not in Fel's head, but a real sound that felt as if it rumbled the ground, even though the dragon hadn't opened his mouth.

"First Mage," this was the title Fel had been told to use, but it felt worse than inadequate now, and made him feel foolish and afraid he was about to fail before even trying. He continued, "I wish to turn back to my human form."

A deep growl came from the dragon. No, laughter. Eerie and strange. "How can you wish for what you already got?"

Fel looked down on his human body, so tiny and fragile, and yet something he'd been wanting so much. "Is this permanent?"

"You tell me. Is this what you want? This pitiful, weak body, when you could be glorious and free?"

At least the dragon hadn't said a word about his lack of hands, and now he felt worse than usual, without his magic, without his metal hands. He would feel self-conscious if he weren't already feeling so small and insignificant in front of such a legendary and old creature. "In truth I want both. But if I had to pick one—"

"You'll choose the weakest? Well, there you are. You can return now."

"What about my magic? The human magic?"

"Oh, so you want it all?" The huge dragon lowered his head, so that it was right in front of Fel. Goodness, he'd be able to swallow him whole in one bite. "Or perhaps you should be clearer about what you want. If it's the stinky, corrupted magic, tell me that's your wish."

"My apologies. I want my body back, but the way it was, with my magic. I wouldn't be myself without it."

"Hmmm..." The dragon was thoughtful. "You know, I've met your father."

Indeed. Like every dragon except Fel. "Really? He came here with a request?"

"Oh, no. He was smarter than that. He came for words."

Fel was wondering why the dragon was veering off subject, but didn't want to offend him insisting on his request, and in truth, he wanted to learn more about his dragon father. He felt that the First Mage was expecting a question, and didn't want to disappoint him. "What words?"

"Wisdom. Knowledge. In truth it's everywhere. You can reach out and grab it. The question is whether you'll use it, that's the question."

"What did he want to know?"

"He was very young, not a hatchling like you, of course, but still young."

A hundred-year-old dragon was probably still a child for him, so Fel didn't mind being called a baby.

The First Mage continued, "I know what people say, I do. They say Ircantari came and got his magic, but it doesn't really work like that. The magic was already his. He wasn't sure if he had what it took to become a dragon mage, and wanted advice. These are the words I told him, and I remember them as if they had been said last year: *Every second you doubt or complain or think you're not good enough is a second you could be working towards your goal. How do you want to spend your time?* Not much, is it, and yet it was enough. But it wasn't the words that did it. You know what made him become a dragon mage?"

"He applied the advice."

"Oh no. Not that. He was lucky." That odd growl again—a laugh. "I'm kidding. Yes, he applied the advice and worked instead of doubting, moving forward instead of wondering."

"And yet he was killed." Perhaps Fel shouldn't have said that, but the words left his mouth out of their own will.

"Indeed. Did you hear anything I said? Or did you imagine

something I didn't? I'm absolutely sure I never claimed he asked me how to become immortal."

"Sorry. It's just... he died so young. If he was so powerful..." Fel sighed. "Do you know what happened?"

"He moved on. Not all of us are meant to stay long in this realm. If you want to know how to remain here forever, I cannot help you. I don't see everything and I don't know everything. Now, what are you here for again?"

"To learn to swap to my human body—while keeping my human magic."

"Learning cannot be given. That said, I can give you your human body, as you can see. I can also give you your human magic, but I need to know I'm giving it to someone who deserves it. I propose a challenge for you. See that peak there?"

He pointed behind Fel, who turned—and saw a huge wall of rock, as if a mountain had been sliced. Previously concealed by the fog, now it stood tall and imposing, extending far in both directions.

The First Mage continued, "There's a nest there. A special nest belonging to a rare, old, golden bird. I need you to climb there and bring me an egg."

Going there would be easy as a dragon, with his wings. As a human it wouldn't be hard either, if he had his metal vest or any metal that he could use to stand on. But like this... "Without magic?"

"Why? Did you expect your challenge to be easy? It doesn't work like that. I must warn you, though, that if you fall, you may die. The bird is not small either, and might kill you. Do you want to risk death? Do you prefer to risk death than to go back to your beautiful, perfect, dragon form? Show me what this human body is capable of, show me, and I'll grant you your nasty human magic."

Fel swallowed. How was he going to climb? "So you want me to bring you an egg from that nest?"

"That's the challenge, yes."

He still had no idea how he was going to get up there, but he was sure it was not going to be easy—or quick. "Is there a time limit?"

The great dragon laughed in that strange growl. "The limit is your hurry, child. I'll be here when you're finished—unless you die, of course."

Fel took a deep breath, then mustered all his confidence. "I'll bring you that egg."

The First Mage lowered his head even more and approached him, so that his huge mouth almost touched Fel. His lower teeth were as big as Fel's legs.

"Pass the challenge, child, and you'll have your human magic back."

"I will."

The huge dragon then disappeared, leaving Fel there alone. It was a cruel challenge. While he hadn't said anything about Fels hands, he'd asked him to do something for which his body wasn't suitable, a task that made him feel weak and foolish. Azir Umbraar had told him many times that he was perfect, but he wasn't, was he? He never had to tell Naia she was perfect because she obviously was.

Climbing that wall would be a task hard enough for most people, even if they were physically strong. For Fel? Impossible. The dragon's laughter came to his mind. Perhaps this was a cruel prank, made to make him quit before even starting. Fel took a deep breath. He wasn't going to quit. He needed his body, needed his magic, needed to be himself again. He wanted a future, a family. And wanted to kiss Leah, kiss her again, this time knowing that it wasn't a feverish dream.

Then he also needed to help his father, help Umbraar. If even dragon magic was better wielded in human form, then it was extremely important.

Wings were nice, but he had to save his kingdom—and make love to his girl. Leah was his girl—had always been, and he knew it now, almost as if turning into a dragon had changed how he perceived other people and his own emotions. He could still be a dragon—in human form. Then he'd feel complete, once he had his magic.

He stared at the rock wall again. How was he going to reach that peak?

THE SKY WAS blue outside the window of the fort. Naia had tumultuous thoughts in her mind, now knowing that everything was so much more complicated than she had imagined at first. But at least River was finally talking, without having to. This was a good change.

He looked at her. "Your magic, it amplifies mine. They combine somehow, they do something, so it was both our powers healing me. That's why you slept, and why we were both so hungry."

Naia had never heard of magic combining like that. "Do you know why it happens?"

He looked down and fiddled with a piece of bread. "Couples do that. Usually. Not always." An odd reaction.

"Why does this fact seem to bother you?"

His stunning eyes met hers. "You haven't said *yes* yet, remember? You were going to consider it. I was giving you the time and space to think it through, the time to know everything about me and only then make up your mind." He paused, then added, his voice a little lower, "Your magic's been telling a different story."

Great. "Oh, so that's how you know you can be a prick and I'll forgive you."

River chuckled. "It goes both ways. It also means I don't want to be a prick to you. And who knows? What if your magic changes its mind? I'm not going to risk it."

Risk. There had been tons of risks. "Then don't put your life in danger again. If it's true that there's something connecting us, it explains how I felt today. It was horrible."

He ran his hand through her hair. "I'm truly sorry, Naia. I swear it never crossed my mind that Ironhold could do that to me. The deal I had with the king should keep me safe—I guess I overlooked the queen. At least I got some information, at least I know something now."

"I hate all of that. I mean, we know Ironhold is awful and wants power. Now, what is this queen doing? And what does she want with you? Why would you be the key to anything?"

River exhaled and shook his head. "Maybe... Maybe she needed Ironhold to be powerful, and that was why she needed me, but that doesn't make sense. They didn't need my illusions to gain power. Maybe... maybe she wants to know how to counter iron magic? Perhaps to fight the Ironholds? I don't know."

Naia thought for a moment. "Could it be your... your mind magic?"

"Mindmelding. How would she have heard about it? No outsiders know about it, and not even many Ancients. And why would my magic interest her? The thing is, she's claiming she's behind Ironhold, she boasted it, so it has something to do with whatever they are planning."

Naia tapped her nails on the table, while awful images of River imprisoned or even tortured crossed her mind. "You'll have to hide. They'll be after you. Is our house safe?"

He had a happy smile. "*Our* house?"

Naia narrowed her eyes. "You know what I mean."

He kept that lovely, breathtaking smile. "Our house should be safe. Ironhold don't have deathbringers or fae or dragons."

There was something else she couldn't believe he hadn't mentioned yet. "We also need to help your Ancient City."

There was a flicker of pain in his eyes. "I'm not allowed to go there."

Naia disagreed. "I think you *are* allowed. What did your father say you had to do for your exile to end?"

He had a bitter chuckle. "Bring a dragon heart."

She smiled. "Did he specify that it had to be detached from the body?"

River shook his head. "I see what you're saying, but you went there on your own."

"Yes, but you could bring me now."

He nodded. "And then they'll want to detach your heart from your body. I won't run that risk."

Naia rolled her eyes. "Well, then, I guess we'll just have to let all the fae in the Ancient City die."

"I'll find a solution."

"You can't do it all on your own, River. And there won't be time. I've thought about it. There's a forest, in the north of Umbraar, the Blue Forest, by a river. Some of your people could come and collect water and fish and then take them to the Ancient City. You could make a fairy circle there. That area, it's far from villages, it should be fine. All I need is some guarantee that your people won't attack humans."

He glared at her. "We don't attack people for no reason, Naia."

Of course. The fae war had obviously been some kind of collective human hallucination. She didn't want to upset him, though, and said, "Just in case. I'll feel better about it."

River was thoughtful. "If we make a deal with them, you could ask for support in the upcoming war. There's a war coming, Naia, and fae warriors are the best of the best."

"And yet..." She paused. Telling him that they had retreated to the Ancient City by the end of the war with the humans would be like poking a wound.

River shook his head, as if sensing her thoughts. "The fae most humans faced were commoners, peasants, families, who used to live peacefully in the land here. I wouldn't want *them* to fight. What I'm suggesting is the help of our warriors. There must be about thirty, forty of them, that's it. And it's about making a deal that makes sense. If the terms are too easy, the Ancients will think there's some trick. They won't accept help without a price they deem fair, it's not our way."

"River, we don't know if, when, or how this conflict is going to play out. We don't even know if humans and Ancients will ever have a common ground to fight side by side. For now, I just want to make sure your people survive. We'll think about Ironhold later. Still, I want the fae to avoid human settlements, avoid being seen, and that's where I want to focus the deal on. I trust you, but I still don't have any reason to trust other Ancients."

River sighed. "You should hate them all."

"No. They were following orders and I have no way to know their opinion about it, and there was a girl who warned me not to follow your father. I did turn back, but I ended up caught."

He perked up. "What did she look like?"

Naia shrugged. "Long white hair, dark red eyes."

River rolled his eyes. "You just described the majority of the population of the Ancient City."

"It's not my fault they all look the same."

"Was she a guard, a noble, a wisewoman, a cleric…"

"Noble. She was sitting by your father. There was a young man as well, but he didn't tell me anything."

"Let me guess, he also looked like a typical Ancient."

"Yes."

River took a deep breath. "The woman who helped you could be my sister. Not the one who died. Obviously. Her twin, Anelise. We never got along well, but when my father exiled me, she seemed… to care. She even gave me a scrying mirror." He exhaled. "Lost when I was pushed into the hollow."

"You think we could talk to her?"

"She doesn't have authority over the Ancient City. You can't get her word for other Ancients."

"So we'll need to negotiate with your father."

"You saw how nice he is."

"I bet he doesn't want the people in your city to die."

River scoffed. "You don't know him well, then."

"What do you suggest?"

FEL CONSIDERED the First Dragon Mage's advice. Doing instead of doubting sounded nice—in theory—but it would be pointless to rush to that stone wall and try to climb it. Believing he could was not going to make him sprout hands or manifest some climbing equipment.

His father, or rather, heart-father, like the dragons said, had once told him that willpower couldn't conquer everything. Most things, yes, but not everything. Some limitations were real, and there was no point banging on them. The trick was to work with them, and not against them.

None of these words gave him a clue how to conquer that wall.

Wait. Azir's words actually did.

There was no point trying to do something he couldn't. Yes, Fel could perhaps climb that wall if he had special equipment—but he didn't have any. But climbing wasn't the only way to reach the nest.

The First Mage hadn't specified how he had to do it.

If only Fel knew how to make those dragon rings! Maybe he could ask for help. No, the challenge was his and his only, and he didn't even know where he was or how to reach any other dragon —or anyone, for that matter. But there was always a way around obstacles.

Fel approached that solid rock. There were crevices here and there. Maybe he could put his feet, then lean on his arms. No, it was too dangerous. Falling to his death had not been his goal when he'd decided to talk to the great dragon.

Perhaps the test had been about patience, not so much physical prowess. He looked at both sides of that long wall. Far on the left, at the limit where his eyes could see, it seemed to be lower. It had to end somewhere, or at least there could be a place where it was easier to climb. Walking around it didn't sound like the smartest solution, but he couldn't come up with anything else right now. After a deep breath, Fel started moving. It would do him no good to stand there, wondering and wishing.

It was a good thing that there were many streams running from that precipice, so at least Fel didn't feel thirsty. The image that came to his mind was his sister as a child, using her hands to get water from a lake, then offering to do the same for him, and him refusing her help. Instead, he kneeled and drank directly from the lake. Even his metal hands couldn't scoop water. But it didn't matter. There was always another way, always a solution. He kept walking until he found a part where the rock didn't look as vertical, but more like a regular mountain—quite a rocky mountain. It was either this or walking a long time to maybe find a more suitable place from where he could go up. Fel decided to take his chances. He made his way carefully, sometimes sitting or leaning on his arms, but slowly, he came to the top of the cliff.

Looking down, he saw such a huge valley beyond him. He wasn't sure if this was still Fernick or elsewhere, perhaps even a different realm in the hollow. But then, the truth was that this continent was much larger than Aluria, and even there, they couldn't always see the mountain range that cut his land in two. Still, what surprised him was the amount of green, untouched green, where forests and vegetation grew undisturbed as far as his eyes could see. With so much unexplored, wild space, it made sense that there were so many groups of fae and elves hidden in this continent. There was so much in here, so much that he wanted to see, even as his heart yearned to go back home and help save them.

The peak from where he'd have to get the egg was visible from here, a protrusion in that cliff, a mountain within a mountain. The way there wasn't easy, though, but rocky with only some rough patches of land. But then, at least if he fell here, he wouldn't die.

. . .

He'd started his walk in the morning, and the sun was already down near the horizon when he got near the peak. Would his cousin be worried? They hadn't discussed anything about time. If his uncle learned about what he was doing, he would likely be upset—and furious. But then, it was for a good reason —hopefully.

The peak was in view, and so was the nest, bigger than he'd expected. One thing he hadn't considered was how he would bring down the egg. But then, had that been part of the challenge? Or just retrieving it? The First Mage's words were a mush in his head. No wonder wisdom got overlooked so often, if he could forget simple instructions for a potentially deadly challenge.

One thing that was worrying him was that he was hearing no chirping or shrieking or any bird sounds. There should be a bird if there was a nest, right? He was sure the dragon had mentioned a bird, not a snake or anything like that. Taking into consideration the size of the nest, that was a potential danger he'd need to be aware of. Fel had no weapons and no magic, and in fact didn't even want to fight an innocent bird who had nothing to do with his problems. But perhaps the bird was gone or something.

Slowly, paying a lot of attention to his surroundings, he approached the nest. There was only one egg, golden, not nearly as big as Fel would have expected, more like an oversized melon. Still no birds. Something about it made Fel uncomfortable, but he couldn't figure out why. If anything, having no birds anywhere would only make things easier. The truth was that the challenge wasn't as terrible as he had expected.

The tricky part now would be to bring the egg down. Fel paused, then decided to make a sling so that he could carry the egg down the cliff. He took off his shirt and was about to rip it, when something about the egg called his attention—an energy, not magic, but something similar to it. He took in a sharp breath and dropped his shirt. The egg—it had life in it—a fully formed bird who would burst through the shell very soon. He'd been thinking it would be an unfertilized egg, not this.

What did it matter? The First Mage had asked for it. Was Fel supposed to feel guilty about a bird now? And if that dragon was all wise and everything, he had his reasons. Fel swallowed. It was better to shut down those foolish thoughts. He had to save his kingdom, had so much to do, he needed his magic and his human form. What was a bird compared to all of that?

Love. Although he couldn't see the parents, he could sense love surrounding it like a blanket, protecting it. This little life had a mother protecting it, perhaps looking for food right now. Could Fel steal this bird from its loving mother?

The Great Dragon had asked for it, though. Maybe he had not known it had a bird in it.

Fel sighed. All this indecision was stupid. His sister enjoyed hunting, and they both ate meat. Not only that, he had killed people, real people who probably had not chosen to attack Umbraar, who were just following orders. But then... It still felt different from stealing a hatchling from a bird who was waiting for it, who loved it. Its mother had to be around, or it wouldn't have survived for so long. It wouldn't be here, about to come to life.

Fel closed his eyes. If he wanted his magic, he'd need to pass this challenge. Perhaps there was something he didn't understand about it, couldn't see, perhaps there was some meaning. Maybe taking that egg wouldn't be that bad.

No. He understood killing in a life-or-death situation, but this wasn't it. There was something about this that felt wrong. Yes, he had killed people, people who likely hadn't deserved it, but this still felt different.

The First Mage's request came to him, and the possibility of death if in case of failure. But he was quitting, not failing—and there was a difference. Hopefully.

After glancing at the beautiful egg once more, Fel turned away from the nest, exhaling in relief. Strangely, it felt odd not to have any fire mixed with his breath now that he was human. Perhaps being a dragon was becoming natural to him, which was great, as this stupid decision would likely mean he'd be in that form for a long time.

Then he sensed something. Fel glanced back—and saw an enormous claw coming in his direction, with golden feathers.

There was no time to react, no time to fight—and he *would* fight for his life—legendary animal or not. If only he had his magic, if only... There was no point wishing.

That claw pushed Fel down the cliff. For a moment it felt unreal, only air below him, the feeling of nothingness around him. Then he was falling, doubting the grass would be enough to save him this time.

14

A RARE RELIC

Naia stared at River, wondering what solution he had for his people.

River paused for a long moment, then took a deep breath. "I'll speak with my father. My way. He's very fond of mind games—"

"Are you going to use your magic?"

He shook his head. "I never use it, and to do it against a king... That could kill me. I mean verbal traps, deals. I also have to make sure I don't hurt his pride. I'll do it. You'll be with me, but don't leave my side. I'll protect you."

"I trust you." And it was true. "But how are you going to prevent a conflict with the humans and guarantee the safety of Umbraar?"

"I'll get my father to agree to send just a few fae, something like ten at most, and they'll promise to be discreet and avoid humans. Would that work?"

Naia thought it was too few fae to feed a city, but perhaps it was a good start, and at the end of the day, River knew much more about his people than she did, so if he thought it was enough, it was enough. "If you think so, I have no reason to doubt you. We could go right away."

River frowned and looked out the window. "Our times are similar. Facing my father is hard enough when he's wide awake. I'm not sure I want to get him out of bed."

"What time can we go?"

"After two."

Naia didn't want to wait, but, again, River knew his father better than her, and it was true that the only time she'd been in the Ancient City was late at night and everyone seemed awake.

"Fine, then, we wait." She exhaled. "Meanwhile, we can try to come up with an idea, a solution, a way to figure out what Queen Kara wants."

"What about the king?" River asked. "You said he wants to declare an Ironhold empire but it's been postponed?"

"Yes. Well, I was in a mirror meeting with Wolfmark, Greenstone, Frostlake, or rather, the Ironhold person who's taking care of that kingdom, and King Harold. We agreed on an emergency gathering. In Ironhold. It's going to be in two days. I think that will be my chance to—"

"Are you crazy? I told you it's much too dangerous."

"They aren't looking for me. I'm not the key to anything, so I don't see the issue. Plus, my father will probably be back by then. He can go. His magic should protect him."

River looked down, as if swallowing something he was about to say.

Naia stared at him. "You don't think he'll be back?"

"I don't know. He might. You're right that he could help us. That is, if he doesn't want to separate *my head* from my body."

"He let me stay with you when I said that was what I wanted. He didn't do it with any joy or pride, but he let me stay. Plus, he'll want to fight Ironhold, he'll want to protect Umbraar."

River looked down. Naia knew what he was thinking. What if her father did not return? But she didn't want to consider that possibility.

He said, "I could go and investigate Ironhold. I can move freely in that castle now."

"River! Now you are the one not making any sense. You don't know what that queen wants to use you for."

"No. Think about it. The only reason she beat me was because of that stupid plant. All I need to do is find a way to counter its effects, and I'll be fine."

"You don't know if you'll be fine, River. You don't know what she wants to do with you."

"It's just a thought. I can try to research it in the Ancient library. They have to have something about that death grass. Then if I can counter it, I can go back to the Iron Citadel and move around unnoticed. Imagine what we could find out? Maybe that's the key."

Naia bit her lip. "Exactly. The key. What the evil queen and the creepy voice want. We'll think of something else. And I don't think Ironhold would be foolish enough to do anything at the gathering."

"Really? You think they can't come up with harsh, apparently illogical decisions? You haven't been paying attention then."

"I've spoken to other kings. Nobody wants to oppose Ironhold openly, but they're not pleased about paying taxes to them and becoming part of their empire. We'll all be together there. There's something else, the Wolfmark king is here. He spoke to me and thinks we could try to negotiate better terms, or even refuse this empire altogether."

"He's *here*? In this fort?"

"Well, he insisted on coming. What was I going to do? And he's a potential ally."

River looked at her. "Ally. And yet something about the way you mention him makes me think you consider him a nuisance—or worse."

She wasn't going to tell him about King Sebastian's outlandish proposal, but she could explain some of her dislike. "My father hates him, so I assume there must be a reason, and I can't be delighted that he's come to visit. But then, you don't need to like your allies, you just need to have interests in common."

River kept staring at her, his countenance suddenly serious, threatening even. "This king, did he bother you? Disrespect you?"

"You're reading my mind now?"

"I'm reading your face, Naia. But now you just answered. What did he do?"

It was better to explain it before River thought it was worse than it was. "He proposed."

"Pro..." His face was puzzled, then, after pausing for a second, he burst out laughing. "He thinks he has a chance? With you? Are all human men that deluded?"

Naia shook her head. "What do I even know?" River found it funny?

River was still laughing. "And what did you say?"

"That I'll think about it. What else can I say? He's a potential ally."

"So you're going to torture the old man, making him think he stands a chance. Cruel, Naia, quite cruel." His tone was playful, and yet there was an edge to it.

Still, in a way, River's pity for the *old king* made her feel better, made her think about Sebastian like a pathetic, deluded fool, instead of feeling threatened by him.

River tapped his nails on the table, then stared at her. "You don't know what else you could say? What about something wild and crazy, like that you are already promised or something?"

"He would ask to whom. What was I going to say?"

River looked away, thoughtful.

Naia feared she'd made him upset. "It's not that I'm ashamed or—"

"I didn't think that." His smiled was gorgeous as he stared at her. "It's just another tricky pickle on our list. Quite low on our list of priorities, I should say." He looked up, thinking.

It was a problem—unless her father banished her for good and declared her dead or something. That would avoid the need for any awkward explanations. She wasn't sure how she felt about it.

River stared at her, an eyebrow raised. "So you think you'll all get together in the Iron Citadel and defy the owners of that castle?"

Naia was glad for the change in subject, or maybe not so much, since this was an even bigger and more urgent problem. "I don't know. River, I don't know what to do. I just needed some time, needed a chance. All I know is that we still have two days to think of something, but I don't have any solution, I don't have any idea. I'm feeling lost. Still, what I can do right now is try to save the fae in your city. They don't deserve to die."

He took a deep breath, extended his arms, and stared at her. "Come here."

Naia got up and stood by him, waiting for him to get up, but instead he pulled her on his lap, wrapped his arms around her, then caressed her hair and nuzzled her neck. "I missed you. I still haven't recovered from almost losing you, from almost hurting you."

True. It had been a little over a day that she'd been in the Ancient City, when the mindmelders had tried to make River kill her. "It wasn't your fault."

"It was. I should have spoken to you more, I should have warned you. I can't even believe you're so good that you're worried about the wellbeing of the Ancients."

She closed her eyes, enjoying their closeness. "Usually the people are not at fault for what their leaders do. It's not right to make them suffer."

"I know."

His lips were close to the corner of her mouth, then he moved them slowly and kissed her. It felt so good to be in his arms, to kiss him again, to feel the touch of his hands, the feel of his tongue, his scent—not really his.

Naia broke the kiss. "You smell like my brother."

"I'm sure it could be worse."

"Not for me. I can't kiss you when you smell like that."

She moved her fingers to the buttons of his shirt. Fel's shirt.

She unbuttoned it carefully, then got that thing of him. There was a faint scar where he had gotten cut, but not much more than that, which was impressive. Naia put her hand on his chest, feeling the softness of his skin.

River stared at her with dark eyes and a serious expression.

Naia moved her hand away, as she obviously didn't want to go through the sheer humiliation of having him push it again. She chuckled. "I forgot. You don't want me to touch you because apparently you can't control yourself."

River tilted his head. "I can control myself. I'm just... You're human. I'm trying my best to court you in a way that's comfortable for you. Your kind waits until you're married—for everything. I always thought it was insane. It *is* insane. But going through this insanity is my way to prove that I care about you, that I'm serious about you. You'll be much happier getting close to me once you decide this is what you truly want for the rest of your life, knowing we're committed to each other."

His words sounded lovely, right, and honorable, and yet somehow they disappointed her. "But is it...black and white? Yes or no? Don't mock my ignorance. It's not my fault. I hate being so..."

He kissed her hand. "You're perfect, Naia. You were raised by a human family, and that's who you are. As to your question... It isn't black and white, no. There's a lot of room in-between extremes. But even that, for humans, it's something they wait."

"I don't even know why."

"I..." He sighed. "It's going to sound as if I'm criticizing your kind, and I—"

"Say it."

"It might be a biased, prejudiced opinion. I heard human men are really bad at...loving stuff. So they want to make sure women are ignorant about it, so they don't realize how terrible they are. "

"That doesn't make sense. They're so competitive. Wouldn't they want to be good at something?"

"Maybe they just want the perception that they are good."

River shrugged. "If there's no competition, then they're the best. Then again, this is a biased opinion from someone who once saw humans as the enemy, but I'm trying to be respectful of your kind."

"So respectful. You think I like to be an ignorant fool who doesn't even know what happens when a couple gets married? Who has some ideas but can't say for sure how exactly a baby is made? I don't even know what you have in there." She pointed to his pants. "I know it lets you pee standing, but I don't know what it is. I feel like a clueless child, and the worst is that you treat me like a clueless child."

"What do you expect me to do? If you decide you don't want me, and if you end up finding a human husband, he'll expect you to be clueless and ignorant."

"Do you really think I'd be interested in someone like that?"

River shrugged. "If he's human, yes. That's what he's going to be like."

Naia couldn't really believe he thought she would pick someone like that, unless... "You really expect to leave me, don't you?"

"I don't. I told you what our magic says about us. I declared my love for you in front of my father, in front of the king. They were one and the same, but it doesn't matter. Nothing can be more serious than that for an Ancient."

She was still sitting on his lap and ran her hand over his chest, down to his stomach. "Then don't treat me like a fragile flower who needs to be kept intact for some snotty human. If you keep doing that, then maybe I *will* end up getting annoyed and picking a human, but you know that's not what I want."

He kissed her ear and whispered, "And what do you want?"

Naia closed her eyes. "Can I want what I can't name? Or am I just something to be wanted?"

"I didn't mean to hurt you."

She shrugged. "I'm whole. Need no healing."

He caressed her face and she ended up looking at him. River

was beautiful, and even his strange kind of beauty was becoming familiar to Naia.

He glanced at her lips, then looked her in the eyes. "You have no idea how much I want you. All of you. How much I've wanted you from the moment I first saw you, back in the dragon lair, so powerful, confident and mysterious, and yet, looking at me with so much sweetness and... I don't even know. You haven't been away from my thoughts since then. I want your heart, your mind, your soul. I want your body too, and you have no idea how much, no idea what so much wanting is like."

Naia chuckled, but it was a wrong chuckle, all bitter, which wasn't quite right after all these words. "River, have you considered that maybe, just maybe, I *do* know what it's like?"

He caught a breath. "I was trying to be good, and I was doing it all wrong." He kissed the corner of her lips and held her close, then whispered, "There is a line we still can't cross—but there are many others we can."

Their lips met. This time there was no odd smell and no anger. Naia realized that this was a decision. For someone who'd been wondering if she should trust him or not, this was a clear sign of where she really stood. Perhaps she should just listen to her magic, and in a way she could feel how their powers blended, how they were stronger together. At the same time, she was curious about those lines they would cross, her heart thumping with exhilaration and excitement.

And still, all they were doing was kissing, while she touched the soft skin on his back, that pleasant feeling of being close.

Slowly, he moved his hands down to her legs, then under her nightgown. He caressed her thigh with the tips of the nails of one hand, those strange nails that gave her goosebumps now. His other hand was lifting her nightgown. Would he know she had nothing underneath it? Would he be surprised? Would he like what he saw?

Death. A bitter price for Fel's moment of distraction.

Falling from a great height, still startled, stunned, he foolishly tried to beat his arms as if they were wings. How he wished they *were* wings. If the First Mage's goal had been to make a point about the fragility of the human form, he had definitely succeeded. Pity that Fel wouldn't be around to appreciate that harshly imparted wisdom.

"Help!" The yell felt pointless and pathetic.

But it wasn't a yell, but a thought—he hadn't spoken it. And for some reason, his beating arms were slowing his fall.

Not arms, wings.

He'd gotten his dragon form back—almost too late to stop him from hitting the ground with a tremendous force, but not too late. Perhaps this was the perk of having failed the challenge. Perhaps... he didn't even know what else to think anymore.

With his heart hammering in his chest, Fel flew to the same clearing where he had first spoken to the old dragon. Indeed the creature was there, waiting, looking even more gigantic than before, now that Fel was a dragon and still three times smaller than him.

Fel waited to see if the First Mage was going to say anything, maybe admonish him, but, hearing only silence, decided to send a thought.

"I beseech you to give me another challenge to grant me my human form." The sentence felt oddly formal and unfitting, but then, what was one supposed to say in a situation like that?

The dragon laughed, and this time it truly sounded like a laugh, unlike before, when it had sounded like a roar. "You think you get two chances? Or as many chances as you wish?"

"I'm asking for an exception. The egg you asked me to bring, it had a living nestling in it, a bird about to come to life. I could feel its energy."

"You felt its magic. Are magical creatures any worthier than non-magical ones?"

Fel paused. "No. Maybe I wouldn't have felt it. Maybe I would.

I... it's an innocent baby bird. I could only assume taking it was not what you intended."

The Great Dragon leaned over, so that his face was close to Fel. It was a lot less intimidating than before, but still ominous. "Why is that? You think I'm merciful?"

The fire within Fel was stirring in his chest. "I thought it was a mistake, that you didn't know."

Another laugh. "Child, it was no mistake. I knew exactly what was in that egg."

A sudden chill ran through Fel's warm body. "Why do you want it?"

This time the old dragon's laughter definitely rumbled the earth. "You think I want it? Do you even think, child?"

"You asked me to bring it to you."

"And that was the challenge."

"I... I'm not going to get that egg, First Mage."

"Obviously not. You think Saka, the great bird, would have let you? You didn't see her at first, did you? She can turn invisible and wait for her prey. Oh, and she likes human meat."

This wasn't making sense. "You wanted me... to become bird food?"

"Hmmm. Interesting theory. I'll give you ten seconds to figure out what the challenge was or I won't help you."

But how would the First Dragon agree to help Fel if he had failed... Unless... Fel stared at him. "You tricked me. You didn't actually want the egg."

The huge dragon emitted a low rumble. "Oh. Finally. It took you long enough."

"And yet I almost died."

"Don't be dramatic. Saka was just, you know, giving you a push. Had she wanted you dead you wouldn't be here talking to me. And trust me, had you tried to get close to that egg, you wouldn't have stood a chance."

Fel was so angry he feared he'd unleash a burst of fire and make things worse. "So that was the challenge? *Not* doing what you asked me to do?" He had to control his thoughts too, so as not to sound so angry, but it was much harder than controlling his voice. "What if I just wanted to touch the egg to make sure there was something there? Would I be dead?"

"No, no. Saka can sense intentions, like all mystical animals. Worst-case scenario, I would have swapped your form in time."

True. A dragon could survive a deadly blow if they swapped forms, which was a good reason to learn how to do that as soon as possible. Still, Fel could hardly believe that the challenge had been a trick. But then, instead of upset, he should feel relieved; he had passed his test.

"I see. So you'll give me my human body back?"

"Is that what you want?" For some reason the dragon's voice sounded quieter now.

"Isn't that why I spent hours walking around that cliff? Why I came here?"

"Oh, boy, let's not pretend you didn't take the easy way. Regardless. You passed, yes indeed. But you know something? I could give you what you want, but it would be the wrong decision. If I swap you to your human form, you'll never again be a dragon."

Was he... going to refuse Fel's request? "I turned once," he protested.

"Then you'll have no problem swapping back, since you're so proficient at it."

"They say it takes years." Fel sighed and decided to be honest. "I need to help my kingdom, my sister. I also plan to get married, and she's human. I can't wait for years. I mean, I'm sure she'll want..." So many things.

"Keep wanting—it's the seed of change, and it will make you stronger. That's my final word, Isofel, son of Ticiane and Ircantari, grandson of Celia, Cassius, Ilaya, and Kasiel, heartson of Azir."

This couldn't be. "But we had a deal."

"Do I look like a fae? I make no deals." His voice was a growl now, and he stood at his full height, managing to be even more intimidating than before. "You came here asking for help, I gave you a test, you passed, and now I'm going to help you, but don't make me change my mind."

Fel had no intention of becoming dragon food, so he had to swallow his words, smother his protests, even though his chest was a burning cauldron about to explode.

The great Dragon continued, "Be thankful. I'm giving you what you need, which is much better than what you want." He held a small necklace in one of his claws, with a pendant with a purple stone. "This is a rare and old relic, and quite a gift. I hope you have the sense to appreciate it. It will allow you or someone you love to go back in time—once."

Going back? When he had so much to do right now? So much he needed? But if Fel complained about it, he'd probably leave this place with nothing, which was an even greater waste of time. "How... how does it work? And how can I carry it?"

The dragon threw the necklace in Fel's direction, and the object disappeared. "The same way you carry your human clothes and objects. It's with you."

"So I'll need to be in my human form to use it." Great! Back to problem number one.

The dragon chuckled. "There's a way to use it in this form, but it's obviously above your pitiful knowledge of dragon magic. It might be for the best, as you're obviously not ready to wield something as powerful as that."

Then maybe he should have given Fel something more useful, a gift that could help him now, not in some unknown time in the future.

The First Mage then lifted a claw, as if to silence him. "I know you're facing challenges. Every dragon has challenges, child."

Fel sighed. This couldn't be it. Perhaps he should ask for something different, a different type of support. He tried to send a thought in a gentle, beseeching tone. "People—and dragons— might die. An evil dragon might return, there's fighting among dragons. In my land, magic is misbehaving. There's something dark and dangerous about to run amok. Can't you help?"

"This is the help I can give. I'm not connected to your world and cannot take part in your fight. But one thing I can tell you: there has always been struggle and strife and yet there's always room for love, for hope, for peace and life to flourish. Trust that." He then made a fire ring between him and Fel. "Goodbye, child."

So this was it. "Thank you." Fel wasn't grateful—he was disappointed and angry, but complaining wasn't going to help anyone.

In truth he was feeling small and deflated. It was horrible to depend on someone else's magic, someone else's goodwill. He'd always hated to feel useless, little, incapable, and this ordeal had only exacerbated the feeling of helplessness within him. And yet. All he could do was return to the dragon city and try to learn as much as he could, as fast as he could.

The sun was already setting on the other side of the fire ring. Fel came across a dark blue sky—not all blue. Bursts of flame here and there disrupted the darkness, while dragon shrieks and roars echoed in the mountains.

As Fel's eyes adjusted to the dark, he realized what he was seeing: dozens of dragons—fighting.

Naia's heart was definitely jumping in her chest. River would soon realize she had no undergarments, would soon touch places that were definitely forbidden. His hand moving up her leg was so close, so close. This was definitely something unmarried couples shouldn't be doing, which only made her want it even more.

A sound of something falling startled her. Him as well, as he turned to the door. The door! That sound again. It wasn't anything falling—someone was knocking. Why did it have to be now, of all times?

Naia approached the door. "Yes?"

"It's me," a muffled voice came from the hallway. It was Arry.

She gestured for River to go to a corner, which he did, then opened the door just a little, so that she stuck her head in the opening and could see her visitor. "Something urgent?"

"King Sebastian is leaving. He wishes to see you."

"Tell him I'm gone. I'm not here. By the way, I'm leaving."

"Where are you going?"

"Somewhere safe."

"Are you going somewhere alone?"

"Don't worry about me." She hadn't meant to, but her tone sounded flippant, so she tried to sound nicer. "Trust me. Meanwhile, I trust you to keep this fort running. Make sure the king leaves, and try to provide him as much comfort as possible. Your father can receive the Haven delegation." They had been informed about it, but it was a good reminder. "And thank you for your help and friendship."

"What should I tell your father or your brother?" he asked.

At least someone else in this fort was optimistic. "They know where I'll be."

Arry nodded and walked away, and she closed the door and turned to River. "Let me get dressed. Can we go back to your house?"

He crossed his arms. "It's not ours anymore?"

"I'd say not yet. But I think it's the safest place for now."

He walked towards her and wrapped his arms around her. "No need to get dressed. You still have clothes there. Can we go?"

Naia nodded. She'd have to return to the fort because of the communication mirror, but for now, she wanted River to be safe, and perhaps she wanted that space that belonged only to them.

It felt as if dark tendrils enveloped her. Somehow, she had forgotten how much she disliked moving through the hollow.

"Naia, you have to look," he said.

She opened her eyes. "I can't see anything."

"If you're a dragon, you should be able to do this. And then you also should have a little bit of my magic."

Naia looked. All she saw was blackness—except for a few lighter points. "I see... dots? And lines going to these dots?"

"They're my circles."

"How do I know which is the right one?"

"In my case, I used to think about it, then the one I wanted shone brighter, but nowadays I just know where to go."

"I'm wondering what all the other lights are."

"Many, many places, Naia."

There was a brighter line and a brilliant circle. She pointed at it. "That one?"

He looked puzzled. "That's... in the castle in the Ancient City."

Strange. Unless..."Perhaps we should go there now?"

His chest moved up and down, in a deep breath.

Naia realized she wasn't making sense. "But then, we do need to get dressed."

"We do." His eyes were on that luminous dot, as if considering it.

Naia knew that he held back a lot of pain about his father, the death of his sister, and his exile. He held her close and one of the dots became brighter and bigger, turning into a circle, but then she felt the darkness around her again, and, unwittingly, closed her eyes. When she opened them, they were standing in front of their house.

The day before yesterday she had told him she couldn't stay here, that she had to take care of her kingdom, but now she wanted to make sure he was safe, and also wanted some peace of mind, some tranquility, a neutral place far from everything to try to get her thoughts together and figure out what was going on. And then maybe she wanted to be alone with River, feel more of his skin against hers, feel the touch of his hands. As if there was any time for that, with everything that was happening, with someone after River, with Ironhold about to take control of Aluria. She wished she hadn't remembered that, she wished they could just spend time together and forget everything outside that clearing, forget that there was anything other than the two of them. But it wouldn't make it true.

Naia turned to him. "I'll get dressed, and I think we should go to your city. If there's a library there, we might find answers." She wished Fel could see her now, interested in books. Well, she wished *she* could see her brother and know he was all right. It was something else worrying her. "The sooner we start, the better."

"Wait. I don't know, Naia. I..."

"You're afraid?"

He thought for a moment and closed his eyes. "Yes. I guess that's the word."

It made sense that he would be worried about her safety. She understood it now, after having seen him hurt. Despite hating what she was about to ask, she figured perhaps it could be a temporary solution. "Do you want to go to the Ancient City without me? But then take me back to Umbraar."

His eyes were lost in the distance. "I don't want to go. I just don't want to return to the Ancient City." He looked at her. "It might be that I'm afraid of going to the place where I went through the worst moments of my life. And yet, in truth, I've always wanted to return, to be accepted again. Helping them, that could be my opportunity." He took a deep breath. "I don't know what's wrong with me. Of course we need to go to the Ancient City. I mean... That's the only place where I can find answers. We also need to help the fae there. And I need you to speak with my sister, it's quite urgent."

It was sweet to see River being honest about his fear and vulnerability. She couldn't imagine all that he had gone through with his father, but the little she had witnessed had to be traumatizing. "Our magic will work together. And maybe it heals not only physical wounds." She turned to the house. "I'll get dressed."

15

BATTLE IN THE SKY

el stared at the battle ahead of him—and noticed a dragon falling down to the ocean. Was it a friend? An enemy?

Large wings flapped near him. Expecting an enemy, Fel got his fire ready, but before he saw the dragon, he heard her voice. Tzaria.

"Follow me. You need to get out of here."

"And leave them?"

"You need to hide," she insisted.

It didn't make sense that she wasn't going to help, that Fel wasn't expected to help, but for some reason her insistence made him follow her, flying close to the mountain and around it, so that they would soon be on the other side—away from the battle.

From the corner of his eye, he thought he saw the sheen of green scales, and recognized a dragon—his cousin, fighting two enemies.

Fel turned. He was going to help him—but then something moved on top of him. A blast of fire, coming from above. He barely dodged it, and felt his wings flapping more slowly. When he looked up, she saw a red dragon, wearing armor, falling on the sea.

"You need to get out of here!" Tzaria's thought was a desperate yell.

Meanwhile, Fel paused. That armor... Fel could feel it, could sense it. Some of his iron magic was returning. Perhaps seeing the First Dragon Mage hadn't been useless after all, or perhaps he was more used to being a dragon and could connect to his ironbringing.

Instead of trusting his physical senses, he closed his eyes, trying to feel more of those metal armors. Only the Boundless wore them, so he would be able to find them.

He felt a faint trace of iron to his right, below him, somewhat far away. Focusing on the metal, he forced all the pieces to get closer and closer together. When he opened his eyes, he saw a dragon falling, strangled by his own armor. Fighting in the air was very different from everything he knew about battle, since he had to pay attention to three dimensions at the same time. It wasn't just a matter of covering all sides, but also up and down.

The iron was here and there, but so far... He dove to help his cousin. This time he just moved the metal armors so that the Boundless near him were pushed down to the water. When two more enemy dragons approached him, he pushed them away. One of them hit the mountain, while the other turned and attacked him again.

Something then stirred in the air. For a moment, he felt as if the enemy dragons had paused—then he felt all eyes on him, both from the enemy and the friendly dragons.

Five Boundless rushed onto him, and he pushed them all away. More and more were approaching—from all sides, below, above. There were too many for him to focus on one at a time and strangle them, so all he was doing was pushing them away from him. A couple of fire blasts came in his direction, and he was able to dodge them. There were too many dragons—some thirty at least—around him.

Some of the other dragons were trying to help him, but it didn't change the fact that all the Boundless were focused on Fel.

His iron magic was strong, but he wasn't sure it would be enough to fight them all. Perhaps throwing them against each other could work. He moved one dragon sideways, and made it hit his companions. But as he did that, two dragons took advantage of that moment and approached him from below. Fel didn't have time to dodge their blasts, and now his wings were too slow to keep him in the air. He was falling, falling over enemies who were trying to kill or hurt him. No, he pushed the dragons below him down onto the sea, and kept them there. Now he could focus on the ones above him.The issue was that his ironbringing was strange, weak, and unreliable, while the enemies were too many for him. Way too many.

LEAH'S MIND. It wasn't a black nothingness, but a large space she could dive into, a place where she could open and close doors, the fountain from where her power sprung.

Perhaps it was foolish, but she decided to surrender and try to learn as much as possible from that mysterious fae, and eventually became able to notice the difference between her own mind and something external to it, after a few hours doing some exercises with eyes closed. The floor where she was sitting was uncomfortable, and yet she didn't complain. After all, learning was one of the things she most wanted.

Through it all, she still felt that familiar pull towards Fel. It was funny that Iona had mentioned using a rope for guidance in the hollow, as that was exactly how Leah felt—and sometimes it pulled her. But she wasn't going to meet him if she thought the Breaker—or whatever that creepy voice was—could spy on her thoughts. Leah still hadn't mentioned the iron dragon to the fae, and hadn't really told her that he was a real dragon. She'd been saying dragon lords, maybe thinking they only had human forms, and Leah allowed her to keep the assumption.

Still, she had learned a lot.

"It's good for now." Iona's voice startled her. "I wish everyone was as easy to teach as you, but we should eat. Aren't you thirsty? Or hungry?"

A little, sure. Would this be the trap? Being afraid of food, when she'd revealed so much, was more than silly. She did have a question, though. "How do you get water and food here?"

"There are lakes and streams. As for food, some fungi and rodents. Not very enticing, I know."

"I'll have some water."

Iona walked out and came back with a wooden bowl with the liquid.

Leah took it and drank it, telling herself to stop with any nonsense. She had been thirsty, after all. "You'll also teach me to disguise my magic?"

The fae looked outside. It was still day, or whatever day looked like in this place. "After night falls. I need you to listen to me first."

"So... what is it you want me to do?"

"The shapers, *kee-lies,* in their language, they are not evil. Yes, they like to eat people, but that doesn't mean anything. We eat animals."

She couldn't seriously be implying that eating people was a minor detail and not a character flaw. Leah was careful not to spit out the water she'd just drunk. "Right."

"They don't like the Breaker either. They are seeing the destruction, and they are willing to fight it."

"Why don't they?"

"He's not... not really here. But to regain full power, he has to go to the second realm, and he'll be there soon. I mean, I'm not sure how soon, but he'll have to go there. Conquering realm after realm had to be a plan to get there eventually."

"Won't the shapers be happy if he moves away?"

"Of course not. He'll be more powerful. He causes discord, war, dissent. He's destroying this place."

"But then, what's the Breaker's goal? If he destroys everything, what's he going to gain? At some point, everything will be gone."

"More and more power, that's it. The second realm is large enough that it could take thousands of years to be depleted or completely destroyed. It would still feed him. If anything, that's his home realm. He won't destroy it completely. You think he cares about this place?"

Leah herself didn't care, and she didn't consider herself a particularly evil creature. "Do *you* care?"

"All life is precious. They are what they are, and it's none of their fault. The important thing is that they could help you."

"How?"

"Let them come to the Second Realm, the ones I know, the ones who want freedom. They'll fight for you."

"Right. And once the fight stops, they'll want to celebrate by having us for dinner."

"You can make a treaty with them. Have them living in a remote location. They don't need to eat people, even if they like it. At least let them survive. I can help. Remember I'm a fae, and my deals are binding."

"How can I call them?"

"Let us come to Aluria. Now. When it's time to fight, we'll be ready."

"You could also wait here."

"Then it might be too late, and I won't be around to help you seal the deal with them."

Everything about it sounded like a terrible idea. "You're talking as if there will be a war with soldiers, but isn't this Breaker incorporeal?"

"He has to assume a form if he wants to come into his power."

"One form, which I'm sure is very hard to kill. What am I going to do? Let loose a bunch of these toothy creatures on him? I'm assuming if he has strong magic, he'll defeat them easily, won't he? I don't see how it's going to work."

For the first time Leah saw a flicker of disappointment in

Iona's eyes. "Sometimes you need to trust that the answer will come."

"No. It doesn't work like that. I told you I got creatures to help me, and in the end they were turning against us."

"Didn't they help, though?"

"For a while, yes. But that's useless if they're going to turn, don't you think?"

"I think you can't just open a passage to creatures without first having clear rules, a clear deal. That was your mistake."

"It was." Then something hit her. "I have a question. You've been here for twenty years. Maybe it felt like less for you." Leah knew that time passed differently in different realms. "You don't even have proper utensils, meaning that you had to improvise. It means you can't leave this place. Why are you truly offering to help me? To return to Aluria?"

Iona closed her eyes. "That was my deal with the ones who found me. To free them. And I can't move on my own. Not from here."

"What if I freed just you?"

"It wouldn't be right. And they want to fight."

"How did you get here?"

She sighed, visibly displeased, but Leah's previous deal about revealing everything was working. "I foolishly tried to get into the Iron Citadel, and my magic went berserk. As I was trying to run away, I got lost and ended up here. What about you? Why did the voice scare you so much? I mean, it seems you were friends with it before, using it to give you power to kill, to win a battle... Then all of a sudden you ran away, realizing the dragon lord was in danger. What happened?" Her eyes were hard. Right. She was making Leah reveal her secrets as a punishment for having been obliged to say that much.

As her throat started constricting, Leah looked outside and saw that it was completely black. Night. She had already learned about the Breaker and even about some of her magic. Fel was tugging her harder than ever. With a lot more confidence that the voice wouldn't find her, Leah decided not to resist the pull, and disappeared into an ocean of darkness. She did feel bad for leaving the lonely, malnourished, sad fae behind, but perhaps she could come back some other time, with a clear mind.

Finally she was going where she most wanted, which was to meet Fel again.

16

THE ANCIENT LIBRARY

R iver had put on a shirt, and watched as Naia came out of the room wearing one of her linen dresses. It was simple, and yet looked so elegant and even regal on her, the white fabric contrasting with her magnificent dark hair and skin. He wished she still had that nightgown, though. No, he wished he had taken it off, then lay her on the bed and kissed her, touched her. They could still wait, while at the same time not waiting that much. But then, the world was falling apart and there was so much that could *not* wait.

He wiped his hand on his shirt before taking Naia's hand, as he didn't want her to notice his cold sweat. His body was telling him that it refused to go to the Ancient City, refused to talk to his father. Perhaps he should just turn away, tell Naia they were going to do something else, but he knew that the city was isolated and wouldn't last much longer without help. He couldn't let his foolish fear of confronting his father ruin it all. And then there were all of Naia's questions... They had to go.

Her eyes were wide as she took his hand. "Something wrong?"

He scoffed. "*Everything* is wrong where my father's concerned. It doesn't end there. Lots of wrong things in Aluria."

She squeezed his hand. "We'll find a solution. Let's trust our magic." That lovely smile of hers was sweet and brave and could set his heart on fire.

Stepping into the hollow was a lot more difficult than usual, even if he wasn't feeling particularly weakened. It was as if even his magic didn't want to go to the Ancient City, but he decided not to listen to it. River squashed by irrational fear, that was a sight nobody should ever see, not even himself. He held Naia close, and this time, it wasn't so much to protect her as it was for him to feel safer.

Everything about this was putting him on edge, but he wouldn't be able to postpone going to his city forever. Perhaps he should have tried to convince Naia to stay in the house, at least wait until he negotiated with his father, but leaving her behind also filled him with dread. It made no sense. He'd been going into Ironhold and had never felt that way. Perhaps it had been his encounter with the queen and being imprisoned, perhaps having his confidence shaken once had been enough to turn his insides into jam. Ridiculous. He was many things—many, many things, some of them rather shameful—but he'd stopped being a coward a long time ago.

His circle surrounded the entire city and the castle, and then there were smaller circles within the circle. The one calling to him the most was the library, which made sense, but he chose to go somewhere else, and then stood inside Anelise's antechamber.

Naia looked around, her eyes curious, even if they also had a tiny hint of fear. "Where are we?"

Just hearing her voice was enough to put him at ease. "My sister's quarters. She should hear us soon. We'd better wait."

"You're worried," she whispered.

"A little." He didn't want to knock on Anelise's room yet, so he wanted to find something to distract him while he waited. "Do you know how to get into the hollow?"

"I don't know anything."

"Can't you feel it? It's a different type of magic. It's like when you perceive a scent coming from one specific direction, or a brief gust of wind. It's there and not there, not all the time, but it's the kind of magic you can sense if you open up."

Naia closed her eyes.

He said, "Nuh-uh. Eyes open. You need to see yourself going into the empty realm, the space in-between things."

"We'll have to practice it."

"I know."

The door to the room opened, and Anelise stepped into her antechamber. "River?" Her tone was worried, not angry. She then glanced at Naia, and seemed horrified. "You? Why are you here?"

"We want to help," Naia said, visibly surprised at Anelise's reaction.

"How?"

Naia glanced at River, who nodded at her. She turned to Anelise. "I think I can unseal your city. I know you just woke up from a twenty-year sleep, and I'm worried you don't have enough water or food."

Anelise frowned, seeming more puzzled than anything. "Why would you worry?"

Naia shrugged. "I don't want to see people dying."

"People." Anelise was thoughtful. "We are digging wells. There's some water to be found deep down. Of course, we wouldn't mind being free."

River thought that it was his turn to do some explaining. "The war ended a long time ago—when we disappeared. But there are things happening in Aluria right now... The Ancients need to avoid contact with humans. Naia here is suggesting an area in her kingdom where you won't be bothered, just somewhere where a few Ancients could go for resources like fish, wood, water. If it's necessary."

Anelise didn't hide the disappointment on her face. "We'd still be limited."

It was true. "For the time being, yes."

His sister nodded. "It would be helpful, but what we really need are new grains, new plants. We have some reserves, but they won't last long."

"I'll try to find some," River said quickly. He didn't want Naia to offer the reserves her kingdom barely had, and didn't want her to negotiate with them either, or offer something that could be perceived as charity, which Ancients hated.

Anelise then took a long look at him. "River, how are you? What happened to you?" Her caring tone was surprising.

"I was suspended in time as well, but I woke up a year ago."

"I see." His sister then looked at Naia. "I'm so sorry for what our father did. I wanted to release you, I was going to, I had some friends who were going to help me, but River was faster."

"Oh. Thanks so much," Naia said, then added, "And I truly want to help you."

Anelise nodded. "I understand. I'm just not sure... I'm not sure it will go down well with my father." She turned to River. "He blames you for everything."

River had a bitter laugh. "I blame myself for Ciara. You can blame me too. You should hate me."

There was pain in Anelise's eyes. "River, after I lost my sister, do you think I wanted to lose a brother too?"

"It's not like..." He wasn't even sure what to say or how to say it. "We weren't that close."

"Because you wouldn't use your magic! You wouldn't help us."

River took Naia's hand and squeezed it, hoping she understood the warning. None of his siblings had any idea about his mindmelding, about the real magic he had always refused to wield.

Anelise continued, "You could make a difference and instead you were squandering your power being lazy, partying and drinking, even when the war got serious. I wanted you to change, I wanted you to do something. Looking back, knowing what happened to Ciara, maybe I was wrong."

Just hearing his sister's name hurt him from head to toes. "I don't know."

"How were you able to get back?" Anelise asked.

"My exile has been broken."

Anelise frowned, visibly confused.

He added, "Our father said I had to bring a dragon heart." He pointed to Naia. "Here's a dragon heart. He never said the heart couldn't still be beating or that it would need to remain in the city."

His sister turned to Naia. "You really are a dragon lord." Lord. Anelise likely had no idea that they could actually become dragons.

"I believe so," Naia answered. "I didn't know that before."

River then realized she needed a better introduction, and said, "She's my chosen life companion. Her name is Irinaia Umbraar, and she's a human princess. Half dragon. You can call her Naia." He then pointed at his sister. "This is Anelise, my older sister."

Naia smiled and extended her hand. "I'm glad to meet you."

Anelise looked at her. Ancients were not used to handshakes. Still, she pulled the sleeve of her dress, so that her hand wouldn't touch Naia's, and shook it. "Metal magic. Id' rather not touch you directly."

"Oh." Naia pulled her hand. "I'm the one who's sorry."

He'd wasted enough time here. The library was calling him. "Anelise, I know you have tons of things to do, but could you take a moment and talk to her? Tell her... Would you mind doing that? I'll be right back."

Naia's eyes were wide. "I thought..."

He kissed her lips briefly. "You're safe here. Trust me."

River didn't even leave the room, but dissolved right back into the hollow and then appeared in the library. His memories of this place were both sweet and bitter. Sweet with so much knowledge he'd gotten, but bitter with the feeling that more and more his only choice had been to become a disappointment to his father.

This library had some thirty rooms, varying from small to medium, with specialized books divided by topics. There was also an area, down below, with some rare objects, and what he wanted was down there.

No, that didn't make sense. He had to research death grass, find information, find a way to resist it. What would he want with that old dagger? Where had that idea even come from? Crazy thoughts.

Why was he getting so confused?

He slipped into the hollow again, and then was in the safe below the library, where the most dangerous objects were contained. There, he saw it, golden with a ruby-encrusted handle. He took it and was taken by relief, satisfaction, and delight. He had what he needed.

FEL WAS able to beat his wings just enough not to hit the surface of the ocean with a damaging impact. He felt the enemies below him, and kept them submerged. That didn't change the fact that some five dragons were flying in his direction. He strangled one of them with his own armor, but that left him four enemies way too close.

He was spreading his wings and floating in the ocean.

Tzaria then flew in his direction. "Get out of the water. Now. Now!"

His wings hurt, but he made an effort, and left the ocean, right as a boundless sent a blast of—what? It was some kind of electric current.

She added, "Stay afloat in the air, no matter what."

So he'd been lucky on his way here that none of his adversaries had that strange fire. Tzaria then flew above Fel, as if to shield him. There was no way she would be able to fight that many dragons at once.

He then felt something different, something on his back. He'd felt it before, but it couldn't be. Then he sensed her: Leah. He wasn't sure how she'd gotten here, but he knew that this was too dangerous for her.

"You have to leave." He sent her that thought, unsure if she would hear it, unsure even if she was capable of going anywhere.

Above Tzaria, he felt some pieces of metal armor. His magic was getting sharper, more precise. He strangled four dragons at once, and then six more. Their bodies fell into the ocean. Then there were no more boundless.

"I'll see you around," Tzaria said. "Be very careful."

She flew away from him, and then the other dragons were flying in his direction. There was a strange murmur among them, along with surprise, relief, and euphoria.

Part of the murmur then got clear. "The iron dragon."

His cousin approached him, with some blood on his neck. His uncle was also close by. Meanwhile, two dragons traced a circle in the sky. A dragon carried a human body through it, and then the six others crossed it.

"Follow us," his uncle said.

Fel did, and came to a strange place over mountains, from where he crossed another fire ring in the air, and came to the dragon city. Tzaria hadn't followed them. They landed right in the middle of the round plaza, and Fel collapsed, careful not to hurt Leah.

"Who's she?" Ekateni asked.

"My betrothed," Fel lied. Well, it wasn't that much of a lie.

"Your magic defeated those dragons?" he asked.

"Yes, my human magic." There was no point trying to hide or deny it anymore. "I couldn't use it before, but I could use it during the battle."

"Are you hurt?"

"My wings aren't moving well."

"Well, then," Ekateni said. "Wait here. I'll take care of the wounded and be right back."

Leah got out of his back and now stood in front of his face.

"Can you hear me?" he asked.

She laughed. "I can! I'm so sorry, I... I didn't know you would be fighting."

"It's fine." He nuzzled her head with his snout.

"I have so much to tell you," she said.

"Same."

There were dragons watching—or guarding them, but standing at a distance. Fel didn't know any of them and wasn't sure what to do or where to go. He wanted to talk to Leah, but didn't want the dragons to hear him.

Someone then ran in their direction. It was his cousin, Siniari, in human form, looking healthy and healed.

"Isofel, how come you were hiding it from us? You're the iron dragon!"

Leah's face darkened, a clear trace of fear in her eyes.

Siniari saw her, and added, "And apparently you can also make damsels appear out of thin air."

Leah chuckled. "I'm no damsel."

"My name's Siniari, I'm Isofel's cousin."

She looked at Fel, surprised, then turned to Siniari. "My name's Leandra. I'm from Frostlake. In Aluria."

He stared at her, puzzled. "How..."

"I'm a deathbringer," she added. "I can move through the hollow. Sometimes. I do realize I got here at a terrible time."

"How's everyone?" Fel asked his cousin. He was genuinely worried about the other dragons, and plus, he didn't want Leah to be grilled with questions.

"They're fine," his cousin said. "Raf and Sonia lost their dragon forms, but their human bodies are unharmed."

Fel didn't know who these dragons were, but felt relieved. It still didn't wash away his guilt. "Was it my fault? My fault you were attacked? If you hadn't brought me—"

Siniari shook his head. "No. I mean, how could it be? They attack us everywhere. We can't stay here all the time. What happened was I should have told someone where I was going, I should have asked for support. Thankfully, my friends found me, and waited there with me. After a while, my father found me. I guess I'm very obvious. He was furious. Still, we waited for you. And then the Boundless came. It was right before you got out of the cave. The iron dragon! Who would have guessed? The Boundless didn't stand a chance."

It hadn't felt like that at the time. And this talk of the iron dragon was making him anxious. "I'd rather say I'm a dragon who has metal magic. That hardly makes me an iron dragon, let alone *the* iron dragon, whatever that's supposed to mean."

Siniari frowned. "Of course you're the iron dragon. There's no other explanation. But it's good. You know what it means? You can defeat Cynon."

"Why?" Perhaps iron magic could do something special. That would be a good thing to know. He still didn't understand why Tzaria had asked him to hide his magic. But then, so had Leah, who watched him with worry in her beautiful blue eyes.

His cousin glanced at Leah, as if making up his mind whether he should say anything in front of her, but then he looked at Fel again. "Dragons can see the future," he said. "Sometimes. Small glimpses. Many years ago, there was a dragon who could see further than most. Most of what he predicted has already come to pass. Among his visions, he said that the iron dragon would defeat darkness. We've kept this saying: *when the world falls into darkness, the iron dragon will be the only flame left to fight it.*"

It didn't sound hopeful. If anything, it sounded like a dreadful prophecy, being alone to fight in a dark world.

His cousin continued, "Of course, we don't want to believe in a savior, you know? But we always thought one of us could be the one, we've always thought that *iron dragon* wasn't meant to be taken literally, that it meant a strong dragon. It was something we could all aspire to be. But now, seeing you, seeing what you've done, there's no doubt it's you. Dragon visions don't tend to be metaphorical."

Fel felt uneasy. How could he help the dragons when he knew so little about himself? "I barely know any dragon magic."

"You have iron magic. Why worry about dragon magic?"

"I'd like to swap bodies, for one."

Siniari glanced at Leah. "I can see why." He looked at Fel. "I guess it didn't work."

"It didn't," Fel said. "Even though I passed the challenge, he wouldn't give it to me." He turned to Leah. "Can you hear me?"

"I can." She caressed his neck, which made him feel better. It was obvious that she understood he hadn't managed to learn to swap into his human form, but she didn't seem worried or upset.

Siniari sighed. "I just hope you won't get in trouble. You can't bring visitors here, and dragons aren't allowed to let humans ride them."

The fire in his chest threatened to leave it. "She rides me when and as much as she wants."

"Hey, calm down," his cousin said. "I don't agree with this rule. I'm just saying what the high council might say. But then, you being the Iron Dragon and all, I don't think they'll mind."

Leah turned to Siniari. "I felt he was in danger and couldn't stop myself from coming. I'm really sorry it was during a fight. But I'm not *riding* Fel; he's not a horse. I'm just lying on his back while he flies wherever he wants. If I had wings, I'd fly *with* him."

She had a point.

"I meant no offense," his cousin said. "And again, I don't think the council is going to care." He smiled. "If you could, I'd bring you to see Sonia and Raf, but they're in the infirmary for humans. It's small..."

"They're your friends?" Fel asked, wondering who all the dragons were in the fight. "Who else was there?"

"Two other friends of mine, a guard who was with my dad," then his expression soured, "and the exiles. They fought with us, but... I don't know. I still think they alerted the Boundless, brought them there. No idea why they insisted on keeping that ruse."

"Tzaria protected me."

"Or pretended to do that."

Could that be? "Well, she wanted me to run away from the fight when I first got out of the cave. I... don't know if she wanted to protect me or what. Nobody got hurt from our side?"

"Our side. I like that. Yes, Sonia and Raf, but they're fine now. I mean, as fine as they can be. Are you and, uh, Le... are you two all right?"

"You can call me Leah," she said. "I didn't even get a scratch. Fel?"

"Some fire hit me, made my wings slow. I don't know if they're back to normal yet, but I don't think I'm wounded."

His cousin laughed. "Of course not. You came out of that cave, and then boom, killed all their dragon forms at once. It was incredible."

Laughing in dragon form felt strange, as if he would accidentally blast some fire, but Fel couldn't help it, hearing his cousin's exaggerated account. "I'm sure that was not how it went."

"Pretty close. It was amazing. I can see you turning the tide for us."

Fel didn't feel half as hopeful, but said, "Let's hope so."

His uncle then landed beside them, and soon swapped into his human form. "I'm sure you'll need to rest. You can come to my house, but she'll have to stay in one of the ground dwellings."

"I'm not leaving her." Fel trusted the dragons, but he didn't want to leave Leah alone in a place she didn't know.

His cousin then said, "They could come to my house. There's room for dragons and humans, and they would be safe."

Ekateni watched them. "I... I'm not sure your mother will like that."

"Of course she won't mind." Siniari chuckled. "She said she wished he'd stay with us. And Leah can stay with my sister. They'll both be as safe as they can be, and together."

Fel's uncle paused. "Perhaps. There will be a celebration

tonight. For the Iron Dragon. I wanted to keep it quiet, but some of the leaders insisted."

Siniari laughed. "You think something like that can be kept quiet? You hide it, it's even worse. The hush-hush and gossip will spread misinformation like seeds in the wind. And we need some fun. And hope."

Ekateni exhaled. "We do need that, and we could certainly use some hope. Can I trust you that you're going to take care of him, or are you going to go somewhere without backup, without informing anyone?"

"I think I learned my lesson." Siniari looked down. "We could all have died today. I almost saw my best friend die, I almost saw *you* die." He stared at his father. "I've been properly reminded of how dangerous the Boundless are."

"Good. I hope you'll keep in mind the importance of our rules."

"No question about it," Siniari said.

Fel's uncle then looked at the three of them slowly, perhaps considering something, then said, "Well, then. I'll see you later. Get ready for a celebration. We do deserve it. If you have any problem, call me, and I'll arrange other accommodations." He swapped his form and flew away. Fel watched his uncle in awe, hoping one day he would be able to do that as well, to pick the form most convenient for each occasion.

"Come." His cousin was smiling and sounded excited. "I can't wait for you to see my house. And for the party!"

Fel noticed that Leah was still serious, thoughtful. He needed desperately to spend time alone with her and understand why she had asked him to hide his magic. She wouldn't have said it if it wasn't important. Now, the truth about his ironbringing was out. Not only that, the dragons were planning on drawing as much attention as possible to it.

Fel's hope was that both Leah and Tzaria were wrong, that perhaps they had been worried for no reason. What were the odds?

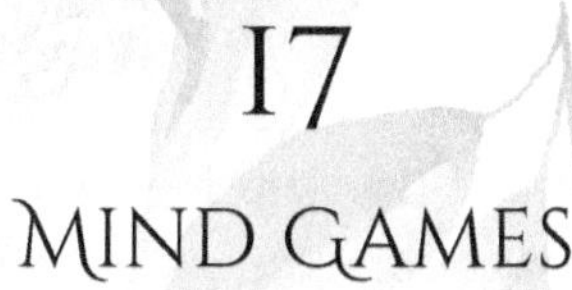

17
MIND GAMES

Naia found it strange. River had told her to stay with him, and now he was leaving like that?

Alone with his sister, she was unsure what to say. Perhaps the best idea would be to go straight to the reason she had come.

"We need to come up with a solution for your city."

The fae was staring at her with those strange, dark red eyes. "Do you love him?"

The change of subject was startling, but Naia decided to answer truly. "I think so." It was odd to voice that feeling so clearly, something she hadn't admitted to herself yet, but it was what she felt was true.

"You're also an ironbringer."

Naia wasn't sure if she heard a hint of accusation in her tone, or if she was imagining it. "I never met my mother, and I think the Ironholds killed her. I hate them. They're also... They're in conflict with other humans. We might have a war upon us. Please don't think I have anything to do with Ironhold."

"Just your magic. It's very dangerous to us." She pointed to a sofa. "Sit."

Naia did so, and River's sister followed. She was very graceful with a white and golden tunic, matching her super long, flowing silvery-white hair. The girl had a strange yet captivating beauty. River, with his horns and reddish eyes, looked almost human in comparison to her.

The fae then asked, "How come your magic doesn't affect him?"

"It did. The first time we kissed. Now he's immune to iron." Naia wasn't sure if it was something she should tell, but if River had left her there, it was because he trusted his sister.

"You haven't married yet, in human terms."

"Not yet."

"So you haven't been together—physically—like a couple."

This was getting oddly personal, but Naia thought it wouldn't hurt to answer. "No."

The conversation then only got odder, as Anelise went on to explain to her about what a couple did. Naia was glad to learn that, but she wished it had been with someone she trusted, not with a stranger. But then, perhaps strange would have been to hear it from her father or brother. The fae explained that human women could get pregnant very easily, unlike Ancients, who could get pregnant only once a year.

"There's a tea," Anelise said. "Ourlisium."

"The one for stomachache?"

"Yes. Drinking it occasionally won't affect you much, but you'll have to drink it every single day if you want to avoid getting pregnant. Every day."

"I see." None of it sounded romantic or exciting when there were all these warnings. Naia realized she sounded grumpy instead of grateful, though, so she smiled. "Thank you. How come you know about this tea, if you don't need it?"

"Inter-marriages were common. I mean, there are some strict rules for that, so they were never that widespread, and became even rarer lately. Still, it was quite common for human women to come to us quite uneducated."

Uneducated—what a dreadful word to describe Naia. The

worst was that it was true. As a princess, she took pride in learning everything she could about other kingdoms, magic, diplomacy, and yet, she'd always been ignorant in that aspect. "It's embarrassing."

"No, it's not your fault. They do it to control you." She sighed. "Humans." There was no hiding her dislike for them. It was a reminder that Anelise still perceived Naia as an enemy. She then added, "Now you'll probably become one of us, so you'll need to adapt. We also need to adapt to you, and can't just assume you'll behave like an Ancient." So that was why River had wanted Naia to speak to Anelise.

The fae continued, "My great-grandmother was human, and since her reign, we've had clear laws concerning human-Ancient marriages. It was also supposed to avoid a conflict, you know? We didn't want the kingdoms of Aluria saying we were stealing or taking advantage of their girls. The conflict happened regardless, of course. For other reasons."

"I'm sorry for the war," Naia said. That was a stupid apology, since it hadn't been her fault, and plus her kingdom had suffered too.

Anelise had a bitter chuckle, and it was eerie how similar it was to River's. "Aren't we all sorry?"

"I hope things will get better. Eventually. And then your people will be able to leave this city."

The fae shook her head. "This was just a city for the royalty and some of us. It should be our safe haven, yes, but not for an entire population."

True, but they'd need to stay there for a while. "Ironhold... they've been lying, saying the Ancients are back, that you are attacking kingdoms." Hopefully she wouldn't need to explain much about it, as she didn't want to tell her what River had been doing. "They want to use this lie to gain control over Aluria. So... these are dangerous times for you."

The fae didn't seem surprised. "Like all the times lately, except when we were sleeping, I guess." Her tone then became sarcastic. "Perhaps being suspended in time was a good fortune."

It had been partly River's fault, worried about them because the dragons had isolated the city. Still, Naia felt that it was his story to tell, his truth to explain to his sister.

Naia swallowed. "Maybe. I think your brother has a lot to say about that."

The girl set those dark red eyes on Naia and smiled. "Ah. You *do* love him."

Uh? "What makes you think so?" Naia was curious, then realized how defensive she sounded, and added, "I'm not saying I don't."

"I can feel it. You're lucky. I mean, he's lucky too."

The door opened again, and in came River, but looking so different. He had thin braids on his hair and wore a red shirt, open almost to his waist. He also had chains, earrings, and rings, as well as a golden circlet on his head. Two daggers were strapped to his belt, one black, the other red, encrusted with rubies or garnets. That was the perfect image of what a fae prince should look like, one Naia wasn't used to. She had seen him well dressed in Frostlake, but that had been human garb. This was all more lacy and delicate, but it suited him. Naia was wearing a simple linen dress that felt too simple now, but this wasn't the time to worry about these things.

He smiled and raised an eyebrow. "Don't I look dashing?"

Anelise chuckled. "Oh, that's the vain brother I've always known. Quite important to look pretty when your city is about to starve."

"Extremely important." He fiddled with his rings. There were four of them on each hand, with colored gemstones and engravings. "I'm going to speak to King Spring, so I might as well be the prince he wants me to be."

Anelise's smile faded. "I think he still wants you exiled, River." Her voice was slow, careful.

River smirked, apparently unfazed. "Then I'll have to change his mind."

His sister stared at him and bit her lip, then pointed to his belt. "What dagger is that?"

"Which one? They're mine. Why?"

She narrowed her eyes, as if examining the weapons, then said, "Nothing."

River approached Naia and extended his arm. "I'll need you by my side."

He expected her to walk beside him like that, looking like a peasant? "You didn't tell me about the dress code."

"The dress code is to look magnificent, so you are perfect for it. I'm just here humbly trying not to be overshadowed by you."

Naia rolled her eyes, but took his arm. He seemed confident and unafraid, which was good. Was it the clothes that were helping?

"River," Anelise said. "It's still early."

"I asked them to wake him up," he replied. His sister had a serious, thoughtful expression. He then added, "Come. I'll also need you."

Naia was also puzzled. Wasn't it going to be harder to speak to his father if he was grumpy and sleepy? But then, River exuded confidence, so he had to know what he was doing. Anelise didn't look so sure, but she followed them.

They descended large wooden stairs, which should have been decorated with vines, except that they were dry now.

Downstairs, they came to huge bronze doors, and then entered a large chamber. This was where Naia had first spoken to King Spring, and the memory gave her chills. At that time, she had been expecting him to be somewhat of a benevolent king who would be interested in negotiating with her. At that time, she hadn't known what River had been doing, hadn't known he was a prince, and had no idea why the city had been under a spell.

So much had changed in so little time. Still, she didn't like being here again. To be honest, if she were to choose, she would rather not speak to the Ancient King. As she had predicted, his sister was friendly, and they could perhaps have tried to make a deal directly with her. But then again, River knew much more about the Ancients than she did, so she had to trust his judgment. She wouldn't want him to tell her how to deal with her father. Her father. That was something she didn't want to think about.

There were fae archers in nooks on the wall, and more and more fae guards were entering the room. As much as Naia wanted to trust River, there were too many ways that this could go wrong. And still, she could sense none of his previous fear. She wished he had told her what he'd been planning, that way perhaps she would have at least some of his confidence. As it was, she had none.

When King Spring entered the chamber glaring at River, she felt certain there was no way they would walk out of this place unscathed, no way even that they would make any deal. The king's eyes had nothing but hatred—all of it directed at his own son.

Naia looked at River, worried about how he was taking it, but he didn't seem upset, anxious, or afraid. Instead, his face was hard, focused on the king, his eyes matching or perhaps even surpassing his father's hatred. Naia stepped away from him, startled to see him like that.

Something bad was about to happen, she had no doubt of that. The issue was what—and to whom.

THE GENTLE TOUCH of warm water on Leah's body was pleasant. This amazing bathtub in the Dragon Eye's house would be extremely relaxing in other circumstances. Right now, Leah still recalled that strange voice echoing in her mind, looking for the iron dragon.

Now she knew that *iron dragon* was a well-known, old expression, which made her wonder if there was any connection between the voice she had heard and the dragons, or even these Boundless. Fel and Siniari had told her quickly about Cynon, this old, not-living and not-dead dragon, who was an enemy. It sounded eerily similar to the Breaker, the creature that the strange fae had mentioned, but Leah hadn't had time to discuss it. She hadn't told much to Fel, fearing her words could be overheard, fearing what could happen if she mentioned voices in her head and the mysterious fae in the hollow.

Another reason the bath wasn't as comfortable as it should be was that she wasn't alone, but with Relia, who was the Dragon's Eye, which was some kind of leader in that community, and her daughter Jacine. The girl was about seventeen, with lovely long brown hair and bright yellow eyes. Leah was used to being undressed in front of her mother and attendants, and didn't mind being seen by other women. Still, it was weird to get to know someone without any clothes on. She felt... naked. Yes, that was the word. Quite appropriate.

Jacine had been asking questions and questions about life in Aluria, fascinated by the different kingdoms and their magic.

"Daughter, dear," Relia interrupted. "We know they have royal families. They are humans with magic." There was some derision in the woman's words.

"I know," the girl said. "It's just... they're so similar to the humans here. It's odd."

Her accent was a lot smoother than her mother's, and Leah decided to ask about that. "Does everyone here speak two languages? Because I heard some Fernian." She didn't understand that language, but knew what it sounded like, and was sure it was what she heard the most among the dragons.

"No, no. We mostly speak one language." Jacine laughed. "And it's not Fernian. It's New Elvish. Not Elvish, really, it's the dragon language, but people call it Elvish. Your language comes from the fae. Some of us study it because there are books in that language. The noxious fae left a lot of things behind..."

"Not that much," her mother said, as if correcting her.

Noxious... Leah thought she knew what they meant, but wasn't sure. "You mean the white fae?"

"Yes," Jacine said. "They were exiled to your continent."

Relia leaned over and got her hair wet. "My daughter likes to talk too much. Interested in magic."

"I'm going to become a dragon mage." Jacine smiled. "I wish Isofel had been raised here, then I'm sure he would become a mage as well. Maybe he can still try it."

Would Fel want to stay here? Would he forget Aluria? Leah didn't think so, but she couldn't be sure. Since they were mentioning him, she decided to ask something that was bothering her. "If this *iron dragon* is so important, is it wise to let everyone know it could be Isofel? Won't he become a target of the Boundless?"

Jacine bit her lip and was thoughtful.

Relia waved a hand. "Oh, no. You need to be a buffoon to believe the words of a loony who spent his days speaking nonsense. There's no iron dragon, and no iron dragon is going to save us. What we need is power, knowledge, strength. That said, words do have power. *When the world falls into darkness, the iron dragon will be the only flame left to fight it.* We've repeated it so much. It's obviously about hope. If we give in, we are defeated before the battle. If we stand with our neck held high, fly with confidence in our wings, then we stand a chance. The iron dragon is a symbol—a much needed symbol when we've lost so much."

The woman's words made sense, but still. "Wouldn't the boundless believe those words, though? Wouldn't they want to kill, hurt, or kidnap Isofel?"

Leah could not forget what she had seen that afternoon, when Fel had been surrounded by enemies on all sides. For a second, she thought they were about to cross the threshold of death together. It wasn't their time, though, thanks to Fel's astounding magic—metal magic, which made him known as the *iron dragon*. There would be no hiding after this. She hoped that whatever danger was targeting Fel was too far away to notice anything. But what were the chances of that?

"For sure they'll try to kill him." Relia's words had the tranquility of someone who didn't see anything alarming in them. "That said, there isn't a day the Boundless aren't trying to kill us —all of us. Or turn us to their side. It's not as if Isofel would be any safer if we were to hide his iron magic. I'll tell you what, girl: he'll be much, much safer now that he'll hold a special position among us. There's something else I need to warn you. I can see you have feelings for him, but if I were you, I would try my luck elsewhere. He's beautiful, he's powerful, and he'll have many more choices."

Leah felt as if she had swallowed a stone.

"Oh, no," Jacine said. "Leah here is also beautiful and powerful, so I think they are a perfect match." The girl winked at her.

Relia sighed. "You think I'm being mean. I'm not. This is the voice of experience. He's his father's son. There's more." She stared at Leah. "You're just human. Dragons can mate in both forms. He's stuck as a dragon for now. What do you think he's going to do?"

"I don't know." Leah's voice was dry. In a way, it was her mother's warning all over again. And hadn't it been true? King Azir had left her. If King Flavio hadn't married her, who knew what could have happened?

Jacine shook her head. "Mom, aren't you the one who always says that we can't know the future, that we can't let fear guide us?"

Relia frowned. "This saying is for war, not for love."

The girl shrugged. "But it works. And love and fear are opposites, aren't they?"

The woman took a deep breath and looked down. "This talk of love... It just reminds me of what I lost."

"I'm so sorry," Leah said, even if she didn't know who the woman was referring to, especially when it wasn't very clear who was related to whom. And her own sorrow was fresh, sorrow for her father and Kasim, but she didn't mention it because she didn't want to stir that pain.

"I know," Relia said. "Perhaps I'm being unfair. Some of us, we have only one love, a love that lasts until we die, even if they go first."

Jacine looked down and fiddled with the tip of her hair, then looked at Leah. "Her love was Isofel's father, Ircantari."

Now Leah was extremely confused. "Didn't you say you were Isofel's cousin, not sister?"

"Cousin, yes. My father, Ekateni, is Ircantari's brother."

Ugh. Had this woman really married and had children with her beloved's *brother*? That sounded dreadful.

Relia looked at Leah. "I see your surprise. And censure."

"No, I—"

The woman put a hand in front of her. "I understand. I've lived through this many times. Many times I've questioned myself. The thing is, we never know what unites people. In my case, it was the shared grief; it was enough to bring us together. Not enough to keep us together, for sure, but at the time we didn't know that we were just leaning on each other, trying to bear the weight of our own pains. And that feeling of hurting a little less, that feeling of having someone who understood my loss, that felt like love."

Leah felt bad for her first impression. "I swear I didn't mean to judge you. And I'm sorry it didn't work."

"Oh, no." Relia laughed. "I'm glad it didn't work. And I'm glad it worked—for some time. Or I wouldn't have had Jacine and Siniari. I just wish... I hope we have calmer times, peaceful times, but I'm working for it. There's no magic that can't be defeated, and at the end of the day, that's all Cynon is; a dragon with magic more powerful than us."

"Is he alive? In this realm?" Perhaps he had nothing to do with the voice Leah had heard.

Relia took a deep breath. "*Alive* is a strange definition once you choose to become immortal. I don't think he's in this world yet, but he's found a way to touch us."

"How does it work? Is it a voice people hear?" The water was starting to feel cold.

"Nothing that simple," Relia said. "If it were, they could just tell it to go away, right?"

"How then, how does it work?"

"We have theories," the woman said. "To be honest, I'm not even sure if he's behind the Boundless. They're just dragons trying to be powerful. When you're the most powerful of all creatures, the temptation to exert your power, subdue others, it lurks in the back of your mind. I don't think you need a powerful dragon to encourage it. Perhaps they want to be greater than us, greater than other dragons, and that's where their hatred comes from. That's why they attack us. It's envy."

Her words were making their conflict seem murkier than the water in their bath.

The woman continued, "But it doesn't matter who the enemy is. What we need is strong magic, what we need is to be united, what we need is to have the will to fight. And that's what I want us to accomplish."

Leah smiled, hoping that indeed the dragons defeated their enemies, but the whole situation was making her anxious. More and more it didn't seem likely that any dragons would be able to help Aluria. It had been a long, dangerous trip to get here, and it was only complicating things. At least Fel had found some of his family. Perhaps he would learn about himself and his magic, and maybe that could help them.

Still, there was no way that Leah could see a celebration for the *iron dragon* as anything other than a terrible idea.

Naia took a breath as deep as she could without calling attention to her, and tried to calm down. River had asked her to trust him. He probably had a plan and this was part of it.

King Spring sat behind a table, and River approached it. "Father, dearest. Enjoying cowering in your little hole?"

"You're not my son."

Naia had once heard those words, which turned out to be true, and yet still hurt. In this case, though, the similarity between father and son was too great for anyone to deny what they were.

The king added, "And you're still exiled."

"How then am I here?" River sneered. "Have you thought of that?"

King Spring laughed. "You want to know why I listened to your summons? To see you suffer." He raised a hand and glanced at a balcony located on the side of the room.

Oh, no. Six of those horrible hooded fae, the mindmelders, were there. They could try to make River kill Naia or even something worse. River looked calm, though, and kept approaching his father.

Every muscle in her body wanted to run, to escape, but she knew it would be pointless. River, River, did he even know what he was doing? It didn't feel like it.

She felt a hand touching her back, over the fabric of the dress. "Stay close." It was Anelise, likely predicting an ugly turn of events. Naia's heart was thumping in her chest, and her hands were cold.

River glanced at the nooks where some archers stood, seeming unbothered. Naia heard arrows being nocked. She kept her eyes on the archers she could see, planning to dodge if they tried to hit her or River. Perhaps she could rip the large copper door and use it as a shield, but that would escalate things quickly, and she didn't want to be the one to make the first move. Not to mention that they would be surrounded regardless.

The archers had their arrows pointed straight across, not

down towards them, which was strange. Even stranger was when the arrows were loosened straight ahead, right on the mind-melders. The six of them were hit at the same time. Naia looked away, dreading the sight of blood. There was no screaming. Either they couldn't yell, or they had been killed fast. Murmurs rose in the room.

King Spring shuddered. "What is this? Guards! Kill him!"

River turned sideways, so that he also addressed the other people in the room. "No. I don't want to shed any more blood from our loyal guards."

A fae ran towards River, sword in hand. Naia was about to try to control his sword, when an arrow hit him, and he fell. Had River spoken to the archers and arranged this? Two more guards ran towards him, but then they stopped, stabbed themselves in the arm, and threw their swords far away.

"Kill him, kill him," the king yelled, his eyes wide, his voice desperate.

Anelise was no longer near Naia, but walking towards the dais.

River saw his sister, and said, "Stop." She did as he asked.

Oh, no. River was using his mindmelding, controlling a few key guards in the room. For someone who claimed he hated this magic, he seemed quite proficient at it. Naia hadn't expected any of this, hadn't expected to see him attack his own people.

The king got up and was about to turn, probably to run away, but he also stopped. Trembling and sweating, he said, "Son, why don't you stop this?" His voice was calm, fatherly even. "I always hoped you could be my favorite."

"Really?" River asked. "Am I in line for the throne?"

"We can discuss it." The king was trying to sound benevolent, but his voice was shaky. "If you stop. Stop it, son."

A horrible feeling came to Naia. River had asked her to trust him, but it was getting harder and harder to believe that this was even him.

"No," River said. He turned to everyone else in the room. "In this castle, in our magical cell, my own father tried to make me kill her." He pointed at Naia, but there was no warmth in his eyes. "He tried to make me rip out her heart—*after* I told him she was my chosen companion. The Ancient law is on my side."

Naia exhaled. If he was mentioning the law, he was definitely going to try to make a deal. It didn't change the fact he had just killed seven fae and hurt two more. He'd killed his own people, after being horrified at what Ironhold had done. Perhaps there was an explanation, perhaps things weren't as they seemed, and yet, it all felt wrong.

Then, fast like a cat, River jumped over the table and stood right across from his father. Naia felt something horrible was about to happen. She wanted to scream his name but it got caught in her throat.

The next seconds were like a horrible nightmare. Naia blinked, wanted to look away, and at the same time she kept looking because she was expecting that false image to disappear. It couldn't be true.

18

A NIGHT FOR DANCING

Naia had to be imagining things, she had to, but that was not something that would come from her mind.

In horror, she watched as River dug his nails into his father's chest—and ripped out his heart.

He climbed back to the middle of the room, still holding the heart, blood dripping over his hands. "The law is on my side. I did to him what he tried to make me do."

Naia felt dizzy and wanted to retch.

River still had that hard face. "I am your new king. Bow."

Shaking, perhaps Naia would just collapse if she bent forward. She wasn't supposed to bow to a king who wasn't hers, but she didn't know anything anymore and was consumed with fear. He set his eyes on her. "Not you. You're my queen."

Naia wanted to turn around and run, but her feet were stuck on the floor, and she didn't even know if he was making her do it or if it was just her shock. Tears ran down her eyes. "No."

"Silence," he said.

If she wished to say any more words, they were stuck in her throat. Before this, she would have been furious if he forced her to be silent. Now, it was just one more thing on top of so much that was wrong.

He turned to the others. "Bow to your queen. No. Kneel."

"River!" A deep voice echoed in the room and a white-haired fae entered. "What are you doing?"

"Appreciating our father's heart." River put his hands near his face, which got all smeared with blood. "Aren't you happy you have a fair king and queen?"

Naia closed her eyes, wishing she could disappear.

The newcomer's eyes flashed with fury, but then he kneeled all of a sudden, and said, "Yes. You're perfect. The best brother." He was trembling, as if fighting whatever River was doing to him. "The... best... king. I... accept you."

Naia perhaps could stop this with her metal magic, perhaps she could hit River hard enough in the head that he would collapse. But then he and she would probably be killed. All she wanted was to run away, but then she felt something—a tendril of darkness.

She closed and opened her eyes, and then saw brilliant lines and circles. Without thinking, she walked to the brightest one and spent a long time there, not knowing how to move back to the real world. What if she was about to be trapped here? Eventually, she lay down, exhausted, and felt something soft beneath her.

It was straw underneath a soft fabric. This had to be the hut where she had lived with her brother for six months, when they had been surviving on their own. As she realized where she was, the darkness dissipated, and she lay down, letting her tears flow.

Who had she fallen in love with? Did she even know River? Had he been pretending all this time? He was good at pretending, and she knew that. Perhaps she had fallen for his looks and his charm, and then perhaps white fae were brutal and she didn't understand them. Even with eyes closed, she couldn't unsee the blood, the violence. She could still feel the lump in her throat when he had made her silent. This wasn't someone she could love. Burying her feelings was like strangling her heart. Heart.

That awful image was still in her mind, except that she felt as if he was holding hers.

Naia tried to look around at the hut. Her memories from this place were good. The food had been horrible, until she realized they could go to the village and barter for salt and herbs. Eventually Fel had planted herbs and vegetables in a little garden.

She walked outside and looked at that old garden. Weeds had taken over the place, but she could still see some rosemary and mint.

The biggest challenge had been food. Food and avoiding fighting when they were hungry. The arrangement hadn't been truly realistic, as her father and some guards passing by, meaning that Naia and Fel were never truly isolated. She once suggested stealing from the royal manor, but Fel didn't want to ruin the challenge. For him it was a matter of pride to do it without ever asking for help.

These memories eased some of the pain, but not enough. Naia took a deep breath. Perhaps this was for the best. What she had to do was plan how to challenge Ironhold, and use all the information she had. Perhaps she could even go to Wolfmark and plan something. She didn't have to agree to marry King Sebastian, all she had to do was make him think he had a chance— regardless whether it was cruel or not. She didn't like to remember River's amusement when learning about the king's proposal. Why did it hurt so much to remember normal River? She had to forget him and focus, focus, focus.

First, she'd need to go to the fort and use the communication mirror. That was a thirty-minute walk. Naia wasn't afraid of the woods, and wasn't afraid of most normal threats, but Ironhold had already sent ironbringers to try to kill Fel, and if they had some bizarre magic, she had no idea what exactly they could do. How had she even come here? Her memory was a blur. No, the worst parts were clear and sharp enough to cut her. What she didn't remember was how she had gotten into the hollow and come here.

Naia had to go to the fort, had to continue to try to forge alliances, had to figure out what Queen Kara wanted, had to find a way to locate her father. Had, had, had. An infinity of impossible tasks. Perhaps she'd come here to remember a time when things had been much simpler, when all she had to do was get something to eat, when her brother had been with her, watching her back, as she had been watching his. Her dragon brother that she loved with all her heart and she hoped would come back soon.

Naia closed her eyes. This wasn't the time to sleep and this house wasn't safe. Still, a few minutes wouldn't hurt her, a few minutes for her to close her eyes and forget everything going on. She could imagine she was a young teenager again, eager for challenge and adventure, blissfully unaware of how lovely her quiet peace was.

FEL WAITED with his cousin Siniari, while Leah got dressed with his other cousin, a girl named Jacine. While the house was big and had room for dragons, it had human-sized tables, chairs... The truth was that the dragons spent the largest part of their days in their human form—which only made Fel even more uncomfortable.

At least Siniari had a dragon-sized room, but even then, he was in human form, getting dressed for the celebration.

He turned to Fel. "You can sleep in my bed for now. I'll ask for another one, then a room for you. You can live with us."

Fel hated to squash his cousin's excitement, but he had to be sincere. "I need to go back to Aluria."

"Yes, that. But you don't need to stay there. And we'll need you."

"Would you forget your people? I mean, your dragons? If you went somewhere in search of help and they asked you to help them, what would you do?"

Siniari paused. "I think... I'd try to help both, but I'd consider which one needed me the most first. I will convince my mother to send a dragon delegation to Aluria, cousin, I already told you that. It's just... whatever happens, I wish you could consider this your home too."

"Thank you." The truth was that his cousin was trying to be nice. "But what about Leah?"

"We'll get her a room as well. It's easier in her case." Siniari chuckled. "She takes less space."

Yes, unlike Fel, who would spend all his time as a dragon. It was also a reminder that he and Leah couldn't be together. And then, like Fel, she hadn't come here to stay and also had a kingdom to protect. The issue would be saying goodbye to the dragons after all the commotion with this iron dragon celebration and all the hope they were placing on Fel. Fel, who knew nothing about dragon magic, who doubted the Boundless would keep wearing metal armor. They couldn't be that stupid. Or were they? A question crossed his mind.

"Siniari," Fel said. "If everyone knows about the Iron Dragon, how come they were wearing metal armor? That sounds illogical."

"It isn't really, if you think that they also grew up hearing that the iron dragon would be the light in the dark. They think they are the light. More than that, they want to be strong dragons, iron dragons in a way, and that's what their armors represent. And they wouldn't have guessed it meant a dragon with metal magic. How could they have predicted it?"

"Well, I'm sure they'll ditch the metal from now on. You understand what that means for me, right? With iron magic or not, I won't be able to do much against them."

Siniari paused and stared at him. "You still have impressive magic. You'll find other ways to use it."

"True, but I doubt I'll be able to defeat a group of enemies on my own again."

"You never know."

He followed his cousin to the common area. At least the doors here were large enough for him, not that he felt any less awkward.

Leah and Jacine came out of a room. They were both wearing leather pants and jackets, in the style most dragons liked to wear. Apparently, the clothes for a special celebration were no different. Leah looked beautiful in a dark brown outfit and he wished he could hug her.

"How are you?" he tried to send the thought to Leah only.

Jacine raised her hand. "I can hear you, just so you know. Before you say anything... you know."

Leah turned to her and narrowed her eyes, but as a joke. "He wasn't going to say anything inappropriate."

"Private," Jacine said. "I was thinking about something private, not inappropriate."

They left the house, and when they were outside, Siniari turned to Fel. "I'll fly with you to the ceremonial arena. Jacine can walk with Leah."

"Walk?" The girl grimaced. "You mean *climb* a ton of steps."

"It's great exercise."

Jacine smiled. "So is flying." In a second, she disappeared, replaced by a black dragon, who soared up into the sky, then dove back, and took Leah with her claws. That didn't look any safer than flying on Fel's back. At least Leah didn't look scared, and was laughing instead.

"Are we allowed to do that?" Fel asked his cousin.

"Not really. Humans should climb to the ceremonial arena, but Jacine always likes to push the rules. Let's go."

Siniari took his dragon form, his light blue scales reflecting the lanterns illuminating the grounds, and then took flight. Fel moved his wings quickly to catch up with Jacine, wondering how the scale colors worked, since there was so much variety even within the same family. The flight was short, just to a mountain surrounding the valley of the dragon city, where there was a plateau and a large round rock formation, looking indeed like an arena. It had a large circle in the middle, and they landed right on its border, in the lower area. His cousins soon took their human forms.

"Are you all right?" he asked Leah.

"I'm fine." She walked towards him and placed a hand on one of his wings.

Jacine took her human form and laughed. "Wasn't it a good idea to get here soon?"

"It was," Leah said.

Slowly, more and more dragons were coming in, landing in the upper areas around the circle. Most of them swapped to their human forms right after landing, but some of them remained as dragons. Humans were coming as well—walking, not being carried by anyone's claws. Fel counted some one hundred dragons in total.

"Is this everyone?" he asked his cousins.

"Young dragons and their parents don't come," Siniari said, then pretended to look confused. "I'm not sure what Jacine is doing here."

She looked at him and grimaced, but it was all in good fun.

Fel couldn't help thinking about Naia, wondering if she was safe, wondering what was happening back in Aluria, in Umbraar, in Frostlake. Would she know he was safe? Would she be worried? Was that fae taking good care of her? He'd never spent so long away from his sister, and being in difficult circumstances only made it tougher to bear. He also missed his father—heartfather, like the dragons said—and wondered what was happening to him. At least Leah was here, and safe. For now.

Eleven dragons landed at the center of the circle, then twelve more dragons landed in front of them, and took their human forms. One of the dragons was Ekateni, and Fel didn't know the others. In the middle stood Relia, in dark red leather armor.

She addressed the benches. "Do you know why we are here tonight?'

A few voices here and there shouted, "The Iron Dragon."

"Yes, yes." She smiled. "Many said there was no such thing. Many said it was a pointless prophecy, but this afternoon we had proof. Proof that the iron dragon is among us, to fight by our side, to smash the Boundless."

"Smash!" someone shouted.

Fel thought it was in bad taste, if it was true that many of their friends and loved ones had joined the Boundless.

Relia had a smile. "I became your Dragon's Eye not for hollow words, but for action, for victory. I am confident we are going to win this minor conflict. I'm confident we are going to spread our dominion across Fernick again. We are going to rule this land, without fear of other dragons, without fear of any magical creatures. And here he is, the Iron Dragon, none less than Ircantari's son. Please come forward." She gestured to Fel.

Great. Apparently he was going to be known as the Iron Dragon, as she didn't even mention his name. Still, he fluttered to the center, as it would look more gracious than walking. Bringing hope to these dragons wasn't a terrible thing. His issue was that he wasn't sure how much he could do for them, and wasn't sure if empty hope was what they needed.

Fel looked back at Leah, who stood by his cousins and smiled, even if she was stiffer than normal. She had asked him to hide his magic, and he had done his best to honor her request—until he couldn't anymore. And now they were celebrating his magic, so that every dragon in that valley knew about it.

Relia stood by him. "The Iron Dragon is in his pure form, and will rarely turn human. He represents the best of us. Three thousand years ago, the One Seer predicted that an iron dragon would be our light in the darkness. I say that we are our own light. But I also say that this is the proof, the proof we are on the right track, the proof we're about to achieve victory!"

At least she wasn't saying that Fel was going to save everyone, but there was a certain edge to it... He couldn't quite figure what it was.

The woman continued, "Tonight is a night for dancing, for

celebration, but before that, we're going to honor our iron dragon, empower him." She turned to Fel. "Stay still, this might tingle. It's just a silly, old tradition."

The thought had been sent to him only, he realized.

The dragons in human form around him approached and touched him, ten hands on the sides of his body, tails, and wings.

Relia addressed the crowd. "Some of our Council members are gifting him with their magic."

Fel didn't sense anything different, except for one woman who was touching his wing too lightly and tickled a little. He closed his eyes and forced himself to stay still. As far as he was aware, magic couldn't be transferred from person to person, but then again, what did he know about dragon magic? Which only made whatever they were doing pointless. If magic could be transferred, it should be sent to someone who would know what to do with it. Then again, they meant to honor him, and he was grateful for their intention.

The members of the Council stepped back, and then Relia took a large cup and poured a dark liquid in it from a bottle. "To the Iron Dragon, the gift of life."

Fel thought she was going to propose a toast, but instead, she approached him and sent a thought. "Just open your mouth. I'll drip it over your tongue, like a medicine."

This was going to be tricky and strange. He didn't control his fire very well—didn't control any part of this body well, in fact, and opening his mouth and sticking out his tongue seemed odd. It would be odd if he were in human form as well. Still, he didn't want to disrespect or disappoint the dragons, so he lowered his head as much as he could and opened his mouth, holding his breath just in case, to prevent any accidental fire from coming out. He didn't want to scorch Relia or anyone in the audience.

From the corner of his eye, he saw someone from the audience jump into the circle. Then something hit Relia's hand—a stone. A strange, golden net flew over the intruder, who lowered her hood. It was Tzaria.

"Execute her!" Relia said. "She tried to kill the iron dragon."

Tzaria was trying to get up, while the net kept her on the floor. "With a stone? Doubtful. You were the one trying to poison Isofel."

"Liar!" Relia turned to the others. "She must be executed."

Ekateni stepped in front of Tzaria. "Wait. Let's hear what she has to say."

Relia's eyes were wide. "The penalty for returning to the dragon sanctuary is death. I want her dead!"

"No," Ekateni said. "Let's be reasonable." He turned to Tzaria. "How did you get here? Why are you saying it's poisoned?"

"Can't you see?" the blond woman said. "Relia is corrupted. Perhaps she doesn't know it yet, but corruption has taken over her. Drinking a liquid is not part of our strengthening ritual. The conclusion is obvious."

Ekateni sighed and glared at Tzaria. "Meaning your proof is nothing but a preposterous guess. I suggest you leave."

"No," Relia yelled. "She broke the law. The penalty is death."

Fel's uncle turned to her. "Since when do we kill our own?"

"We kill murderers, traitors."

In a brief second, Tzaria assumed her dragon form and took flight. Before disappearing in the sky she let out a shrill scream, and then she landed again with a spear in one of her wings. In a second, she was human again.

Ekateni swapped to his dragon form and landed above her. The thought he sent sounded like a thundering yell. "If you want to harm her, you'll have to go through me."

Relia's face was red, and she screamed from the top of her lungs. "Don't try me. I will not hesitate to have both of you killed."

Ekateni roared, then sent a thought. "I don't think so." From his mouth, he sent gigantic blasts of fire in all directions. Some of it caught Fel, giving him that strange sensation of being immobilized. His uncle then took flight holding Tzaria. Fel wished he hadn't left, but then, it didn't seem like he'd been given much choice. It also felt uncomfortable to see Relia's anger towards Tzaria. But then, if she had killed Ircantari... Either way, Fel couldn't fly after them, as he couldn't move.

Relia, who had fallen, got up. "They're both traitors now. Both enemies."

Fel turned to see his cousins. Jacine was in dragon form, while Siniari looked at his mother with wide eyes. "He was just protecting her!"

"Protecting a traitor. Your father is no more."

Jacine took her human form again, and had tears in her eyes. Leah bit her lip and stared at him. That inner rivalry wasn't good when they had so many external enemies. But then, perhaps Tzaria *was* dealing with the enemy. Fel couldn't forget how well she had fought against those three dragons on the way to Fernick, and then again, back on the mountain of the First Mage. Fel wasn't sure he'd be alive without her. Now both she and Ekateni were gone.

Relia then smiled. "None of that shall disturb our celebration. Let's get back to the village. Tonight is a night for dancing." She then turned around and headed to the stairs.

Fel tried to move, but couldn't. He had been somewhat close to his uncle, and caught in his fire. The guards who'd been around them were immobilized as well, while dragons on the far benches were already taking flight. He took a look at the broken cup. Could it have been poison? Or had Tzaria just been paranoid?

Leah approached him. "Are you hurt?"

"I just can't move very well. It's something that happens with dragon fire. What about you?"

"Siniari shielded me."

Fel looked at his cousin and nodded, or at least tried to do that, thankful that he had protected Leah. She then looked up and pointed. "Are they back?"

For a second it seemed like it, until he realized it wasn't only two dragons flying towards the arena—but about thirty. They were not coming from the side of the village, but from the other side. A horrible feeling came over him.

A scream broke the silence. "The Boundless!"

They were coming—with no metal armor this time.

Meanwhile, Isofel couldn't even move his wings.

LEAH KNEW little about the dragons, but even she could feel a sudden change in mood, a sudden change in the air, and didn't need to know much to realize that the dragons flying in their direction were a threat. This place, which should have been a sanctuary, was being breached.

In the arena, few dragons remained, not enough to fight the attackers, especially when most of them were still in human form. Leah stood by Fel. His cousins, both in human form, were a few steps from them.

"You should run," Siniari told her. "Dragon fire will kill you."

Leah was almost doing it, but realized it would be foolish. She could get caught mid-escape, unless the invaders ignored her, but she didn't want to bet her life on it.

"My wings won't move," Fel then said. "Come under me."

"Don't," Jacine told Leah. "They'll set fire to the floor."

"On my back," Fel said, and she jumped on it.

That position didn't provide her any cover, but she felt safer being close to him. She felt him tense beneath her, as if focusing, then a spear and many swords flew in the direction of the incoming dragons.

Fel was using his ironbringing. Some of the Boundless formed a wall of fire in front of them. When swords met it, they fell back, as if they had reached a shield.

A voice, a real voice, sounded in the sky. "Give us the iron dragon, and you'll be spared."

There was no way this city would protect Fel, not when their houses and families were in danger.

Most of the dragons in the arena were stuck to their places, which seemed to be a side effect of Ekateni's fire blast.

"Hold tight," Fel said. "I know what to do."

The ground trembled. Was Fel really going to do what she thought he was going to do?

Soon the entire arena was floating up in the sky, and then moving away from the incoming dragons, towards the edge of the valley.

At some point, the arena stopped moving. "I can't get it out," Fel said, "I'll have to land it."

Leah felt the floor moving sideways, as they landed at an angle, over some spiky hills. A few of the dragons that were on the corners took flight. Fel's cousins swapped forms now, and stood by Fel.

"Fly away," Leah yelled. "It's him they want. Get help."

Even then, many of the dragons did not take flight, and she wasn't sure if it was because they couldn't. All this time, she'd been thinking about slipping into the hollow in case there was too much fire, in case she was a liability for the dragons, but maybe she wasn't thinking this right.

"Trust me, Fel."

"Always."

That reply warmed her heart, even if she wasn't sure it was deserved, even if she wasn't sure her idea was going to work. Could she do it? Technically, going into the hollow with someone else should be hard enough. She had no idea how hard it would be if this someone else was that much bigger. Even then, she tried to go to that other place. Instead of stepping into it, she tried to feel as if she were dissolving in it, bringing Fel with her.

Keeping in mind the danger of getting lost, she kept an eye on her reality, and they got back into the real world not far from the arena, on another part of the mountain.

He said, "This is great, Leah. We can draw them out. Can you yell?"

Draw them out? Her idea had been simply to try to escape,

but he had a point. If she didn't attract their attention, the Boundless would look for Fel in the valley and cause destruction there.

Leah took a deep breath and yelled from the top of her lungs, "Here's the iron dragon. Come and get him!"

She waited until she heard wings flapping in their direction, then dissolved again in the hollow, but just enough not to get lost. They reappeared a few steps from where they had been at first. "Here!" she yelled again.

This time, she would need to try to go a little further, but carefully so as not to get lost or trapped somewhere where she shouldn't. They were on the mountains, but there was no sign of the dragon city anywhere. "What—"

"It's normal," Fel said. "The city is hidden."

"Will the Boundless see us?"

"Yell again."

"Here!" She had barely said the word when a dragon appeared in front of her, as if coming from out of nowhere, then sent a blast of fire in their direction.

Fel met the fire with his own, and Leah let out the most relieved sigh she had ever had. Still, she knew more dragons were coming, so she tried to slip into the hollow again—and couldn't. It was as if Fel's fire was keeping them on this level, unable to slip through.

But then, these dragons couldn't keep blasting fire ceaselessly. She kept a sense of the darkness, the in-between, that other place. It was almost calling to her, but to her alone, and she had to bring Fel with her.

The attacking dragon stopped its fire for a moment, and Fel did the same. Leah took the opportunity to jump away. For a moment, she feared getting lost. It was like slogging through black mud, walking in a thick curtain of smoke. This wasn't good at all, and if they kept like that, they could end up somewhere where they shouldn't. Then she recalled her difficulty in going to the hollow a few seconds before. "Fel, I need you to produce fire."

He did—and then they stood on another mountain ledge.

Leah didn't know if they were near or close to the dragon village. She heard no screeches, no wings flapping, no dragon fire, only now realizing it had a distinctive sound. This was still Fernick, this was the human, normal realm, she could feel it, but that was as far as she knew.

"Are we far from the village?" Fel asked.

Leah swallowed. "I don't know. I don't know if we're near, far, I just don't have any idea where we are. I got lost for a moment. I'm sorry."

"Why sorry? You saved us."

"Well, you were doing pretty well moving the arena. How did you do it?"

"It had some metal beams in the base and was over a rock with some metal ore. I'm surprised it worked, actually."

"Your magic is amazing." Leah looked around at that strange place, in that strange land. "But now we're lost."

Fel was quiet for some time, but then he said, "Dragons can sense other dragons. Someone will find us soon. The question is whether they will be friends or enemies."

The wind was the only sound she could hear, even if she felt her own heart thumping in her chest. "We can't stay here, then."

His chest moved up and down, slowly. "My wings are almost good. I'll fly us somewhere where there's a lot of metal. My magic could keep us safe if a large group attacks us."

She caressed his scales. "Eventually you'll have to rest, though."

"I know. Leah, I'm sorry I didn't find the answers I was looking for, I'm sorry I brought you here."

"I think you found out a lot, and even found some of your family. Eventually you'll reconnect with them. And there's something I've been meaning to tell you. This... Cynon... The way they talk about it, that it influences people, I think he was in my head, Fel. That was what I heard; someone looking for the iron dragon, and that was why I had to leave."

"You heard? How?"

Leah jumped from his back and stood in front of him, so she could see his eyes, which were green like his human ones, beautiful in a different way, but still beautiful. "In my mind. It's odd to say it, but it was like I had a bridge to this creature, and then it saw you. I blocked it now, I can feel it's blocked. But I think it was with me before. It's so similar to what they're talking about, this Cynon. I spent some time in a realm in the hollow, and a fae helped me and mentioned a Breaker, which was similar as well. I think maybe it's the same creature, but I feel it is in Aluria already."

"Maybe it's everywhere."

She reached out a hand and caressed his face. "Maybe." She tried to think. "But it has to be related to the dragons, right? If the creature had a reaction to seeing you, if they wanted the iron dragon?"

"Likely. I'm lost, Leah, and I don't mean just that I don't know where we are and have absolutely no idea how to navigate this continent. Where do we even start? How do you fight an enemy if you don't even know what it is, where it is, and what it wants?"

"It seems to want you dead for some reason."

"Yes, the *iron dragon*." His tone was mocking. "As if I could do anything. All I can do is move metal and blast fire. I can't even take my human form yet."

Leah kept caressing the soft scales on the side of his face. She knew he'd been worried about being in this form, and she understood his worry, but at the same time, this was also who he was. "It's not a problem."

"You know it is. If we get back, how can I do anything for Umbraar?"

That was a good question, for which she had no answer. He couldn't act as a prince like that. Still, she tried to cheer him up. "At least you're looking good. Not that you didn't look good before. But, you know, considering our situation, I suggest we start looking at the little positives."

"We're both alive."

Leah chuckled. Yes, it was great that they were both alive, both together. It wasn't something they should take for granted. The question was how long that was going to last. "Do you really think we should just wait for other dragons to find us?"

"For now. Eventually we'll need food, water. When the sun rises, I'll have a sense of direction and then we can fly south. If I fly really high, I can do it during the day, and eventually we'll reach Aluria."

Eventually was an uncomfortable word when so much was happening, when so much was at stake. Plus, they could be east or west of their continent, in which case, flying south would not bring them home. But repeating out loud how lost they were wasn't going to help anyone. She smiled. "We'll wait, then."

"Actually, no. Get on my back. I think my wings are strong enough to get us to a place with more metal, or at least metallic rocks, or else we'll be easy targets. I doubt they'll take long to find me."

Leah did as he told her, but a light caught her attention. A fire ring, on their right.

Dragons were coming.

19

THE FAE KING

Fel knew the boundless wouldn't leave them alone for long, and yet this fire ring, so soon, was still unexpected. There was no metallic rock near him, so if enemies flew through, he'd need to try to fight with his fire—his pitiful dragon magic.

Perhaps Leah could manage to get them out of here, but she'd done a lot already, and was perhaps about to overuse her powers. The last thing he wanted was to see her passed out, weak, to feel the life slipping from her. He stared at the circle forming near them, feeling his own fire burning in his chest, his own power wanting to be released.

A dragon flew in, a familiar blue dragon. Fel relaxed.

It was Ekateni.

There was barely room for him to land, as Fel was on the only flat surface in the area, but his uncle took his human form right as he landed, so that he didn't take up as much space.

His uncle said, "You need to go. The Boundless will find you soon."

Was that supposed to be some groundbreaking information? "I know. We've been running from them for a while, and don't intend on lingering. I'm just waiting for my wings to get better."

"Of course. I mean you need to get back to Aluria. The Boundless won't realize you're there."

"How come?" It was Leah who asked.

"The way there through the hollow has been closed—for most dragons. So they need to fly, which will take them some time. The other reason is that they won't be able to sense you. I think human magic masks dragon magic, and you won't be as easily found there."

"We were planning on getting back regardless, and it will be much easier to do with your help. How's everyone? Did they survive?"

Ekateni rubbed a hand against his forehead. "Your cousins are alive. The village, I believe most dragons escaped."

Fel felt horrible thinking he had ruined that sanctuary. "I'm so sorry. For bringing them there."

His uncle shook his head. "You know it's not your fault. It's not like you insisted on coming, or that you wanted to announce that you were the iron dragon. That was foolish. Our mistake was believing that we were more invulnerable than we actually were. Lesson taken. That city was only ten years old regardless. No history left behind. We will regroup—likely not in such an easy target."

"Tzaria was right, then. How is she?"

His uncle's face became hard as wood. "Alive. Not that she will apologize—or explain anything. Oh, no. No explaining."

Leah then said, "She might have saved Fel."

Ekateni closed his eyes and snorted. "Saved him? Do you really think Relia would poison Isofel? The *iron dragon*? Even if we were to assume this as a possibility, there's no way she would do it in front of an audience. Relia has many flaws, but *incredibly dumb* is the extreme opposite of how I'd describe her."

"What about Cynon?" Leah asked. "Couldn't he be whispering ideas in her mind? Corrupting her, like Tzaria said?"

"It doesn't work like that." His uncle shook his head. "You need a long time in contact with his energy, a long time, something Relia wouldn't have had the opportunity to do, being in the dragon city. You often need an object, which works like a conduit. It's... I have no doubt that some Boundless are in contact with Cynon, but I doubt that's the case with Relia."

"Why then did Tzaria try to stop her?"

"Tzaria..." Ekateni sighed. "I think she meant well, truly. It must be guilt consuming her. I do think she wants to protect Ircantari's son. But her hatred for Relia blinds her."

"I'm glad you saved her." Fel still wanted to talk to her, still wanted to understand what had happened to his father, and, more than that, he would have hated to see her executed.

Ekateni shrugged. "Principles are principles, even if it means defending a dragon I despise." His nose wrinkled, as if he truly meant these words. They were a huge contrast to his feat in the arena, unleashing an incredible wall of fire. Fel hadn't seen many dragons, but the little he's seen of them fighting told him that what his uncle did had been far from ordinary. He looked down. "But my actions made you vulnerable to the boundless, and then it makes me wonder if Tzaria did it on purpose, if she brought them, but then... She's the one who told me how to get you back, how to open this way, and then she's kept your existence a secret for years. She knew my brother had a child, she knew it, and didn't bother telling me." He rolled his eyes. "To protect you. So then I find it unlikely that she'd bring the Boundless upon you."

"Will... anyone come to Aluria? We need help."

He nodded. "Of course, but first I have to make sure my children are safe, and I have to hide a traitorous, exiled dragon who can't return to her winged form yet. Cynon is upon us. I know your human magic is impaired and you're having issues with a kingdom, I know that, and I won't forget you."

It didn't sound as if Aluria was a priority to them, though.

Leah then said, "Ekateni, I think Cynon is in Aluria. It might be the explanation for much of what's happening. I heard something in my head." Her voice was strained. "I think..."

"I will go and check. It's a promise. Still, my understanding is that the human magic in Aluria has degraded a lot. Death-bringers can contact other realms." His uncle had been informed about Leah's magic. Everyone had, as seeing someone materialize in the middle of a battle wasn't a regular occurrence for them. "It's no surprise you'll hear voices. It doesn't mean it's Cynon."

"What if it is?" Leah insisted.

Ekateni shook his head. "Cynon can influence dragons, yes, and that's dangerous on its on. The real danger, though, is if he finds a vessel, a vessel through which he can come back to this realm. We need to prevent him from doing that. That's our priority."

"The vessel could be in Aluria." There was a tension, a warning in Leah's voice.

"A human cannot be a vessel," Ekateni said, "even those of you who have magic. It doesn't work, it's not compatible. And that process would need a lot of contact with Cynon's energy. We're talking months, years maybe. It has to be someone among the Boundless, someone who's been influenced for a long time. And they also need anchors, objects infused with Cynon's magic. You wouldn't have those in Aluria. Once the vessel finds these objects, they could open a portal, but you still need to be in a place with dragon magic, so it can't be in your land. Also, the process is thankfully quite complex."

"Couldn't it be a white fae?" Fel suggested.

"Unlikely." Ekateni exhaled, seeming annoyed. "I promise, I will go to Aluria, and then we can discuss all of that, but you have to leave now unless you truly want to give the Boundless time to catch up. I'll open a ring for you, to fly through. It will take you to an archipelago near Aluria, slightly to the north of it. There are no dragons in that region, and you'll be safe. Even then, make sure you hide. I'll come and find you."

"How?"

"Tzaria knows a way." He swapped into his dragon form, then made a fire circle in the air. "Go. Quick."

Leah was safe on Fel's back, and he flew through the ring, a thousand questions still on his mind, and yet aware there was no point trying to figure out anything when they had enemies so close after them.

Indeed he came out of the ring over some islands, and he thought he could see Aluria far away, in the distance.

"How are your wings?" Leah asked.

"Better." He felt he could get to Umbraar, and he was going to try it. Something she said came to his mind. "You didn't tell me about voices."

"I didn't have the chance to tell you anything, Fel. There's so much."

"I'm so sorry for all you went through. I was so stupid, Leah. The moment you showed up in my room, I should have held you and never let you go."

She leaned over him. "We're together now." After a moment, she asked, "Where do you want to go? In Aluria?"

"I need to find my sister." This was one reason he'd been wanting to get back so desperately.

"Where is she?"

"It's a long story—but I think she's in Umbraar now, and..." It was odd to say it. "I'm worried about her. It's as if I can feel a hint of her pain, her fear, her worry. Something bad's happening to her, Leah, and I need to find her."

Fel could feel Leah resting her face on his back, her arms spread around him, in what felt like a soothing, calming hug, even if she couldn't even reach the sides of his body. His wings felt better and better, and he was on his way to Naia. After that, they would need to figure out what was going on in Aluria—and try to find a way to save his and Leah's kingdom, perhaps even the whole land.

None of that sounded easy.

Naia awoke with a start. It was night, and someone had a hand on her shoulder. She was about to scream, when she realized it was River. Her relief exhale got stuck in her throat when she recalled what he had done. The blood, the deaths, and then his harsh, hateful eyes.

"What are you doing here?" she asked, trying to sound calm.

"I... woke up alone.. and came to find you." This was the sweet River she knew well—or thought she knew. He was still wearing the earrings and the fancy garb, including the daggers strapped to his belt, but had a black, clean shirt on, and apparently had washed the blood from his hands. It didn't erase it from her mind.

"Right." She didn't even want to ask him how he had found her. And how come it was night already? Had she slept that much? When they had such few days to plan anything against Ironhold? She got up. "I'm... going to the Royal Fort. I'm sure you'll be busy in the Ancient City." She wanted him to leave her alone for a while, give her the space to stop and think and do everything she had to do.

He frowned, seeming confused and worried. "Naia, what's wrong?"

A day before, she would have yelled at him and his stupid question. Right now, she was too uneasy to confront him, so she made an effort to smile and look relaxed. "Nothing. I mean, everything. There's so much to do. Or try to do."

He stared at her. "Are you *afraid* of me?" He sounded concerned, not angry or anything.

Still, a nervous laughter escaped her. "You think so?"

He touched his horns and seemed confused. "Something happened. Wait." A golden circlet made of entwined threads appeared out of nowhere around his head. "Why am I wearing this?"

"You're asking *me*?"

"Naia, this is the Ancient crown. The real one. It's invisible most of the time, but..." He stared at her. "Only the king can wear it. I don't understand."

Naia froze. "What do you mean? What is it you don't understand?"

"Let me see you." He extended his hand to her forehead. Naia wanted to step back, but she was still somewhat afraid of him. When he touched her, she felt something around her head. "You have it, too," he said.

Naia closed her eyes. Did he not remember? Or was he pretending?

His crown then disappeared from his head, and she felt it disappearing from hers.

He looked at her. "And you're not surprised. What happened?"

A horrible feeling was settling in the pit of her stomach. "You don't remember what happened when you *talked* to your father?"

"No. I went to my bedroom." He paused, looking down at his clothes. "To change, I guess. But then I fell asleep. I woke up and sensed you weren't in the city anymore. I was terrified that something had happened to you, and came here. Now... did something happen?"

Naia could swear that she could hear her heart. "Is it true you don't remember? Or are you saying it so I don't get angry?"

"Angry..." It was as if it took a while for him to understand the word. "Naia, I can't lie."

"Well, you're immune to iron."

"What does it..." He snorted. "Right, you think I'm here pretending to be confused and lying. Meanwhile, you're not telling me whatever happened."

It was better to go straight to the point. "You killed your father."

He chuckled. "That's impossible. Do you know how many guards he has? How many mindmelders..." He paused, and his face blanched. "Wait." He swallowed and stared at her, his eyes wide. "I did sleep too much." After a deep breath, he said, "Seems like I did the impossible, didn't it?"

Naia was partly relieved he was not suffering from memory

loss or anything worse, partly horrified that he could talk about it so casually. "So you do remember?"

"I do." He scoffed. "Isn't it hilarious? The mighty King Spring, defeated by his own worthless son."

"It's not funny."

River stared at her, and his eyes had that odd coldness from before. "What? You're upset? Upset, Naia? I'm thinking you would have preferred if my beloved father had made me rip out your heart. Is that it? Or do you miss his magic prison? What is it?"

Naia got up. "Don't you have any remorse? Any feelings?"

"Oh. That's what it's about. Would it have helped it?" He pretended to hold a heart with his hand, then mock cried. "Oooooh, father, it hurts me so much, but I have to do this..." He smirked. "Is it what you wanted? I can still cry if you absolutely want me to."

She closed her eyes. "You... it's like you aren't yourself. I feel that I don't know you."

"Aren't both things true? How much do you know me? How much have you seen me with my family? And then, no. I wasn't myself. I was the son my father wanted me to be: ruthless, powerful, unafraid to use his magic to its full extent. I guess I did find a way into his heart, after all these years..." He laughed, and that laugh gave her shivers.

Indeed she had no idea who River was and didn't want to keep arguing. She just needed time to get her thoughts straight, time to swallow it all, time to bury her hurt. "Right. So... You need to get back, right? You're the king. I... need to do things here."

He stared at her, concern on his face. "You don't want me?" Somehow, he managed to sound hurt.

"It's not that." It was, in a way, but it was also so much more. And she did want him, but she wanted the real River, not this cold-hearted stranger speaking to her. "We just... The world is falling apart, isn't it?"

"That's when we should be holding each other." He closed his eyes, then took a deep breath, as if trying to calm himself down.

As if to show her he wasn't going to hurt her, he pulled out the daggers from his belt and put them on the table, then sat by her. "I can sense your disapproval about the way I dealt with my father. All I can say is that it was the only way I could do it. Ancient law is very strict, very precise. Had I killed him in any other way, I'd be imprisoned and trialed for murder. Now, we have other problems. Aluria and the Ancient City have other problems. I can't, Naia, I can't fight inner and outer battles at the same time. I can't. I had to find a solution, and I did."

He had a point, and yet... "You never told me what your solution was. You told me to trust you, and what I saw was a bloody spectacle, and I could not recognize you."

River shrugged. "I hadn't planned any of that. It just... came to me. I looked at myself in the mirror and said: I'll be the son my father wants. At that moment, that was what that son would do. Would I want to see my father dead? No. In my worst hours, I never imagined him dead, I imagined him regretting all his harsh words, regretting exiling me. In my worst, angry moments, I dreamed of humiliating him. I never thought I would kill him. And yet it happened. I'm not sorry." His eyes were cold.

"You also killed the mindmelders."

"That was my only option. They were my father's shield. And to be fair, their lives were horrible. I did them a favor."

She rolled her eyes. "Oh, what a wonderful justification for killing. I mean, most people have hard lives. It's not up to us to decide if they live or die."

River shook his head. "Had the mindmelders' lives been wonderful, I would have done the same. Too much at risk here, Naia. Responsibility means making hard decisions."

Naia sighed. She did understand that, and yet, this whole thing made her uneasy, nauseous, the way he'd done it... "But you don't feel any remorse."

He scoffed. "What's remorse going to do? What difference does it make? Does it bring anyone back? It doesn't. And you know who didn't have any remorse? King Spring. No remorse. He would have been delighted had all the humans in Aluria died. He wanted me to kill them. Every. Single. Human. Families, children, peasants. Innocent, honest people who had nothing to do with that war. We would never have peace with him. Ancients always say that the humans started the war, that the humans did everything, but now, seeing the things my father's capable of, I have questions. You can't honestly be upset he's gone, especially you, knowing what he tried to make me do. I don't think you have the right to judge me. He tried to make me *kill* you. Can you imagine what it did to me? Perhaps that's what happened. I snapped. Too much pressure, and one breaks."

He sat down and leaned his head on his hands, making the tip of his horns point up.

Naia was still shocked, but some of what he said made sense. She sat by him and put a hand on his shoulder. "River..."

He stared at her. "Oh, it's *River* now." He mimicked her tone. "Now that I said I could be broken, you want me back, and yet, when I'm whole and powerful, you don't like it."

Naia pulled her hand. "I don't like it when it seems that you don't have feelings."

"Oh, I have feelings, tons of feelings. I feel that my father was an asshole and deserved to die. Is that a feeling? Or it doesn't count for you?"

She sighed, unnerved at his reaction. There was another thing bothering her. "How did you manage it? That much magic? You said that trying to use mindmelding on a king could kill you. It seems that you used it on him and a bunch of fae at the same time."

He shrugged. "I guess I had been grossly underestimating my magic. Or rather, *our* combined magic."

"I see." He'd used her magic to increase his? To do that? It explained all the sleeping. "I still can't understand it, I still can't erase that horrible image from my head, but I'll accept that you had no choice but to kill your father, that it was either that or you. Or me. I can accept that the dreadful way you killed him was your only choice. It's still horrific, but maybe you're right that it was the correct decision given the circumstances. Still, doesn't some of it strike you as..." She closed her eyes, at a loss for words. "Off. I can't explain it. There's something wrong. I swear it wasn't you, River. I couldn't recognize you. I can barely recognize you now."

He stared at her and thought for a moment. "Then you have only one option: you need to lock me up. Put me in a prison, Naia. I think the magic cells will hold me."

"You think you're not yourself?"

"I think I'm fine. Just so you know, I don't rip people's hearts on a daily basis. I've never done it before and didn't even know my claws were sharp enough for that." He stared at his hands, then looked at her. "I had never killed anyone before, but I think I'm myself. Do I love everything about what I did? No. Do I wish it didn't have to come to this with my father? That's a stupid question."

"Did you have to become king, though?"

"Had I let Forest take the throne, he would kill me. He hates me. And he's just as brutal as our father. Anelise is fine, but... I don't know. I don't know where she stands."

"And why do I have that crown too?"

"That's obvious." He smiled. "The magic of the Ancients thinks we are really good acquaintances."

"No, but... I'm pretty sure you have to be married for something like that—which we're not."

River looked away, then back at her. "Do you want to know the truth?"

"Don't ask me that question. I always do."

"What do you think it means when I declared my love for you to my father?"

"Wouldn't I have to say something as well? Don't I get a choice?"

"If you were an Ancient, you'd need to do the same. In your case, you would need to say that to whoever, let's say, is somewhat responsible for you, a parent, a guardian, a king... That would be enough.”

“But I—” She was going to say *didn't,* but then she paused. “I just had to say it? There are no special words?”

“We can't impose the way you communicate with your family. As long as you clearly tell them you're choosing one of us as a life companion, and they agree, you're fine. Your brother agreed. Your father agreed, in a way.”

“That's unfair. What if a human's family is against it?” Naia was thinking about her mother and the story she had always been told, even if it wasn't true.

“I think the idea was to prevent conflicts, and the communication with a parent or a person of authority was to assure nobody started thinking we were stealing humans. What I can say is that we're very good at creating verbal traps, and that's something that can be learned... The human would need to get an approval, even if not that genuine. There are more rules regulating human-ancient relationships, but once you're considered an Ancient's life companion, you are subject to Ancient's law, and cannot be harmed, unless it's fair punishment for a misdeed. Not even the king is exempt from that law.” He bit his lip. “As you clearly saw.”

“And would rather forget. So you're saying we're married, according to Ancient laws.”

“We don't use that word. Marriage is a contract between two people who might not even like each other. A life companion... It's a choice.”

“I never made that choice.”

“You were still thinking, I know that. And yet, the moment you chose to leave the Frostlake castle with me, the moment you chose to stay with me instead of going home with your father, you were making a choice.”

“Don't we have to consummate the union for it to be valid?” At least now she knew what that entailed.

“No. What we do or don't do in bed is nobody's business. But I know that the Ancient law doesn't count for you. I know that. It's just... so you understand."

Naia took a deep breath. She almost asked if there was a way to break this life companion thing, but didn't want to hurt or upset him. At the same time, she wasn't sure about anything, she wasn't sure how she would feel if he touched her with those hands that had been covered in blood hours before. "I was scared today. And horrified. I don't think I know who you are."

He blinked slowly. "I trust your judgment. I can go to the magical prison. I'd hate to leave you alone, I'd hate to—"

She didn't want to lock him somewhere, away from her. "It would be horrible. And someone—like your brother, for example —could try to kill you. We have too much to do. Too much to plan. I haven't even opened the Ancient City. You do realize that, don't you?"

He raised two fingers in the air, with those sharp dark nails. "The city can last two months. Let's wait and see what happens in the next few days. I think we will need to join forces and fight Ironhold. I think we'll have to do much more than just open a faery ring to bring goods to the Ancient City."

They could work together with the Ancients, with River in control of them, but this idea had many issues. "I bet the Ironhold king is dying to accuse Umbraar of working with the white fae. They might be spreading the rumors already."

"In which case, why fear a retaliation that's coming nonetheless?"

Naia shrugged. "I don't want to make it easy for them. And you, you need to take care of your city, don't you?"

"Anelise is doing the work for now."

"Why not appoint her queen?"

He ran his hand through his hair. "Because then she could abdicate and let Forest take the throne, she could order them to imprison me for investigation... tons of possibilities."

"It seems you really thought this through..."

He got up and ran his hand on the edge of the table, making a line where he removed the dust. "I didn't, and I think it's dreadful, Naia, but I also don't think I had a choice." He turned to her, then looked around. "What's this place?'

"I used to come here with my brother. We're near the Royal Fort, but not that near that walking is safe."

"A house is even less safe."

That made sense. It could be a resting spot for rogues, thieves, or soldiers. "I didn't come here on purpose. And we're not close enough to the fort to draw much attention."

"Still. I'm going to glamour this house, just so that strangers don't notice it. Give me a minute."

He walked outside. Naia almost said that she would rather return to the fort, but she let him do the glamour, as it gave her a moment to think.

Something inside her hurt seeing him. He looked so familiar, so hers, and yet, the side of him she'd seen was none of that. It was a monstrous stranger, one that scared her, one that she didn't know if she could love. And yet they were *life companions*, whatever that meant. She wanted him to hold her close, and yet, couldn't quite forget the blood in those hands, the callousness with which he had killed his own father. And now she didn't know what to do.

20

RECONNECTING

River stepped into the woods surrounding the little cabin, while Naia remained inside, looking at him, her face serious. A small, isolated house, with just the two of them, should give them a moment of peace, an opportunity for reconciliation. It was like their house in the clearing by the Ancient City, that little pocket of space just for them. He just had to make sure strangers didn't see them, that people who passed by felt compelled to walk away. It was complicated, old magic, but something that could be useful in a case like this. And yet, as much as he protected the house, this would never be their sanctuary. Naia's face when he first found her here still distressed him. Fear. She'd been afraid of him, as if he were a stranger.

In a way, she had been right. He hadn't acted like himself. The blood on his hands would never wash away, the horror of seeing the life fleeing from his father would never leave his mind. And yet, that had been the son King Spring had always wanted; ruthless, putting duty ahead of feelings, ignoring any sense of mercy. River hated him. Could he blame Naia for hating him as well? He looked back at the house. She was no longer by the window, probably still upset. Would she be able to forgive him? Maybe. But would she be able to forget? Or would she think he could turn into a stranger at any point in time, that he could become unrecognizable? He didn't know the answer.

But then, what was the alternative? Let King Spring rule and make things difficult for the Ancients? Let him threaten Naia?

And yet, it hurt to see her pretty dark eyes staring at him with suspicion. Perhaps if he explained, if he told her how he felt, perhaps she'd understand. Understand what? That sometimes he acted like someone he was not? That sometimes he lost control? He could remember clearly how he had gone to his room, how he had been determined, with this newfound confidence, when he decided to become the prince his father wanted.

River circled the house twice and then figured it was glamoured enough. It wouldn't hide it from someone who knew this place, but the danger was assassins or soldiers from Ironhold or other kingdoms.

He walked back in slowly. "Naia?"

She was sitting on the bed, but got up. "I need to get back to the fort, you know that." There was still that lingering coldness, lingering formality in her. Lingering fear?

It was true that they didn't know each other that much, it was true that perhaps things had moved somewhat fast, but then, there was this wonderful magic when they both got together, and he couldn't forget the moment he had first seen her, so many years before. There had been much more than all these short moments between them.

"I want to apologize," he said, even if he was struggling with the words. "It doesn't change anything, it won't bring my father back, it won't make you understand my decision..." He looked down. It was strange to talk like that. "I'm not brutal. I understand you don't like to see me like that. What I can say is that it was one moment, one moment when I had to make a decision, and it was the only solution I found."

She stared at him, her eyes wide. "It felt like it was another person, River."

"I told you it was. I was trying to be something I'm not." He bit his lip. "Not trying. I obviously managed it."

There was still suspicion in her eyes, as she looked at him, as if searching for a hint, an answer. "Something... Something happened, River. You were going to the library, remember? Did you even get there?"

He paused. It was true. He'd been thinking about researching the death grass... and yet, he must have forgotten about it.

"I... I remember going to my room. I had that idea, that I was going to be the son my father wanted." He frowned, thinking, trying to recall that moment. "I didn't research anything. I don't think I even went to the library."

Naia's dark eyes were on him. "You left your sister's room saying you were going to research death grass. What changed? How?"

River took a deep breath. His memory of that time was a little fuzzy. Perhaps the truth was that he was also in shock for what he'd done. He couldn't blame Naia for feeling that way. Still. What had happened? He knew. "I had the idea. I think I was worried about talking to my father, then I had this idea and everything got clear."

She nodded. "I know he was horrible, but you said you could have waited and woken him up later. You didn't even do that."

"The prince my father wants—" He looked down for a moment. "—wanted—doesn't wait for anybody, Naia. I... I guess I thought it would solve my issues with him, but it didn't. Maybe I made a mistake. That said, it's true he has threatened you, so he got what he deserved, and I don't feel sorry."

The only sad part was that his father would never see who River would become, that he would never have to apologize for all he had done. Those were still disturbing thoughts.

The suspicion didn't fade from Naia's eyes, but she said, "I guess you did what you had to do."

"To protect you. Make no mistake, Naia. I will do anything to protect you."

She snorted. "Maybe I should be glad you didn't force me to sleep. Is that how it goes?"

Naia was still angry about that. He didn't blame her. "I won't do that again. And with my father, I had no choice. Now you're looking at me like I'm a monster."

"You're not a monster, River."

"Fine. A stranger, then."

She tilted her head. "You know it's true. You said it."

He stepped close to her and took her hands. "I'm still myself. Now. I'm myself. The same person you've chosen."

A lovely laugh escaped her lips. "Don't we make foolish choices?" Still, her tone was playful, and she didn't pull her hands.

He kissed her temple, then wrapped his arms around her. "I'll make sure you never see anything like that again."

Her head was resting on his shoulder. "I'd rather know, River."

"We'll talk, and you'll know what's happening, and we'll decide things together."

She scoffed. "You're so full of promises."

"My promises have value. My word has value. I look back at this morning and don't appreciate what I did either, Naia, so perhaps we agree on that."

"Then couldn't you have found a different solution?"

He ran his hands through her magnificent, thick black hair. "Maybe. But at the time, I didn't. It's done now. And I have to say that it has many positives. We can't fight ourselves, Ironhold, and then the strange voice. It's too much. If we are united, we have a chance. It's not that big to start with, but it will be none if we're fighting each other." He'd meant the humans and Ancients, but it was also true for him and Naia, and he hoped she'd realize that.

She took a deep breath. "I know that rulers sometimes have to make harsh decisions, I know that. I know that one life, or half a dozen lives, doesn't compare to all the lives at stake in a kingdom. I understand that." She moved her head away from his chest and faced him. "It was just that you didn't seem to be yourself, and it was terrifying. Perhaps I was afraid of losing you. Perhaps I'm still here, wondering if it's still you, or if my River is gone."

"I'm here, Naia. It's me. The same me you saved at the Dragon's Lair, a long time ago. Now that, according to you, wasn't really you, and I'm not here complaining." He smirked.

Naia chuckled. "Have you found an explanation for that?"

The world was full of magic he didn't understand, and that was just one example. He took one of her hands and pulled it to his chest. "Our connection transcends time."

"Pretty words. And what do they mean?"

"I don't know, but the more I get to know you, the more I'm sure it was you. Now, if you think *this* is not me, you should imprison me."

There was less suspicion in her beautiful eyes. "You remember everything, right? Do you remember making those choices?"

"It wasn't as if I spent a long time debating. Choice might not be the right word, more like a reflex—but it was me, yes. As brutal and horrifying as it was, I remember killing my father. At the time, I thought it was the right thing. I..." The memory felt strange, even to him. "I still think at that point I had no other option."

Naia sighed. "Well, it's true that it might be better for your people." It felt as if she was trying to convince herself. She then looked at him. "We need to plan, River. Plan what to do with Ironhold, that queen, that voice. We need to figure out what they want with you, what kind of herb they used. It's too much."

He kissed the top of her head. "I know. What if we just stayed here? If we just forgot about everything everywhere?" It was a joke, but he was also exhausted and unsure of what to do.

"Neither of us can, and you know that."

His arms wrapped tighter around her. "I could... for a time. I watched friends, even family dying, and did nothing. Nothing. It's true I didn't want to become a mindmelder, but I could have done something."

She raised her head to look at his face. "Didn't you go to Fernick to steal a staff? That doesn't strike me as nothing, River."

"I know... It's just... A lot of what I had been planning hinged on getting King Harold's trust, on having them building castles made of cards, and yet, they were making other castles all along. Even the carefully crafted illusions might not have mattered that much, not when they can reawaken the dead. It's as if... as if gaining power was a front."

Naia broke the hug and stared at him. "What if it is? What if the queen's plan has nothing to do with Ironhold's plans?"

River paused. "Possible, very possible. The queen was anything but devoted to her husband. But perhaps she needs them to be strong."

"But we know it's her."

He smiled. "See, my information was useful."

Naia reached out a hand and caressed his face. "Of course it was, but I hated to see you almost dying. Now, hear me out: Ironhold, that's something we can deal with later, we can use politics, we can try to defeat them in ways I understand, in ways even you understand. Now, the queen and that voice, that's what we need to get rid of as soon as possible. We need to get rid of that freaky magic. That's what we need to focus on." Her eyes were bright, filled with hope. "If I have to let them declare the Ironhold Empire, so be it. That's not the biggest problem. We need to focus on the worst enemy first."

He took a deep breath. "I can still enter the Iron Citadel."

"No!" There was horror and even anger on her face.

"Listen to me. I could follow the queen—"

"River! How well did it work last time?"

He had his hands on her shoulders and was careful not to squeeze them. "Just listen. What if I figure out what's in that death grass? That was the only reason she defeated me, Naia. Then I can go there and find out what's going on."

"What about the whole thing about you being *the key*?"

"I escaped. I escaped, Naia. As long as I don't get caught again, I'm not going to be anyone's key."

"And that's why you shouldn't get anywhere near the Iron Citadel." There was fear in those pretty dark eyes. So much fear, so much worry, so much...

He exhaled, relieved that at least one of *his* fears was false. "You don't want me to get hurt."

She frowned. "Did you hit your head? Of course I don't want you to get hurt. Why are you saying this nonsense?"

Because I thought you didn't love me anymore. I feared you'd never be able to love me again. He couldn't come to voice any of those fears, as they sounded silly and ridiculous even in his head. Now. They had seemed true a few minutes before. River pulled Naia and kissed her.

Naia did kiss him back, but then pushed him. "River, we need to decide what to do. We need to plan. And you still didn't answer my question."

He ran the back of a finger over her beautiful face. "We need to kiss, Naia. Kiss and forget everything. It's a matter of strategy: decisions shouldn't be made over troubled minds. It's been too much. Too much for you. Too much for me. I say we take a break before we break."

In truth he just wanted to hold her and forget everything about that horrific morning, everything about the events in the last few days, everything, everything—just for a moment.

She rested a hand on his face and he kissed it, as he noticed that she looked at him with her usual softness, that look that was so soothing, calming, that could put his heart at ease even when the world outside was falling apart.

"Let's rest at the fort," she said. "If anything happens, I'm there to make decisions, to talk to other kings." Her voice then got strained. "And if my father returns, I'll see him."

River tried to be playful and cheer her up, and grimaced. "Oh no, all my work glamouring this house is for nothing, then."

She smiled. "I didn't ask you to do that." Her tone was playful, but then, all of a sudden she got serious, thoughtful. "Let's stay. A little. A couple of hours."

What did she want to do in two hours? The only theory that came to his mind didn't sound that plausible at that moment, but it reminded him…"You spoke to my sister, right?"

"Uh?" She frowned, confused, then slapped his arm. "Oh, you're talking about *that.* You can't seriously be thinking… River, really?"

"No. I wasn't. I wasn't. I was just curious about something, but now I do realize it sounded awful. I just want to make sure you know what can happen between a man and a woman—when they're alone. Because we are alone, and then it reminded me. I do realize you have no intention of benefiting from that fact, though. But I'm glad you know… things… now."

He wasn't sure if she remembered that he had given his word to wait until they were married—in human terms, but he didn't want to mention it and risk making her even angrier, thinking his mind was going there.

She looked away. "It's all complicated and not at all romantic, River. But I'm glad I spoke to her, even if now… She probably hates, me, right?"

Anelise was a mystery to River himself. He raised an eyebrow. "She hates *me.* Not sure she hates you."

"And yet she agreed to rule the Ancient City for you?"

He shrugged. "It was an order, not a request. But she wouldn't have lied to you. I just wanted to make sure you knew, you knew everything, otherwise you can't say *yes,* you can't say *no,* you don't know what you're getting into."

Naia sat on the bed. "I don't want to get into anything—for now, at least."

He sat by her and caressed her hair. "It's fine. Fine, Naia, and I shouldn't have brought any of that up. I just wanted to know. Come here." He hugged her and held her close, holding her tight. "I wish we could stay this close forever, you know?"

"We can."

"You do realize Ancients go to the chamber pot, just like you humans. How can I go there holding you? I mean, I can, but—"

Her laughter was like music. "Don't be silly. I mean from time to time."

River held her tight, feeling her heartbeats so close to his. She probably hadn't realized what she had said and what it meant. Humans were careless with their words. And yet it meant so much being able to hold each other from time to time—for eternity. That, if they survived.

NAIA'S EYES WERE CLOSED, basking in that moment of silence, peace, quiet, still with that odd feeling that she shouldn't leave the cabin—at least not yet. A long embrace, as if it could last forever. Naia and River just sat like that, matching each other's breaths to a slow, calming, steady rhythm. River was now leaning his head on the space between her shoulder and neck, the rough texture of his horns on her neck strangely pleasant.

She realized that he needed this moment more than she did, he needed the comfort.

He kissed her neck, sending shivers down her spine, then said, "You make me sane again, Naia."

She closed her eyes as she considered his words. "Were you crazy before?" She wasn't sure about her own opinion on this, but wanted to hear his.

He still had his head buried on her neck, but chuckled. "Every second away from you is a soft, subtle agony, perhaps not enough to make me realize it, but I see it now."

Naia almost reminded that she had been there, right there, almost beside him, when he'd become unrecognizable, a cold-hearted murderer, but she didn't think he'd want to be reminded of that. Not right now. Instead, she chuckled.

"I think all you can see right now is my hair."

"One of the most beautiful things in the universe. How could

I complain?" His chest moved up and down, in an even slower, deep breath. "Naia, I understand you were scared earlier, I do."

She wasn't sure what to say, so she only made a non-committal grunt. "Hmm."

River moved his head away from her body and looked into her eyes. "I want you to know one thing: I'll never hurt you." He took her hand and put it over his heart. "Trust this. It's for you."

Dreadful images from that morning flooded her mind and she pulled her hand. "Bad metaphor, River."

He closed his eyes, but then smiled. "All of me, then. Definitely all of me. Trust me on that." His face was serious, focused, without its usual amusement.

She kissed his lips softly, then said, "Trust is earned, not granted. But I... I believe you won't hurt me. I do, River. If I ever let you take me away from my family, it was because I trusted you."

He pulled her hand and kissed her fingers one by one. "Because you're wise."

Now he had an amused smirk, and it made her breath catch. It made no sense. She wanted him to be open and honest, and yet was drawn by his playful, even deceitful nature. Perhaps because it was who he was—and she truly liked him.

Naia shook her head, then looked straight into his eyes. "I'm foolish." Foolish for him, and wanting indeed every part of him.

Why was it that eyes could communicate so much? The moment changed, the energy in the room shifted, and then he was kissing her, a kiss that was all passion and yearning, making the world tilt around them. Not the world; they shifted positions, the soft cover of the bed behind Naia, part of his weight over her, one of his legs on the mattress, and other bent, his knee finding a place between her thighs. One of his hands was moving to her hip, and the other moving up her stomach, right under her breast.

He suddenly stopped, his breath hitching, eyes wide. "I... you said you didn't want..."

"I changed my mind." Naia stared at him while she ran her hands down his back, and then right below it, her own heart making a racket inside her chest. "Also," she added in a lower voice. "I would like to inspect all that's mine."

River smiled and kissed her temple. "Any time, my love."

Love? Her hands almost froze in place, but she didn't want to make a bigger thing out of it. Why would it be a big thing, when he had said their magic united, when he had claimed they were *life companions* according to Ancients? Perhaps it was just that words had power, and this word was one with so much weight— good and bad, that to hear it from his lips was magical. A fae's lips, someone who didn't play with words.

He stared at her. "Something wrong?"

Naia wanted to tell him she loved him, but then changed her mind. "I'm scared." She wasn't sure of what.

River must have misunderstood her words, as he moved away from her, so that he was lying beside her, and ran a hand over her face. "I'm glad you told me. Time is our friend."

Was it, though? Would they survive? He meant that they could go slowly, which was a good idea, of course. Then at the same time she wanted to tell him to do everything, everything right now. And she could. It was a matter of saying the words, letting him know that fear was a common companion to bravery, that sometimes fear and desire walked together. And yet the words were stuck, as if they had been stifled for so long that they couldn't believe they were allowed to come out now.

Why was it that just talking about it was so hard? But then, it was a language she did not speak, on a topic she knew little... As Naia tried to gather her thoughts, a sound outside, like wings, and then twigs breaking, caught her attention.

River raised a hand and whispered, "They won't see the house."

It wasn't that she was afraid of what was out there, but something else. Her feeling was more like worry and curiosity. "I need to see it."

She was up in a second, River after her, his horns and eyes glamoured, his ears covered by his hair. Still, he said, "Naia, we're safer inside."

"I don't think it's an enemy."

River stood by her and placed a hand over her shoulder as she unlatched the door and opened it—then couldn't believe her eyes.

A huge silver dragon sat there, and she knew who it was. Naia ran to him and put her arms over the side of his face. Tears of happiness were threatening to come out of her eyes. Her brother was alive, was unharmed, was here!

"Fel!" Her voice came out mingled with a relieved laugh.

"Naia?" The word sounded as if inside her head, and yet it was her brother's voice. "Can you hear me?"

"I can! I can!" She stepped away and looked into his huge green eyes. "How are you?" Only then she noticed a girl climbing out of his back—Leah. Naia stared at her. "Hello." Her voice sounded cold, but then, that note the girl had written still gave her shivers.

"Hey." Leah waved as she stood beside Fel.

River stared at Fel in admiration and nodded. "What can I say? Looking good. By the way, I can also hear you."

Naia tried her best to ignore her annoyance at Leah, then asked, "What happened? Where have you been?"

Now the Frostlake princess pointed at River, who no longer had any glamour. "You?"

River smiled and raised his hands. "In person. No need to thank me for saving you; it was done for him." He pointed at Fel.

"What saving?" her brother replied in that strange voice that came from nowhere.

Leah shook her head. "I'll explain later."

Fel's huge dragon eyes were on the princess, then he turned to Naia and River. "We went to Fernick. Met other dragons, including some of our family, Naia."

She swallowed. The idea of being a dragon hadn't yet settled well in her mind, so the thought of having family also felt strange. "Family? Like... a father?" A father who was not King Azir was also incredibly unsettling.

"He's dead," Fel said. "Died a long time ago. His name was Ircantari—"

"I met him," River muttered, and then sucked in a breath, while staring at Fel. "Your eyes. They're almost like his. They were more yellow."

Fel straightened his neck, making him look taller. "How old are you?"

River chuckled. "I was eighteen when I saw Ircantari, and then I got lost in the hollow after that, frozen in time. I came back about a year ago. I'm not sure how old that makes me."

"Lost in the hollow?" Leah asked. "I met a fae like that."

"Who?" River's tone was calm, but Naia could sense the urgency behind the word.

"Her name was Iana," Leah said. "She also disappeared after the fall of Formosa, but before the end of the war. She didn't know it had ended."

River was thoughtful. "Iana..." He frowned, thinking. "What did she look like?"

"Dark red eyes, long pale blond hair, almost silver, and white horns, shorter than yours." The princess said it as if her description meant anything, unaware that her words were as helpful as saying someone had two eyes, a nose, and a mouth, when it came to Ancients.

River was staring at her, eyes wide. "Was she short, tall, old, young? Shape of her face?"

Leah looked up, thinking. "Youngish. Not a teenager, but a young adult. Face..." She shrugged. "Normal? She was also very beautiful, like very, very—"

"Did you mention me?" River asked.

"I did. She told me it was impossible, that no fae would be able to enter the Iron Citadel. But you did, didn't you?"

River looked down and nodded. He then pulled Naia's hand

and kissed it. She was unsure if he wanted to comfort her or him, and knew well that he had hoped perhaps that Leah had met his dead sister, but the name was different and the description too vague to mean anything. At the same time, holding his hand felt so good, so natural. She could barely believe she had considered leaving him only a few hours before.

Leah then asked him, "And what's your name?"

"River." He looked down and squeezed Naia's hand tight, then added, "Of the Second Dynasty."

Fel asked, "Weren't you River Annoying? Or had no last name?" If he had been in human form, Naia was sure he would have raised an eyebrow.

"I got my name back," River replied, an unsuppressed strain beneath his casual tone. It was clear that the events of that morning had also hurt him.

Naia wanted to change the subject, especially because trying to hold back her anger wasn't working. "Fair. Meanwhile, I just want to know one thing." She looked at Leah. "How come you're here? With him? After writing that note?"

"Sis, it wasn't her fault," Fel said, and the words sounded menacing when coming from a huge dragon protecting his rude beloved.

"What note?" Leah asked. "All I did was ask him why he hadn't proposed, and if something was happening." She frowned, thinking. "Did you receive something else?"

"Your mother," Fel said. "She must have faked a note."

Leah shook her head. "Not my mother. Ironhold. They could be capable of that, and they needed that wedding. Bastards." She stared at Naia. "What did the note say?"

Could it be? Could it be that her anger at the girl had been misplaced? That Fel's anger had been wrong? "Uh... bad things. Like..." Naia didn't want to repeat it, but the girl's questioning eyes meant she had to give her an explanation. "You wanted a partner who had..." She swallowed. "Physical integrity."

"What?" Leah turned to Fel. "You thought I could write something like that? Really?" It was odd to see the girl, who wasn't tall or strong, yelling at a huge dragon.

"I thought your mother had made you do that," Fel said.

"No!" There was anger in Leah's voice. "If that was the case, I would write that I was sorry and changed my mind, that I had to break up our engagement, I would write something decent!" Engagement. They had been a lot more involved than Naia had suspected. The girl had tears in her eyes. "I had agreed to marry you and you never proposed! You wished me good luck."

"I did propose," he said. "To your mother. She clearly didn't pass on the message."

Leah sighed and covered her eyes. "That's different. Still bad, but different. And she probably thought we were siblings."

What?

"Siblings?" Naia repeated, unsure from where that word had come from.

"She's a deathbringer," Fel said. "I think she's our father's daughter. I mean, not Ircantari, but Azir."

Naia almost said that it made no sense, but then... She recalled the look his father had given the Frostlake queen and it all fell into place. Almost. "Why then didn't he marry—"

Leah waved her hands. "Some men are dishonorable and use then abandon women, that's all."

Naia frowned, still stunned. "My father is not perfect, but I don't think anyone can say he has no honor. He wouldn't do that."

Leah shrugged. "We don't know our parents, we don't." Her voice was cracking.

Naia felt bad for the princess, but then Fel pushed the girl closer to him with his wing, and she rested her face on his beautiful scales. Leah was so obviously enamored of him, even in this form, that it made Naia regret her past anger. All she remembered now was the girl's smile while on stage, when she and Fel had stared at each other like nothing else existed in the world.

"I'm sorry," Naia said. "Sorry I believed that note was yours." And in fact she had found it strange, she had thought there had been something wrong, and yet, she had allowed anger to blind both Fel and her. Her brother had been so hurt... and for a lie.

The Frostlake princess shook her head, then caressed Fel's scales. "It's all in the past. And we have more important matters to discuss. We found out... a lot. I haven't even had the chance to tell Fel everything."

River still held Naia's hand and said, "We also made our own discoveries—and we have a lot to plan. I guess it's time to compare stories, isn't it? I can start."

He glanced at Naia, and she gave him an encouraging smile. It felt that this was his way to let her know that he intended to be open and honest about things, and that his openness included his family.

Leah opened her mouth, as if about to say something, perhaps anxious to tell all her news, but ended up listening.

River summarized some events that he had already told Naia, about the war against the Ancients, his incursion into the dragon lair, to retrieve a staff, then his return and discovery that it would kill all humans in Aluria, which led him to destroy it.

He looked at Leah and Fel, and said, "You may think the white fae are terrible for considering doing this, but it was desperation, desperation that led us to this dark path, this dark thought, this horrible possibility." In a way, he was justifying his father's choices, which was odd. "And yet, despite everything, despite our losses, I couldn't carry on with that much destruction. And I don't think we caused the disaster in Formosa. We don't have magic that would do that kind of physical damage."

"But you don't know," Fel said.

River shook his head slightly. "I can't be sure."

He then talked about his meeting with the dragon lords. Naia hadn't paid that much attention the first time he'd told her about it, but now it had another meaning, if their father had been among those dragons, and seemed to be their leader.

Naia had to hold back all her questions, otherwise they'd spend forever asking about what might have been, about so much... River then told them about his city being frozen in time, him getting lost in the hollow, and finding Naia. Her cheeks got hot and she almost stopped him. After all, this was also her secret and her story to tell Fel, but then, at least he omitted the kiss, saying that *touching* her had almost killed him. It wasn't a lie, of course, and ended up being important when he told them about helping Ironhold and creating illusions for them, including the fae attack in Frostlake.

"What about the watersnake?" Fel asked.

River sighed. "I don't know who or what caused it, and I didn't hear anything about it from Ironhold. I'm sorry." He looked up, thinking. "How it came to that lake... It confounds me. I can see how it would be a good opportunity for Ironhold to get rid of you two." He glanced at Fel and Naia. "But I don't know. I don't think they'd want to risk hurting her." He pointed at Leah.

Surprisingly, he told them that he hadn't been forthcoming about his past and even identity to Naia, and he told them about their house in the hollow and that she had found a way into the Ancient City, from where he had to rescue her.

When he started telling them about his recent discoveries in Ironhold, Leah's eyes widened in alarm. "Cassius' been revived?"

"Yes," River said. "I... don't know if it's really him, though. I haven't had the chance to check."

He then detailed following Queen Kara, and how she was connected to a mysterious entity, then something about the vessel, and that River was the key. He ended up telling them that he killed his own father, without specifying the method of murder.

River swallowed. "He wanted to kill Naia. I... It's not what I would have wished to happen." He had a bitter chuckle. "And here we are. The advantage is that if we need, we can count on the Ancients as allies. We want to defeat Ironhold as well."

We for River meant both the Ancients and... Him and Naia? Everyone who opposed Ironhold? She didn't ask him, but proceeded to tell her brother some of what she'd seen in the

Ancient City, how it was all dead, then the meeting with the other kingdoms, the upcoming emergency gathering, and the visit from the Wolfmark King, without mentioning his odd proposal. River didn't let that slide, though, and had an amused smile at the mention of King Sebastian.

Leah then told them about going to Ironhold, that she remained mostly in her bedroom, and never saw the king and queen.

Fel asked, "Why?" So it was new to him as well.

The girl took a deep breath, closed her eyes, then said, "I was a prisoner, all right? I couldn't come and go, I couldn't do anything. They are horrible."

Fel said, "I can smash that castle, Leah." His voice was gentle, as if consoling her, but also threatening. He definitely meant to destroy the Iron Citadel.

Naia raised a hand. "We'll wait and plan what to do with them." She feared her brother would fly there at that very moment and demolish that dreadful castle, and they still had a gathering to attend.

Leah nodded. "Agreed. Hot heads won't help us now."

Fel blew a small flame in the air. "Can't help it."

At least they all chuckled, despite the gloomy revelations. Leah then continued, telling them about slipping into the hollow by accident and ending up in Umbraar—in Fel's room, who immediately realized what was happening and spoke to his father, who took her back to Ironhold.

That made no sense. "Why would you go back there?"

Leah's voice was laced with pain. "I feared they could retaliate against my parents if I disappeared. I was wrong. They had already attacked."

Fel then said, "That's where our father, uh, I mean, King Azir went."

Naia almost reminded him that Azir was still their father, but then she glanced at Leah and realized how complicated this story was for the two of them. And there were more important issues. "If he's in Frostlake, we have to rescue him."

"I went there," Leah said. "Nobody knows where my mother is and I guess they're together. They... someone told me she died, but I don't think it's true. I believe he went into the hollow with her."

"And got lost." The words popped out of Naia's mouth. It was the only explanation that made sense.

"Maybe," the girl said. "We have to hope they'll be able to find their way out."

21

CYNON'S MAGIC

Fel was not surprised that his sister could hear him, but found it odd that the fae could also hear his voice. Regardless, it made it easier for them to talk. And then, River held Naia's hand and looked at her with so much tenderness that perhaps it made sense that he could also hear Fel. But there was so much to do.

Leah's tale was surprising, about hearing a strange voice looking for *the iron dragon*, then finding a fae lost in the hollow telling her about a creature called The Breaker, who had been conquering realms. It explained why she had told him to hide his magic.

River frowned. "You think it's the same voice as the one I heard?" Fel had the same curiosity.

"Seems like it, doesn't it?" Leah replied.

She then told them that Iona, the fae she had met in the hollow, helped her close her mind to that strange voice, then asked her to let the creatures from that realm lose.

"Wait, wait." River seemed confused. "You're telling me that a fae taught you something just to be nice? Without a deal? Then *asked* you something without proposing anything in return?"

"We *had* a deal," Leah said. "For me to stay and listen to her. I didn't trust her at first."

River rolled his eyes. "Incredible."

Leah clicked her tongue. "Maybe... maybe it has to do with magic. Maybe she couldn't make a deal for me to open up that realm; she had to convince me. But then... I feared for Fel. Since I didn't think that voice would see me anymore, I decided to find him, and came to Fernick. Now, I'm sure he can tell you about it better than me."

Naia stared at Leah wide-eyed. "You can go to Fernick through the hollow?"

Leah shook her head. "I can find Fel, no matter where he is. If he's there, I can find him, but I don't think I'd be able to go to Fernick now, for example."

"Still impressive," Naia said, then turned to Fel, "And you? Did you fly there?"

"I did," Fel said. He told them about traveling to Fernick, the Boundless, Tzaria and Risomu, the dragon village, Ekateni, his cousins, his encounter with the First Mage, the festivities for the *iron dragon*, the attack, and their return. It was all so much, condensed in so little time, in such few, small words that failed to convey even half of what he had experienced. And yet talking about it made it all seem a lot more extraordinary than it had felt.

His sister approached him and tried to hug him. All she did was put her arms around his neck, without managing to close them. "I'm glad you're back and safe, Fel." She stepped back and looked at him. "Do you think... we'll ever meet them again?"

Their family. "Ekateni said they would send some dragons to check what is happening here, and I could try to travel back there once things are quieter. For now... they thought Aluria would be safer for me." He then added, "Also, I didn't tell them about you. Just in case."

For some reason, she looked down, slightly disappointed.

"It's for the best," River told her quietly, as he wrapped an arm around her. He then turned to the others. "It seems we all met some version of the same creature, doesn't it?"

Naia grimaced. "Unless they are two or three different ones."

Leah shook her head. "The one I heard wanted *the iron dragon*, just like the Boundless. It had to be a dragon to know that, to know anything about an iron dragon. Based on what Iona told me, this voice is the Breaker. If I came in contact with him in the Iron Citadel, he could well be there, which explains what River saw. I think it's all Cynon."

Fel agreed with that. "My uncle mentioned the need for a vessel and anchors. River, you said Queen Kara mentioned a vessel, right?"

The fae nodded. "Yes, but what are the anchors?"

Fel tried to recall his words. "Objects infused with Cynon's magic. The risk is that a vessel could come in contact with the anchors and open a portal, but it needs to be in a place rich in dragon magic. It must be in Fernick."

The fae scratched his chin. "If we assume it's the same creature, then what was he doing in Ironhold? Why isn't he in Fernick, taking care of these rogue dragons or something?"

"Perhaps he is," Leah said. "Nothing prevents him from being in more than one place at once."

"Still..." Fel agreed with River. "Why even bother with Aluria?"

Naia bit her lip. "Maybe he didn't exactly bother to come here, maybe he was called. Maybe Queen Kara or someone from Ironhold communicated with him, perhaps as a way to get more magic, and this is just an extra place he has access to. Maybe his main goal and main activities are still in Fernick. But we still need to get rid of him."

River sighed. "Anchors, you said? One of them might be the statue."

"Wait," Leah said. "Wait. Vessel? It has to be Cassius. Maybe this Cynon, Breaker, whatever, is here because it was where he could find a vessel."

Fel puffed a breath that ended up having some smoke in it. "Ekateni said it needed to be a dragon. Still... We need to speak to Tzaria. She would know more about it." And something about Cassius being the vessel sounded off for some reason. "I still think... Shouldn't Cynon want a better vessel? If not a dragon, someone with magic at least?"

"Cassius has magic," Leah said in a small voice. "He's an ironbringer."

"True," Fel agreed. Funny how he often forgot that his cousins from Ironhold were also ironbringers—which made no sense, considering the kingdom they were from.

Naia sighed. "Let's consider what we know so far. Queen Kara is communicating with something, probably this Cynon, Breaker, something. Prince Cassius was part of a very macabre ritual, and was re-awakened. Ironhold is trying to take over Aluria, using magic that shouldn't even exist, and they are horrible people. Anything I missed?"

"No," Fel said, still trying to figure out how everything was connected. "What Ekateni told me was that Cynon needed a vessel to help him come back to this world. Maybe they are wrong, and it doesn't need to be a dragon. I... Yes, it could be Cassius."

Naia frowned, thoughtful. "I... think we'll need to kill him." Her voice was hesitant.

Leah turned to her. "I don't know why you sound sad about it. He should be dead already, if anything."

River looked at Leah. "You killed him with your deathbringing, right? With a voice you thought was Cynon's?"

She was close enough to Fel that he felt her shiver. "Yes."

Fel understood where the fae was trying to take the conversation. "You think Cynon wanted Cassius to be dead or almost dead? So he could take him?"

River shrugged. "I don't know. It's a possibility."

"Again," Naia said. "We need to kill him, and make sure he stays dead this time."

A shadow crossed over River's face. "I can get into the Iron Citadel. I could go there and kill him. Right now."

"No!" Naia protested. "They might trap you with that death grass."

"They didn't have it everywhere in the castle." River rolled his eyes.

Leah sighed. "If he's killed, they might cancel the gathering. I was thinking of going there—through the hollow. Show up, tell the other kingdoms what happened in Frostlake. I know they won't openly defy Ironhold, but it might open their eyes."

Fel hated that idea. "Too dangerous, Leah."

She turned to him. "I need to do something for my kingdom."

"No doubt." Of course Fel understood her urgency. "But showing up in Ironhold is reckless. If you want to talk to other kingdoms so badly, try something with communication mirrors, something safer."

Naia sighed. "We will have to take risks. It's not like not doing anything will keep us safe." She looked at River while saying that.

"That's debatable," the fae replied. "If you hide well you can be safe." Naia was glaring at him, and he added, "But I know that you feel responsible for your kingdom, and you're not going to want to hide like a coward. I understand that."

"Also," Leah said. "If this... Cynon wins and comes to this world, will there be any place safe enough to hide?"

RIVER FELT a cold prickle down his neck as they kept discussing what to do. One thing was to have an idea of what they were up against. Another thing was knowing what to do, or even knowing exactly what their enemy wanted and what his next steps would be. Good strategists usually observed the enemy, but what was there to observe in a mysterious voice?

Another strange thing was to hear a dragon's voice inside his head. A real dragon, something he had never imagined possible before, even though he'd been in a dragon's lair and seen the huge doors. And yet this was Isofel, Naia's brother. One thing that made River relieved was that Fel hadn't told anyone in Fernick about Naia, so at least it was one less worry—as if they didn't have way too many already.

They kept debating ideas, ideas that made him feel all sick inside. Perhaps Cassius had to be killed, and he didn't want to let Naia do it, and wouldn't ask a full grown dragon to do it, so he had no option but to volunteer. If they didn't use the death grass everywhere in the iron citadel, River could do it easily. Almost too easily. His father's glassy eyes stared back at him in his mind—a strange memory that River didn't want to revisit. If he could, he wouldn't return to the Ancient City, and that thought made no sense, since he'd been trying his hardest to save his people. And now they had to find a way to fight a mysterious enemy.

Naia was set on going to the gathering in Ironhold, to the point that he gave up trying to dissuade her. Instead, he had another idea.

"I'll come with you."

Her dark eyes were filled with worry. "What if they have—"

"Death grass?" River interrupted her. "They won't have it all over. I can pretend to be Isofel. I think..." He tried to recall the last time he'd seen Naia's brother. "We're about the same height. The glamour shouldn't be too hard, and it means I'll be with you."

She narrowed her eyes. "Show me."

River glamoured his horns, made his eyes bright green, almost yellow, that unnatural, strange color, then made his skin brown, and his hair darker, that beautiful black tone like Naia's hair, but straight.

"What do you think?" he asked.

Naia frowned, while Leah burst out laughing. "You look nothing like Fel."

That was unfair. "Bright green eyes, black hair." He pointed to his head and was going to say no horns, when he realized he still had his dark nails. He was almost glamouring them to look human, when he realized his mistake. "I'll wear gloves."

Naia was staring at him. "I never thought I'd say that, but you look too... pretty? And you look like you, like River. They'll recognize you."

River glamoured his nose to look bigger. "What about now?"

"My face is longer," Fel said. "And I don't have a big nose. At least not in human form."

River tried to glamour his face to look thinner and longer. "You two know him well," he told Naia and Leah. "The other kings don't."

Naia raised an eyebrow. "The people in Ironhold know *you*, though."

River undid all his glamour, annoyed that they weren't awed by his incredible display of magic. "I won't look like myself, but I'm sure they won't look too closely at me if my eyes, skin, and hair are the right colors and if I'm pretending to be Prince Isofel."

"We'll think about it," Naia said, sounding unconvinced.

To be fair, he wasn't certain if going to the Iron Citadel was a good idea, but then, was *not going* a solution? What was the solution? What were they supposed to do?

Naia then sighed, almost as if she could hear his thoughts. "The gathering is tomorrow. We still have time to think." She turned to her brother. "Aren't you exhausted? I bet you need to sleep, but I'm not sure where—"

"I'll go to the mountains," Fel interrupted her. "Find a cave or ledge or something. I doubt anyone will find me there."

She nodded. "You should go soon, so that nobody sees you. We can meet again here tomorrow, two hours after sunset. Then we decide what to do, after we sleep on all the information we got."

River was relieved that she was saying this, even if part of him felt this meant admitting defeat, admitting they didn't have the answers, and saw no clear path to move forward. But then, perhaps it was true that they needed to sit on it.

"Sounds good," Fel said. River still found it strange to hear his voice like that.

Naia turned to Leah. "You can come to the Royal fort. We'll get a room for you."

"No." She stepped closer to Isofel. "I'll stay with him."

"There won't be beds in the mountains." Naia glanced at Leah and her brother. "And it might get cold."

The girl shook her head. "I'm not leaving him."

"Fair," Naia said. "I'll bring a communication mirror tomorrow, so we can be in touch."

Leah was thoughtful. "Are we going to spend an entire day... doing nothing?"

"I need to communicate with the other kingdoms," Naia said. "And you need to rest. Maybe you'll recall an important detail, maybe you'll have an idea. Maybe..." She bit her lip.

"She's right, Leah," Fel's voice echoed in River's mind. "Come."

He helped her climb to his back, then extended his wings as much as he could in that clearing, and took flight. River watched with fascination as his scales glinted in the moonlight, but then soon he was high up, at a distance where he could be confused with a bird. Magnificent—like Naia. But hiding her dragon identity, even forgetting about it, felt like the right thing to do for now. She also looked magnificent as a human, and stared at him, poorly concealed worry in her eyes.

River turned to her and kissed her cheek. "You want to go to the iron fort, then?"

"I have to."

He could feel her apprehension and worry floating between them, so many words that were not being said and yet lingered in the air. River himself had an ominous sense of dread, a fear of never seeing her again, a fear that he would lose everything he cherished, that he would fail. Was this really the time for these baseless fears to creep up on him? He didn't want to go to the Iron Citadel, didn't want to try to do anything. If he could, he would hide somewhere far away. These were a coward's thoughts, and he wasn't going to entertain them.

River walked back to the hut and took his daggers.

"You didn't use them before." Naia stared at the objects with curiosity.

"They were in the Ancient City, and I couldn't go there." He put the black dagger on his belt. For a moment, he didn't recognize the red dagger, and almost left it there. Weird thought; it was his favorite weapon. He put it on his belt then was ready to leave that place.

A nauseous feeling came to him, but he preferred not to say anything. It was just fear. Just nerves, and a horrifying feeling that something was wrong, very wrong. But again, of course something was wrong. *Everything* was wrong and Aluria was about to be taken by something they didn't even know what it was for sure.

When River took Naia's hand, her touch felt like a cool breeze dissipating a foul, fetid smoke, healing that strange nausea, as if her magic could suppress all his worry, all his fears. Perhaps it could.

This hut was within a circle, so it would be easy to take Naia back to the fort. "We're going through the hollow," he said.

The walls around them disappeared, giving way to darkness. A part of him was screaming inside him, screaming "No, no, no," as if he were walking to his death, walking to his doom. But he was just walking between circles.

LEAH HAD NEVER IMAGINED she would one day visit the mountain range that split Aluria in two. Well, she'd never imagined she'd fly on the back of a dragon, seeing everything from up high, higher than she had seen when flying with Fel still under the dome in Frostlake.

These mountains were covered with green vegetation and trees except for their rocky tops. The weather was cool, but not cold enough to cover the peaks with snow, as they were fairly north. Leah wasn't sure if Fel would find a nice cave to hide in or if they would need to sleep on an open, flat terrain, under the stars. The thought was good, except that if it rained, it could get uncomfortable quickly.

Fel was flying by the top of the mountains and landed on a chasm between two rocks. So indeed there would be nothing over their heads other than the black sky and gray clouds.

They had so much to do, so much to decide, to think, to discuss, and yet she felt how tired he was just based on his silence, his movements. He lay down with his wings folded and curled his tail.

Leah leaned her head on it, while lying over his back paw, which was folded by his body. His scales were warm and soft, and for a moment, she could forget everything going on outside these mountains.

22

IMPROMPTU GATHERING

Naia swallowed. Going through the hollow still felt uncomfortable. Holding River's hands usually helped, but this time she couldn't stop noticing how close his nails were to her skin and wonder what it would take to rip it. The memory of what he'd done to his father insisted on intruding in her mind—as if it would ever fade. Eventually she would need to come to terms with it, come to terms with the idea that sometimes people had to make terrible choices for the greater good—including River.

Leaving Fel didn't feel right either, but it was true that he would be safe in the mountains, and they would meet again, hopefully with a clearer idea of what path to take.

Naia realized she had her eyes shut and opened them, wanting to see the circles connecting places through the hollow, hoping to learn more about moving through it, but the darkness was already dissipating, being replaced by Fel's room in the Royal fort.

River had a tight-lipped smile that didn't reach his eyes. "Here we are."

He was nervous, that was obvious, even under his sheen of pretend confidence.

"I need to go to my father's office." She wanted to check if there had been any messages, and was a little upset that she had spent so long away. "You can wait—"

His horns were disappearing under his glamour. "I'll come with you."

Naia didn't say anything, which he took as encouragement enough, considering he was following her. There was something inappropriate about walking around the fort with this man nobody knew, but then, Naia had already been disowned, so it wasn't as if anything worse would happen to her. And then, there was nobody in the hallway.

She opened the door and ran to the communication mirror, which was brighter than usual, indicating some recent activity.

Of course. Obviously.

This was the time to make alliances, to attempt to forge a plan with the other kingdoms, and she had squandered it by... sleeping. Sleeping because River had likely siphoned her magic to commit brutal murder. Naia closed her eyes to prevent glaring at him—anger wasn't going to solve anything.

Naia wondered if she should wait until the next morning to contact someone—but then, it wasn't that late, and these matters were urgent.

She tried Wolfmark—and was surprised by being seen right away. On the other side of the mirror stood a young counselor.

"Princess Irinaia Umbraar. We've been waiting to hear from you."

"Apologies." She was going to say she had been busy, but what did it matter? And what explanation did she owe?

The counselor then said, "Wolfmark is hosting an impromptu gathering—without Ironhold, and my king wished you'd come, but it might be too late now."

No, no, no. This couldn't be. "When does it start?"

"They're meeting right now, your highness."

"Now?"

"Their dinner just ended, and they proceeded to the meeting room."

River was gesticulating beside her, pointing at something. Naia wasn't sure if he meant they should go or wait or what, but she turned to the mirror and said, "I'll try to get to you right away. Thank you. You can sever the communication."

Naia turned to River. "This is terrible."

"I can take you there through the hollow."

"You happen to have a circle there?"

He nodded. "And in many of the kingdoms I visited with the Ironhold delegation."

Naia's mind was whirling. "We should tell Leah, tell my brother."

"I don't have circles in the mountains, Naia, and we'd better hurry."

She stopped to think. She had to be presentable for such a meeting, not wearing a ball gown, but at least something nicer. "I need to go to the manor. For clothes."

He already had black hair and no horns, and pointed a finger at her. "I'll glamour you."

"And if your magic slips, I'll look ridiculous."

Even as she said that, her dress was changing into a dark green velvet dress, with black embroidery in its sleeves, and a high neck. It wasn't fancy or flashy, but simple and elegant.

River looked at her with his fake green eyes. "If my magic fails, we might have bigger problems. That way we can go right away." He lifted a hand—gloved, at least. "I know what you're going to say: that I don't really look like your brother. I don't think they will notice it."

Probably not, even if River still looked very much like himself, despite the long, straight black hair, brown skin, and bright green eyes. Plus he was too pretty, not that Fel was ugly. It was odd to even try to describe it. But there was a bigger problem.

"Won't they find it strange if we show up like that? Without carriages? Right after getting the message from the mirror?"

"Your excuse will be that you're a deathbringer. You'll need to say it. Remember that the glamour still doesn't let me lie. I'm the same truthful River."

Naia rolled her eyes. "So open and honest."

She had meant it as a joke, but he didn't smile. Instead, he looked down, before reaching out his hand to hers.

It felt so sudden. So many things could go wrong.

River raised his eyebrows. "Changed your mind?"

"What's the plan?" She didn't expect him to know much more than she did. It was more like voicing her thought aloud.

He tilted his head. "We observe."

"Everyone will be observing, won't they? Afraid of making the first move."

"It seems that Wolfmark has already made the first move." River put a gloved hand on his chin. "The question is whether Ironhold knows it."

Who would be foolish enough to tell them? Out of the nine other kings, eight in fact, considering Frostlake had already been taken, there could be one bold and stupid enough thinking this would grant them favors. "They probably know. They might have spies." Naia frowned. "This could be a trap."

River shrugged. "Not necessarily. We don't know if they are openly conspiring against Ironhold. I... don't know. But it's better to go and find out, isn't it?"

"Yes." In reality, Naia was shocked that he wasn't admonishing her that going to this meeting could be dangerous, wasn't even warning her. But then, he had told her he wanted to change, and he knew as well as she did that they would need to act if they wanted to defy Ironhold and defeat Cynon. Telling her that it was dangerous would be a waste of time.

Naia took his hand—and soon found herself in a dark place, seeing bright circles in the distance. Most of them looked as if they were made from a brilliant substance, like gold stars, while a few of them, far away, looked more like fire. Then, far away, she saw an upright circle that was black, like a door leading into a tunnel with dark smoke. No, a pit, as if a person would fall into it if they got too close.

She looked away as she felt goosebumps, but pointed at it with her free hand. "What's that?"

"What?"

"The black one."

"I don't know all the circles, Naia."

He didn't sound worried or impressed. Perhaps circles like these were common. She'd need to ask him all about it, ask and learn and eventually be able to move in the hollow by herself.

They walked to a circle close to them, with faded light, and then it was as if that environment of the hollow was peeled back to reveal the entrance to a majestic castle made of grey granite, bordering a plateau. Its entrance had a golden door ten times her height. It was iron, she felt its force and weight, even if the finish was plated in gold. Many lamps and torches illuminated the grounds. Four guards came at them at once, pointing their swords.

"State your purpose."

"We're coming from Umbraar. To the impromptu gathering," River said.

The man widened his eyes. "How did you..."

"Deathbringers," someone muttered.

Naia then remembered she had to do the talking, and said, "I'm princess Irinaia Umbraar, and this is my brother Isofel." Lying so obviously felt strange, and perhaps it was an impression, but she felt a prickle in her throat.

"Follow me," another guard told them.

The man, with two more guards, led them to a smaller door, from where they reached a white, brightly illuminated corridor, and then a thick wooden door with engravings representing animals like wolves and birds. This was a wildbringer kingdom, after all.

The door opened to reveal a room with a long wooden table, where six kings were sitting. Some people were missing, but she would need to look at them carefully to figure out who. A large window led to a starry sky outside.

King Sebastian was at the edge of the table, and got up. "Princess Irinaia." He turned to River, and, in a drier tone, said, "Prince Isofel. We thought you wouldn't come."

"Apologies for our lateness," Naia said, while looking at the table. She recognized the kings from Karsal, Eaglehold, Haven, and Varana. "I was making sure our kingdom is safe."

"Any news from Azir?" Sebastian asked, sounding curious, but not worried.

Naia sighed. "Still indisposed, unfortunately."

King Sebastian smirked, and she wanted to punch him for that. Of course they all knew this was a lie, but she was hoping they would think he had gotten hurt in battle, when Umbraar was attacked. She also hoped her father wasn't gone for good.

The Wolfmark King then asked her, "Would you like to tell us about the strange attack in your fort?" He furrowed his eyebrows, as if thoughtful. "Apparently they *looked* like they were from Ironhold." There was no subtlety in the way he emphasized that word, making it clear what he thought about it.

Naia took a deep breath. "It was as if about a hundred or so Ironhold soldiers came and attacked us. Of course, why would they do that?"

A middle-aged man then said, "I was explaining to them that my men inspected the area, and there were indeed signs of battle. And bodies dressed in Ironhold garb."

She recognized him now. He was the Haven king, and Naia felt bad that she hadn't been in Umbraar to greet his committee. "My apologies for my absence. I was making sure the kingdom was safe. I hope your men were well received."

"They were allowed to see as much as they wanted, which I'll take as a sign of your friendship and courtesy," the Haven King said.

Naia smiled. "More than friendship. We are allies and should support each other." Actually, last time she had checked, nobody cared about Umbraar, but mentioning that didn't feel like a sound diplomatic move.

"We'll resume our discussion, then." King Sebastian sat down again and gestured to a chair beside him. "Princess Irinaia, this is for you."

Naia didn't like that and didn't like the look the man was giving her. When she glanced at River and caught his amused twinkle, she felt more at ease, now thinking of King Sebastian as a poor old deluded fool. Despite having been ignored, River stood there looking unbothered and even proud, as if standing up was a much greater honor than sitting. Thankfully nobody there knew Fel much, as he would be upset at the slight, and wouldn't just stand there looking like he owned the palace. Looking like a king—and River *was* a king, even if she would like to forget it.

King Sebastian then said, "We want to make sure we come to Ironhold tomorrow all of the same mind."

"Which is?"

It was the Eaglehold king who spoke. "*No* to the Ironhold empire."

That was quite direct. And bold. "Sounds wise." The part she wasn't sure was how they were planning on giving that information in person and walking out of the Iron Citadel alive. "And yet, are you still intending to attend the gathering in Ironhold?"

"We'll send emissaries," Sebastian said. "Men we don't mind losing."

Men who would probably be taken hostage and tortured. Naia looked around the table to see the kings' faces, to check if the thought disgusted anyone, but they all had neutral expressions. Some of them could be pretending to reject Ironhold's proposal, and be ready to go to the Iron Citadel the next day and tell them everything.

"And if Ironhold retaliates?" Naia asked. She would otherwise listen more and talk less, but she still felt that the king was giving attention to her.

Sebastian frowned. "Not if. When. We'll need to be ready."

They were planning for war. A coldness settled in her stomach. At the same time, there was something promising in his words: the idea of all the kingdoms in Aluria united.

Naia nodded. "If we all work together, we can defeat any enemy." She was rather thinking of Cynon and his strange magic, but the idea was the same.

River then walked up to the table and stood by her. Naia wasn't sure what he was about to do, and feared it would perhaps make everything worse, but all he did was address everyone. "You all need to leave *now*. This castle has been compromised and Ironhold has planted strange magic in this room. It's going to explode." Coming from River, it couldn't be a lie. She turned to him, but saw no alarm on his face.

Sebastian scoffed. "How would they do that? And how would you know?"

River said, "They sent guards to all the kingdoms, not only to spy on you and extend their influence, but as a means to attack from inside if necessary."

The Wolfmark King still didn't seem bothered. "Our visiting guards are safely sleeping—somewhere from where they can't leave."

"A prison?" Naia asked. "They have ironbringers in their midst. They could escape."

River put a hand on Naia's shoulder. "We're leaving. And I suggest you do the same. Evacuate the castle as well."

Sebastian got up, his face red. "So you came here to create panic?"

Naia stood in front of River. "He's telling the truth. Listen to him."

She felt River's gloved hand grabbing hers.

He told the kings, "I'm just warning you. Sharing information freely is a gift, not a threat." Oh, River, why was he speaking like a fae?

Darkness surrounded them before she even had the chance

to tell him anything, and she asked, "Do you think they believed you?"

"Not really." He was too calm.

"Is it true? That the room might explode? Then they're going to die."

"They were warned. I can't control their choices."

"Why didn't you tell me? That this could happen?"

"I..." There was confusion in his reddish-brown eyes, the glamour all gone. "Maybe I didn't recall. There were things I couldn't tell you. I couldn't tell anyone."

It made sense. Perhaps when River had traveled with Ironhold, he might have seen them placing the contraptions, might even have agreed to create illusions in case these things were used. She would need to ask him to tell her everything he knew, every little thing. Sometimes one detail could make a difference.

He then looked around. "We can talk about it later. I'd rather not spend more time here than necessary." His voice was strained, tense.

Something about it felt wrong, even if she obviously knew that the hollow was no place to have long conversations. Naia buried her questions and worries, waiting for when they reached Umbraar.

But when the darkness dissipated, she found herself with River in a room she didn't know. It looked like a storage room with empty wooden shelves and jars, with stone walls and a metal door, but this wasn't in any place she'd ever been to.

"Where are we?"

His jaw was set. "We'd better get this over with."

SOMETHING WAS WRONG, but all River could think was that he had to act fast, act before something happened, even if he wasn't sure what it was.

"Where are we?" Naia asked.

"The Iron Citadel." He didn't love the idea of bringing her with him, but he didn't want to leave her behind either, and had to deal with dueling feelings, dueling fears. Something horrible was either happening or about to happen, and, having no means to prevent it, at least he was trying to do the best to keep Naia safe.

She took a deep breath, then whispered, "I should have noticed it. So much iron. Even the air... But why—"

"If Cassius is the vessel, we'd better do something. Soon. Waiting won't fix anything." That was his reasoning, and why he'd rushed here, hating to have to kill again. But then, considering Cassius should be dead, did it even count? "We can plan the rest later."

She nodded, understanding in her eyes.

He then added, "If you hold my hand, I'll glamour you." She seemed confused, and he added, "Not to be seen."

He slipped into the hollow just enough to see and feel more of the castle, then went to the area where the royal quarters were. He knew well where each member of the family resided, but wasn't sure if the crown prince would be in his quarters or undergoing some other strange ritual.

Cassius was in his room, though, lying in bed, his grandmother sitting beside him. They didn't notice either him or Naia, not that the prince was in any condition to notice anything.

The first feeling that came over River was pity, pity at seeing that once proud prince lying like that. He was resting on many pillows, so that he was almost sitting, but his eyes were glassy. It was as if there was life in him, but at the same time there wasn't...

Lady Celia held one of Cassius' hands. "Wake up sweet boy, wake up. I'll get you orange cake and we'll travel to a lake. Remember that song?" She started singing. "Her heart was sad and broken and gone. Her life was all alone. And then the sweet little boy came to make her smile again. With laughter, grace and even farce, he brought her back to life. Sweet little boy with the smile that never dies..."

River froze. That song was similar to one of the Ancient's songs about a sweet child, a sweet child healing the wounds of a parent who had lost a loved one. It was often the case when mothers died in childbirth. This song celebrated joy and life, it was a way to deal with the pain.

His father had never sung this song to him. Nobody had, in fact, other than friends playing this lullaby as some sort of joke. A couple times, the servants had sung the song around him, but it had never been for him, with the feeling it required.

A lullaby many Ancients heard even if both parents were alive, a lullaby celebrating the mere existence of a child. Not River's. His existence had never been celebrated, other than when his father had found out about his mindmelding. And yet River had rejected the only reason his father had ever loved him for. A silly lullaby. Something so simple, so common, except for those who had never had it sung to them. And then what did it matter now? All River had done was make absolutely sure that his father would never have the opportunity to sing anything to him.

"River," Naia whispered in his ear.

Lady Celia stopped singing and looked around. "Hello? Did you come to take him? It's not his turn yet, not his turn. Not my sweet grandson."

Could it be that he was waiting for Cynon? That the vessel would be like that while waiting? Unless... River tried to think. Perhaps... Perhaps Cassius was just the sacrifice. But then who was the vessel? If there even was a vessel, if Cynon or whatever was real and was affecting Ironhold. As for the Ironhold crown prince, in this state, he was harmless.

River wondered if Naia would agree with him, wondered if it was worth it to simply walk away. No. This young man had done horrible things. Perhaps it wasn't River's place to decide who was worthy of living or dying, but he had no reason to feel bad about Cassius' death. And then, what if the prince *was* the vessel? Quite an empty vessel right now, but for how long? He held Naia's hand tighter, hoping it would give him courage. And then there was the matter of how he was going to kill the prince. He could make Cassius kill himself, but that would mean using mindmelding in its most horrific form—all the while keeping a glamour on him and Naia.

The truth was that River was no murderer, and yet perhaps it was too late to realize it now, since he'd promised to get rid of the Ironhold prince. And then what got him was how he'd killed his father. How? He couldn't even kill this horrific prince. It made... no sense. Not that he wanted to go back to that moment and figure what his thought process had been—if there even had been any thought.

As River struggled, trying to decide how to kill the prince, a dagger moved towards Cassius' neck—and cut it right in the biggest vein. A fast, precise cut that should kill him immediately. Naia's work.

Lady Celia let out a deafening wail, and River got to the hollow again, then to that abandoned deposit.

He stared at Naia. "I'm sorry. I should have—"

"It was easier for me." Her voice was low, and her expression was serious, thoughtful. "Hopefully it will help."

So she didn't think Cassius had been the vessel either. If he wasn't, then had all their conclusions been wrong? Or just some of them?

Then a thought hit him like a block of ice, freezing him all over. How could he not have seen it? Naia stared at him, eyes wide, so beautiful, as always, and the sight brought him pain, the horrible pain of losing her. River had to find a way to save her, a way to protect her, against impossible odds.

NAIA COULDN'T BELIEVE she'd killed someone—and in cold blood. Cassius probably deserved even worse than that, perhaps deserved to live for many years and suffer, and yet killing felt horrible.

Now she stood in this strange deposit in the Iron Citadel, wondering where to go from here, wondering what to do now, when River sucked in a breath and stared at her in horror.

"River?"

"I..." He frowned. "Part of me... still..." He closed his eyes, then exhaled, looked at her, and said, "I know what to do." His tone had become confident all of a sudden.

Naia should be relieved, but the memory of the last time he'd been that confident made her tense. "What?"

He smirked. "We'll go down to the belly of this monster. They have earth from Mount Prime there."

"Mount Prime..." It was connected to the Ancient City. "Does it have Ancient magic?"

He pressed a finger to his lips. "You'll see."

Naia wasn't sure what he was about to do. Perhaps he had found a solution for his people? For a second, she wished she could slip away on her own and run far from this dreadful castle, far from River.

Far from River? Her own mind was telling her strange things, and then there was the memory of Cassius's blood, now mixing with King Spring's blood in her mind. Could she even be upset that River was a cold-blooded murderer, when she was also one?

They slipped briefly into the hollow, then reappeared in a room that felt gigantic, even if she could not see much. There was so much iron that its smell overwhelmed her senses. Iron on the walls, floor, even the high ceiling. It was strange that she could almost *see* the place with her metal magic. Perhaps she should light a flame in her hand to illuminate that room, but somehow it didn't feel safe or wise.

His hand still held hers, so she pulled him closer and whispered, "What are you planning?"

"We're getting there." He spoke clearly, in a normal voice, unafraid of being overheard.

"I don't like this," she said.

"I know."

Naia let go of his hand. Something was wrong. "River, is that you?"

There was a flickering sound, then he had a lit torch in his hand. "Are you afraid?"

"Of course. You're not telling me what's going on."

"Come. I'll show you." They walked to the middle of the room, where there were tall and wide iron cylinders. "They have Mount Prime earth in them. But the real treasure are the rocks."

They walked to a wall, which had a small door, leading to a different room, where indeed there were rocks of various sizes, lying there. Most of the rocks were about as big a wild pig, while a couple were as big as a horse, and then there was a dark rock in the middle, almost as big as a hut. They had some kind of primordial magic in them, Naia could sense it, but she couldn't really identify what it was or what it could do. Somehow, it felt different from all the magic she'd sensed in the Ancient City.

"Why are we here?" she asked.

River placed the torch on a sconce by the wall. "That's quite a complex question."

Non-answers. Great. Perhaps she should be relieved that this was the real River. No. It all felt strange. Could she get to the hollow by herself? She'd done it once. But then she would never know what was happening. And then again, there was nothing threatening in his behavior. If anything, being vague and doing things without telling her was typical of River. The puzzling thing was how she had ever found his demeanor charming. It wasn't charming now; it was terrifying and yet all she could tell herself was that she was exaggerating.

River approached the biggest rock and buried his red dagger in it, as if the stone were as soft as an apple. That was one of the daggers he'd taken from the Ancient City. Again, this had to be some kind of magic for his people. The only thing she didn't understand was how come he had never tried it before and why he hadn't told her anything about this place and about what he'd been planning on doing. For someone who'd promised to be more honest, open, and forthcoming, he was letting her down again.

A few seconds after the dagger had been stuck in it, the rock started to glow with an eerie, blue light. River exhaled and laughed what at first felt like a relief laugh, then took on a sinister note.

This was the time for Naia to escape, and yet she couldn't stop looking at him, trying to figure out what was happening, trying to make it make some sense.

He picked the red dagger from the stone, then turned and pointed it at her. For a second, she feared he was going to throw it, and tried to focus on the metal in the weapon, so as to throw it back or change its direction if necessary. It wasn't easy because of all the metal energy in that room. Either way, she didn't need to block the dagger, as it never left his hand. Instead, a circular wall of ice encased her in less than a second.

Naia knew what was happening, she knew it. She also knew that the answer would be to move that dagger, move that dagger and do the unthinkable, and yet her breath caught. The wall of ice made a shield around her but didn't touch her, and yet her insides were freezing.

23
CLARITY

Leah rested her head on the side of Fel's long body, while she lay between his paw and tail, as he was curled up and asleep. The slow, up-and-down movement of his breathing was a soothing sound. Still, a knot in her chest kept her awake. Perhaps she was afraid of what she would see if she fell asleep, even if she knew that her dreams had power—strange, uncontrollable power that she understood way too little.

And how much did she grasp about anything? It was highly likely that Cynon—or whatever he was called—was affecting Ironhold, perhaps behind the invasion of Frostlake, and yet they didn't know what his goal was or how to stop him. And the worst was that Fel was in danger. Regardless of whether that prophecy was true or not, *the iron dragon* would always be a target.

"Leah." Fel's voice sounded in her mind, as if it were part of her own imagination, except that it wasn't.

"You should sleep."

He'd flown so far. Even with Ekateni's help, who had taken them to an island far from Fernick, Fel had still flown for more than two hours, not to mention he hadn't rested since facing the boundless by that mountain, when completely outnumbered.

She felt rather than heard a chuckle. "Isn't it too soon for you to be tired of my company?" His voice was playful.

Leah ran her hand over the scales on his tail. She adored those scales, now reflecting the moonlight. "I'm not tired. But I didn't fly."

He took a deeper breath, which now felt more like a crashing wave. "There's so much to do. So much to think. And I don't like the idea of you going to the Iron Citadel. I failed once, when I shouldn't have let you go. You don't want me to repeat my mistake, do you?"

Perhaps Leah should be upset that he wanted to control her, to tell her what to do, but the truth was that she was also afraid— and confused. "What do you suggest?"

"If you ever step foot in that dreadful place, I want to be with you, and yet I can't. I'm powerful—and powerless." He paused, then added, "I want to kiss you—and I can't."

Leah planted a kiss on the scales of his tail. "I'll do it for both of us."

Fel took another deep breath, his silence more eloquent than any words.

"I know," she said. "Not that kind of kiss. I've dreamed about you, though. In this form... And..." Oh, no, had she just been about to tell him that he'd caressed her with his tongue? That she had enjoyed it? She didn't even know what it would be like if it happened in real life. Would she want him to do that as a dragon? She could still recall the soft feel of his tongue on her skin.

But she said something else. "I... I like you this way too." But then, she also wanted to touch human Fel again, to touch him and know that it was reality and not mistake it for a dream. The touch of his human tongue had never left her memory. If she thought about it for a little longer, it would blind her senses to anything but bliss—and want. Oh, what would she give to have him undressing her again, this time with purpose, knowing it was her, then kissing her in more places than she ever thought possible.

Fel curled his body some more, so that she was staring at one of his huge green eyes, then he moved his paw from under her, and ran a talon over the side of her face. Leah closed her eyes, then he pulled her closer. She could feel the warmth of his body, then the lovely scent of his breath. It was fire and iron, but most of all, magic and power. That insane, intense power that made him so magnetic, that had always entranced, captivated her. There was something thrilling and exciting about being so close to such a huge, powerful creature, knowing he could kill her in the blink of an eye if he wished to, knowing that breath could become destructive fire if he wanted to.

"Kiss me," she whispered. She didn't think he'd dare it unless she asked.

His tongue caressed the side of her face so, so softly, while he asked, "Does this count?"

Leah chuckled. "Yes." It was so nice that he could lick and speak at the same time.

He stopped. "I wish I had my human form now. You have no idea how much I'd love to see you again, all of you, to touch you again, then make you mine. If you allow me, of course."

Leah caressed the side of his face. "I can't be yours—physically—right now, but it doesn't mean I can't..." She paused, the words stuck in her throat.

"Say it. I want to hear it. Say it, Leah, say what you're thinking with no fear and no shame. We're better than that."

"That night when I came to you. I wish you hadn't stopped. That night you came to my bedroom, I wish you hadn't left. I wish you had ruined me there and then. And now... I know things are crazy and we have so much to think about and plan, but..." There was where it took some courage. She unbuttoned her top. "You can still see me. You can kiss me if you want. And then tell me what *you* like. I don't know anything about human men and nothing about dragons, but I can learn."

This leather armor was a little uncomfortable, with pants instead of a skirt, but she was glad to get rid of the top, then remove her slip, and feel the night wind caressing her breasts and bringing a chill to her body, then Fel's breath warming her again. Not only his breath, but her own heat now, aching for his touch, a touch like she had dreamed once, that had lulled her to sleep in infinite bliss. Her silver dragon was real, and they were together now.

Leah unbuttoned her pants, and was wondering how to remove them gracefully, when a light caught her attention. Not a light, but a round line on the rock beside her. A fire circle was being formed on the ground. Dragons.

"On my back," Fel said.

She grabbed her jacket and underslip and jumped on him as fast as she could.

How could anyone have found them here, in such a desolate, unreachable place? And most importantly, *who* had found them?

FEL WOULD HAVE to make a decision quickly on whether to fight or fly. Perhaps Leah would also use her magic, but it was better to be prepared just in case. At least the circle being formed was on the ground, meaning that whoever was coming was in human form. Not that it would help much, depending on how much magic they had—and who and how many they were.

He watched closely as the line became a full circle, from where smoke seemed to come in. Fel prepared a blast of fire.

Two people stood in the circle. He almost blasted them, but then he noticed that it was a blond woman and a dark-haired man. In a few more seconds, he recognized Tzaria and Ekateni.

The heat in his chest cooled down. More than relieved, Fel was elated; he and Leah needed help, direction, guidance, and Ekateni and Tzaria were the right people to give it. He did wish they had arrived at a slightly better time, though. Leah jumped from his back, thankfully fully dressed now, and stood near his face.

He then noticed that Tzaria was leaning on Ekateni, and then sat on the ground slowly, as if having difficulty.

"Are you all right?" Fel asked.

"I'm still recovering," Tzaria replied. "That spear was poisoned."

Ekateni walked away from her, so that he was standing as far from her as he could. "She could've died," he said between his teeth, staring at the distance. His anger was palpable, but Fel wasn't sure who it was directed at.

After a moment of awkward silence, Fel realized then that Tzaria didn't know Leah, and said, "This is my betrothed, Leandra, or Leah. And this is Tzaria." Not that he had to introduce the woman, but he felt it would be polite to name her.

Tzaria stared at Leah with some mix of admiration and curiosity. "You can walk in the hollow. And quite far."

"I'm a deathbringer."

It was odd to see her claiming that magic as hers with confidence.

Fel then turned to both his uncle and Tzaria. "I thought you wouldn't come to Aluria."

The woman shook her head. "In normal circumstances, it would be unwise. Some of us can sense dragon magic, dragon energy. There wasn't any in Aluria, and that was why it was safer not to come here, so that the Boundless wouldn't come looking for you. But something changed... I can sense dragon activity in this land. I'm not sure it's you, or..." Her tone became grim. "Perhaps you have company."

Another dragon. Naia was the first thought that came to his mind. Unless... There could be many, many possibilities. Still, should he tell them about his twin? He should definitely tell her about all that had been going on. But instead, he asked, "What do you think has changed?"

Tzaria shrugged. "Again, it could be you. You're in your dragon form, and it might be easier to detect it. Then there could be Boundless in Aluria. I'm sworn to protect you and—"

Ekateni scoffed. "Great protection. To leave him to fend off by himself. Away from his family."

"Nobody knew about him," she said. "It worked."

Fel's uncle turned to Tzaria. "It worked by luck. Sheer luck. Because you never bothered telling me about him, never bothered telling me what happened to my brother."

She rolled her eyes. "You were so willing to listen."

"What happened?" Fel asked. "What happened to my father? You never finished your story." Perhaps they had more urgent matters to discuss, but he felt uneasy with these questions in his mind, uneasy not knowing what had happened.

Ekateni threw his arms in the air. "Oh, she won't say it. Better to keep it all a secret."

Tzaria shook her head. "The secret was to protect him. Now that he's been found, I don't need to hide anything."

Fel's huge heart was beating fast in his chest, with the anticipation of the truth he was about to hear. How could the most powerful dragon mage have died? It didn't make sense. Leah was close to him, her hand on his neck, a touch that brought him some steadying calm.

"So?" Ekateni's voice was still hard.

Tzaria took a deep breath. "I already told him that we came to check on the noxious fae. Their city was isolated, but there was a possibility that the tragedy had been caused by Ironhold, so we went there. Ircantari met princess Ticiane, who ran away with him."

Ekateni frowned. "Wasn't my brother engaged to Relia? He wouldn't—"

"No." Tzaria shook her head. "He never had anything romantic or serious with her. She lied. Lied in order to get attention, sympathy, power. Lied to pose as Ircantari's widow." Tzaria laughed. "I have to admit, her plan worked. But it didn't make any of that true. He fell in love with Ticiane, a princess from Ironhold. You know how we can sometimes see glimpses of the future? He recognized her. He knew she was the one, his companion until his death. He obviously had no idea it would be so soon."

"How?" Fel asked, still puzzled about his father's death.

Tzaria closed her eyes. "We were at an inn. In Umbraar. From where we could check the ruins of Formosa. Ircantari was agitated and planning to leave the next day. He didn't want a confrontation with Ticiane's family, and they had soldiers all over Aluria looking for her."

Ekateni glared at her. "That makes no sense. My brother could easily deal with a few dozen armed human soldiers."

Tzaria shook her head. "At that point, all he feared was a possible confrontation and the repercussions. Also, he didn't want to hurt or kill any innocent. But that morning, that last morning, he woke up and Ticiane was not by his side."

She closed her eyes and took a deep breath. "She left a note, saying she was going to say goodbye to her sister. It was a very small inn in a tiny town with only a tavern and a market. She was at the tavern. When he got there, the place was surrounded with more than thirty men, heavily armed. Someone was holding her by the hair, with a knife on her throat, asking her to take them to the man who had, in their words, dishonored her. As Ircantari approached, they knew it was him right away. Perhaps they recognized him from his visit to Ironhold, or perhaps it was the way he looked at her or she looked at him. These things can be hard to hide. Two guards advanced towards Ircantari. He was going to swap forms and fight, but a thought stopped him."

Tzaria stared at Fel. "He realized Ticiane was pregnant. I doubt there was any recognizable energy in her belly at that point, but perhaps he glimpsed the future. I do not know. He'd been studying Cynon for his entire life, planning to fight him, and recognized Ticiane's child for what it was: an ironbringer dragon. The meaning of it didn't escape him. He realized that if he fought, there was a chance she could be hurt and even killed. Also, if he swapped forms, many people would realize that a dragon had been in a relationship with an ironbringer. Their child would be in danger.

"It killed him to have to do that, to have all that power, all that knowledge, and then, at the time it mattered the most, to have to give it all away. And yet, for him, who had sought knowledge most of his life, it was what made the most sense. It was the only way he could be sure you would survive. He sent me a thought explaining his choice. It was not just words, but an image, a feeling, so I know exactly how much it hurt him to have to have to give up everything, to have to make that huge sacrifice, to have to abandon Ticiane."

She continued, "At that moment, he realized that the only way he could truly protect you was by letting them kill him, letting them think he was just a regular human, someone of no importance, with no magic. He asked me to leave Aluria, to avoid coming here, so that nobody would suspect your existence. That's what I did. Risomu also received his message, also knows what happened. To honor our friend's sacrifice, we did our part. As time went by and I saw how much the Boundless were infiltrating every dragon group, I understood the wisdom of keeping silent, of hiding this truth from everyone, regardless of the personal cost."

"You could have told me," Ekateni said.

"Right." Tzaria snorted. "Because you love your brother's child so much that in the first opportunity you found out he was the iron dragon, you agreed with having a big party, so that he would be an obvious target."

Ekateni exhaled. "They already knew about his ironbringing. It wasn't a secret anymore."

"You didn't have to announce it to everyone, make such a deal out of it."

"It wouldn't have made a difference," Ekateni said. "They would have found him regardless."

Tzaria shook her head, as if in disbelief. Her words were circling in Fel's head. Ircantari's death had been tragic, but he still wasn't sure Tzaria had handled it the best way. "You couldn't have known I would survive. I..." It felt odd to say the words aloud. "I was born without hands, and because of that, I was almost left to die."

"Almost," Tzaria said. "Ircantari asked me to trust that his spirit would look over you, would protect you. I assume you were raised with love and in great privilege, were you not?"

That was true. "I was. My father... adoptive father... He's great." He felt Leah's hand flinch. She had her own reasons not to share the same opinion about Azir, which he understood, and wished he could comfort her more.

Tzaria nodded. "To let go... To trust... It's hard. You have no idea how hard it is. How hard it was to be sitting in Fernick with no idea if you had even been born, if you were alive, if you were well, and yet I had made a promise and planned to keep it."

There was something else bothering Fel. "Do you think I can make a difference? Against Cynon?"

"Yes, but I don't think you should see it as a burden, as a responsibility, as something on your shoulders. Nobody does anything on their own. I'll help you. Even your grumpy uncle here will help you. Perhaps all you'll have to do is to be a link in a chain. Either way, Ircantari also protected you out of love, not because he thought you'd be a weapon. If he hid you, and meant for you to survive, it was because you were his son. He knew that the words of the seer would make you a target, but I don't think he was sure how literally those words should be taken."

Fel took a slow, calming breath, even if he wasn't sure how slow any breathing would be in these powerful lungs he didn't quite understand. Were they even lungs, if they produced fire? "If Ircantari's spirit protected me... Is he still..."

"The dead don't often communicate with the living, unless they have to, and don't usually do it after so much time has passed. He made sure you'd be protected, and perhaps you have to trust what he set up for you."

Fel was trying to digest these words, trying to grasp the enormity of this revelation, trying to understand how such a powerful dragon had given up his own life for him.

They were silent for a moment, until Leah said, "We're glad you came, as we need help. We're pretty sure the vessel is here. In Aluria."

"What makes you think so?" Tzaria asked. She didn't sound concerned, probably still deeming it impossible for Cynon to be on this continent.

Leah proceeded to tell her what River had told them, about the ceremony that had reawakened Cassius. Neither Tzaria nor Ekateni were surprised that a fae had been in the Iron Citadel, probably unaware of the effect of ironbringing. Still, Leah told them that River had previously met Ircantari and that he was interested in defeating Cynon as well, and managed to avoid mentioning Naia. Fel wasn't sure if keeping her existence a secret was a good idea, but it didn't hurt to be extra careful. Leah also told them what she had seen in the hollow, with the white fae talking about a being breaking barriers between realms and conquering them, and how it all fit.

Tzaria bit her lip. "There are many ways Cynon can affect people. The easiest way is when he influences them and they don't know it, but there needs to be an opening for that, an affinity, let's say. Now, what you're talking about..."

"When was the ceremony?" Ekateni asked, his tone urgent.

"Yesterday or the day before," Leah said. "We want to plan a way to kill Cassius—for good this time, but—"

"This time?" Tzaria narrowed her eyes. "What do you mean this time?"

"I killed him. Or thought so." She raised both her hands. "Look, he deserved it."

Tzaria and Ekateni exchanged grim looks. The woman said, "The *vessel*, it's different. It means Cynon himself is among us, using someone like a puppet. Now, a few conditions must be met. The vessel needs royal blood, which is obviously the case, and needs to have been in the realm between life and death, which, again, seems to be the case. It will allow Cynon not only to influence people here, but to use his magic, and to come to this world."

"We understand that," Leah said. "And that's why we want to kill Cassius soon. We just need a proper plan."

Fel added, "Now that you're here, we're hoping you can help us."

Tzaria shook her head. "Soon might not be good enough. What the vessel can do is open a door to another realm. If he opens our world to the eleventh realm, I can't even imagine what he could do. That is the job of the vessel: to allow him to come."

Leah sighed. "I can take you to the Iron Citadel and you can kill him."

"It won't be that easy. He'll have access to Cynon's magic. We need to think..." She sighed.

Ekateni was scratching his chin, and said, "We could find the place where he's building the frame for the fissure. I don't think it would go unnoticed."

Fel asked, "What should it look like?"

"A circle," Tzaria said. "Dragons travel in circles, sometimes called faerie circles. But... to open to another world, it would need to be massive. I don't think it would use stones, but iron." She sighed. "If he's been influencing people in this land, they might have been building something like that."

Leah was pale and covered her mouth with her hand. "Would a dome around a city work? A dome made of iron and glass?"

NAIA STILL COULDN'T QUITE UNDERSTAND why she was surrounded by a wall of ice and what was happening. "River?"

He stared at her. "You still don't know what's happening?"

"I'm not sure."

"No." He scoffed. "Of course not. There's a difference between knowing and accepting something, isn't there?"

Naia stared at the dagger. It felt faint and distant now, and the metal in the room wasn't overwhelming her as much. This wasn't just ice, but something that blocked part of her magic—but only part of it. She could still kill River. The question was whether she wanted to.

Unless this was not what she was thinking.

"Tell me what's going on," she said, with a faint trace of hope that he would give her an answer that would contradict her fears.

"I'll do even better. What about some company? Someone who likes to babble and babble and babble? I'm sure you'll love it. Meanwhile, I have things to do." He frowned. "Places to go."

How could he stare at her, so confident, while he had an iron dagger on his belt? Did he underestimate her magic that much?

"You're the vessel, aren't you?" There. She asked it.

He approached the ice in front of her, pressed a hand against it, and leaned on it. "A vessel is empty. I'm full." He was so, so close. Naia could feel the energy of the iron in his dagger thrumming, calling to her. It would be as quick as she'd done with Cassius—and yet she hesitated.

He smiled. "Oh, if you could kill me. Wouldn't it solve everything? Save all your people?" He was taunting her, and it didn't make sense. The dagger was just there. On his belt, yes, but it would be as easy to cut his throat as if she were physically holding it against his neck. Her hands trembled while she tried to gather the courage to do it, to end it all. Tears dripped down her eyes and still she did not dare do what she had to do. He then added, "Don't worry. As long as you amplify my magic, you won't be harmed."

He then disappeared in a cloud of black smoke.

Naia almost called his name, but it would be futile. He was gone. How long had he been gone? Had he been controlled before? Could she get River back? Or was he dead? She didn't know anything.

One thing she knew, though. Only a complete idiot would

encase her in a wall of ice, in a room with so much metal. It was almost as if he wanted her to escape.

Unless...

Naia recalled River's last words, when he had still seemed scared and confused. *Part of me... Still...*

Then he had leaned so close, telling her that killing him would solve everything, daring her. And yet she had failed. Failed, failed, failed.

No. If Cynon was from another realm and was just using River, how much would it have helped to kill the vessel? Perhaps it would have delayed Cynon, delayed him long enough for her to find a solution, to save her people.

Dizzy and with a bitter taste in her mouth, she was unsure what to do and where to go. She had to find Fel and warn him as soon as possible, but she wouldn't be able to reach him now. They had to redo their plans, think. And yet it all felt so empty without River. Where was he? What was he doing?

Naia lit a flame on her hand, about to melt that wall of ice, then recalled something else he'd told her. She would have company. Someone who liked to babble. The flame faded.

Never show your true power to your enemies. Her father's words sounded appropriate now. But then, if Cynon was using River, wouldn't he know everything? Maybe not. Maybe yes. Questions, questions, so many questions and uncertainty in this horrific reality.

Someone who liked to babble. Hopefully it was true and she would get some answers. Naia was not afraid. Even with the strange ice around her, she felt safe in this room with so much metal—unless she had to fight ironbringers, which wasn't an impossibility, considering she was in the Iron Citadel.

Naia could try to escape now, while alone, while she had a chance. Or she could trust River's word and wait. If he still had his magic... he was still a white fae. He couldn't lie. The wall around her was real ice, truly cold. Was it fae magic? She recalled River telling her about the Dragon Lair and how he had almost been encased in ice, and yet his account had been different. It had not been a barrier, but something that was making him cold, that could kill him quickly. This was just a strange prison, with some magic-blocking property. What kind of magic was this?

What was River thinking or feeling right now? Was he conscious? Was it truly a part of him that had wanted to keep her safe, or was she trying to cling to a comfortable lie just so she could forgive herself for failing to stop him? The moment she'd seen him killing his father, there had been something wrong, and yet she had never suspected anything. She still didn't know since when River had been a vessel.

The iron dragon. Oh, no. If Cynon could see everything River saw, then he would know where Fel was. Naia had to warn him. But how?

If she left now, what was she going to do? Try to climb the mountains? Naia was so angry. Why hadn't she taken the time to give Leah a communication mirror? Or perhaps she could wait for this person who was going to come and *babble*, wait based on the hope that there was a part of River trying to help her. She had barely learned to trust him. Could she trust a part of him that might have been influenced by Cynon?

24
ALONE

Naia was in the Iron Citadel, down in its entrails. So much iron, so much iron magic, more than she had ever thought was possible. Inside her, a cold, hollow space. And some regret. She *had* noticed River had not been acting like himself, *had* noticed there had been something wrong, and yet had chosen not to see to the truth.

And her truth now was that she felt lost, with no idea what to do. She couldn't even call her brother or find him, and didn't even know if she would be able to step into the hollow. The idea of leaving through a hidden door down in the abyss didn't feel that appealing when she considered the possibility of facing giant spiders and even some Ironhold forces. Well, she did still have her magic, which was quite handy in a place with so much metal. Perhaps she could face a couple of spiders. And then perhaps she could use her other magic—and try to walk in the hollow. It had felt so easy with River. Had it been him? Or something else? *Part of me still...* What did it mean?

Her heart was pounding in her chest, pumping blood through her body, as she stood and waited, while the truth of what had just transpired washed over her. A bitter feeling, a bitter taste, and so much anger at herself were her companions. She had known something had been wrong in the Ancient City, she had felt that it hadn't been River, and then... All the evidence had been standing in front of her, while she'd been distracted with his lovely face. Lovely, lovable, sweet—a face she adored—now a vessel for some ancient evil. Would there have been a way to prevent it? Or had they always been doomed? She had failed to kill him—and would keep failing as long as she thought there was a chance to get River back.

She touched the surface of the ice, and realized it didn't melt even with the heat of her hand. There was something magical about it, unnatural. What if her fire wouldn't destroy it and she'd been imagining things, imagining River trying to help her? What if she was about to be trapped here? She could still try to slip into the hollow—unless this ice wall had some magic blocking it. And yet she stood and waited, leaning on a foolish hope that she was about to get more information, about to learn something that could make a difference. She trusted the wisp of River that might have been still in that vessel.

A sound from behind her made her turn. There was another door there, a door made of iron, now moving and revealing someone walking in. The image was blurry through the wall of ice, but the steps were feminine, walking in her direction. *Someone who liked to babble*. It was true. Naia knew who it was: Queen Kara.

"Look at that," the queen said as she approached her. "The Umbraar princess. A filthy harlot just like Princess Ticiane, opening her legs for any scum who'll take her."

Those words about her mother, they would have been infuriating in any other circumstance. As it was, Naia was too numb to feel any anger. "At least they'll take me. Can *you* say the same?"

The queen laughed. "Funny you. I, too, had my prime. And I have a secret to tell you: it fades. Beauty and youth don't last, silly girl. Only power lasts."

"And you have power?" Naia was quite curious.

"Do I? Oh, no." Kara then made a mocking voice. "Of course I don't. I'm the silly little queen, chosen at a contest, picked like an animal to breed ironbringers to this family. I'm so little and insignificant and powerless, poor little me." She pouted.

Naia recalled some of what River had told her, hoping it had been truly River. "You're behind everything, aren't you?"

The queen laughed. "Am I? What is *everything*?"

So this was true, at least from her point of view. Fair, the woman was babbling, but Naia had to make her give up some information instead of spouting nonsense.

Power. Perhaps the key was power. The queen didn't want to be seen as useless. Naia had to work with that to her advantage.

"I guess not. You're just helping your husband, aren't you?"

Kara laughed again. She seemed to be enjoying the conversation. "My dear harlot princess, my husband is nothing. Nothing. He thinks he's king, he thinks he owns me, he thinks I'm useless. He's wrong."

"But your husband was behind this, wasn't he?" Naia insisted, hoping she'd incense the woman. "Planning the army of ironbringers?"

She snorted. "Army of ironbringers... It was an excuse. An excuse. When he realized he could bend the magic laws of Aluria, he came up with this idea. It meant he had the sacred duty to impregnate other women. Poor King Harold, made so much sacrifice for his kingdom. But you see, while he was busy, I was busy too. Busy connecting to a greater power. Soon Harold will be dead—and I'll be greater than him—and immortal."

That made no sense. "Everyone's soul is immortal."

"Exactly. It's why I choose to have my soul continue to live in this world, instead of going who knows where."

Was the plan to have Cassius be king? One of his brothers? Why? Naia had to keep prodding, keep trying to find out something useful.

"Cassius will be king, then." No, he wasn't going to become anything in this life, but Naia didn't want to confess that she knew he was dead. In fact, why was this woman here instead of up there, mourning her son?

"Cassius..." Kara snorted. "Just one of the little monsters I made for King Harold. An empty monster now. There's nothing there. He's not going to be king, he's not going to be anything. But he was useful. His life energy fueled the magic of someone much more deserving."

Naia was disgusted. This woman had sacrificed her own son? And didn't even feel bad about it? "So you're serving this someone who's much more deserving?"

"I serve nobody," she snarled. "I serve no one. Never again. The great one depends on me, he's gaining life again thanks to me. Me. I'm the master."

Naia doubted that it was the case, but didn't think it wise to tell her. Instead, she said, "I'll break this ice and defeat you, then."

"Oh, silly princess. You think you can break this. Let me tell you a secret: only dragon magic can undo this ice."

Naia chuckled involuntarily. Did she really not know what Naia was? This... this was great.

From behind the ice, Kara smiled. "You think it's funny."

"I mean... dragons. Who still believes in dragons?" She tried to look sad. "Am I going to die here?"

Kara sighed. "That's what it looks like, doesn't it? Don't ask. Don't beg. I can't do anything about it. I just came to take a look at the princess who caused me so much grief."

"I did?"

"Nothing too bad, I guess. You should be dead, you know? You and your brother. Alone, in a desolate lake, in another kingdom. Who is stupid enough to do that? I guess you and your brother. Harold had explosive magic, and he thought the fae was working for him. Poor thing, he thought it was his idea. They both thought. The fae was going to create the illusions, and you two were going to be killed—tragically, I must add."

The fae... illusions...River? But he had said he didn't know anything about the watersnake. "Why didn't we die?"

"The Frostlake princess was there. How or why, I do not know. The plan was abandoned. Some explosives still went off, and the fae did his part."

"He brought a watersnake to the lake?"

"The fae is not a wildbringer, harlot princess. He does not command animals. But he can create impressive illusions."

True. Had River lied to her? "Was it you who convinced the fae to work for Ironhold?"

"It was the great one. Found him between life and death, a stroke of luck, the perfect vessel. It was easy to bring him to the Iron Citadel, both my stupid husband and the silly fae thinking they were tricking each other. The fae was being *prepared*. His body now houses someone much more deserving."

"Everything's happening because of River?"

"River." Kara scoffed. "What a silly, girly name. But no, nothing is thanks to your River. When you're a hunter, you wait. You sit, wait, and watch. Eventually, the prey shows up. He is perfect, mind you. I'll make sure to get rid of those hideous horns, of course." What? She planned to mutilate River? "But other than that, he doesn't look bad. And he has so much magic, magic that's now serving the great one."

Naia was fuming at the thought that someone wanted to use River as if he were a piece of meat. "If this great one is so great, why does he need someone else's magic?"

"The body has its limitations, my stupid princess. He will transcend that body, of course, he will get his own body back, but, meanwhile, he has just gained access to some incredible magic. It's a pity all you can do is amplify his magic, and you have none of your own. He said you didn't even have ironbringing like your brother. So sad."

Kara... didn't know Naia was an ironbringer? If she had gotten this information from River, he wouldn't be able to lie. Wait. *No ironbringing like her brother.* It was true; her ironbringing was not like her brother. Sneaky sentence. "Why would you be happy if I had magic?"

"Why? Take a guess."

Naia had no idea. "You'd love it if I killed you right now?"

"No. Absolutely not. You don't think your body is going to be wasted, do you?"

"Oh, you plan to inhabit it?" She almost said *over my dead body*, but that was literally the point.

"I will, my dear princess, I will. To be fair, if I could choose, I'd pick someone prettier, but the natural magical affinity between you and the fae will help my union with the great one."

Oh, gross. The thought was disturbing. Naia had to escape as soon as possible, before River and whatever was inside him returned, but she also had to get some answers.

"Call me sceptical, but I doubt you could conceive such a grand plan and elude everyone, even your husband." She hoped she didn't sound too desperate for an answer.

The woman burst laughing. "You think it's hard? You are really a dumb princess, aren't you?" Her satisfied tone was a good sign. "Let me tell you a secret: men are dumb. And yet they think they are so smart. They had been bringing earth from Mount Prime, happy to elude the magical laws of Aluria, unaware of the guidance it also brought. Men don't pay attention to voices, to whispers. I did, and I found the great one. Then, when Formosa fell, Ironhold thought it was their chance to dominate the sea—but it never happened. They were so silly, focused on gold, on trade. And yet, they didn't realize what their deed opened. When your silly fae appeared, I was told what role he could to play, and helped convince my husband to take him in. The fae thought he was serving Harold, but, meanwhile, I was making sure he was being surrounded by the energy of the great one. The fae was easy to work with, pliable like mud, until the gathering, when he started having his own mind. The great one told me a girl was interfering with his magic. At first, the plan was to kill you, but then, we had a better idea. Eventually, to get the fae back on track, I had to keep him for an entire day in a room with Cynon's magic, lying to him that it was death grass."

She laughed. "Death grass, what a nonsensical lie. Then I made one of my stupid sons overhear something and release him. Poor little Venard, he probably still thinks he has played hero. The fae was supposed to escape—to continue his plan, to open the gates to the Great Mage's magic."

There was so much satisfaction and pride in her tone, and yet, Kara was not that important after all, just someone who heard Cynon and did his bidding. "So you're working for the great one," Naia said. "You do know that, don't you?"

"Working *with* him. There are only two kinds of people: the powerful and the pathetic. I choose to align with the powerful."

"No." Naia suppressed her laughter. "You choose to *serve* the powerful, which makes you pathetic."

"The great mage *loves me*, and together we'll be the greatest of all."

"You're a pawn. Can't you see?" Naia didn't even know why she was saying it.

"You are jealous because you just realized your fae is worthless. You're jealous because you're powerless."

"What about your sons? You don't care what happens to them?"

"Little monsters bred for a pathetic excuse of man? No. I do not care. Love only makes you suffer. They made sure I had an iron heart, and I became what they made me. Never again would I love a powerless creature. It leads to pain."

River's words telling what had happened to Kara's family came to Naia's mind, and she felt pity. "You were afraid you'd lose them. But isn't it a greater loss to never love?"

"My love is given to someone worthy, and nobody less."

Goodness. That woman thought she loved Cynon, and worse, thought he loved her back. Who knew? Perhaps he did like her. Naia had to focus, had to try to get information. "Was it Ironhold who destroyed Formosa?"

She shrugged. "No idea. What would they tell silly little me? All I know was what I felt right after: like a door had been opened, a door to a greater power. Death and pain, they have incredible magical properties—if you know how to use them. I don't think Ironhold knew the power they had just accessed. Pity."

"So now you'll take my body and do what?"

"Become Ironhold's new queen, of course. As long as someone who resembles Harold sits on the throne, nobody will question much."

Of course. River could pretend to be a different person.

The queen continued, "They'll pretend I died, and he'll have a new wife."

Yuck. "I'm King Harold's niece!"

Kara waved a hand. "Nobody will care. And it's not like your body is going to touch Harold's body. It will only touch the fae's body—without the horns, of course. They're so disgusting. And those nails!"

Naia had had enough. And enough information. She ripped a piece of one of the doors and made it fly towards Queen Kara. She meant it to nick her neck, the way she'd done to Cassius, but the piece came with too much speed and ended up severing her head.

Horrified, Naia turned around as she heard the body thudding on the floor. It had been so fast that the queen hadn't even screamed. It had been a clean, merciful kill. All Naia could feel was pity for this woman void of love, void of feelings, thinking she was finding freedom and yet setting her hopes on another man, allowing herself to be used for him. She had even sacrificed her own son! Cassius had been horrible, but still.

After a deep breath, Naia lit a flame on her hand and directed it at the ice, which started to melt fairly quickly, freeing her in a matter of seconds. Naia stepped out, but then noticed something on the floor. A black dagger. River's. She remembered the first time she'd seen him wearing it, in the Ancient city, and his sister had found it strange.

No, she had asked about the *red* dagger, not the black one.

This was River's, and had been left under the ice. Naia took it. *A part of me...* Had he left it for her? It had magic, she could feel it, but it was familiar magic... his magic. She closed her eyes and slipped into the hollow. So many circles, and she had no idea where to go, and how to start. Naia had to stop Cynon. She knew he was in River's body, and could also be pretending to be Ironhold's king. Could be pretending to be anyone.

The question was how to stop him.

Fel sensed Leah trembling. Could it be?

Tzaria perked up. "You have something like that in Aluria? A large iron circle?"

"Yes." Leah's voice was cracking. "In Frostlake."

A portal to a prison realm opening in Leah's city would be a disaster. Fel was hoping that wasn't the case. "That dome has been there for a long time, though."

"Sixteen years," Leah said. "And my father was friends with king Harold, from Ironhold. If Cynon has been affecting them..."

That couldn't be true. "For that long?"

Tzaria was thoughtful. "Time passes differently in other realms." She paused. "We'll have to destroy that dome. Just in case."

Leah's eyes widened. "It's winter down there. The city won't be prepared."

"I'm sure cold is preferable to dealing with denizens from a prison realm." Tzaria's voice was hard.

Leah looked down. "I guess I could try to warn the people."

"Can you take us there?" Tzaria asked. "Just to check?"

Fel hesitated, fearing it would be a long flight. "It's just a matter of following the mountains towards the south, but it's quite far."

Tzaria glanced at Ekateni, who nodded. She then turned to Fel and Leah. "That's not a problem. We have to check this dome.

If it's the kind of circle that could be used to bring in the eleventh realm, we have no choice but to destroy it as soon as possible, before Cynon gets to it."

That part didn't bother Fel. "I can do that easily with my iron magic. If we're sure it needs to be done."

"We'd better go," Ekateni said, then asked, "Can you just show us the way?"

"Of course." Fel had never meant to imply that he didn't want to help.

Leah then climbed on his back, while his uncle swapped forms and took Tzaria in his claws.

The cool night wind caressed Fel's wings as he glided over the mountains, Ekateni beside him, in his beautiful dragon form.

Fel wondered if he should have warned Naia, but then, they were just going to check the dome. The night should keep them hidden and safe, even in a kingdom controlled by Ironhold. He'd try to remain near the mountains and check Frostlake City from a distance. And then they would still need to figure out a way to take down Cassius and defeat Cynon.

Too much to do.

Too little time.

Fel was expecting to have to fly all the way to Frostlake, but then heard Ekateni's voice.

"I'll make a circle for us, but you have to be quick, as it won't last long. It will take us south."

A bright fire ring appeared in the sky, and Fel flew through it, followed by his uncle. He was still over the Aluria Mountains, but the air was colder here.

He sent a thought to Leah. "Tap on my back when we're close to Frostlake City. Can you recognize it from here?"

"It should be visible from the mountains," she said. Her voice was muffled by the sound of the wind, but somehow he could still hear it.

It was a good thing they had gone through that ring, as his wings were still tired from flying from Fernick. There were now some flurries in the sky, and the top of the mountains had a white blanket of snow. He could sense that the air was cooler, but he didn't feel cold in the way he would in his human form, as something unpleasant. Instead, the temperature was still comfortable for him. His worry was for Leah, leaning on top of him, wearing clothes that were not warm enough for this freezing weather. Hopefully his own body heat would be enough to keep her comfortable.

"I think we're getting close," she whispered, that odd whisper that could still be heard even with the wind in his ears. "I can see a river that's not too far from the city."

Fel was unsure if his uncle heard her, and said, "We're close to the—"

"I heard her," Ekateni said, then added, "But look. What's that?"

In the dark, it was hard to see, and Fel almost flew lower to get a better look, when he realized that would be stupid. Instead, he glided near the mountains.

Down below, several tents bordered a stream. "Is this a village or something, Leah?"

"No. There shouldn't be anyone here. It looks... It looks like a military campground, but I'm not sure."

Fel was trying to understand what was happening. "This is north of Frostlake city. Would they be moving to attack Ironhold? Or to join them?"

"I can go and check," Leah offered.

That was a dreadful idea. "Too dangerous. And it's not like they'll have signs saying what they're planning to do. Soldiers sometimes don't even know where they are being sent or why, and generals aren't going to be spilling plans out loud in the middle of the night."

Tzaria then said, "Let's not worry about it yet. What we need to do is see the dome over the city." Her voice was also clear.

"We're almost there," Leah said, and Fel was thankful that she didn't insist on the idea of going down there to check on troops that could have Ironhold soldiers.

They kept flying south. Fel still didn't understand that odd movement of troops. If they were walking, they would take some three days to reach Ironhold. Well, it was possible that they were gathering armies from allied kingdoms in Aluria. The question was for what. The dreadful possibilities made his insides curl.

Something else that was bothering him was the possibility that the Frostlake dome would need to be destroyed. He hadn't missed the disappointment and sadness in Leah's eyes when Tzaria had suggested that. Hopefully it would turn out that the dome could not be used as a faerie circle, dragon ring, or whatever, and they would just leave it alone. They still had to kill Cassius and stop Ironhold and Cynon, and that was already more than they could handle.

More and more snowflakes fluttered in the air. Even though they were falling slowly, they hit Fel's face with some strength because of his speed, so he had to squint not to get snow in his eyes. Again, it wasn't so much the cold, but the physical sensation of something striking him. His worry was for Leah, who was now leaning down with most of her body touching his back. Hopefully the snow wouldn't hurt her face. Tzaria's position, cradled in Ekateni's claws, started to make more sense. She was probably more protected and warm.

At least they should get there soon. Perhaps it had been hasty and irresponsible to come here like this, without much planning or thinking. But then, Tzaria was worried that the vessel could be opening this portal right now. It seemed unlikely, considering that the troops were north of the city, but checking couldn't hurt anyone.

"I think it's over there," he heard Leah's voice in his head.

"Where there's a light?" Fel asked.

"Yes."

It meant flying away from the relative safety of the mountains, but again, they were high enough that nobody would hear their wings.

There were a few houses outside the dome, with thin trails of smoke coming from chimneys. Further down, he did see the majestic dome, where he had once floated holding Leah in his arms. Now he was truly flying. Still, he wished he could float again in his human form, wished for peace and quiet, wished to spend days reading by a fireplace, then talking about books with Leah. He wasn't sure if any of that would ever be real. Some dreams were so simple and yet simple sometimes was so distant.

Leah shivered and tensed on top of him. "Something..."

"What?"

Ekateni approached them, and Tzaria asked, "Can you sense the magic?"

Yes. Now that he paid attention, it was obvious. Fel could smell it the same way he could smell a forest fire kilometers away. This... It was not deathbringing or ironbringing or anything he knew. He wasn't sure what it was and felt a sudden chill in what felt like his stomach—if he even had one.

"Yes," he said. "I don't know what it is."

Ekateni said, "It's similar to dragon magic, coming from the city. Quite strong. And... Maybe..."

"Fire ring magic," Tzaria added.

"Should we..." Fel was going to say turn back, but realized it didn't make sense. It wasn't as if they could go and get reinforcements if things were really going wrong. "What should we do?"

"We'll approach," Tzaria said. "If the ring is being activated, we'll have to destroy it as soon as possible. If there are people protecting it, we'll have to fight them."

They would be outnumbered. But then, he and Ekateni could overpower a small army.

Leah said, "They won't have forces protecting the city or the dome. They're away. Our army was small. Even with the reinforcements and invaders from Ironhold... There won't be much resistance."

Still, approaching Frostlake city could be dangerous. "Leah," Fel said, "Perhaps you should stay back."

"It's my city and my people. I know them well. I know the dome. Drop me off near enough so I can support you." Her request was fair.

"Fine."

Fel's thunderous heart was beating with more force than usual, perhaps partly from the effort in flying, partly in anticipation of what he was going to see. Hopefully nothing had been activated yet and they could just destroy the dome and be gone. Yes, it would be tragic for the people in the city and even the castle, but they should be able to survive the night. If the dome was only sixteen years old, most buildings should still have the infrastructure necessary to withstand the winter.

Ekateni lowered his flight, and Fel did the same.

Even his worst fears had not prepared him for what he saw.

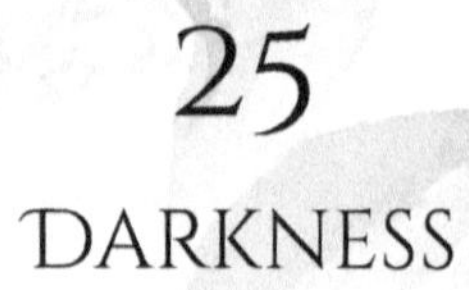

25

DARKNESS

As darkness dissipated, Naia found herself in a hallway with dried vines on its walls. The Ancient castle. The last time she'd been here was when River had decided to become *the prince his father wanted*. He had to have been himself to make such a personal decision, and yet, it hadn't truly been him.

"Stop!" a man yelled.

Naia turned to see two Ancient guards, both of them with red eyes and white hair, pointing bronze swords at her. Disarming them would be incredibly easy, but this time she wasn't going to run.

"I'm your queen, and I'd like to see princess Anelise." She hoped it would work, hoped there wasn't some strange loophole that would invalidate her authority. But then, she could always fight, and there was no lack of metal in this castle, even if they didn't use iron.

The guards lowered their swords right away, then bowed slightly. No hesitation in their movements, and she wasn't even sure if they knew who she was. But then... as far as she knew, there was magic binding the guards to their rulers, so perhaps they had sensed it. It had been smart of River to name her queen. Hopefully she would know what to do with that power.

The same fae who had yelled then said, "We'll take you to her right away. Follow us."

They couldn't lie, so he couldn't be tricking her. Technically he could take Naia to Anelise and then kill her or something, but he wouldn't take her anywhere else, like a magic prison, for example.

The prison.

Could that place contain River? Contain Cynon? And if it did, how could she bring him here? Anelise would have some answer —if she even wanted to talk to Naia, after everything.

The guards descended two flights of stairs and Naia followed them closely, trying to ignore how much that palace felt dead and barren. The dry vines lining the walls were a horrific reminder that this place would soon face its end, unless someone did something. And then, wasn't all Aluria about to fall into an abyss of despair? Unless someone did something. But who? And what?

The guards stopped at a rough, small wooden door. Without knocking, they opened it, revealing a small room with wooden shelves and a dark wooden circular table. Five fae were looking at a map. If they were saying something, Naia didn't catch what it was, as they stopped and stared at the door. Anelise was sitting by another female fae, also with white hair and red eyes, but hers were a little lighter. There were three more fae there: two men and one woman.

Anelise glared at Naia. "What do you want?" Then she added, in a mocking tone, "Your Majesty."

"I need to talk to you. Alone."

"We can talk here," she said. "We have no secrets."

"Alone, please," Naia insisted. The other fae in the room were likely trustworthy, but not enough to listen to what was happening to River. "Somewhere where we can't be heard."

Anelise exhaled, then turned to her friends. "I'll be right

back." She got up and walked towards Naia. "Where would you like to go?"

Did she expect Naia to say she didn't know? Was she meaning to humiliate her or something? It wasn't going to work. "I want you to lead me to a place where we can talk and won't be heard. You know this castle better than I do."

She bit her lip. "Of course."

They climbed three sets of stairs and went to her bedroom, that same room where they had talked before, when things had been so different. The guards remained outside.

Once they were alone, Anelise scowled. "Was it a plan? Were you and River—"

"No. I had no idea he was going to kill his father—and neither did he."

The fae blinked slowly. "What do you mean?"

"He's..." It felt strange to say these words out loud. "At that time he was being influenced by this... immortal dragon who lives in another realm. Dragon lord, as you call them. Now this evil dragon has completely taken him over. And it's disastrous." There was a chair on the corner, and Naia collapsed there, unable to hold it any longer. "And your city is all dry, and everything is wrong." She took a deep breath and pushed down the tears threatening to come out. "You care about River, I know it. I need help."

Anelise stared at her for a while, then said, "So you mean that it wasn't really River who killed our father?"

"I... It was partly him, had to be. But something changed in River, it was as if he was no longer himself. The moment he walked back, all dressed up, with those daggers." Naia recalled that detail. "The red one, it did something. Do you know that dagger?"

A shadow crossed her eyes. "Maybe. We had objects like that, but tucked deep within..." She stared at Naia. "The vaults in the library."

"It's where he said he was going..."

Anelise swallowed. "Before we go on, swear that you had no intention of stealing our throne."

"No! I didn't know he was going to do that. And if you think about it, it's horrible. From what I understand, your king has tremendous power over you, which means this immortal dragon could have access to your people, your warriors, your resources, weapons... And you wouldn't be able to do anything. Unless there's a way to remove River from the throne, without..." She looked down. Perhaps the easiest way would be to kill him, and perhaps her hesitation would put too many innocents in danger.

"Killing him." Anelise had the courage to spit the words Naia could not. "I wouldn't want that either, and we can't even do it. Not without a good reason. The magic binding us to our king—and protecting him—is quite strong."

That magic could have horrific consequences. "Which is a problem, considering he's no longer himself. And then we still need to at least find a temporary solution for your city. I don't want you all isolated and dying here. I need a strategy to at least... mitigate this mess."

Any trace of anger was gone from Anelise's eyes. "Tell me more about this evil dragon, and I'll tell you what we know. That dagger... if it is what I think it is..." She bit her lip. "I might have answers for you, but I don't think you'll like them."

FEL REMEMBERED the dome over the castle in Frostlake as something delicate, brilliant against the snow around it, alive with the lights of the castle and the houses at night. This was a city he had seen from above before.

What stood before him was something completely different.

Dark tendrils of smoke spread within the dome. The circle itself, around the city, shone with a subtle but strange reddish glow. There was no doubt that he'd need to destroy that dome, but then, what exactly was inside it? For a moment, he feared tearing down that dome and unleashing unspoken horrors upon Aluria. But that made no sense. The city was the most inhabited place in a large radius. If anything, they had to try to protect the people inside it.

Leah's anxiety was palpable, even if he couldn't see her. She asked, "Do you know what's happening?"

He was about to reply when he realized the question was for the other dragons.

"They..." Tzaria's voice was quivering. "They opened it. He already opened it."

Ekateni then said, "They look like they're from the fourth realm. Not the worst yet. We need to destroy the circle, so that we won't see more of these things."

"We'll need to fight them too," Leah said. "These things are dangerous."

From that distance, it was hard to make out their shapes, but perhaps... The magic was not that alien. They were like the creatures Leah had summoned in Umbraar, the creatures which had helped them win for a short period, but then could have taken their lives.

"Cynon will be here," Tzaria said. "This won't be easy. Isofel, you should turn back."

What? "That makes no sense. If I'm supposed to make a difference because of my iron magic, if it was something that was foreseen, why would you stop me from using my ironbringing when it's needed?"

He got no reply, only silence, until Ekateni said, "Let's be careful."

"I will."

Fel's impression was that Cynon—or his vessel—would be inside the dome. That dome. All the metal in it called Fel, spoke to him. Reaching out and breaking it would be as easy as grabbing something with his metal hands. So far there were no guards and nobody outside the city, so they were unopposed. For now.

But there could be other problems. "When I destroy the dome, these things will be unleashed, won't they?"

Tzaria's voice was grim. "They would be unleashed regardless. I'm sure they'll break the top of the structure so they can get out and still use it as a portal. The longer you take to break it, the more creatures will come."

"I'll be quick. Then what?"

"Fire," Ekateni said. "If they are the ones I think they are, dragon fire will stop them."

Fel almost asked *what if they aren't*, but he figured it was best to focus on the dome for now.

"Leah, where can I leave you?"

"I..." He could sense her fear, her hesitation. Her home was being destroyed, defiled with unimaginable horrors. "I have to go, Fel. I'll be right back. I have to do this." She meant going into the hollow. At this time, in this place, when all this was happening? It was madness.

THERE WAS a secret vault under the Ancient library, and Naia was following Anelise there, after telling most of what she knew about River and Cynon. In retrospect, even some of River's previous behavior had been odd. His motivation for being in Ironhold had always struck her as flimsy and poorly founded, and then there had been so many little things here and there that made no sense. If he had been slightly affected by something else, it explained a lot—unless she was trying to make excuses for him. This would be the perfect excuse: *it wasn't me. I had an evil voice inside my head.* Naia didn't even know if it was a voice or what.

Anelise had heard her with attention, agreeing with most of her points, then brought her down here. Naia wouldn't have imagined that she would be following a fae to a secret vault mere days after being imprisoned in this city. But then, Anelise had never threatened her.

They were in a corridor under the library, when the fae said, "To be honest, ambition was something that River never displayed. It was the opposite, in fact: a complete lack of interest and involvement... But then, if he's a mindmelder and feared his power, I guess it might explain why he didn't want to use it."

"What's the problem with mindmelding? Other than the obvious. I mean, it takes away people's free will." And now this power was another weapon now wielded by Cynon.

Anelise paused. "It's an old kind of magic and only our kind has it, few of us—most of them now gone, thanks to River, who killed them. It was part of our tradition, even if it was not very fae-like. But then again, few ancients can wield that power, and they are born with it. We saw it as a gift to our kind, and mind-melders as special fae. That said, mindmelders had no family or personal interests, they lost their own minds in the years they developed and used that magic. I feel... maybe that's what River feared: losing his sense of self. Now, that type of magic is confined to the Ancient city. It won't work elsewhere in Aluria."

Naia exhaled. This was one piece of good news amid so much despair. "It means River won't be able to control anyone if he's not here."

"I guess not." Anelise sounded a lot less certain and relieved than Naia would have liked. She ran her hand through her pale hair and sighed. "Do you know how the Ancients came to Aluria?"

"They came..." Naia had studied the history of her land. "About a thousand years ago, right?" She didn't know much more than that, or why they were the only magical race on their small continent. "I'm not sure about the details."

"Nine hundred years, to be precise. Do you want to guess the reason we came?"

Naia tried to think. If no other fae or elves were here... "Was there some kind of conflict?"

"Yes. Again, this is not a story we usually tell, and not a story you'll find in our books, but it's been passed on in hushed voices through generations, especially among royalty. The Ancients came right after the Great Mage was defeated. That's where our history gets obscure. It seems that some of our people had some role helping him, something with mindmelding. As a punishment, we were exiled. Our mindmelding and some of our magic was contained to this city. The dragon lords also sent some humans to Aluria and gave them limited magic, so that we wouldn't grow too powerful."

The fae let out a bitter chuckle. "I guess it worked. Nobody knows the details of what exactly happened, what our kind did. They kept it hidden so that history would not be repeated. Still, we have relics from that time, from Fernick. These relics could well have been in contact with The Great Mage's magic, and I'm assuming this Great Mage is the one you're calling Cynon."

They were in front of a heavy wooden door. Anelise took a key, spoke some incomprehensible words as she inserted it in a keyhole and turned it, opening the door to reveal a dark room. From the tip of her finger, she sent golden sparkles towards the four corners, reaching lanterns and igniting some kind of light in them. It wasn't fire that they were burning, but something magical Naia had never seen before.

That eerie golden light illuminated a long, thin table with some objects on them: a golden crown, a cloak, some silver plates, a golden bronze sword. None of them seemed magical, mysterious, or extraordinary in any way.

Before Naia could ask anything, Anelise said, "The red dagger's missing." She covered her face with her hands with those dark nails and took a deep breath, then balled her fists and stared at Naia. "I saw it and I knew it. I knew the dagger looked familiar. I knew there was something wrong about it, but then River said it was his..."

"We couldn't have guessed it." *We*, because Naia had also missed obvious signs, had ignored her own voice telling her that something had been amiss. But then, how much could she have done? "And perhaps there was no way to stop him."

River's sister shook her head. "Perhaps. And now it's not as if we can retrace history, understand what happened years ago. I've got very few answers. No idea what this dagger was, no idea how to stop Cynon."

Naia swallowed. "At least we know something. The dragons will know more about it. Maybe they'll come." Dragons. A thought hit her. "So this city was made with dragon magic?"

Anelise nodded.

"And connected to Mount Prime? Mount Prime, in Ironhold, now destroyed." Naia recalled that huge chamber where River had stuck the dagger in a dark rock. "I think they dug Mount Prime and brought it to the Iron Citadel and the earth and rocks they brought had dragon magic. I'm assuming Cynon then used the magic in Ironhold, not in Fernick. Meanwhile, the dragons thought he would never show up in Aluria because they didn't realize the dragon magic here could be enough. Maybe even... Maybe that was why they kept us apart. Kept the Ancients far from the dragons... So that..." So that... It made sense that perhaps they didn't want the dragons here, but the answer eluded her. "I don't know."

"Perhaps the dragons thought we'd bring Cynon back or something. And yet, despite all their effort, here we are. Stupid dragons." She looked at Naia. "I mean, sorry. It's just..." She sighed. "At least they should know we were asleep during all the time Ironhold was concocting their plan, and I'm sure it was Ironhold."

"True. What about Formosa? Do you think it was them as well?"

"Look at it this way: no magic can break rock. No Ancient magic, at least. Who has the weapons that could have collapsed that cliff?"

"So you're sure? Not even River was absolutely certain about it."

"Was he right in the head, though? The proof of whatever happened is in the Fernick ruins, not in the Iron Citadel." A light chuckle. "What was he expecting to find? A written account of how they did it?"

That was true. "Well, he was already being manipulated, having his mind poisoned, when he went to Ironhold." Naia shook her head, still in disbelief of how much she hadn't noticed. "Before you judge me, let me state that I tried to confront him about the reason he'd been going to Ironhold, tried to ask him about his *great plan*."

"You got yourself in a dangerous position."

It didn't feel like it. "No. If anything, he tried to spare me, tried to keep me away from the conflict, tried to protect me. Perhaps deep down he sensed something, even if he wasn't aware of it. Even now, I'm sure there's a part of him still in control. The question is how to get him back."

Anelise stared at the objects, then back at Naia. "The answer might be in your connection. You've made him immune to iron, he must have passed on some of his magic to you. Usually this intermingling of magic only happens with more intimacy, but a kiss seems to have been enough in your case."

"What are you suggesting?"

"I'm not suggesting. I'm trying to think. And I don't know what to do either."

Naia took a deep breath. "We know he's a mindmelder and that magic works only here. I need to open this city, and I think I can. Do you think we can send your warriors away? River won't be able to control them if they're not here."

"It would make us vulnerable. And even outside the city, they'd still be sworn to our king. That said, if you can open a passage, it will be helpful. Our city still needs to survive."

"I can do that." Perhaps this was the answer; focusing on what she *could* do, focusing on now, focusing on the matters in front of her. And yet... "What about River? Do you have any advice?

Any…" Anything, anything. Naia would grasp onto a sliver of a chance of saving him.

"Your hearts are connected. Trust yours. Trust that your answer is brewing somewhere. Ideas are like wine, they need to ferment in our minds."

"I don't know if I'll have time for that."

"Of course you don't know much. That's the whole point of trusting."

Trust her heart? That same silly, oblivious heart that had shushed her voice telling her there was something wrong with River?

They were all doomed.

LEAH STEPPED INTO DARKNESS, her heart beating fast, a cold chill all over her body. She had never imagined that something so awful could happen in her city, in her naive illusion that the Iron-hold invasion had been the worst that could happen to her kingdom. The sight of dreadful creatures inside her dome was breaking her heart.

Those were the same creatures she had called once, except that they were much more numerous now, and a permanent passage was being built in Frostlake. Her heart tightened thinking about everyone in the castle, in the houses in the city, wondering if they were safe, if they had been able to go to the shelters. The city had been left defenseless, considering their army had been sent away—probably not by coincidence.

The creatures were from the fourth realm, according to Tzaria, which matched Iona's account as well. Odd that Leah had once connected with these creatures enough to call them to this world, and yet it had felt different at that time. This felt a lot more permanent, more real.

And that was why Leah had to get help, and quickly. Why

hadn't she done this earlier? Maybe because she hadn't thought it through, hadn't realized it would come to this point.

She found herself in that desolate landscape where she had met the mysterious white fae. This time Leah was not in the path among mountains, but near that tree under which she had spent time learning to close her mind, getting some skills to even walk in the hollow—until she left. It had been Fel in danger that had pulled her away. He was in danger again, but the answer was not to go to him, but to bring help.

Leah went to the tree and yet this time she could not find the entrance to it. It was likely enchanted to keep intruders away. She was about to call the fae, when a rustle of leaves behind her made her turn.

Iona stood there, those eerie, dark pink eyes staring at her. "I can see you considered my proposal."

Leah nodded. "Can you control them? Once they're in Aluria?"

"They have their own minds—but a deal with an Ancient is binding."

"I want them to help us defeat Cynon. They can remain in Aluria, in the islands, but—"

She was going to say that she didn't want them to attack humans or fae, that she wanted some kind of guarantee, but then she tasted something bitter and felt as if she were falling into a dark abyss. It was that odd feeling that something was calling her away, almost like being pulled. Fel was likely in danger, but rushing back to him empty-handed would only make things worse. Still, her body was feeling cold all over, a dreadful chill from her feet to her scalp.

Iona stared at her, and then Leah gathered her courage and said, "I want help in Frostlake city, and later. Against the one you call the Breaker." Hopefully it was indeed Cynon. "But no harm to humans. The inhabitants from here, the ones you said can help me, can then live in the southmost islands."

"I fear they'll deem those islands too cold."

Likely. Leah was out of ideas. In fact, she could hardly think, that emptiness inside her becoming unbearable. And yet she had to do something. "Find a solution then. One that doesn't harm humans. And get them to Frostlake as soon as possible."

Everything was turning black and Leah barely heard what Iona said. I sounded like *deal*, but she could be imagining things, perhaps hoping for an easy solution. How easy, when she was basically putting the fate of Aluria in a stranger's hands?

FEL COULDN'T BELIEVE Leah had just gone into the hollow. "Don't go," he wanted to tell her. "We'll figure it out."

He had many more words to assure her that they had it all under control, to assure her they would protect her city, to assure her that she could just wait, wait in safety, while it would all be fixed.

The words never came out, as there was no point, since she was already gone. Gone to the nowhere between realms or another dangerous realm, where she knew so little, and where evil didn't only lurk, but roamed unchecked. And yet he was powerless to stop her, powerless to convince her to stay.

The dome. He had to focus and at least do his part, hoping Leah would return.

Tzaria then said, "Don't blame her for also wanting to use her magic."

"I'm not blaming her." His voice came out a lot more strained than he had expected.

"I know." Tzaria's tone was kind. Fel then sensed that her words were no longer for him. "You can leave me on that hill. I wish I could help more."

"You brought us here, Tzaria," Ekateni said. "Your knowledge played a great part."

He placed her softly on a rocky part of a hill near the city. They were still far enough not to be seen. From this distance, Fel could already connect with the metal of the dome, but he would need to get closer to be able to move it more easily.

"I'll have to approach the dome," Fel said.

"I'll be right behind you," his uncle replied. "Once it's ripped, be ready to fight."

Fel had fought these creatures once. Burned them with his fire, and there had been many of them. The prospect shouldn't frighten him now, considering he and his uncle were two huge dragons.

And yet it did.

This time, something was different.

As they got closer to the metal and glass structure, Fel reached out with his magic. He wanted to break the dome with the least possible damage, as he imagined that the falling glass could have disastrous consequences, not to mention the metal beams. But then, those creatures were disaster enough, and he had to break the circle quickly, before anyone had the chance to stop him.

Sitting atop the city, the structure looked like a cake dome, but in fact, there was a lot more to it, buried deep in the earth, long rods of iron stuck like roots in that frozen soil. Perhaps he could rip out the entire structure at once, but then the ground would tremble. He could bend the top, but that would leave the circle intact. No, he'd have to rip it out as carefully as he could, hoping the vibration wouldn't damage the city too much.

The night sky didn't provide as much cover for Fel as he wished, and yet he got close to the city without facing any resistance. So much iron, in and around it, so much iron everywhere, but what he focused on were the roots of the dome, those long filaments—and moved them up.

Long ago, he had realized that the weight of the object he moved didn't matter as much. When he had control of metal, it was like being able to float something in water. Still, this time, the soil held back the dome, as if unwilling to part with this long-time companion.

It wasn't more strength that Fel needed, but focus, focus on the metal only. He could feel it being lifted, until something, again, held him back. It wasn't the frozen soil, it wasn't the weight of the structure. It was something working against him, keeping the dome firmly stuck. It was... magic.

Ironbringers.

"They're keeping it down," he told his uncle. "With metal magic. But I'll try—"

"I'll go in," Tzaria said. Fel was stunned that he could still hear her, when she'd been dropped off far away, and when she was still in her human form. "And stop them."

Fel wondered how she was going to find the ironbringers, but assumed she knew what she was doing, just by the certainty in her voice. As a dragon, she was likely capable to sense magic and sense whoever was wielding it. Still, going into the dome on her own, when she could barely stand, sounded quite dangerous.

She added, "I'll let you know when you can try again."

He thought his uncle would warn her against it or at least tell her to be careful, but instead his words were directed toward Fel. "Be ready when she tells you to do so. And then leave. Go. Let me deal with whatever has come through."

These were words for Fel only, as his uncle could control that. So he meant to fight the creatures from another world on his own? Well, he was a dragon, and an extremely competent fighter. Still.

Tzaria's voice sounded in his head. "I got one of them."

One. There were likely many ironbringers—but not that many. Fel could sense the structure yielding to his command. As if they were the metal parts of his hand, he pulled the rods from the earth slowly but firmly, making them float in the air. He was about to squash the dome, so that it would no longer be a circle, when he saw those creatures, some fifty of them, coming in his direction. Fire should take care of them, but he was unsure how to wield both types of magic at the same time.

"Leave them to me," Ekateni said.

Fel threw the metal structure away from the city, to an area without houses or people, then bent it. Most of its glass finally fell, crashing on the ground with a thunderous sound. At the same time, his uncle sent a gigantic blast of fire toward the incoming creatures, burning most of them. Fel was free to send his fire towards the rest. Unlike in Umbraar, they didn't burn like paper, but much slower, like thin pieces of wood, and they fell while still burning. The black smoke slowly dissipated to reveal a severely damaged city, with roofs broken or missing, and a few buildings on fire here and there. Even the castle had broken windows and damaged turrets. Among the ruins, many of those creatures still roamed while some of them flew towards Ekateni and Fel.

As much as his uncle had told him to turn around and flee, he wasn't going to leave Leah's city at the mercy of these creatures. He focused on that feeling of fire on his chest, getting ready to burn the approaching creatures, when he noticed his uncle was also flying towards him. That was reckless, to give his back to his enemies. But there was something odd about him, not any specific feeling like anger or fear or worry, but rather an absence of any emotion. Perhaps he was just focused on the battle. Still.

"Ekateni?"

His uncle opened his mouth, then sent a huge blast of fire towards Fel. This was a hundred times worse than when he had been blasted by the Boundless on the way to Fernick. He could no longer feel his wings or any part of his body, and hit the ground with a huge thud. A loud buzz didn't let him hear anything, feel anything. Still, he saw the sheen of fire on blue scales. His uncle's blue scales, flying towards him.

It felt unreal, as if it was happening to someone else, those huge teeth getting buried on his neck, so much dark blood flowing, and his life fading. A shrill, loud scream echoed in his head. Was it his?

And then there was only darkness.

26

THE AMULET

Leah didn't quite understand that dreadful feeling, didn't understand what was happening, except for that gigantic, devouring anguish. She found herself on that hill again, watching her city burn, horrible creatures flying above it, and the dome gone.

Fel was flying low. No, falling. At least his uncle was close by. Leah wanted to run to him, but there were too many creatures there, and she would be a needless distraction.

But then her eyes could not believe what she was seeing. Was she seeing it? Or was it one of her horrific nightmares? Unwittingly, she tried to cross her hands—and felt them touching.

And yet, how could this be? It couldn't be real. The image she saw was Ekateni attacking Fel. It made no sense. He was now biting his neck, so deep and so hard that dark blood gushed from the wound, and here Leah stood, unable to help, unable to do anything, even her scream stuck in her throat as she felt her skin turning into ice.

Nobody could survive a wound like that, not even a dragon.

She'd seen Tzaria changing forms after being wounded, and maybe that would be a possibility, but Fel hadn't been able to swap into his human form. Leah realized that she was now running to him, running to call him, to see if maybe he could find his human form, to see if she could maybe help him somehow.

The already dark sky was getting darker with those creatures flying towards her, even if the worst darkness was inside her, while the fire from the city illuminated the night. At least Ekateni took flight, leaving Fel's body alone, but then the blue dragon flew straight into one of the broken beams from the dome, which traversed his body. Leah couldn't grasp what was happening, but at the same time, she was more focused on Fel, lying still, his life gone or fleeting.

Three flying creatures were advancing towards her. She had commanded them once, and yet felt empty now. Perhaps it had been an impression of commanding them, when in reality she had been doing their bidding by opening a passage to this world. Perhaps she could try to bring in something from another realm to help her, use her deathbringing, and yet nothing came. While she stared at that absurdity, all that came to her was a deep sense of nothingness. Was that a sense? Or would she fall into the space between space, the gap between realms, the real hollowness that was that in between?

A circle of light appeared in front of her. Tzaria was there, and spread her arms, as if to stop Leah, stop her from running.

"We have to leave," the woman said.

Leave? Was she insane? "I have to get to Fel."

"There's no more life in his dragon form. There's nothing here. I can't fight these creatures. Not in my current state."

This was the time when Leah should do something heroic, should have a brilliant idea, should come up with an amazing solution, and yet all she felt was pain. At the moment when she most needed to think, all she found was emptiness.

She felt the woman holding her hand, then tracing a circle on the ground, saw the flying creatures approaching, then saw everything turning black. That inviting blackness, where she belonged, that nothingness where nobody could feel pain.

Perhaps she could dream about human Fel, find him in this

place, find him before he left for the land of the dead. Even her city was now at the mercy of those creatures. Everything lost. If only she had considered Iona's proposal earlier, if only she had planned better, if only she could turn back time. Now she had this scar in her soul, and the guilt of not having done enough.

"Leah?" Tzaria's voice echoed, but it sounded far away. Everything was far away, and here she stood in darkness. There was something sticky in front of her, something that didn't let her move, and she could no longer feel Tzaria's hand. Leah was hopelessly lost, with no idea in which realm she was, and yet being lost was so small in comparison to the enormity of everything she was losing.

No, she couldn't give up. She had to hold herself together, had to find a way. How? When she couldn't even move? Something had definitely trapped her. The question was what.

BEING a sovereign meant ignoring her own pain for the sake of her people. Naia had heard that many times in her childhood and had always imagined that it meant going to a meeting even after bumping her pinky toe. Those had been simple times, when she hadn't yet understood all the different types of pain.

Now she realized what her father had meant, as she grappled with the fear of losing River, her own regret for her failure, her worry about Aluria, and so many more troubles clouding her mind, numbing her senses. And yet she had been named Queen of the Ancients, and wasn't going to shirk her responsibilities.

Naia stood with Anelise on the banks of the Blue River. Coming here had been so simple, just a matter of watching the fae walk through the hollow and step into existing circles, and yet somehow Naia had unsealed their city by doing that. At this moment, she wanted to forget everything that was happening to River, all her anxieties, and focus on making sure the Ancients would have some kind of access to food and water from outside their isolated city.

Anelise had brought two of her friends, Gaelle and Barton. They both had the typical fae looks, but now Naia was getting better at differentiating them. River's sister had a slightly darker complexion than her friends and a rounder face. Her friend Gaelle was a cute girl with pale horns and light nails, her face a lot more angular than Anelise. Barton was a young man with white-blond hair cropped below the ear, his skin even paler than his companions and his eyes a much brighter red, rather than the usual dark burgundy of most of the Ancients.

River's sister looked around. "So only I and whoever I allow can come here."

"Yes. I mean, I wouldn't know who to bring. You can fish and hunt, and take some water to the city."

Anelise paused, then said, "Had you been a stranger granting us a deal, I would appreciate this small gesture, but as our queen—"

"It's good for now," Gaelle interrupted her.

"It's not," Naia agreed with Anelise. This was far from enough. The Ancient City had very little land, and even if they could bring water, it wouldn't heal soon enough to feed anyone. Animals had been gone. "You need to bring people back to Aluria, to live off the land, I guess, but this is unfortunately not the time for that."

Gaelle sighed. "We're actually not farmers. We used to do a lot of trade. Before."

Before the war.

Anelise turned to her companion. "This is not the time for trading, though."

"No, but if we could go to other kingdoms, other places..."

"You can," Naia said. "I mean, I don't know if I need to do anything to allow you to do that. As long as you don't attack or steal from humans, and as long as you do your best to stay hidden, you can."

"A verbal agreement is enough," Anelise said. "But if we eventually want to trade, we can't stay hidden."

"So don't." Naia didn't want to impose too many conditions, knowing their dire situation. "But don't harm humans."

Gaelle said, "We weren't the ones who started the war. And Aluria is our land as well. The Ancient city was just a safe haven and a place to seal some of our magic."

Mindmelding had been restricted to the Ancient city. Still, Naia knew so little about the Ancients. Perhaps she should let them decide their own destiny. "You know what? Do whatever you want. Come and go as you please, just don't attack humans for no reason."

Naia realized that this was a very ambiguous sentence. What did *no reason* mean? When could the fae attack? And yet, perhaps the right thing would be to give them back their freedom, which had been unjustly taken away because of a suspicion that they had destroyed Formosa. True that King Spring also would have killed all the humans in Aluria without remorse, but then, she knew that some humans would do the same if given the chance. And right now, the enemy was another one. If anything, if Cynon turned his eyes to the Ancients, perhaps they would need a place to hide.

Anelise stared at her, eyes wide. "You could have bargained for that agreement."

"I would, in different circumstances." Naia shrugged. "As your queen, it's my duty to make sure you're safe, to think about your well-being first."

Gaelle sighed. "So you do see yourself as our queen." The girl didn't know yet about River being corrupted and possessed by Cynon, and perhaps thought of Naia as a power-hungry human, which was fair, considering everything.

Naia scoffed. "It doesn't matter what I see or don't see. What matters is what it is."

Anelise put a hand on Naia's shoulder. "We're lucky to have you."

Of course. Lucky that it wasn't only Cynon's vessel in charge.

Perhaps hiding River's true condition was a mistake, but Naia feared that they would kill him, and she still believed that there was a part of River fighting Cynon. As long as she thought that he was still there, she wasn't going to give up hope.

A twig cracked behind Naia and she froze, then turned and saw River, standing by the trees, wearing some fae finery.

He was staring at her and said, "I'm the one who's lucky to have you."

Naia wanted to run to him and embrace him, wanted to feel relieved that he was himself again, but she knew it wasn't true.

Still, she smiled. "Why is that?"

River shrugged, then glanced at Anelise and her friends. "You. Out. Out of here. Out of my presence."

The three fae disappeared quickly. They were still in a fairy circle, after all. Still, Anelise could at least have given Naia a guilty look for leaving her alone with Cynon's vessel, but no.

Stepping towards Naia, River said, "You didn't wait for me."

He didn't sound angry, but she didn't know what he was going to do. "It was cold," she said.

He was close enough to her that he took her hands. "You know what I like about you? You amplify my magic."

Naia hated that. Hated... A thought hit her. The amplification wasn't only one way. She could also have some of *his* magic, amplified on top of that, and if she got the mindmelding...

There *was* one way to mix their magic. Naia swallowed and her stomach chilled. She ran a hand over his chest. "I could amplify it even more. You're still River, aren't you? Just... more powerful."

He smiled. "A lot more powerful. And improved."

So many thoughts going through Naia. If only she could recreate their first kiss, recreate that intimacy, that exchange of magic, except that they wouldn't be able to kiss for the first time anymore, but they could get close to another first time.

Naia tried to quiet down her anxiety and worry, as she didn't want him to notice it, and said, "I think that if you're still River, there's no reason for us to be enemies. I want you to be powerful. Let me amplify your magic to its fullest potential."

River grabbed her chin. "Speak clearly."

It wasn't going to be easy to recreate the feeling of their first kiss with this weird River, though. And perhaps it was all Cynon, which would be quite disgusting, if she thought about it. And she wasn't sure if he would even be interested in her.

But she had to try to work with that part of River that was still there. "Make me yours." The words had come out and there was no way to pull them back in, and yet Naia felt as if she were falling from a tower up above, falling, falling.

He stared at her for a long moment, while she listened to her own heart, trying to figure out what was going on through his mind. Would he kill her? Laugh at her? These were only two dreadful options among so many. Why was he taking so long for such a simple, yes-or-no answer?

After the agonizing eternity of a few seconds, he finally said, "Let's do it right."

Naia found herself in the hollow again, unsure where she was going, terrified of what she was about to do, unsure if it was even going to work.

EVERYTHING WAS SO BRIGHT, and then dark again. Fel opened his eyes and saw stars. Different stars, not the ones he was used to. There was soft grass behind him, and... he was human.

As much as he had gotten used to being a dragon and felt like himself in that form, this was him, the way he'd known himself for most of his life. He was wearing the same white shirt and brown pants he'd worn... In Umbraar, when fighting the Ironhold forces. There were pieces of metal by him—his hands.

Fel sat up. Was this the after-realm? He'd always thought he'd have to cross a hallway, something, and that there would be someone to greet him. He took another look. All the moonlight and the glow of the stars allowed him to see was a valley surrounded by a ravine. He heard a bird's cry and the rustling of leaves. This place... he knew it. This was...

His mind felt fuzzy and confused, and then a memory shook him. His last moments as a dragon, and Ekateni attacking him. Ekateni, of all people—or dragons. So strange. Leah's city on fire. Now he was here, and didn't even know if he was alive or what was happening.

"Feeling thankful yet?" a familiar male voice asked.

Fel got up and turned, and saw a tall man with blond hair, dark skin, and yellow eyes. Yellow eyes like everyone said his father had, but this wasn't his father, this was someone Fel had met before.

After some moments trying to figure out why he recognized the voice, it hit him. "First Mage?"

This was odd because Fel had been told that he didn't have a human form, but this was the place, and it was also his voice.

The great dragon chuckled. "Surprised to see me like this?"

"A little," Fel confessed. "What am I doing here?"

"Surviving. Aren't you glad I kept your human body safe?"

"You did?" Safe? Did it mean... Could he be that lucky? "So I didn't die?"

The First Mage shook his head. "Sturdy, stubborn creatures we are. Unless we put both forms in danger, unless we don't swap quickly enough. But you're here. And you can go home now if you wish." He pointed at Fel's chest. "Don't forget your gift."

Fel looked and saw a necklace with a purple pendant. "This... the amulet?" He had even forgotten about it. "Can you explain more how it works?"

"You know how it works because you already used it. If not you, then someone you love. Just put it on and remember."

Remember... No, that didn't make sense. "I haven't used it. How am I going to remember anything? Isn't this supposed to change the past?"

The First Mage shook his head. "Time is a circle. You can't change what's already been changed. Eventually you'll realize or remember when the amulet was used. Then you can hold it and think about that time."

Fel wished he could change so much, but then, if it had to be something that had already been changed, it would always lead to this moment, when so much was wrong. Unless... "What if I make a mistake? What if I use it for something that I didn't use before?"

"You could rip the fabric of reality."

Great. Nothing to be worried about. "You're joking."

"No, I'm serious."

"That's..." How could he even word the enormity of it? "A lot of pressure to get it right." He removed the necklace and held it between his metal fingers. "I don't think I want this responsibility."

"It's meant for you."

"How can something so little destroy the world?"

"I didn't say destroy. I said rip. It might be catastrophic, and then it might not. Time is a tricky thing. I understand you're wondering why I gave this to you. Well, I didn't choose it. You think I'd pick a nitwit to hold that? Of course not."

Fel still held the necklace and ignored the jab. "I do have a sense of humor, but if it's a joke, tell me."

"It's not a joke."

"But then... If time... If everything has already happened, then what's the point? It's all set, isn't it?"

"Nothing is set. Summer and winter come and go, and the leaves are never the same. You still have to do your part, or else you will change it."

"Won't it rip the fabric of the universe then?"

"Of course. Why do you think we have all these realms?"

Fel sighed. "Fair. So I need to recognize the moment I already used it, and then use it. You're saying I need to hold it in my hands. Do you realize I have a bit of a problem here?"

"No. You have hands."

Sighing, Fel put back the necklace. "What's going to happen to my dragon form? Is it lost?"

"The dragon form will reemerge again, after some time. You should wait."

"Will I be able to swap forms?"

"Who knows what the future will bring?"

"I thought it was all written."

"No. Only the past is written, even if it's the past you changed from the future. There's a lot of room for variation in what's coming."

What was coming. Everything so dreadful. Fel thought about his sister, Leah, his father... "Aluria is in trouble. Cynon is there, and has a vessel."

"Indeed. And isn't Aluria the land of the iron dragon? There's a great plan at work. Things happen when the time is right. An apple doesn't mature before its time. Things happen for a reason."

Fel shook his head. "I doubt there's a reason for suffering, death, pain—"

"The pain is not part of the plan, Isofel. Neither is the suffering."

"Easy for you to say that when you remain here while we go out there and fight." Perhaps this was disrespectful, but Fel was getting desperate.

The First Mage didn't seem bothered. In fact, he chuckled. "Quite easy because I know what my part entails, and I know its value." He raised his hand and pointed behind Fel. "There. Through that circle."

It was a floating fire ring, like the ones the dragons flew through, but small. "Am I supposed to jump through it?"

"You can always stay here to chat some more, but I might not be in the mood to grant you passage home again. I'd jump if I were you."

Again Fel would leave this place knowing nothing, with more

questions than answers, with more confusion than clarity. But then, he wasn't going to risk his luck. He jumped as if he had to go over a high fence.

On the other side of the ring, he found an abyss. He was near that cave that led to the passage to meet the First Mage, except that he'd jumped too far and now he was falling on the water. No way he would be able to swap forms now, and the height was too great, meaning that the impact on the water could be deadly. Was he supposed to turn back time or not? How would he do it if he was dead? Unless it was an illusion, a trick. Goodness, he had to think fast, or the surface of the ocean would squash him.

NAIA STARED at the water around her, still half in disbelief at her plan. At first she'd been in shock, when River had ordered her to be sent to a room, and then these two fae women came, armed with swords and bows... But all they did was fill a bathtub with water. They were servants doing double duty as guards and chambermaids.

Now they stood in the room, watching as Naia bathed. This was someone's bedroom, but Naia didn't know whose. She did think that a bath was a huge waste of water, considering the situation in the Ancient City, but she didn't have much say when the order had come from the king himself.

She wondered about the magic keeping her as a queen, and how much power she truly had. It was more than a queen consort, and yet less than River, which was a problem.

The door opened and Naia wondered how many people exactly were going to see her naked. While nudity was not taboo among fae, or even among human women, she had grown up only with her brother and father, and appreciated some privacy for these moments.

At least it was only Anelise, which was a relief. The fae was

Naia's only ally in this place, perhaps the only person who understood what she was going through.

"Stay where you are," River's sister ordered the two guards, then she kneeled by the basin, put a hand inside, and started shaking the water. Smart. She wanted to muffle their conversation. "Should I assume you have a plan?" she asked Naia.

"Not... exactly. But I want to mix our magic."

Anelise nodded. "It will make him more powerful."

"It goes both ways."

"And then what?" She stopped moving her hand and stared at Naia, then seemed to recall why she was doing it and continued.

Naia tensed. The truth was that she wasn't exactly sure what was going to happen. "I'm hoping I'll figure it out."

Anelise looked at the water, then whispered, "Are you going to try to kill him?"

A bitter taste came to Naia. This was one possibility, and could be a necessity. "What if I do?"

"You might not survive your attempt."

Naia had rather been expecting some censure about trying to kill Anelise's brother. Not that she was going to do that. Still, she had a question. "I gave you power to act in my stead. If something happens to me—"

"Your order will be void. I will have no more power."

"What if we both die?"

"The next in line is Forest."

Naia didn't really like him, just based on what River had told her, but then, he couldn't be worse than Cynon's vessel. She decided to be even more honest. "I want to save River, not kill him. Do you have any suggestions? Advice? Ideas?"

Anelise took a deep breath. "Delay. Delay as much as you can. Allow yourself to soak up his magic as much as you can, and then do what you have to do." Her tone was grim.

"You still think I'm going to kill him."

At first, the only answer Naia got was silence, broken only after a long while. "You will be in a privileged position. Few will be able to get that close to him." Her voice was so quiet, even Naia could barely hear her. "Shall you waste your chance? And what is the alternative?"

The truth was that Naia didn't know. She was acting on a hunch, a very vague hunch, and hoped that there would be another solution. "You think I should kill him."

"No. I truly don't know what to think, but I don't want to see my brother used for a sinister scheme either. He wouldn't want that. And then, I don't know who was the person ordering this bath, I don't know who you'll meet in that room. If Cynon is an old, extremely powerful being, he won't be fooled so easily. This could be a test and he could be prepared. Be careful."

True. But then... "When the price for inaction is so high, why not be reckless?"

"Because you can still temper his power, you can still make sure the Ancients don't fall into an abyss."

"I can also absorb his magic. Didn't you just say I was in a privileged position and should do something?"

"Do something if you can, don't do it if you think you might fail." Anelise then pulled her hand suddenly, as if the water had burned her.

That worried Naia. "What happened?"

"Iron magic. Got in the water." She glanced at the guards, who weren't even looking in their direction, then said, "Good luck. And count on me—whatever happens." Sadness tainted her voice. Whatever happened, would there be a way to get River back? If it was really a matter of killing him, would Naia be able to follow through? She was alone in her decision, alone holding the responsibility of trying to find an answer.

Before leaving, Anelise turned. "Love is powerful too. Just so you know."

Love. Could love undo the mess under which she was buried? Or was it the excuse she'd give to forfeit her duty?

27

FIRE

After Naia dried herself, one of the fae guards gave her a dress. It was light purple, with embroidery so much finer and more delicate than anything she had ever seen or even imagined. True that she hadn't seen much finery in her life, but none of the royalty dresses in the gathering could even come close to this. It was no wonder that the Ancients had traded with humans before it had all gone sour.

Naia put it on slowly, with no help from the guards, who could not touch her because of her ironbringing. The dress was laced in the front, and not complicated, which was helpful, but even then she struggled, as her fingers were trembling.

The part that was making her most worried was realizing that River—or Cynon—was taking her proposal seriously, making sure she had this bath with scented herbs and all. Unless he thought she usually stank, but then he wouldn't agree with this, would he? Troublesome thoughts. Who was in control of River? If it was Cynon, he could think whatever he wanted. If it was River... Perhaps he just wanted to do this right or maybe give her time to think. Time. It was only increasing her worry and mortification, and she doubted she would be able to recreate their first kiss in that state.

Had desperation turned her mad? And then, would she be able to look into his eyes and tell him she had changed her mind? Perhaps she would need to do that, but then that would mean no kiss, no exchange of magic, and her plans would all go to waste. As if she even had any plan. No, she was sure that if she had access to his magic, she would be able to do something.

"Are you ready?" one of the guards asked.

"Yes." A good thing she could still lie, even if it prickled a little, even if her voice was shaky.

"Follow us, then."

Naia was startled. Somehow she had thought she would need to wait, that perhaps she would have more time. Crazy thought, considering how long she'd spent in that bath. She followed the two fae to a large bronze door. At least she would have easy access to a weapon if it came to it.

The guards opened it to reveal a room immersed in darkness, except for the light of about fifty candles, spread all over the place, in nooks on the marble floor. There was no bed, only a mattress on the floor as well, and a table with two chairs by a corner. River was sitting there.

Naia felt the door closing behind her and the fae leaving. She was alone with River. Alone with Cynon's vessel—and in a room with a lot of metal and fire. What was she going to do?

Her stomach was about to somersault, and yet she noticed more metal in the room; swords and shields hanging on a wall. A thin silver tray with some fruit on it lay on the table. Who would agree to be alone with an ironbringer in a place like this? The answer was obvious: someone who didn't think she was a threat.

Naia sat across from him, wondering if River was even there, if he had a plan, or if this was truly a suicidal idea. If dying was what he really wanted, if it was the only solution, she'd have no choice. Three candles were burning on the table, between them, while he looked down, resting his head on his hand. Was he exposing his neck for her?

"River?" She had to look into his eyes, had to find a clue, an idea.

His eyes met hers, so beautiful reflecting the flames in their own fiery color. He was beautiful, dressed all in black with a loose shirt that seemed to have some of that same fine embroidery.

He took a knife and fiddled with it. "So you truly want to amplify my magic?"

"Aren't we allies?"

He chuckled and shook his head, then raised an eyebrow. "You know what that entails, I assume?"

"You talk of it as if it were something dreadful."

He smiled. "Undress, then."

Before she panicked, she realized she had better act like herself. She chuckled. "So crude. Why? These laces are too hard for you? And I didn't get all dressed to get it off that soon." *Delay, delay, delay,* Anelise had told her. "And I want to eat first." But then, how were they getting to the kissing? Naia plucked a grape, still unsure.

He was staring at her. "I don't have an eternity for this."

"Isn't it odd? Young people are always in a hurry, while the old ones are patient, when it should be the opposite." She was trying to gain time and think, staring at the flames as if they could give her an answer. This was all going wrong, and she didn't have an eternity either.

Perhaps she was overcomplicating this. They had mingled their magic with a kiss before. Why should it be different now? At least they were alone, undisturbed.

Naia got up and stood by him. "Kiss me, then."

He put a hand on her chin and then their lips were touching. Naia wanted them closer, so she sat on his lap and wrapped her arms around him. This was not the time to wonder who she was kissing. This was the time to remember River, and remember why they were connected.

She recalled the River that had comforted her after her argument with her father, recalled his music, his words, his smiles, recalled the day she'd been captured by the Ancients and how he had come to her. Even in his worst hour, he had named her queen, perhaps to protect her, and then made sure she was somewhere from where she could escape.

He was not only beautiful but fun and kind. She enjoyed watching the stars with him, enjoyed having him close. Could she feel his mind if she reached out? Could she interfere with his thoughts?

She felt his hands lifting her, then placing her on the mattress. He stared at her, all sweet River, then undid her laces, removing her dress. Naia was half naked, exposed, and yet the feel of his hands, the feel of his nails against the soft skin of her breasts did something to her, ignited a surge of desire—and magic. She pulled his face for another kiss. Kiss, kiss, kiss, and mingle their power, that was what she was here to do.

Shadows danced on the walls from the flames. Flames. Fire. She was resistant to her own fire—and fire was purifying. Was her idea insane? A lot of what she was doing was. He removed her dress and underclothes, so that all her body lay bare to him. Naia then pushed his shirt up, so that they would be skin against skin. Now she could definitely feel an overwhelming surge through her, a power that wasn't hers. They *were* blending their magic. Magic, fire, magic. The ideas were still blurry, but coming into focus.

"Undress," she whispered.

He smiled and didn't take long to do what she had asked and get rid of his pants. Naia avoided looking, then rolled over to the floor, the cold marble cooling down her body, her thoughts, sending another odd shiver through her body. "Here."

She had expected him to find it weird, but that didn't seem to be the case, as he was above her in less than a second. It meant that there was nothing around them that could burn.

Naia pulled him close to her, wrapped her arms and legs tight around him, then whispered, "Don't move." She tried to put power and intention in her words, tried to weave some magic in them, hoping she was doing it right.

Even if she wasn't sure if her suggestion had worked, she immediately conjured the strongest blast of fire she could, involving them in a pillar of flames.

River's yell was a horrifying wail that soon faded. Naia held him tight, glad that she couldn't feel him burning, and yet still kept that fire alive, thinking about love, thinking about how she had been called to him and vice versa, if it was true that he had seen a light leading him out of the hollow. There was a power connecting them, and Naia surrendered to that power, imbuing her fire with her love for that part of River that was still there, still fighting to get free.

Naia held the flame, held the fire, for what felt like forever. Only when she could no longer hold that powerful flame did she stop, terrified about what she had done.

River lay motionless over her, his eyes closed, as if sleeping. At least he hadn't gotten burned. Naia rolled him on his back and put her ear near his heart, hearing only silence. She put her hand in front of his nose and felt no breathing.

No, no, no.

Her heart was beating loudly inside her, a drum to accompany her dread.

If death was the only answer, if River had made sure to be here alone with her, she shouldn't regret what she had done. And yet.

"River."

She placed a hand on his chest, his skin still warm from the fire, but she wasn't sure if there was any warmth inside. But then, if he survived, she wasn't sure if this would cut the ties with Cynon, and that would mean she would be in danger.

"River," she called again, even as she saw no sign of life in him.

Was this the end, then? A good thing, of course. A good deed. Bitter good deed.

Naia kissed his lips softly. "River, come back. Come back for me. If you can."

A tear dropped from her face, falling right on his chest. And then another. None of this was what she wanted, and yet, even his sister wouldn't censure her. If anything, this was a heroic act, something only she could do. She still couldn't quite understand how he let himself be so vulnerable. And now he could be gone.

FEL WAS APPROACHING the ocean very fast. Too fast. And he had no wings. How he wished he was in dragon form again. Wishing wasn't going to save him. What could save him, then?

It came to him in a flash: his magic.

There were still some pieces of the armors of the boundless floating in the ocean. He moved his body to the horizontal position, then pulled as many pieces of metal as fast as he could, placing them under him, at the same speed as he was, but then decelerating them slowly, until they stopped, supporting him mid-air. More like low air, almost touching the surface of the ocean.

This had been close. That crazy old dragon mage had almost killed Fel. What a great help he was. And then he had the nerve to talk about ripping the universe or whatever he had called it. Fel took a deep breath, glad to be alive for the second time today, but now wondering how he was going to get back to Aluria.

Around him there was only ocean and pointy, rocky islands. The shore wasn't far, but what shore? He had absolutely no idea where he was, not even a rough estimate. While he assumed this was Fernick, he wasn't even sure of that.

He made the pieces of metal lift him higher until he found a flat surface where he could at least sit and think. His metal hands were still with him, and he let them rest beside him. The stars could tell him where he was and where to go—if he knew about them. Naia had been the one more interested in astronavigation, and even she would be unlikely to find her position in such an unknown land.

And then, he could go back to his original plan, which was to wait for the sun to rise and then fly south. Or rather, float south. Eventually he would end up in Aluria. Probably too late to do anything, as he would take forever to get there without the powerful propulsion of his dragon wings.

The truth was that he was exhausted, and yet he feared the boundless could find him here. While he could defend himself with the scattered pieces of metal, he wasn't sure for how long and against how many foes.

The best thing to do would be to get to the shore, away from these islands, away from this place where other dragons could find him. The land would likely provide him a place to hide and rest, before his long journey back. At least he was alive, and for that perhaps he should have thanked the First Mage.

Slowly, he let the pieces of armor support his weight and allow him to glide to the rocky shore, which didn't provide much protection. He would need to go further inland to find a forest where trees could provide cover for him.

Before he did that, however, he heard the now familiar sound of dragon wings in the distance, and descended to the ground, where he hid behind some rocks. It wasn't a great hiding place, but hopefully the darkness of night would provide enough cover for him.

Peeking from the rock, he noticed that there were only two dragons. One of them landed by the cave that led to the First Mage and swapped forms, then yelled something. It was hard to hear due to the distance and wind. The other dragon flew in circles, as if looking for something. It was a dark dragon, likely black—like his cousin Jacine. It was hard to see the person by the cave, but it could be his other cousin.

Fel decided to float up and wave. "Siniari? Jacine?" he yelled, hoping it was indeed the case, then added, "It's me." If by any chance he was wrong, they were still only two dragons, and Fel could deal with them.

The human swapped forms again, and both dragons flew in his direction. All Fel sensed was calm and relief. As they got close to him, he realized that they were indeed his cousins, and they soon landed beside him and swapped forms.

"Isofel?" Siniari asked.

"Yes. How did you know I would end up here?"

"We didn't," Jacine said. "But dragons can sometimes feel a pull towards a place, and it just happened to us. I'm glad you're alive."

"We should leave." Siniari's voice was tense. "Can you swap forms?"

"My dragon got hurt."

"I can carry him," Jacine offered. "Then you can make a ring for us to fly through." She turned to Fel. "Can you come with us?"

"I need to get back to Aluria, but—"

He was going to say that he could maybe float through the circle, but Siniari interrupted him."Let's get out of here, then we talk."

They swapped into their dragon forms in a flash, and then Fel was caught by a dragon's paw and flown through a fire ring.

Dream web. Or rather, nightmare web.

Azir was covered in it, the material weaved by a rare and dangerous spider, meant to trap its prey forever, keeping them in a strange, pleasant slumber, unaware of the real world. His doze hadn't been *that* pleasant, but certainly illuminating. At least now he was awake.

He had always heard that dream spiders sucked people's blood, but he didn't think that was the case, as he had no marks. Still, if they were going through all this trouble to enchant their victims, they had to be feeding on something. His best guess was that they were feeding on his emotions.

Delight, shock, betrayal, hatred. If that was what the spider wanted, it explained the dream web, explained how he'd been reliving those strange moments in his life, moments that he had believed forgotten, but still hurt like sharp new blades.

And yet he had seen a sliver of truth.

Truth? Or deception? Pointless hope?

It wasn't pointless. He had come to the hollow with one goal in mind—to rescue Ursiana. What was the point of risking his life for her while clutching old wounds as if they were diamonds? What he had seen in his vision—Prince Sebastian tricking him— made a lot more sense than anything he had ever conjured in his delirious, hateful, wounded mind. And now what hurt most was having wasted so many years of his life duped by a silly lie.

The spider keeping him prisoner was likely enjoying these morsels of shock, hate, and regret, while he restrained by that sticky material. Still, he was able to reach for a dagger in his coat pocket, and then ripped that dream web all out at once. Then, in a swift motion, he stabbed what looked like the ceiling of a low cave and was met with a shrill, loud scream. Perhaps the books were wrong in claiming that these spiders sucked blood, but they were right about the right way to kill them.

Azir stepped out of that small "cave" and looked back at the huge creature that had been above him, now twitching. Long tubes came out of it, looking like veins, connecting with other spiders like that, over small hills. He was in the bottom of a circular chasm, and had to get out of here as soon as possible. He didn't think these creatures would attack him, but it was like they had something in the air that would make him lose consciousness and fall into that strange trance-like state. But then, in theory the mere fact that he was aware of these spiders' trick would make him resistant to it. Hopefully it was true.

Ursiana should not be here, but in another realm. All Azir had to do was find a place from where he could move into the hollow. These lower levels were dense, difficult, and strange, not to mention he had never truly studied what to do in case he ended up here. And yet here he was, which should tell him that deep down, he had never believed Prince Sebastian's lies, or maybe even if he did, he still cared enough about Ursiana to risk his life for her.

He found a slope by the stone walls and climbed it quickly. At a higher ground, he felt the hollow calling to him, and slipped into it easily. From darkness, there was an infinity of paths, infinity of ways, circles, portals, passages. He could find himself on the edge of the third realm, clutching the handle of the light-shield and hoping that it would protect him from the deatheyes. He was in a dark cave again, perhaps the same as before, and yet this time he couldn't hear anything outside. No roars, only silence. After unsheathing his sword, he walked out slowly, making sure his steps didn't make a sound.

The landscape had an odd, bluish tone. He saw the cave through which he'd escaped—leaving Ursiana behind. Before it, there were vines, many, many dark vines on the ground. Beside them, a fallen creature. Even before seeing its face, Azir realized it was a deatheye—dead. A few more lay nearby. What had happened here?

Azir followed the vines. Some of them were dry and looked old, though. How long had he been under the dream spider's spell? It had felt like an hour at most, and yet, time perhaps slipped by while he had been stuck in that daze. He hoped it hadn't been that long.

These vines had to be Ursiana's. Most of them led to another cave, which he entered slowly. Thin streams of light came from the ceiling and entrance, and there, amidst vines, he saw her, lying down. He kneeled to check if she was breathing, when a sudden movement startled him. It was a sharp vine, coming in his direction, almost reaching his eye, except that he cut it in the nick of time. She had used her magic to attack him before, but never with that much violence.

"Ursiana, it's me. Can you wait to kill me? Wait until you're back in Aluria and safe?"

No sharp words met his, and he realized he missed them. No movement, and for some time, not even vines—until something circled him. Another vine, which he cut. If it was her magic, it was a good sign, even if she was motionless, with her eyes closed. He needed to take her back, but the issue was how to carry her in that state—especially if she could try to impale him at any moment.

Slowly, he touched her face. She was still warm, and still breathing, even if softly. Perhaps if he talked to her she would listen, would realize she was safe... Or else try to kill him again. Right as these thoughts crossed his mind, another vine came in his direction and he blocked it.

Azir took a deep breath. "Ursiana, you're safe now. The deatheyes are gone. It's Azir. I..." He saw no reaction in her, but took it as encouragement to keep trying. "I'm truly sorry I didn't try to talk to you. Sorry I believed in lies. I know these words don't change anything, but..."

In reality it was hard to say this. "I was wrong. I was wrong to shun you without a single explanation. I was wrong not to even try to confront you, not to attempt to listen to what you had to say. I was wrong to believe something horrible about you, wrong to walk away and not even tell you why." He took a deep breath. "I'm truly sorry. Think of it this way: if you survive, you have until the end of your life to punish me, to berate me, to yell at me and tell me all those angry words that perhaps you kept stuffed inside. I also had angry words, but if anyone needs to hear them, it's myself. We'll yell at me together."

Ursiana was still motionless. Azir swallowed. "Give me the chance to let you yell at me, yell at me for all your pains, for everything you went through. Give me that chance. Wake up."

Her magic had probably been depleted and it was likely that she would remain like this for a while. He could carry her—as long as he could be certain that she wouldn't attack him.

"It's me, Ursiana," he insisted. "I still remember you as the girl who wanted to travel around the world, who wanted freedom. You can go back and travel." He almost said *once things quiet down,* but he didn't want to remind her that there were still so many struggles ahead.

She looked small and fragile lying there among those dreadful vines, and yet, she'd slayed the creatures around these caves, she had been the one responsible for the vines and deaths. Appearances could be deceiving. He was going to wait by her side, and if she didn't attack him again in a few minutes, he'd carry her back. There were more foes in this realm.

"Ursiana, it's me. I'm going to carry you. Please don't try to hurt me, or we both won't make it." There was one person she still loved, and perhaps it would be a good idea to remind her of that. "Wait until you're in Aluria, until you meet Leandra again. I'm sure you miss her."

Mentioning her felt odd. He wasn't sure if saying *our daughter* or *your daughter* would upset her more, so he hadn't risked any of those. She was right that Leandra's father had been Flavio, the man who had raised her, and yet it didn't mean Azir didn't care. If anything, he had cared for her just by knowing she was Ursiana's daughter. Hopefully she was safe.

"Ursiana, I'm going to carry you." He spoke these words as softly as he could, then he sheathed his sword and was about to take her in his arms when a sound behind him startled him. It was just a big rat, now impaled by a vine. Ursiana was unconscious but fast.

He decided to carry her over his shoulder. Inelegant, yes, but at least he could still have one hand free and carry a sword.

When he was about to lift her, she murmured something, but too softly for him to hear.

"Could you repeat what you said?" he asked as gentle as possible.

"It sounds romantic," she said, even if her voice was weak.

Azir was delighted to hear her again, and yet surprised at her words. "Me carrying you is romantic?"

Ursiana opened her eyes. "Me yelling at you."

He was relieved to see her awake and smiled. "I agree."

She then sighed and closed her eyes.

Azir said, "I'll carry you, don't strain yourself. It's not going to be comfortable, though, but we need to leave."

"I can survive here. I survived."

"I know. And I'm impressed. But I'd rather go."

He took her and put her over his shoulder, holding her with one arm.

They walked outside and met no creatures, then entered the cave from where he'd left that other time, leading out of this dead end, this point of no contact with any passages. Last time he'd been here, he had meant to protect her, to make sure she survived, even if it cost his life. It was a relief to know that they were leaving together, both of them getting out of this together.

He was about to find the path to Aluria, when Ursiana said, "Put me down."

"Can you stand?"

"I don't know. We have to stop. Stop, Azir. Or put me down and go. I'm not leaving."

"What is it?"

"I... put me down."

"We're in the hollow, there's nothingness here. I can't put you down."

"We can't go to Aluria. Not yet."

She could be delirious. Still, he tried to understand what she meant. "Where do you want to go?"

"My daughter."

IT WAS strange to wake up from such a long stupor. River still tried to parse out all that he'd done. How much had been his own free will, how much had been Cynon's influence, and then, how much had been plain old stupidity?

Yet this was not the time to untangle all the threads, to trace back the steps that had brought him here, but to try to identify what could be useful. Clues, resources, plans, there was a little bit of each here and there, if only he could settle his mind and smother his guilt and shame.

River now remembered—in clear details—the horrific way in which he had killed his father. And yet he also remembered when he had made Naia sleep, believing he was worried about her, and yet not knowing why. There had always been this nagging sensation that something was wrong, but it had been blurry, confusing... Even then, he should never have taken Naia's free will, and yet, what was that compared to the long list of his regrets?

He still failed to remember completely how he had come back to Aluria after being thrown in the hollow by Naia's kiss, and yet he remembered his stubbornness, his plan to go to Iron-hold. Where had that come from? And there was more. His stomach chilled.

River had been a prisoner, confined to a dark, horrific place, until he fought to get back. With a lot of strength, all he got were some glimpses, pieces of himself. Now he saw his chance to set himself free, and wanted to kill that dreadful creature who had dared take his place, had dared enslave him.

Darkness dissipated, and he realized with horror that he had his hands on Naia's throat, and pulled them out quickly. "Naia?"

"River?" Her voice carried a smile. "Is that you?"

He was going to say, *Who else could it be?* when it all came back to him in a flash. In the last few moments, having glimpses that he had to be killed, he had been putting all his effort into ensuring Naia would have the chance to do so, and yet he was back, feeling as if a weight had been lifted from him, a veil had been ripped, chains had been broken.

"It's me, Naia. What did you do?"

There was concern in her pretty dark eyes. "Are you hurt?"

"You freed me." River closed his eyes, as memories and memories made him mortified. He sat on the mattress and rested his face on his hands. "I don't think I was normal, Naia. From the moment I came back again..." A horrible bitter feeling came to his mouth.

"I know." She smiled. "To be fair, I did tell you that your excuse for helping Ironhold made no sense."

Naia then took her dress and pulled it over her. This was the first time he was seeing her undressed, as he had been careful with that and given her time, knowing it was a big deal for humans. He had been confused in the glimpses he had, but had known she had a plan. "You were afraid the fire from the clothes would burn me?"

She looked down, a little shy. "Yes."

"How did you know fire would free me?"

Her lips formed a straight line. "I didn't."

He exhaled, so much relief, horror, shock, especially after spending his last minutes believing he was trailing the edge of death. "I thought you were going to kill me."

"And you didn't resist?"

This was a little complicated to explain. "No. I... I could see a little, I was partly aware. It wasn't me, I wasn't in control. And yet I still had some magic, some mindmelding. I could convince this horrific thing inside me that you were harmless, that this was a great opportunity to amplify his magic." He swallowed. "I trusted you."

Naia chuckled, such a lovely, musical laughter. "Didn't the dumbass realize we're in a room with tons of metal?"

This was another complicated concept. "I don't think he's truly aware of your magic, Naia. I don't think he knows about your *nature* either."

"But if he knows about Fel..."

"He doesn't know that much. He could influence me on what to do, but not see my mind. That until I did that thing in Ironhold, with that red dagger." A horrible feeling came to River, now that he had mentioned Naia's brother. Horrible, dreadful. He stared at her. "Naia."

Her eyes widened. "What?"

How could he tell her that? How could he *not* tell her? River swallowed, trying to find the words. It was like having to bury a dagger into someone, while trying to find the angle to hurt the least. "Your brother was a great warrior, a magnificent dragon, and he would die fighting, you know that?"

"Tell me, River."

"In Frostlake. I... Cynon...." River shut his eyes. There was only one way to bury a dagger with the least damage—and it wasn't by meandering. He looked at her. "Killed his dragon form."

"What?" The color faded from her face.

"He was with another dragon, an ally." Naia stared at him open-mouthed, while he scrambled for a way to explain what he'd seen. "Cynon used mindmelding on this other dragon and made him kill..." He took a deep breath. "Isofel. I..." How could he have been so stupid? "I did not predict it, I had no way to stop it, Naia. I was shocked. When I found a way to counter his magic, it was too late. The other dragon killed himself. I... have no words to express how sorry I am."

She stared at him for a while, then said, "It was not your fault, and you know that." Her eyes were wet with tears and her voice dry, emotionless.

But it *had* been his fault. His fault for not seeing what was happening when he could still do something, his fault for walking straight into a trap, for not even listening to her when she pointed out all his inconsistencies, but this wasn't the time to argue or make the case for his blame. He wanted to console her, but he didn't know how to do that. Would she want him to hold her, or would she want to stay as far away from him as she could?

Naia dried a tear, then asked, "Why Frostlake? How did he even get there so soon?"

"Cynon was opening a passage there. It was the whole point

of the dome. Your brother destroyed it—with little damage to the city. His act was heroic." He then added, "Not that it will bring him back." River knew what the pain of losing a sibling was like, and it wasn't something he wished upon anyone.

Her eyes were unfocused as she shook her head. "No. He's not dead. He's not dead, River. I think I would know it."

He wasn't sure if that was her way to cope or if it was indeed an intuition. "Maybe. I know very little about dragons." Now that River forced his memory, he could recall Cynon looking for Fel's human form, watching to see if he would change, but nothing happened. And yet he didn't want to tell this to Naia and kill her only sliver of hope. If that hope was what it took to keep her going, at least for now, then he wasn't going to smother it.

River finally decided to pull her close and embrace her. "I'm sorry, so sorry, Naia."

"At least it's you now. Welcome back," she whispered.

They spent a long time in silence, the candles burning and their breath the only sound in the room. River's memories from the time he hadn't been in control were getting clearer and clearer, and they only made him anxious, but this was the time to comfort Naia, not think about all the trouble ahead.

When she broke the hug she had a faint smile. "At least Cynon is gone. We won."

Oh, no. All he felt was a horrifying dread all over his body. He had to tell her the truth, but didn't think this was the time to ruin her only consolation.

Too late. He must have told her with his face alone.

She frowned. "What? What, River? He's not gone? You're still in danger?"

"I'm... I think you truly severed the bond. Your fire... it did something. I don't think I'm going to be used as a vessel anymore, but—"

"I killed Cassius."

"There are other people in Ironhold who can be the vessel. King Harold, for example. I think that was the plan all along, until Cynon found me—a mindmelding Ancient, resistant to iron. It must have been like coming across a pot of gold."

She rolled her eyes. "I love how humble you are."

It was good to see some playfulness in her, but in truth it wasn't something River found funny. He had never asked to be born with this magic, and was horrified that it had been used for such atrocities.

And yet he smiled and touched her face. "You should be glad I'm pretentious, or I'd never have asked you to run away with me." And then perhaps it was the wrong thing to say, as maybe if they had never gotten together, maybe... What could he have changed? How much could he have done differently?

Beneath her sadness, there was a hint of a smile on her face. "I'm glad you did."

Despite everything? Despite what I've done?

He swallowed these questions and pulled her close. "I'm so sorry. For everything." So much to make up for, and such little, empty words. Ancients hated saying they were sorry. What was the point? If there was a debt, they'd rather make a verbal deal, and yet, that was all he could say now.

Naia kissed his cheek, then broke the hug. "So we still have to defeat Cynon?"

He nodded.

"But now we have more information." She couldn't hide the sadness in her voice, but now she sounded more determined.

"We do." Information that should make them all panic, but it was information nonetheless.

She sighed. "There's one thing I don't understand. Isn't mind-melding confined to the Ancient city? How did—"

"Not in my case, it's not confined. Aluria has very precise magic rules, and the rules for humans are different. Human royals have magic everywhere on our island. I'm human—partly, but I guess it's enough. And a prince. It's an odd loophole."

She stared at him, clear understanding written on her face. "And that was why you could have made a difference in the war."

"Yes. Add that to my list of regrets. But this magic has a price... To use it against humans... I couldn't see it having a happy ending, Naia. And then, what ending have we found?"

"Maybe you were wise." Her tone was so sweet, so soothing.

"I was a fool. Even if I didn't want to use my mindmelding, I could have at least tried to do something. So many lives were lost. And yet I can't turn back time, can I?"

"We can make sure we don't repeat our regrets. We can still try to save some lives, even if we can't go back and save everyone." These words sounded heavy with the weight they carried. Of course Naia was thinking about her brother, while he was thinking about Ciara, about so much, so much that had been lost. She then asked, "What's going to happen? What are Cynon's plans?"

River held a strand of his hair and stared at it. "So much. And yet I know so little of everything."

"Tell me what you know. Instead of berating the past, let's be grateful that we got to have this glimpse into him."

Such a small glimpse. River was still consumed by guilt, as he doubted her brother could have been that easily killed without his magic, but he didn't say any of that. Instead, he tried to organize his thoughts, revisit his memories. He wasn't even sure from where to start. If he could, he would spare Naia the truth, but that would only make everything worse. She had that sheen in her eyes, claiming for a fight, claiming for revenge.

He wished he could be sure that she'd get her revenge, that she'd defeat her enemies. He wished he could assure her that everything would be all right—but he owed her the truth.

"Wait," she said. "Your sister must be dying with worry. We need to talk to her."

Anelise worried? He was still trying to get used to that idea. Still, he got up. "Let's go."

Naia stared at him, an indecipherable look on her face.

"Something wrong?" he asked.

"You're naked."

28

THE FINAL STRIKE

Naia watched as Anelise hugged River, that long hug with so much relief, thankfulness, and love. A part of her wondered if she would ever give Fel that same hug. Had he truly been gone? She couldn't believe it, couldn't accept it, but wasn't sure if it was a hunch or plain old denial.

For now all she wanted to do was try to contact the other kingdoms and warn them. After that, she'd need to plan what to do.

When River and Anelise broke their hug, the girl approached Naia and kneeled. "Gratitude binds me to you. Now and always."

Naia was embarrassed at such a formality and had a nervous chuckle. "I... wanted him back, too. It was a selfish thing."

Anelise got up and stared at her, or maybe glared.

River held Naia's hand, then turned to his sister. "If anyone is worthy of the of the greatest honor an Ancient can give, that is Naia, even if she doesn't quite yet grasp it."

Grasp... Perhaps late, but Naia understood it in a second. Apparently what his sister had just done was huge, and Naia had dismissed it. She smiled at Anelise. "I appreciate it, and appreciate your love for your brother."

Anelise nodded.

River put a hand on his sister's shoulder. "We're leaving. I'm sure the Ancients will be in good hands with you." He then lowered his voice. "When this is over, we'll solve this whole king... thing." It was pretty obvious that he hated what he had done to his father, hated the way he had ascended to the throne, but it was true that this was not the time to fix it.

"Don't worry about it," Anelise said. "And remember you can count on me." River squeezed his sister's shoulder, visibly moved, and she added, "You should go. Don't lose the scrying mirror this time."

At least they'd be able to connect with her. Naia wished she had given a communication mirror to her brother, or that she hadn't lost the one he'd given to her, thinking it didn't work.

River took Naia's hand and then they were encompassed in darkness, until they stepped into a brilliant circle and were in the woods by the fort, a faint light from the sunrise filtered by the trees. Everything seemed quiet.

Too quiet, like the calm before a storm.

"What does your sister's gratitude binding mean?" Naia asked.

"Basically you can ask anything of her. At any time. Without a deal and without asking for anything in return."

"That is..." Naia couldn't even grasp what it meant for an Ancient. "Huge."

"Unheard of. Of course, while you're queen, she will be bound to you, but it's different, and I don't know for how long..." He inhaled, as if trying to find the words.

"I know you don't like being king. I know you regret it. The only reason I didn't abdicate was because the alternative was giving *him* all the power over your people."

"I know." He had a bitter chuckle. "I make mistakes, but try to fix them."

"It was not your fault. And you did your best."

"Did I?" He raised an eyebrow. "I'd like to hope I could do better than that if such a horrific situation ever presented itself."

"From the vantage point of looking back, already knowing the result, it all seems simpler than when we're in the midst of it. I also didn't notice anything strange."

"You must have thought I was an asshole."

Indeed. She gave him a smile. "A redeemable asshole, though."

They arrived at the side door of the fort and Naia knocked. She hoped that nobody had attacked this place in her absence, that everything would be the way she had left it, but wasn't sure. And Fel, where was he? Was he truly dead? The thought was a dagger in her heart, and hurt too much for her to even entertain it.

The guard who opened the door was a blond young fellow whose name Naia didn't recall.

"Princess." He bowed slightly. "There are visitors. Waiting for the prince or the king, but I assume..."

"I'll see them." They were probably emissaries from another kingdom. She hoped it wasn't King Sebastian, even if she knew he could be a key ally. In fact, she didn't even know if they had escaped the attack in their castle.

The young man took her to the refectory, where a man and a woman were having soup, two other guards watching them. The woman had light blond hair, still darker than most Ancients, and the man had black hair and brown skin. They were dressed not like nobles or emissaries, but rather like warriors. Naia could not identify where they were from, as there was something different about them and their clothes.

The woman looked at Naia and opened her mouth in surprise. Could they be dragons? Fel had mentioned Tzaria, who was blonde. The man... Naia wasn't sure. Her uncle? That other exiled dragon?

But she preferred not to ask leading questions, not to give an intruder an excuse to lie. "I'm Princess Irinaia Umbraar. How may I help you?"

"So there are two of you," the woman said. "I'm Tzaria, from Fernick. This is Ekateni."

"My uncle." These words were barely audible, as she looked at him, a piece of a lost past, lost history.

He nodded.

There were a million questions she wanted to ask, but all she did was lead them to her father's office, River beside her, glamoured to look human.

When the door was properly locked, Naia turned to them. "A dragon, can they survive after their dragon form dies?"

Tzaria looked at her, then glanced at River. "So you know what happened to your brother?"

No. She was missing the most important part. "I don't know if he survived."

"I believe his human form was safe," she said. "Even if I'm not sure where it was, or how he swapped."

"But he couldn't swap forms," Naia said.

"He would come back here, wouldn't he?" Tzaria asked. "I say we wait."

Agonizing wait. Naia looked down.

Tzaria then looked at River. "I know you."

He unglamoured himself. "Same. I asked you to spare the Ancients and all you did was push me away."

"Ircantari did that. But we went to Ironhold to investigate. We took your claims seriously, fae."

"Oh, yeah." River gestured vaguely at Naia. "I can see how focused you were on the investigation." He then changed his tone. "But I'm glad you're here. We'll need your help."

It was true. The dragons would know more about Cynon, would know more about what River had seen, and perhaps, if they worked together, they would stand a chance.

Someone then knocked on the door. Naia was hoping it wasn't any nonsense, but opened it regardless.

Emotion swelled up in Naia's chest, and tears in her eyes.

IT FELT like forever that Fel hadn't hugged Naia. Holding his sister in his arms was pure joy. He kissed her forehead, then saw how tearful she was.

"I feared you were gone," she said, so much emotion in her voice.

Fel chuckled. "Can't get rid of me that easily."

He then noticed Tzaria and Ekateni and was overcome with relief. "You're alive too." River was also there. And yet someone was missing. His joy fizzled. "Where's Leah?"

"She went into the hollow and hasn't returned yet," Tzaria said.

Like his father. Would she be lost like him?

River put a hand on his elbow. "Time can be different there. And she's a deathbringer. I'm sure she'll return."

Fel's father was also a deathbringer, and yet... Tzaria and Ekateni then noticed Risomu, who had brought him. It had been a long flight, and yet the dragon had carried him all the way to Umbraar, after his cousins had contacted him.

"This is Risomu," Fel said, more to Naia and River.

"I know you too," River said. "Now, as much as I'd love to have some long introductions and explanations, I'm afraid of what's about to happen. But I'm glad there are a few dragons here, as we'll have to plan."

"And be fast." Tzaria nodded. "I know."

River told them that he had actually been the vessel, and had even made Ekateni kill Fel. This was surprising. He rushed through the details of how he had used a dagger, then even killed his own father and taken the white fae throne. He then told them about something that Ironhold had left in each kingdom, something that he feared could be activated, and something important in the Iron Citadel. "I know this is all quite vague," he explained.

"It is not," Tzaria said. "It's lucky that you were the vessel, and could gather so much information."

Fel wasn't sure about that. It was quite obvious that the Iron-hold castle had something important, and if they had been visiting other kingdoms...

Tzaria continued, "To come back to this world, he needs both forms. What's probably in the bottom of the castle is his dragon form. Hopefully still as an egg. Now, as to the gifts to the kingdoms, he can give them something like... The best description would be eggs, though the form will vary. They can also open gaps and bring creatures from other realms. My guess would be the eleventh realm."

More gaps? Fel couldn't believe it. "But what about the circle in Frostlake? Doesn't it mean anything that we destroyed it? That we stopped him from connecting with those realms?"

"We closed one circle, and a huge one, but his entire plan couldn't have depended on that," Tzaria said.

"Shouldn't we return there?" Fel asked. "Destroy those creatures?"

The woman shook her head. "There weren't that many left, and they would be spread out by now. We're better off focusing our efforts on Cynon and preventing more harm."

It made sense, even if leaving Leah's city helpless pained him.

River was thoughtful. "It was a trap. A circle made of metal and glass? Who would it attract? My feeling, what I got from it, was that the portal in Frostlake was important, but not that much. He was satisfied when he killed you, or thought he did, not disappointed that his circle was gone. I know my impressions are vague."

"What's the priority now?" Naia asked. "Destroy his dragon form? As for the eggs, I want to warn the kingdoms, but I was going to wait until the sun has risen properly and they're awake. I'm still not sure what to say or how to convince them."

"Fel should talk to them," River said. "They'll think he was the one who warned them about the attack in Wolfmark." He looked up, thinking. "Of course, if there was no attack, they'll be unlikely to hear anything we have to say."

"Let me try."

The others stood to the side while Fel activated the mirror. This was one of those times when he wished his father had been friendlier to other kingdoms. Sometimes it was just a matter of getting them to hear you.

He tried Wolfmark first, but nobody was there to answer.

"Try Haven," Naia said. "They also came to visit."

Fel tried and got the same lack of response.

River shrugged. "Either everything is quiet and they're all sleeping—or they're all already dead."

Naia scowled at him. "You can't be so flippant."

"It's not like I'm celebrating it," the fae said. "If anything, I was the one who raised the concern."

"They were your enemies," Fel said. "It's understandable."

"Were." River chuckled. "You're so optimistic." He changed his mocking tone. "Now, it's true that we do have a common enemy." He turned to Tzaria, Ekateni, and Risomu. "Oh, mighty dragons, how shall we defeat the evil that you allowed to grow in our land?"

Naia rolled her eyes. Ekateni was staring at River, and asked, "Are you a mindmelder, or was it Cynon?"

River stiffened. "Me. And before you ask, I also happen to be partly human. And royalty. So my magic works everywhere, at least in Aluria."

Tzaria was staring at the fae. "Did you really destroy the death staff all those years ago?"

"I did."

The woman still stared at him. "Our kind has feared your people for so long, and yet, one of you might be our salvation."

"I'll be happy to save Naia, Fel and our land," River said.

Fel didn't miss the implied meaning that he was not doing it for the dragons.

Tzaria looked satisfied. "At least we know we can trust you."

River rolled his eyes. "Fae can always be trusted. Our words are true."

She looked at him. "I know you're upset about your city, but we saw that there was a spell keeping it in stasis, we thought that we could wait, and that would give us—"

"You ignored us." River scoffed. "That's fine. What a small, little thing."

The dragons had stayed away from Aluria to make sure nobody found out about Ircantari's child. It sounded reasonable when Tzaria had told it to Fel, but now he agreed with River that it had been a cruel thing to abandon the white fae in those circumstances.

"I'm truly sorry," Tzaria said. "For what sorry is worth. If it helps, dragons feel great shame in having to accept help from someone they wronged."

"Really?" Naia looked at them in disbelief. "Instead of being ashamed of wronging?"

"Dragons are odd creatures," Ekateni said. "I tend to think that I'm better than that, but it might be pride speaking."

Naia exhaled, annoyed. "So is there a way to kill Cynon, kill the egg or dragon, is there something we can do?"

"There is a way," Tzaria said. "Your father spent his life researching it. We need to find both forms and kill them at the same time. For now, the vessel counts as his human form. I believe just killing him, like you kill any person, should work, but the texts talk about a specific way..."

Naia raised her eyebrows. "What way?"

Tzaria sighed. "Clear him of his blood, as in removing all his blood in one swift stroke."

River clapped. "Aren't we lucky? Isofel can do that."

"What?" Tzaria turned to him, and the other dragons stared at him open-mouthed.

Fel felt awkward with the attention. "I did it once. I was being attacked, and had no more weapons." He didn't even had his hands anymore, but didn't want to share that detail. "I connected with my attacker's blood—the iron in it." The memory disgusted him, but of course he'd do it again to save Aluria.

"Cynon is Harold," River said. "He was his second choice. And he's in the Iron Citadel. Its defenses were being reinforced. The ironbringers were being called to the castle to protect it from an invasion or something. But I can get in there—incognito, and even take a person with me. That said, I can't be in two places at once."

"So you could take me to Harold," Fel said.

River nodded.

"I could also get in the castle," Tzaria said. "With Risomu, since he still has his dragon form. And find Cynon's egg. I can sense dragons."

River looked at her. "How are you going to deal with the security? There will be guards."

Naia was thoughtful. "There wasn't anyone in the bottom of the castle when we were there."

"He planned it like that," River said. "He wouldn't leave this other important thing undefended." He closed his eyes. "It's even under that. Underground. Tightly secured. I'm... not sure how. I just got this feeling that it was safe." He took a deep breath. "I could get in there, though. No place in that castle is off limits to me."

Tzaria stared at him. "And you could move elsewhere quickly, right?"

"Yes."

The woman shook her head. "I don't think *at the same time* means exactly at the same time, it's just close enough that there's no time for him to recover. We could go down there, destroy the egg, and then find King Harold and kill him."

Naia was frowning, thoughtful. "I doubt it will be that easy."

Tzaria nodded. "There will be complications, that's granted. Do you have a better plan?"

"We should go in two groups," Naia said.

River shook his head. "I'm the only one who can move all over the castle and be invisible. I could make two of my companions invisible. If anyone else here has that glamour, then maybe..."

Naia sighed. "So you and Fel are going to risk your lives? While I stay here, terrified, hoping and wishing?"

River took her hand and kissed it. "I've come back from worse, Naia, so you should trust me."

Tzaria looked at them. "Perhaps we could try to plan better, but if we don't do anything, we'll also be risking our lives, and the more time passes..."

Naia crossed her arms. "It might get worse. I know."

Fel then recalled the strange amulet he had been given and realized it could work as a safeguard and a way for Naia to know she was important.

He removed his necklace and extended it to his sister. "This was given to me by the First Mage. He's... a special dragon or dragon spirit, I'm not sure. The amulet can turn back time, but he said we would know when it was used, since it has already been used. He said it was for me or for someone I love. I trust that you'll know what to do with it."

Naia nodded, then frowned and turned to River. "What?"

The fae blinked. "What what?"

She narrowed her eyes. "What do you know about this amulet? And don't give me your fae non-answers."

River seemed confused. "Why do you think I would know anything?"

"Because you're giving me a non-answer. Have you seen this before?"

"No," River replied. "I've never seen it before today. Happy now?"

Naia raised an eyebrow, but then turned to Fel. "So this was already used? And yet we're in this situation? What crap did we do?"

"I don't know." Fel had the same questions. He turned to the other dragons. "Do you know anything about this?"

"No," Tzaria said, which was quite disappointing. She seemed to always have an answer for everything.

River pointed to it. "Perhaps this could be our key. Instead of trying to figure out when or if it was used, we could be strategic about it and go back to the moment when everything started."

Tzaria closed her eyes. "It's never one single event, but a series."

River shook his head. "There's usually a trigger. We see things as a series, but there was something that caused it."

Right. Except that using the amulet in a wrong way, in theory, could rip reality or something. And then, was it a bad thing to rip a reality that was about to turn horrific? There was only one thing Fel had to say about it. "We need to return to a time we remember."

Naia frowned. "I guess if you die or something, I can come back to this moment and say that the plan flopped?"

"In theory you would have already returned, so no."

River shook his head. "I say it's nonsense to try to find the moment it was used. It's a tool we can use for the best."

Tzaria was thoughtful. "It's probably quite dangerous, though."

River rolled his eyes. "Everything is."

Fel was getting anxious with this conversation. "Shall we move? Go to the Iron Citadel and get Cynon while he's sleeping?"

"What's the hurry?" Naia asked.

Tzaria took a deep breath. "Once he latches on a proper vessel, he can... do more things. Like what happened to that iron dome. And if his egg turns into a dragon, it's going to be even harder. At the point things are, it could happen at any minute."

"Right." River smiled. "Aren't we glad we're in the nick of time? I mean, it's not like the dragons could have figured it out earlier or anything."

"The timing is perfect," Tzaria said. "There's evil in this world, but there's also a greater plan. We needed you to have been the vessel, and to be able to go everywhere in that castle, we needed the iron dragon to have been born and raised, and to be strong in his magic. This is the time. And we can act on it."

Naia shook her head. "One hour planning won't hurt us."

Ekateni sighed. "One hour arguing, you mean."

He had a point. Maybe. This decision was too sudden.

Tzaria then said, "Risomu should come as well because he has his dragon form. We might need fire. I can also walk in the hollow, and while we don't glamour ourselves as well as fae, we can walk unnoticed in a castle."

"We could split, then," River said.

"You'll grant us access there. And a bigger group is better. In case we face trouble."

Naia touched the necklace with the amulet. "If you take too long to return, I'm not going to think twice before using this, no matter the cost. So be careful."

Tzaria got up. "Let's go, then."

"No," River said. "Let's at least get some weapons, shall we?"

"We don't use weapons," Tzaria said. "We only use magic."

The truth was that Fel was the same. Even when he had used swords or a bow and arrows, he was still using his ironbringing to control them.

River shrugged. "It never hurts to be extra protected." He turned to Fel. "Can you lend me a sword and also arrows and a bow, if you have them? I can't guarantee I'll return the arrows."

Fel opened a cupboard that had some weapons, and passed them to River.

Naia's eyes were wide. "Really? Now? This is hasty and reckless."

Tzaria put a hand on Naia's shoulder. "Imagine you're hungry and you want a cake. You have all the ingredients, you have wood for the fire. Would you wait?"

"If it was morning, yes." Naia shrugged. "I'd wait for the cook to arrive or for Fel to wake up so I wouldn't have to do it myself."

"What if you *were* the cook?"

Naia took a deep breath. "I don't like it."

River took her hand, then kissed her cheek. "And I hate it. I hate everything that has happened and that is about to happen.

And yet I would hate even more to look back and see that I failed. That I could do something and I didn't..."

"But I'm not doing anything."

River took both of her hands. "Connect with the other kingdoms. Make sure this place is safe. You've done a lot for the Ancients, and you also need to rest, Naia."

She had a half smile. River's lips got close to hers, then he looked around and stepped back, as if they made him embarrassed or maybe he thought it would be inappropriate to kiss her in front of Fel and the dragons. Fel wished he could tell River he could kiss her, but then he figured they would be able to kiss a lot in a few hours—if everything went right.

Fel hugged his sister and kissed her forehead, like he'd done so many times since they were little. He knew that part of her problem was being left behind. She was brave and wild and eager to prove her worth, and staying here waiting was likely a torture for her. But perhaps he was selfish, as he was happy to know that no matter what happened, she would be safe. His own heart was ripped in shreds thinking about Leah. He couldn't bear to risk any more losses. And in that sense he understood his sister, who was watching him and River go.

Fel took Tzaria and River's hands, who took Risomu's, so that they formed a circle. Naia was right. This *was* sudden. He wasn't sure if it was hasty and reckless, though. Waiting and doing nothing sounded a lot worse. And yet.

River had to be in control of stepping into the hollow because this was unlike anything Fel had seen in Fernick. There was no circle traced on the floor, and yet they were soon in this odd, uncomfortable dark place, then in an empty chamber.

"Where is it?" River whispered.

"Lower," Tzaria said.

Darkness surrounded them again, then they were in another chamber, this one much smaller. Fel could sense a huge amount of metal around and under him, so much that it almost numbed his senses.

"In that room." Tzaria pointed to a huge door.

This time it felt as if darkness was squeezing his body, then they were in a room with metal floor, walls and ceiling. A red linen cloth covered a huge bundle in its corner.

"Run." It was a dragon's voice, but wasn't a voice Fel recognized.

"Let's go," Fel said, not willing to stay and figure out what was wrong. He had no doubt that this was not right.

"Oh, shit." River chuckled. "Not this again."

"What?" Fel asked.

"We're screwed, brother."

RIVER HAD ONLY HAD this sensation once—when he'd been caught in that room by Queen Kara. Now he felt it again, even if there were no leaves on the floor, and that story of death grass had been a lie anyway.

"I can't feel my magic," he whispered.

Fel looked at him. "I can still..." His hands fell on the floor, metallic thuds echoing in that chamber. "Nevermind."

Tzaria approached the red fabric. "We'll escape without magic." She pulled it to reveal a strange thing, some kind of mangled leather.

Oh. River's stomach chilled as he realized what he was seeing. It was a dragon, so skinny that the shape of his bones was visible beneath his skin. Most of his scales had fallen, and the ones still on his body were rough looking, like old tree bark if it were gray. There were also some cuts in his body.

"Who are you?" Tzaria asked.

"Can't... talk. Run." The dragon didn't exactly say these words, but sent them as a thought.

"I think we should just follow his suggestion," River said, checking the room for visible doors. He couldn't see any and assumed there would be something specially conceived for an ironbringer—and now Fel was powerless.

The sound of metal against metal made River look up. King Harold was there, or rather, Cynon, looking at them through a hole that was like some kind of small trapdoor.

"How lovely," Cynon said.

River took his bow in less then a second, then loosed an arrow towards that dreadful face. It hit a barrier and bounced back.

The creature looking at them from the top chuckled. "So now you know you're trapped. Trapped in a trap. Incredible how people can be so gullible. Enjoy your time there."

River still sent another arrow and another and another, even though they all bounced back. This was a human bow, different from the ones he was used to, but he was able to put enough strength to send them at a good speed, and yet there was no way they could reach the ceiling.

The trapdoor was then closed, and they were left alone. River tried to reach the wall, but came across a barrier.

"What's this?" he asked the dragons.

"It's a dragon barrier, by all means," Tzaria said. "Except that it's much stronger, and interferes with magic. All kinds of magic, it seems."

River scoffed. "And I assume he let us live thinking he'll over-hear some yummy morsels of gossip or something."

"Probably," Tzaria agreed.

He wanted to strangle them all and this stupid idea. While he wasn't afraid of dying, he didn't want to let Naia down. She had warned them, and yet he had trusted these dragons. He then remembered the amulet Fel had given her. Should such a rare and powerful object be used simply to save someone's life? It felt like a waste. Perhaps everything could be different if they used that object right this time.

The truth was that now he remembered it, remembered Naia wearing it, when she had rescued him in the dragon lair, so long ago. He hadn't lied to her when claiming he had never seen it. In truth, he hadn't noticed it then, and yet now the amulet was clear in his memory. But why should it be used to save his life, when so much more was at stake? And yet, if she didn't use it for that, what would happen to him? Die? Disappear? He wasn't sure.

One thing he realized was that his theory that Ironhold had a dragon heart was actually correct. He hadn't imagined the heart would still be attached to the body, but there it was. It was even more useful for Ironhold, as they were probably also using the dragon's blood.

Tzaria was close to the huge creature, caressing his wings and whispering some soothing words. Fel was thoughtful. Risomu was... anxious? There was something odd about that dragon, or else it was just that River didn't know him.

Tzaria turned to River, Fel, and Risomu. "His name is Kaneyo. He was an exile. Ended up here a long time ago—and got caught. It seems it was Ironhold's doing."

"Evil attracts evil," Risomu muttered.

She nodded. "Indeed. You need compatibility to bring something like Cynon."

"Not necessarily," River said. "I think." He hoped, at least.

The woman shook her head. "One thing is bringing him all the way from the eleventh realm. Housing him temporarily is another. And it seems you were not an easy host. He targeted you because of your power, not because of compatibility."

"Amazing power. Aren't you all in awe?" River couldn't believe he had fallen for such a silly trick. "And what about that thing we were looking for? Where is it, then?" He didn't want to mention the egg or Cynon's dragon form, fearing they were being overheard.

"We'll find it," Tzaria said. "There's a reason for everything."

"Oh, yes," Fel said. "It explains why my father died."

She put a finger over her mouth. Indeed he was stepping into dangerous territory. If Cynon realized he had his *iron dragon* right here... And then, what would he do? Imprison him? Take away his magic? But it was callous to talk about a reason for everything in front of Kaneyo, who likely had suffered for years.

River approached him and put a hand on his snout. "I feel for you. Some things do not have a reason. I wish you hadn't suffered."

"Noxious fae," the dragon whispered, so softly that it was likely meant for River only. He would be upset at being called that, but this dragon was so weak that he was likely not measuring his words. "I thought your kind was dead. I didn't know you could talk to dragons."

"I can," River whispered. He wasn't sure if it was because of Naia or because of his mindmelding, but he could definitely communicate with dragons.

"You shouldn't stand so close," the big dragon said. "His plan is to make me eat you. Eventually, I might."

River was going to make some joke about indigestion, but then realized the starving state of the dragon. "I appreciate the warning," he said, then stepped back. After all, being careful didn't hurt. He turned to the others. "Please tell me someone has an idea before we all become dragon food."

Pointing up, Fel said, "We'll need to have ideas and yet not discuss them."

Well, it was obvious. River waved his arms in frustration. "Just tell me you have a plan, fool me before death."

Fel got close to him and whispered in his ear, "The only plan is to wait. I trust my sister."

River also trusted her, but he didn't want her anywhere near this place. "Well, I want her to live a long, happy life, not get caught like us."

Fel frowned, thoughtful. "You think she can be happy without you?"

"I sure hope so." If something happened to him, he would want her to be happy. If they ended up using that strange amulet to save the day, he would also want her to be happy, even if the mere thought hurt him. And yet he also hoped that she longed for him the same way he longed for her, even if he was thinking that perhaps there would be no future for him. Their time had been so short—and he'd been partly out of his mind for most of it. This couldn't be the end.

"There's always a way." Isofel hadn't given up on his optimism.

"Sure." River pointed at Kaneyo. "I'm sure he just didn't think hard enough."

"He was alone, though. We're many."

Many dumbasses. Still, River gave Fel a smile, as if he appreciated his optimism. He hated it. If something didn't happen soon, they'd certainly all die.

29

FORGIVENESS

Something was wrong. Naia knew it. Or maybe imagined it. Maybe it was her mind full of fears fantasizing the worst for River and her brother. She touched the pendant hanging on her chest. Too early to even consider it. And then, she didn't think she would know how to use it—and should have asked Fel more about it.

With a slow, deep breath, she told herself to calm down. It wasn't as if they'd been gone for hours.

Ekateni was in a nearby room. Too tired even to sit, probably still hurt from technically dying, the best thing he could do was rest, so she had sent him away. But it meant that now she was alone with her thoughts.

A light in the communication mirror caught her eye and she pressed her palm on it.

King Sebastian's face showed up on the other side. If Naia were to follow her instincts, she would run from the room, but she needed to know what was happening elsewhere.

"Your Majesty." She bowed softly.

"I figure your king is still *sick*?" Was there an edge of mockery in his tone?

Maybe she was imagining it, and even if she wasn't, she

needed to pretend that was the case or else she would want to climb into the mirror and punch him. That was unfortunately impossible, and even if it wasn't, it wouldn't be a good way to treat a potential ally.

"Some things take time. Apologies for leaving your gathering. I still don't know what happened afterwards."

He narrowed his eyes. "Interesting. For someone who was so intent on disturbing our meeting, your concern for the other kingdoms is quite touching, princess."

"I was delayed. Securing our borders. These are tense times."

The king tapped his fingers on a table. "Tense times are when you seek allies."

This talk was annoying her. Yes, she shouldn't have disappeared, but it hadn't exactly been her fault. "Was there an explosion or did we miscalculate?"

He stared at her. "There was. And yet, there's no consensus on who could have caused it."

"Who do they think did it?"

"Some think it was Ironhold, some think it was... Umbraar. You knew about it, after all."

That was ridiculous. "True, but we didn't send people or resources to your kingdom. That's something that needs to be planned in advance."

He took a dagger and twirled it in the air. "It's all speculation. Quite empty. Pointless. I can steer their mind on the right path, of course." He was staring pointedly at her, as if it was a threat.

Naia wasn't sure how to respond, so she decided to smile. "Much appreciated."

"I haven't yet, princess. I can defend my wife, not a suspicious kingdom with no allies."

Oh, gross. She'd been hoping his proposal had been a delirious moment. The challenge was controlling her face not to show her disgust, then she quickly tried to come up with something to say. "But if you defend your wife-to-be, they'll think you're biased, and your word will be worthless."

"A marriage alliance will show them that Umbraar is repenting from their rebellious ways, and willing to cooperate."

There were so many things she wanted to tell him, starting with where to stick that dagger he was holding. This was not the time for it, though. She smiled again. "Your words are wise and will be considered." Quickly, before he insisted more, she changed the subject. "And what of Ironhold? And their gathering?" Only now she realized she'd completely forgotten it.

The king sighed. "Yes, that. Somehow, they caught hold of our impromptu gathering, and used it as an excuse to cancel their gathering and declare the Ironhold Empire. Instead of asking permission, they decided that they could declare it by default. Anyone who opposes them is declaring war."

"Then *Ironhold* is declaring war." She didn't understand how it fit with Cynon's plans, or perhaps it didn't and was just King Harold being King Harold.

"Perhaps they think nobody will step up and defy them. Perhaps they hope some of us *will* step up and can be turned into an example."

Unless... "There's something important. I got information from someone closely connected to their delegation. They left something in each kingdom, a magical object, something that will trigger..." She stopped short of saying *something* again, realizing how vague her words were. She wanted to mention Cynon, explain, but didn't think he'd believe her. This was so much harder than she had imagined. "I mean, if they can cause an explosion, imagine what else they can do."

"Which is why many fear to defy them, princess."

"You could try to find what it is, try to get rid of it."

King Sebastian shook his head. "Retreating is part of war too. Sometimes we have to concede defeat, wait, then strike when they are not expecting. Not now."

"So the kingdoms are just going to accept their rule, hoping that one day they can stab Ironhold on the back?"

"You summarized it well, princess."

It wasn't a terrible idea. Now was not the time to try to confront Ironhold, unless... There could be some kind of magic that needed Harold to rule the entirety of Aluria.

"King Sebastian, I beseech you to reconsider it. Ironhold has old, dangerous magic. There's a good possibility that they need to control Aluria due to some kind of magical law, perhaps some way to put something in motion. You have to refuse their rule and help me tell the other kingdoms to do the same. You don't need to openly defy them or tell them that."

"Irinaia, your cute lips are so adorable when you beseech. You can have me on my knees for you, if you say the word. Say yes to my proposal and I'll help you."

Naia was trembling in anger. "King Sebastian, with all due respect. Umbraar was not dumb enough to let Ironhold come in, station their troops, and put a stupid magic egg here. *We* don't need anything. It's your kingdom and others I'm worried about."

He laughed. "Princess, with all due respect. Who do you think will be the first kingdom Ironhold will attack? Do you think they'll bring a couple hundred men like last time? I don't think so. Your kingdom is about to be squashed. I'm the only one who's even willing to extend a hand, to ignore your family's tarnished past, your mother's ruined reputation. Your king is dead or about to die, your brother is a cripple. Who will—"

"Quiet," Naia roared. "Dare say a word more about my brother and I'll personally kill you. And you know what? I don't care what happens to your kingdom."

She put the palm of her hand so hard on the mirror that it even hurt. Now Naia wanted to go to Wolfmark and kill King Sebastian, as anger burst inside her. How dare he? So he'd proposed to her under the assumption that her father was dead? How sick was that?

Naia rested her face on her hands. Great. Now she had to worry about an attack by Ironhold.

She paused. No. Harold and the Ironhold family were the ones with the hatred towards Umbraar. Would Cynon care about that when he had all the kingdoms? When he had so much more? He could care because Umbraar was one of the few kingdoms, if not the only one, without that stupid egg or whatever. Unless... Visitors *had* come here. And attackers as well. They could have placed an object anywhere. But then, maybe it needed to be accepted as a gift or something, and maybe it had been Kara or River delivering it. Naia was so confused. Meanwhile, Fel and River were in the Iron Citadel and all she could think was that something was very wrong, and yet she had no idea what to do.

She took the communication mirror and stared at it, hoping for a sign, something. Hoping for a miracle.

AZIR DIDN'T UNDERSTAND why Ursiana didn't want to return to Aluria, especially if she was worried about her daughter. "Leandra's in Ironhold, and I need to get her out of there." This had been worrying him since he'd learned about their attack in Frostlake.

"She isn't." Ursiana's voice was failing, and he feared she would become unconscious again.

"Then where is she?"

"I... can't you feel it? Like a faint song. Maybe not so faint. I can stand. Can you put me down?"

He got her down from his shoulder, but laced his arms around her, holding her tight.

"Better?" he asked.

"Maybe." Ursiana was thoughtful. "She's in one of these realms, but I don't even understand what this place is, how to move here, I can't..."

He was about to wonder aloud how Leandra could have gotten in the hollow. What a stupid question—she was a death-bringer. Untrained, on top of that, carrying the weight of his magic, unaware how heavy it was. It was quite possible that she would end up lost if there was any trouble in Ironhold.

"Do you have a sense of direction? Any..." What could he say? *Clue, tip, image*? He was still unsure how Ursiana could sense their daughter, but then, there was so much more magic at work in the world than anyone understood.

Ursiana closed her eyes, thinking, then looked at him. "You have to find her, not me."

Azir truly did not know how to do that, and yet didn't want to disappoint her, didn't want to leave Leandra lost. "How?"

She thought for a long while, then said, "I poisoned my heart with hatred, thinking it made me strong. Maybe it did. Maybe it did give me the push to carry on, and yet it kept me in the dark. It dampens the senses, Azir, overpowers logic. I'm sure it messes with magic too. Maybe it empowers it, maybe it was what gave me those dreadful vines, life-saving vines, and yet, I don't think hate ever gave me clarity."

He wasn't sure where she was going with this. "Anger is a natural emotion."

"Yes. Yet clinging to it is a choice. I made that choice, and I was wrong." She looked at him. "I heard what you said, and I want to apologize. I blamed you, and you only for what happened."

"Well, it wasn't *your* fault."

"It wasn't yours either. You were duped. I might have berated you for thinking the worst of me at the first chance you got, and yet, didn't I do the same? I assumed the worst. Maybe you didn't try to talk to me, but I didn't try it either. Yes, it's more complicated for women, but still... I mean, maybe there was nothing that could be done. Maybe there's no point trying to look back and imagine what could have been different, and yet, clinging to anger doesn't make anything better. This is what I wanted to say. *I forgive you* sounds wrong. It's still placing the blame on you. I meant to say that I don't want to hold on to my resentment, I don't want to carry that hatred anymore. I understand what you did. Would I have done anything different had the situation been switched? I don't think so."

He held her hand. "We can talk when we get back. And you can still yell."

She shook her head. "You need an unburdened heart to find clarity. You need a clear mind to find your way in the darkness. I know I'm not a deathbringer, but..."

"I regret what I did, Ursiana. It was wrong."

"It all turned out well, though." She closed her eyes. "I mean, Leah should never have been sent to Ironhold, but if she's here, it means she has escaped."

And yet, where was she? How could he know in which realm? "It's worry that burdens my heart."

She put a hand on his chest. "I know. You have to let go of that."

There was a sweetness in that voice coming from her lovely lips. He'd kissed them so many times that he still remembered their taste. And yet this was not the moment to think about that. And then, if he needed clarity... Perhaps there was something he wanted to know.

"Ursiana, you said you'd forgive me."

"Not forgive..."

He put a finger over her lips. "Hush. I know. I know you don't want to blame me. But I have a question. You said we shouldn't look back to what has been lost, to what could have been different, and maybe there's wisdom in that. Now, is there a way we can make our futures different? Pick up where we left off?" It took some courage to say these words, to lay himself bare and vulnerable, open to be rejected. "Start over?"

"Two days ago, I would have said *over my dead body*." She snorted. "It felt so good to hate you. Bitter, but good. And yet I could never truly hate you. I thought I was hurting you, and yet I was just drinking poison."

"You want to torture me with your riddles."

He then realized he was touching her lower lip with his thumb. Ursiana kissed it. "Do I?"

She followed it with a quick swirl of her tongue. It was like fire bringing back memories, taking him back to a precious moment many years ago. A moment when nothing else existed but the two of them. Those lovely lips that could weave funny words, smart words, that were so sweet, and could also weave magic.

He barely felt when his lips touched hers, and then for some reason he was back in the ruins of the Formosa castle, right where he had retrieved the lightshield. Now that there was solid floor beneath them, his hands were free—free to undress her. It felt unreal, a strange dream, to see her body again, to feel her hands lifting his shirt, opening his trousers. Perhaps want was also a burden and he didn't want to think how heavy his heart had been with it.

This place would be the last he'd choose for a romantic moment. It had no bed, no soft carpet, no pillows. The solution was to hold her again, this time against one of the few parts of wall still standing. He'd wanted this for so long. With each thrust, he let go of his anger, let go of his shame, his regret, his sadness. As much as he'd said it was all his fault, he'd still been angry, carrying that dreadful grudge like a rotten treasure. He wanted to let go of everything, let go of all parts of the past that had hurt him. He was letting it all go. Back where he belonged.

When it was over, it was like waking up from a long daze again. He took her face in his hands and kissed her lips quickly, then said. "I missed you. Every day without you was a torture."

"I missed you too." She was serious, though.

Of course, they had more important things to do. He grabbed all of their clothes, then took her hand. They were back on that strange beach he'd ended up after escaping the deatheyes.

"Nothing like the ocean to cleanse our souls."

"Souls? I'm pretty sure that's not what that word means." Ursiana chuckled, but ran to the waves.

Azir followed her, but soon they were back, and got dressed. Part of him wished he could take her somewhere safe and then go on his own, but part of him felt she would be important to help him. Hopefully Ursiana was right, and all that he needed was a clear, unburdened heart. He didn't think he could ever feel lighter.

WHERE HAD her pain led Leah, other than to emptiness? The great empty, the space between spaces where nothing existed— not even loss. This wasn't the land of the dead, the bridge to the other worlds, that place of waiting in the long line before the next life. It wasn't living or dying, just an infinite numbness.

Leah felt no difference with her eyes open or closed. She had to leave this place, she knew it, and yet her body didn't want to move. She tried to think about her kingdom, think that perhaps it needed her, but maybe it would be presumptuous to believe that it depended on her. What had she done so far? It had fallen to Ironhold, had its dome used as a horrific portal, and she had foreseen none of it. Not to mention her father and Kasim...

Those were the thoughts she wanted to escape, the thoughts that had led her here, where nothing hurt as much. And yet nothingness also hurt. That big emptiness. The world was about to fall apart, and here she was, unable to go back and fix her mistakes. And then again, could she even fix anything?

Her breath was slow. There was still air here, even if she felt suffocated in her thoughts.

And then there was also some light, faint at first, then brighter. Leah would run if she could. Perhaps she should. And yet all she did was stare as that light approached her.

All she could see was brightness and a hand in it. A hand to pull her out of that place, and yet she did not know whose hand it was, did not know where it would lead her, did not know how much it would hurt if she left.

"Take my hand," someone said. A man. Leah didn't trust men. Didn't trust anyone.

"Leandra," the man repeated. "Your mother wants to see you. She's alive. She's here."

Leah reached out at once, and then was pulled away, pulled away from that darkness and even from those dreadful thoughts that kept telling her she was useless and everything was meaningless. They hadn't really been her thoughts.

She realized she was holding King Azir's hand. How would she tell him what had happened to Fel? And yet the shame and regret wasn't as great as before, when in that strange place. Another hand found hers, and she recognized it at once.

"Mom?"

"Yes, darling."

So much weight was lifted from Leah all at once, so much relief inundated her heart. Her mother was here, was alive! Leah wanted to hug her, but didn't want to let go and risk getting lost again.

They moved to a dark place that had brilliant circles in the distance and an eerie light all over it.

Azir said, "I'll take you to Umbraar, to the Royal Fort. For now."

Slowly she recognized the same room where she'd spoken to the Umbraar King a few days before. So long ago. Naia was sitting there, her head resting on her hands. And then Leah sensed something else, a familiar pull. Fel. He was alive, he was. She wanted to hug her mother, she wanted to talk to Naia, and yet, it was as if she was being dragged out of that room.

"I'm going to Fel," she muttered, before disappearing into the darkness.

Perhaps she heard something like *no* or *wait*. While she understood why she should be cautious, she had no strength left to fight the pull of his magic—their magic.

She saw herself in a strange room where four people stood. Among them, Fel, in human form, looking regal, powerful, and beautiful, as if all his might and power as a dragon could be condensed in that form as well.

"Fel," she said, or rather choked the word. Tears were running down her eyes. Purifying tears.

He pulled her into a hug. "Leah."

She held him tight, so tight, she wanted to hold on to him and never let him go. "I thought you were dead."

"I'm here."

His lips touched hers and then they were kissing. She'd been wanting this kiss for ages, a true kiss, without any burden between them, a kiss like their first, when the dome in Frostlake still stood, when they thought their love would be so easy and simple.

Someone cleared their throat, and Leah turned to look. It was River. "We can all look away and give you privacy. If you want."

Fel frowned. "We're just kissing."

The fae shrugged. "It's a suggestion. In case we realize we're stuck here. I mean, if you're going to die, die in style, with no regrets."

"Die?" Leah didn't understand what was happening, then realized they were in some kind of Ironhold prison. It had to be Ironhold, due to the amount of metal. On a corner, where she thought there was a bunch of old leather, it was... She felt sick in her stomach. A dragon, so weak... There was no door, just metal everywhere. Couldn't Fel... She didn't even finish her mental question, as she noticed the parts of his metal hands on the floor. His magic wasn't working. Tzaria and another man, probably a dragon as well, were also in the room, their faces somber.

Fel bit his lip. "This is a prison, Leah. Can you try to leave?"

"If you do, would you mind getting us some help?" River asked. "You're welcome to stay, of course. The more the merrier. I'm sure Fel is happy to see you."

"Can you feel your magic?" Fel asked.

She adored his voice, soft and deep, and yet, it wasn't a question she could answer. "I... don't know."

NAIA CLOSED her eyes and took a deep breath. Wouldn't it be wonderful if air could give her some answers? Just once. She was still shaking with anger, thinking about King Sebastian, still wanting to kill him. What a stupid waste of energy, when she should be focusing on defeating her true enemies. More than anything, she wanted to know if her brother was well, and if something had happened.

Then she heard a voice in the office. A woman's voice. "Let her go to your son. It's what she wishes."

Naia looked and saw her father and the Frostlake Queen. Here. Inside the Royal Fort. Was she hallucinating?

"Dad?" She then recalled his last words to her. "I mean, King Azir?"

He circled the table she was sitting, and then pulled her into a strong embrace. "Naia, I'm so sorry."

Naia was happy, but also startled. "For what? Where were you?"

He kissed her forehead. "I was lost. And had time to mull over my words. Of course you are my daughter. Will always be. I should never have said you weren't."

Tears were pooling in her eyes. "Is this real?"

He broke the hug and held her shoulders. "It is." He looked around. "I'm glad you're back home."

Did she think she had left River and that was why he was being so nice? Would he still accept her if she told him the truth? But this wasn't the moment to think about any of that. "I... we're having... quite a few problems."

Her father nodded. "Why don't you tell me?"

First, because she didn't even know how to start. To be fair, he was looking at her the same way he did when she came back from a hunt or found something interesting, all ears for what she had to say. And she had told him he had never listened to her! In things that mattered, perhaps he hadn't. But had she ever tried to say anything? And then, none of that mattered right now.

"Aluria is in great danger, there's something dreadful in Ironhold."

"I know," he said.

Technically, he didn't, but it was true that he had hated that family for a while, perhaps sensing their dealings with dangerous magic.

Then Naia heard another voice, saying, "Can you hear me?" Her brother! She gestured to her father to wait, and to the queen as well, who was standing in a corner.

"Fel? Where are you?"

"Naia, can you hear me?" The voice spoke again.

He was communicating like he'd done as a dragon, which probably meant he was close, and yet there was no relief or victory in his tone, only worry, as if he was about to tell her something serious. She tried to send him a thought. "I can hear you. What is it?"

"Naia!" At least some relief in his tone. "We're in a room down in the Iron Citadel. Our magic is mostly blocked and we can't leave. It was a trap."

Her father was staring at her in curiosity, and she gestured to him again to wait, then sent a thought to Fel. "I can try to find you."

"No. If you get here, your magic will be blocked. Leah has just arrived, and she can't do much either. River is saying you should try to find his sister—"

"Ancients, I mean, white fae can't get into Ironhold."

"I know. He means she might be able to help you. There is a way for the Ancient City to contact the dragon council. You'll need to tell them."

Naia shook her head. "Fel, you think Cynon is going to sit around that long?"

"We're trying to find a way out. There has to be one, Naia. We're alive and unharmed, so don't worry about us."

An idea came to her mind. "You think it's Cynon's magic keeping you there?"

"Likely."

There was a solution. "Fel, I'm going to get you out."

"Naia, don't come here."

"Not there. Give me some time and then try to talk to me again. I'm going to do something that might help."

"What are you—"

"Fel, I need to focus. Give me some fifteen minutes."

Naia stared at her father. "You can get into the Iron Citadel, right?"

"Yes, why—"

"I need you to trust me, just this one time. I can't explain it all because it's very complicated, but I need to find King Harold and kill him."

Azir frowned. "I can kill him."

"No. It's a special way to kill him, only an ironbringer can do it. Just get me close to him."

He sighed. "It's dangerous to carry someone across—"

"The hollow, yes." She pointed at the Frostlake queen, still standing in a corner. "Looks like you did it just fine. And the thing is, you always said you can't transport someone who doesn't have the magic to go through the hollow, but I have it."

"Naia..." He said it slowly, apologetically. "You're not a death-bringer."

"I know! I'm a dragon."

He grimaced. "You what?"

"Too complicated to explain. I swear, it's a matter of life and death. Fel's life." She almost mentioned Leah as well, but then again thought it would be too complicated and invite unnecessary questions. It would also make the queen worried, and calming her down would be another unnecessary complication. "Trust me. Take me to King Harold. It's not really him, but an evil creature. If you want to help, protect me. But let me kill him. Please. This is the biggest and most important favor I'm asking—"

"Naia, for you I'll do anything. I'm just worried."

"Then trust my power. This time only. Please."

He nodded slowly, then turned to the Frostlake queen. "I'll arrange—"

"Go," she said. "I'm fine here. I'll wait."

"Let's go," her father said, then held her hands.

This was very different from moving into the hollow with River. It wasn't like picking a circle in that dark place, but more like whooshing from one place to another. She saw the Iron Citadel from above, ugly and artificial, brimming with metal magic and so much metal, like a perfume so strong that it felt like it burned the nose.

"It won't be easy to find him and he'll be quite protected," her father said. "Are you sure you want to try this?"

She was. For the first time in her life, she realized she could do something, she could make a difference. Instead of resenting the burden, she welcomed the responsibility, welcomed the challenge. "I'm certain."

Of course, her heart didn't seem to share her opinion, as it was beating like crazy, perhaps thinking it could sway her from that decision. It couldn't. She would risk everything to save Fel. She would risk everything to save River. There were no words to explain how much she'd risk to save them both.

30

THE OTHER ONE

Naia stared at that horrific, artificial monument to Ironhold's greed, the Iron Citadel. She had never imagined one day she'd float above it.

Her father looked down at the castle, his expression thoughtful. "You said King Harold has some... other creature controlling him. What kind of magic are we dealing with?"

"Dragon magic."

Her father was silent for a few seconds, then asked, "What does it do?"

"I'm not sure. I think he's more powerful than most dragons and to be honest, other than fire, I don't really know much about dragon magic. And he also has ironbringing, of course."

Her father grunted. "What I could do is make it dark once we find him and kill any guards protecting him. Do you think it can help you? Can you do what you need to do without seeing him?"

"I'll have fire, but some darkness might be enough to distract him. Getting rid of any guards might be good too. Thanks."

Rooms in the castle whooshed before her. Bedrooms, a throne room, meeting rooms. What kind of magic would Cynon have? If Naia reached out, could she sense it? She'd been close to him and knew the difference between regular River and River with Cynon. If only she could isolate, identify the difference...

"Upstairs," she said. "Really up. I think." It was a hunch, a guess, an idea that a dragon would miss the heights and not want to be buried deep within the castle.

"I'll try the observatory," her father whispered.

They came to the top of a tower. Suddenly everything went dark, as if the sun had disappeared for a moment. She'd glimpsed Harold standing there, with guards outside. In a second, she shut the iron doors, then shot him a blast of fire.

Tzaria's words were about fire and then removing the blood, so she thought she had to use the fire first. It should also immobilize dragons.

King Harold, or rather, Cynon, turned around and laughed at her. "You think you can use my magic against me? Silly girl. Only the Iron Dragon can kill me."

"Really? What a coincidence." Naia focused. With so much iron in that castle, something as subtle as someone's blood was easy to miss, but it was also life, magic. In this case, it had an odd, tainted feel to it. It was true that Naia, unlike her brother, couldn't manipulate many different objects at a time, but she could sense his blood as one thing. In a swift motion, she removed it, then blasted him with fire again.

She then said, "I happen to be an iron dragon too." Too bad that he couldn't hear her, as his body was shriveling and burning as if it were made of thin wood. She kept burning it, wanting to end everything.

"Naia." It was Fel's voice.

"I just killed Harold. Where are you?"

"I was able to escape, and now I'm going to find his dragon form."

"Good."

He had to be quick to ensure Cynon's ties to this world were cut. Meanwhile, she burned Harold until his body became ash. Perhaps it wasn't fair to kill him if he was just a vessel, but his actions had led to Cynon being here. And then perhaps there was no way to defeat this evil without killing this king. She couldn't believe she was feeling bad for Harold. True that he was also her uncle.

Naia sighed, then glanced at her father. He was alert, keeping an eye on the door, not at all fazed by the sight of blood and death.

"Do you think this is enough?" she asked.

He looked at the remains on the floor, mostly ashes. "There's nothing left of him, but I don't know if there's some magical rule..."

Naia blasted more fire. "I'll burn him more—just in case. Thankfully the floor here is granite. Imagine if it was wood."

"And the windows are open, or I'd be roasting here. I guess you don't mind the heat, but I do."

Naia smiled at his attempt at levity. To be fair, she usually felt just as hot as anyone else, except when it came to her own fire, or maybe even other dragons' fire, except that she had never experienced it. Now the body was gone, something that wouldn't be possible with a regular human or animal body, and she knew how long a wild pig took to roast. Odd magic.

"Can we go?" Her father asked.

That would be wise, before the guards opened the doors, although they weren't even attempting it. Something then came to her mind. "Why do you think he was up here? It's as if he wanted to see something."

"Maybe. I think we can leave now."

Naia looked out the window at the cliff surrounding the castle and, further away, bare plains with no houses or people, unsure of what anyone would expect to find. Or it could be something in the sky. Dragons? Or something more sinister?

"Yes. Let's go."

She took his hand and felt that strange darkness involving her. One thing she knew: this wasn't over.

FEL TOOK A DEEP BREATH, almost regretting having contacted his sister, fearing she'd do something reckless. He was glad to see Leah, but also horrified that she was now sharing his fate, trapped here.

She had her eyes closed, thinking, then stared at him. "I can feel it. My magic. I think I can get you out." She glanced at the others. "We can return with help."

"See?" River was standing near them and chuckled. Hopefully nothing inappropriate was going to come out of his mouth, but Fel doubted it. "Look at what the need for privacy does to people."

Fel wanted to tie the fae's horns together.

Tzaria was standing close to them as well, and whispered, "If you do manage to leave, find it."

The egg, she meant. "How?" Fel didn't think he would be able to find anything in this gigantic castle.

"Wait," River said. "It has to be here, at least not far. There's a dragon to mask its magical signature, there's a magical trap to ensure anyone who comes close can't do anything." He turned to Tzaria. "How big is a dragon egg?"

She shook her head. "We reproduce in human form. A dragon egg is a magical encasement for the dragon form."

"How big?" River insisted.

"I've never seen one," the woman said.

River frowned. "And yet you were sure you could find it."

She shrugged. "I can sense dragon magic."

Fel and Leah exchanged a glance, as she seemed to realize that finding this egg would be next to impossible.

River then got close to Fel and whispered, "It's under our impaired friend, Kaneyo. There's a compartment there."

"How do you know it?" Fel asked.

"I... sense it, not know it. But we'll need our magic. Yours, to reach it, and maybe mine, to ensure the dragon won't try to stop us."

From the corner of his eye, Fel saw a blast of fire coming in their direction. He barely had time to push Leah away. The blast almost hit River, but now the fae was standing still, staring at the dragon, who didn't try to burn him. At the same time, a host of sensations came back to Fel. The room came alive with an energy he knew well: metal magic. He pulled back his hands.

Meanwhile, without moving his stare from Kaneyo, River said, "Now. Go, Fel."

"I'll get the egg." Then a new clarity hit him. "Naia is after Cynon."

River stared at Fel wide-eyed. "She what?"

At that same moment, another blast of fire came towards River. Fel pulled a panel from the wall, but couldn't move it fast enough to block the fire. Horrified, he watched the fae engulfed in dragon flames. Fel looked again, unsure if his eyes were playing tricks on him. River was not burned or hurt. He stared at the dragon, and said, "Go. I'll keep him still."

Tzaria was saying calming words to Kaneyo, who was oddly motionless, like River. At the same time, Risomu was taking his dragon form.

Fel sensed an opening on the floor right behind Kaneyo, protected by a metal pane, which he pulled. Perhaps he pulled it too much, as the floor beneath him cracked.

Tzaria took River in a circle, so that they would leave this room before the floor collapsed. Leah held Fel's arm. His hands were working again, but he understood she wanted to be sure. The only reason Fel didn't fall into a huge abyss below was because he was able to control the part of the ground beneath his feet, since it was iron. He wrapped Leah in his arms, aware that he needed her. If things got too dire, she'd be able to take them away. It was all dark, but this felt like an enormous chamber, more like a natural cavern.

Fel then heard it, like someone taking a breath, but the sound was more ragged. This was a dragon about to blast fire. A gigantic one. It could be another prisoner like Kaneyo, and then perhaps Cynon's dragon form was no egg after all.

He felt the odd whoosh of darkness, then was standing at the bottom of the cave, while a blast of fire illuminated stalagmites on the ground. Part of the ceiling was broken and led to the chamber from where they had fallen.

As a dragon, Fel had been much more attuned to other drag-ons' sensations, intentions, feelings, but he could still sense some of that. All he found was darkness, like a hollow pit of hatred. He hoped he wasn't wrong in his assumption, hoped Tzaria wasn't wrong in what she had told him. At once, he pulled all the drag-on's blood. It wasn't enough. He needed fire. "Risomu!" he yelled. No, it wasn't what was needed.

Fel tried to reach out to his sister, through thoughts, asking her to come here, asking her to find him.

"Fel!"

It was Naia, on the other side of the room, with their father. He was alive!

Fel would like to go there and hug them both. Instead, he shouted to her. "Blast the dragon! It has to be you."

She raised her hands the way she always did before using her magic, which always gave away her intentions, but this time he was glad to see her doing that and burning the body of the dragon. Hopefully she was burning Cynon's dragon form.

Hopefully this nightmare was about to be over.

A small circle appeared on the other side, near Naia. There were pieces of metal that had fallen from the room above that Fel could use as a weapon, but it was just Tzaria and River. Kaneyo's fire seemed to have dampened the fae's magic, but he embraced Naia, visibly relieved to see her there.

"We should go," his father said, yelling so that he was mostly talking to Fel. "I'll take them to Umbraar, then come back for you."

"I'll follow you," Tzaria said. "And take him."

"Oh, the humiliation," River grumbled.

First Azir and Naia disappeared, then Tzaria traced a brilliant circle and was gone with River.

Fel was left alone with Leah, and she rested her head on his chest. "I still can't believe you're alive." It was as if only now she was able to voice her fears, voice her worry.

"I missed you too," Fel confessed. "I was so worried that you disappeared."

"And yet you were still here, fighting. I..." She looked down.

He kissed the top of her head. "It's over for now, that's what matters."

She looked up at him. "You think it's over?"

The truth was that he didn't know, and was wondering the same thing as her. "For now, it is. Let's hope *now* lasts a long time."

RIVER FELT as if all his bones had been broken and if he moved, they would fall apart. Of course none of this was true. He'd just been blasted by dragon fire—and probably saved by some of Naia's magic that still coursed through him. In his state of incompetence, he allowed Tzaria to carry him through the hollow. It felt strange to trust a dragon, especially considering she'd been among the ones who had isolated the Ancient City, who hadn't listened to him. No, they had listened, but then something obviously happened. A trick of destiny.

He let Tzaria hold his hand and draw a circle on the ground. They moved differently than fae, even if the principle was pretty much the same. This was something that Naia would have to learn. For now, he was glad Cynon had been defeated—or at least seemed to be—and they had escaped.

The woman lingered in the darkness, in the space between everything, and stared at him. Great, what a time be have a conversation—when none of his magic seemed to work.

"You controlled that dragon." Her voice was a whisper, as if afraid of saying it out loud.

River wasn't sure where she was going with that. "Did I? You think I wanted to get blasted?"

The woman shook her head. "You lost control, sure, but you held him. Don't worry, I won't tell anyone. I'll even try to convince Risomu he must have been confused."

River wasn't sure why she was saying that. "You all heard me tell you that I controlled that other dragon and made him kill Naia's brother."

"You were the vessel then, and Cynon has powerful magic. Now it's different." She stared at him. "You don't understand, do you?"

"Obviously not."

"Many will say that the noxious fae were exiled due to their role in helping Cynon."

Noxious. He couldn't even move his arms, or else he'd consider slapping her. "Can you not use that term?"

"Sorry. They say that's the reason the Ancients were exiled, and yet, it doesn't make sense. There were Ancients fighting on both sides. The thing with Cynon, that was an excuse to isolate you. You know why? You're the only creatures who can subdue a dragon. It was fear, not justice."

"I see. As someone who cares about justice, that's why you did your part, and made sure we got our freedom back. Oh, wait."

She looked down and shook her head. "It was a long time ago. I used to trust the High Council back then. It's incredible how much you can see once you get out of the box. I'm truly sorry I didn't come back for your people. I was trying to protect Ircantari's child—children. And I thought the Ancients were safe."

"Well, tell your dragon friends then that most mindmelders are dead, it's a dreadful power, and they can stop fearing us."

"I might. But I'll make sure nobody ever knows what you are. It must be kept a secret."

River nodded. "Can we go? I want to embrace Ircantari's daughter."

She smiled and they appeared in the king's office in the Royal Fort.

Naia was the one to find him first and wrap her arms around him. "I was so worried."

"I'm... almost fine."

The Umbraar king was not there, and neither were Leah and Fel. There was a woman standing at the corner, looking anxious. The Frostlake Queen. Leah's mother.

River felt that at least his arms could move and held Naia tight.

A few seconds passed, and three people appeared in the room: King Azir, Fel, and Leah.

The time had come. River whispered in Naia's ear, "I have some reparations to do."

He approached Azir and kneeled, even though it hurt to do that in his state, looking down at the ground. He'd never humiliated himself like that to anyone before, but he knew that this was the honorable thing to do after his mistakes.

"Your Majesty. I, River of the Second Dynasty, pr—" He choked, unable to say *prince*. "King of the Ancients, or White Fae, as you call us, humbly approach you to apologize." His heart was beating fast.

He realized that this position, staring at the floor, didn't let him see Azir's expression. It was perhaps comfortable for when someone was speaking from a place of great shame, but it just made him anxious, unsure how his words were being received.

River continued, "In my foolishness, I convinced your daughter to escape Frostlake, to leave her family, leave everything she loved, for me." Now that his mind was his own, he didn't understand how she hadn't punched him in the face. "It caused her great grief, and I assume must have caused you grief as well. As much as perhaps I wasn't totally myself then, I was committed to protecting her, committed to making sure she stayed safe. I told myself that was why she had to be sent away from everything, but I didn't realize that it split her in two." Talking about this was hard. Not only confessing his mistakes was difficult, it was even hard to express what exactly had gone wrong, and why he'd done all that.

"Get up, River," Azir said. "I'd rather face you when I speak." River was up in a second, staring down at Naia's father, who wasn't angry. He asked, "You're their king?"

This was the last thing River would like to talk about, but there was no way around it, so he tried to make it short. "I plan on abdicating my crown soon."

Azir sighed. "River of the Second Dynasty, future ex-king of the Ancients, I'm absolutely certain that you would never have convinced Naia to do something she didn't want to. She has a mind of her own. I do hope you noticed that."

She was observing them in silence, and smiled with her mouth closed when hearing this.

River agreed with his point, but it didn't free him from his own responsibility. "I know. But I played my part in all this. Had I never asked her to escape with me in secret, had I approached you and asked for her hand like any decent human man would have, it would all have been different."

"River," Naia finally intervened. "You were not yourself."

He waved a finger. "The only part in my mind that was clear was the one concerning you. I knew I had to protect you, even if I wasn't sure from what. And yet protecting shouldn't turn someone against their family." He turned to Azir. "Apologies are a great deal for us." He bowed slightly, with his head only. "I apologize."

Azir pointed to Naia. "Apologize to her."

"I have. But I would like to have your consent to court her and ask her to marry me."

Naia's father had a raised eyebrow. "A bit too late to ask for that, isn't it?"

That wasn't true. "Not late, not according to human customs. We haven't—"

"I don't want to hear it." Azir waved his hands in front of him and grimaced. "Please. The only person who needs to give you permission to marry her is Naia. If she's happy, I'm happy."

"She won't be happy if she's estranged from her family," River insisted.

King Azir glanced at Naia and sighed. "From my part, as long as she's happy, and it's what she wants, you have my blessing."

River nodded, then took Naia's hand and kissed it. There was something different in the way she looked at him, just a little sweeter, more open, more trustful, which made this apology worth it. Of course she'd been right to say "no" to him before, and at least now he understood what an idiot he'd been.

Fel then said, "Speaking of marriage, I'm going to marry Leah, authorization or not." He glanced at the Frostlake queen. "Oh, and we're not siblings."

"What about her husband?" Azir asked.

Fel smirked. "He's not her brother either."

The Umbraar king rolled his eyes. "You know what I mean."

"We'll annul it," Leah said.

"If they cause us trouble, she can always become a widow," Fel added.

These two didn't seem to be in the mood to apologize to their parents, but then, they hadn't eloped. King Azir shook his head, but Naia smiled, probably glad to see her brother happy.

River was thinking of going to the Ancient City to check the situation there, when someone knocked on the door, and he disguised his horns and eyes quickly. The hair was already covering his ears.

It was a messenger, who widened his eyes seeing Azir. "Your majesty."

"Yes, it's me," Azir said. "I'm back."

The young men caught a breath. "We have a visitor. She

wanted to speak to Princess Leandra. She's waiting in the safe room. She's..." The young man swallowed. "White fae."

If only everyone feared the Ancients this much, perhaps they would have won the war. But then, perhaps the war had happened because of so much fear.

Leah stepped forward. "I'll go."

"I'll come with you," Fel and Azir said at the same time.

"Can I come too?" River asked. "If she's fae..." His best guess was that this was Anelise, and his worst fear was that something bad had happened, but why was she looking for Leah and not Naia?

"Of course." It was Naia who replied, and then was pulling his hand out the door.

He should have told her that he still felt as if his bones were cracking. Actually, he had to say something. "Slower."

She stared at him, those stunning dark eyes marred with worry. "Are you hurt?"

"I got blasted with dragon fire."

"It didn't burn you? Do you need care?"

"It just... for a moment I couldn't move or use my magic. I'm fine now. Sort of. I want to see who is here."

"Probably the fae Leah found in the hollow."

True. Part of River's worries quieted down, realizing it was unlikely to be Anelise, but he also felt a slight disappointment. What had he been expecting?

When he and Naia got in a room with a heavy wooden door, Leah and Fel were already there. The fae had her back to him. Even then, his heart sped up. Was he imagining things?

"Ciara?" the word slipped from his lips, even though he didn't really think his sister could be there.

NAIA SAW it in River's eyes, the moment the fae turned. A spark of joy, relief, and love. He embraced the fae, sobbing, his body shaking. The girl held him tight too, tears also streaming down her eyes.

Emotion came to Naia's chest as well. River and Ciara reminded her so much of Fel and herself.

River stepped back, pulled Naia's hand, then told sister, "I wanted you to meet her."

Ciara smiled. "Your life companion. I can see that." She reached out a hand, but Naia didn't raise her own.

"I'm an ironbringer." As far as she knew, Ancients couldn't touch her.

"Oh. I see." She turned to River. "I can't wait to get back to the Ancient City. Is everyone still alive? Anelise, Forest, our father?"

Most of the joy faded from River's face. "Our siblings are fine. I killed our father."

"Odd circumstances," Naia said, trying to soften the blow. "He didn't mean it."

River chuckled. "Oh, I meant it. Of course I meant it. While I had an odd influence, the act is all mine."

He was strange. Naia knew he regretted killing his father, didn't even like to talk about it much, and yet it was as if he wanted to bear the blame for it, even though Cynon had been whispering in his mind.

Ciara took his hand. "I'm sure you had a valid reason." She reached out her hand to his temple, and then that strange crown became visible. "See? You wouldn't be wearing it if it wasn't justified." She stared at him with a sad expression. "I'm sorry for whatever happened that caused that."

"You need to come to the Ancient City."

"Yes, but..." She looked at Leah, who was standing away from them, with Fel. "I have debts to settle."

Leah approached her. "I'm sorry I left..."

Ciara shook her head. "I choose to believe that you were meant to leave. But you later called us. You remember that, right?"

"For Frostlake? I don't think we settled..."

"We didn't, but it was a request strong enough that I was able to bring the shapers across. They helped protect Frostlake. Not perfectly, as they can't fly. And there are still a couple of those creatures out there. The Ancients could help hunt them, depending on how things are with the humans…"

Right. Frostlake and the breach. Tzaria had told Naia about it, and now it made more sense.

Ciara continued, "The creatures from the sixth realm will need a place to live. It was the price for them to come, for them to free me. I need to take them to their new home"

Leah stared at her. "How many of them are there?"

"About five hundred."

"There's an island, in Frostlake waters, but far from the shore, called Lost Heart. Nobody lives there, and it should be big enough for them."

"They feed on human emotions, though. They'll die if they're that isolated."

Naia had an idea. "Can't you just send them to Ironhold?" It wasn't totally serious, it was just that she was fed up with that kingdom.

Leah took a deep breath. "Can they promise not to hurt humans?" She glanced at River. "Or Fae? Or dragons? Can their descendents keep the promises?"

Ciara shook her head. "They're immortal, and yes, the promise will bind them."

Leah turned to Fel, then to River and Naia. "What do you think? We could just let them be, could we not?"

River clicked his tongue. "I'm sure there was a reason they were in a different realm, though. Ciara, what do you suggest? We don't want another war."

His sister nodded. "They could go anywhere, and promise to stay hidden and not interfere with humans or us."

"Then do it," Leah said. "I am thankful they helped save my city."

Ciara nodded, then turned to River. "I'll have this settled, then I'll be back."

Naia wondered if his sister had omitted anything in her words, if there was something they were missing. But it was unlikely that anyone would find out a mistake any time soon.

Her father then appeared at the door. "The guest is gone?"

"She had to leave," Fel said.

Azir then took a long look at them. "You all look like you've been awake for a week. I'm fetching baths and a meal, then you can explain some of what happened, and I suggest you rest for now. Tired soldiers can't fight a war."

Naia was still anxious about those eggs or whatever that could open in all the kingdoms, even if part of her knew that it could happen now just as much as it could happen in a thousand years. "I wanted to warn the kingdoms. There's a trap left in each of them. And watch the communication mirror."

"I'll watch it," Azir said. "I'm here, and it's my duty to relieve some of this heavy burden you've been carrying."

THE WATER WAS tepid and Naia almost felt like screaming, but it felt refreshing to wash away any traces from Ironhold, from Cynon, wash away the blood from Harold's body. She jumped out of the water quickly and then put on fresh, clean clothes, then got down to the refectory, where they had a soup with rye, some vegetables and meat. Ursiana was sitting by Leah, who sat by Fel. The woman was here because Azir had rescued her, and yet... There was just something when the Frostlake Queen and her father looked at each other that Naia couldn't shake. On the other side, Tzaria sat between Risomu and Ekateni, who was still recovering. Naia wished she could talk more to them, ask about her family, ask about dragon magic, but the opportunity would hopefully come soon. Naia herself was sitting between River and Azir.

Naia's father turned to River, Tzaria, Ekateni and Risomu. "My excuses. Our accommodations here are simple. Nothing worthy of a king or dragon lords."

Tzaria shook her head. "Our ways are not extravagant."

River stared at him. "If you'd like me to leave, please ask clearly." There was no anger or hurt in his voice, just blunt curiosity. "We don't deal well with dubious hints."

Naia took his hand. "He doesn't want you to leave. He's just saying that this isn't a castle."

"Exactly," her father said.

River chuckled. "You should put me in the dungeon, not feel sorry you can't offer me luxurious rooms."

Her father gritted his teeth. "You think both feelings can't coexist?" He then smiled. "I'm joking. I want Naia to be happy."

River kissed her hand and said, "Then we're of the same mind."

Naia and Fel tried to explain to their father some of what had happened. Azir listened. He was calm enough that no detail shook him. At this point, if he'd stood still while Naia murdered a man in cold blood, just trusting her word that it was the right thing to do, she didn't think anything would faze him. Umbraar men truly didn't flinch—and maybe women too.

When he learned that Ekateni was their uncle, he reached a hand to greet him again, and said, "Thank you for looking after Fel."

It was subtle, but Tzaria rolled her eyes. Perhaps not that subtle, but nobody else noticed the reaction.

Her father took both Naia and Fel's hand. "You are my pride, my joy. I'm proud of what you've done." He glanced at Leah. "Proud of you three."

Leah just looked down, embarrassed. This had been an acknowledgement that she was his daughter. Naia had suspected it for a while, and yet it was still strange to see it, especially considering Leah and Fel's situation.

Perhaps to diffuse the tension, Azir turned to River. "Proud of my future son-in-law too."

River raised an eyebrow. "Really?"

"I'm sure you protected Naia. Cynon or whatever his name that was taking over Harold wasn't expecting her to be able to hurt him, didn't even know she was an ironbringer or a dragon. That was your doing, wasn't it?"

"I tried." River looked down, then back at him. "I tried to make him think Naia was harmless, to forget her, not to see her power. I did do that, yes. Even when she used fire on me, he thought she was using his own power."

"So your role was key, River," her father said. "Welcome to the family." He then added, "To be fair, had you done nothing, you'd still be welcome."

Had it always been that easy, had her father always been so accepting and Naia had refused to see it? And then, maybe something had happened in the time he'd been away. All he'd told her was that he'd been trapped with Ursiana, then trapped alone, suspended in a daze. Perhaps it had done something to him. And then, perhaps the truth was that Naia had never asked her father for permission to marry, had never told him what afflicted her heart, had never opened up, fearing to upset him.

River was right in one thing: she wouldn't be happy while estranged from her father. Her father, because he was. She wanted to know more about Ircantari, and appreciated his love and his sacrifice, but that didn't erase what King Azir had done for her and Fel. It felt good to have their family back together, even if not everything had yet been solved.

Naia could sense evil lurking, could feel that something was about to happen. She saw it in the eyes of the three dragons, who looked alert rather than relieved. Then there was the Ancient City and all its problems, but it was true that her body couldn't go on forever and resting for now was the best she could do.

3I

TOGETHER

Peace and quiet for a while, even if it was a short while, was amazing. Fel could barely believe it as he lay in bed, realizing he was indeed exhausted—but happy. He even got an apology from Ursiana. He hadn't asked about the note, but heard Leah mentioning it to her mother, who didn't seem to know anything about it. The important thing was that now she approved their union, which made him happy, even if they still would need to deal with Venard.

He wondered if Cynon was really gone, if this was it, and yet his mind couldn't focus much on that, so tired, already drifting into sleep. Still, Fel waited, wondering... Leah had been assigned her own bedroom, but he was still hoping she'd come here, since she could move through the hollow. Last time, his mind had been addled, thinking this was a dream. And yet later on, wide awake, she had undressed for him on those cold mountains, even if they wouldn't be able to get together properly. But then, she was probably tired and had to sleep. Their time would come. It was just that it felt so good to hold her with his human arms, kiss her...

Perhaps *he* should get up and go to her room. Or perhaps he should let sleep take him. Her mother was a few doors down. And his father—her father. Fel really didn't want to think about that. He closed his eyes, drifting off, leaving all his worries behind.

"Fel?" Leah was sitting on his bed, wearing a nightgown, even though it was day, looking so beautiful under the sunlight coming through the thin curtains.

"I was waiting for you."

He lifted the sheet covering him.

Lying beside him, she smiled. "How did you know I would come?"

"I only hoped." He pulled her close and kissed her cheek.

Their eyes locked. He wanted to undress her, wanted to do so much, and yet wasn't sure she was ready for it, wasn't sure this was what she wanted, and yet he feared that asking would be too bold. His heart was hammering in his chest.

"You're tired." She looked down, suddenly.

"Never tired for you." He kissed her shoulder. "We can get married now."

She sighed. "After we deal with Venard."

"I can make you a widow. Just say the word." He wasn't joking.

She shook her head. "He's the least evil in that family, and could be a potential ally. Plus, he's your cousin."

Fel chuckled. "I'm supposed to love my Ironhold relatives now?"

"No. Your grandmother is a monster." Any trace of playfulness or joy was gone from her face.

Fel pulled his metal hand that had been resting on the mantelpiece and caressed her hair. "I'm sorry you went through all that. Sorry for my part in it. I should have tried to speak to you." He still felt so guilty for not having intervened, for having let her go to Ironhold.

"I made the same mistake." She held his metal fingers and smiled. "I love your hands." She then let go of them. "But you don't need them now."

Fel stared at the sheet, feeling uncomfortable to be reminded of that.

She said, "You can keep them if you want."

With his eyes closed, he guided the pieces of metal to his corner desk. The truth was that he felt naked and vulnerable without them. It had been easy when he'd thought this was a dream.

He felt her lips kissing the tip of his arm. "I love you the way you are," she said.

"My hands are part of me."

"I know."

He caressed her temple with his arm. "I love you." He chuckled, suddenly reminded of something River had told him. "These words sound small when trying to convey what I feel."

She had her eyes closed, a smile on her face. "Show me not with words, then."

There was no need to ask twice, although he was still not sure how much she wanted. Perhaps it had been easy for her when he'd been in dragon form and nothing could truly happen... But now...

Still, he was kissing her shoulder, then lowering her nightgown, until he revealed one of her beautiful breasts, its tip so soft, so inviting, so sweet. He hadn't forgotten its taste, and couldn't help but caress her nipple with his tongue. She then placed a hand on his chest and was lowering it towards his belly.

It was definitely better to ask. "Do you want to wait?" His breath was more ragged than he'd expected. "Until we're married?"

He couldn't believe she didn't stop moving her hand and smiled. "What do you think?"

"I'm asking."

Her lips were by his ear, forming a whisper that brought shivers down his spine. "I'm answering."

Her hand moved even lower, the feel of her delicate fingers against his skin more wonderful than anything he had ever felt. Fel closed his eyes, lost in the feel of her touch, then opened them to get rid of her nightgown. Her lovely body lay bare before him, but trembling.

"You're afraid," he said.

She tensed. "Many worthwhile things are scary."

"No, you have to relax, Leah. I'll kiss you until you're ready."

Her smile was enchanting. "I won't mind that."

His lips were on hers for a long kiss, then he kissed more of her body, down, down, down to that special place where he could weave magic with his tongue. From tension, her trembling changed into something different. He moved his body so that he could look into her eyes—lovely fiery eyes.

"Fel." It was a moan, a demand, a question, so much.

He moved up, kissed her lips again, then felt her hands pushing down his trousers. Her touch was bliss.

Neither of them had any more clothes on as he lay on top of her, feeling the soft touch of her skin against his body. Her eyes had desire and love, those amazing, sweet blue eyes that looked at him the way nobody else did. Now her eyes were closing, her lips parted, as he entered her slowly, carefully, their bodies moving together, a soothing, gentle motion. *This* was pure bliss.

NAIA WAS TIRED OF WAITING. She wanted some time alone with River to talk, and more, and now, even though he was the one who could move through the hollow, there was no sign of him. The alternative was to get up and tip-toe to his room, hoping nobody saw her.

At least some luck was on her side, as indeed the hallways were empty. She knocked quickly and he opened.

"Naia." He didn't even give her a smile.

"Something wrong?"

He was tense. "Your father will make assumptions if he learns you were here."

She stepped into the room. "So what?"

"Humans consider it a grave offense."

Naia rolled her eyes. "Oh, you're going to teach me about human customs now?"

River finally closed the door. "I can tell you about some of our old treaties..."

"Shush. I thought fae were wild and free-spirited—"

"The very reason why such strict treaties were written in the first place. Humans are weird."

"Why. Thanks!"

He finally smiled. "Come here." He pulled her close and embraced her. "I am so glad you're safe, so glad we're together. It's as if we've climbed most of the mountain."

"Most? You also feel this isn't over."

He nodded.

There was something else she'd been dying to ask him, but knew it had to be in private. Before getting to her point, she decided to test him. "Well, if anything happens, we still have this." She touched the amulet. "And can go back in time, right?"

"Uh-huh." His stiffness gave him away.

"River. Tell me now what you know about this amulet."

He frowned, apparently confused. "Why would I know about it?"

"Because you're evading the question. Fel said we'd remember it. Do you have any idea when it was used? Yes or no?"

He stared at her. "What difference does it make? This is a powerful object. Imagine how many lives could be saved."

"You haven't answered it, so I'll take it as a yes. When was this used?"

"I can't be sure."

"River," she growled.

"They'll hear us."

"I'll scream even louder if you don't answer."

He sat on the bed and crossed his arms. Only now she realized he was using some kind of human sleeping clothes, cream loose shirt and pants that looked strange on him. She was too angry to laugh, though.

After a deep breath, he said, "When I was rescued in the dragon temple. It was you. I swear I didn't recall seeing this before, but once I saw it, I suddenly remembered you wearing it, but it could be an impression maybe."

The dragon temple. Many years ago. It made sense. "Why didn't you tell me?"

"Why? You have an object that can change the world and you're going to waste it by saving me? Let me rot in that temple, Naia. I probably deserve it."

"But then the dragons wouldn't come to Aluria after you. I wouldn't be born."

"Maybe they would still come after Formosa."

"I wouldn't meet you. That's what you want?"

River set his lovely mahogany eyes on her. "Do you really think we won't meet? Do you really think all we have is this brief life? Do you not think we've met before? We'll see each other again."

Naia exhaled. "So nothing matters then. I'll have to defeat Cynon without your help."

"You think I helped?" He laughed.

"I only found him because I knew his energy, I could recognize him. As my father already stated, it was a miracle that he didn't know what I was, and that was because you concealed me well."

"I used all the magic I could to make sure he wouldn't harm you."

"It worked. I don't know how gone he is, but at least he isn't King Harold anymore."

"It's just..." River exhaled and shook his head. "How could I have been so blind, so oblivious?"

She had also been oblivious. "I can say the same."

"Naia, I'm really charming, so you have a great excuse." He wasn't even joking, he was truly pretentious like that.

"Oh. What about me? Am I not charming?"

"You are. For you I should have done better. Much better."

"But you didn't. And it worked. If you remained stuck in that temple, we wouldn't know what could have happened. So I'll use it to save you, just to be sure. Your life is valuable."

He sighed. "Every life is valuable. I lost friends. I lost a dear cousin. He was the most beautiful of all the Ancients, with dark black hair and black horns." He looked at Naia. "Gone."

"I'm sorry for that. I don't mean to minimize your pain, but I lost my mother. My blood father. I would have liked to have met them, to have had a mother's touch."

"My mother died too. She died so I could live." He chuckled. "I don't think my father thought it was a fair exchange. Maybe it wasn't."

"No. A mother should live to see her children, but fate sometimes has other plans."

He snorted. "Fate."

"Do you hate your life that much?"

"I hate many of the choices I made. Many, many. But I'm happy we're here together. I've been in love with you from the moment I first saw you, in that dragon temple. And now we're here."

"Yes, and yet you want me not to go to that temple and perhaps puff you out of existence."

"I don't want that, I just didn't want to be selfish."

"I'm selfish, River, and I'll use this thing to save you. It's *my* wish."

He took a deep breath and closed his eyes. "Fair."

"You need to rest."

"I can't rest with you here. Humans think sleeping together means doing things together, and I can't do it under your father's roof if we're not married."

"He's not my father."

"Your guardian, counts as the same."

"Are you always this annoying with your stupid fae rules?"

He chuckled. "Isn't River Annoying one of my names? I agree the rules are stupid, Naia, but they were made to appease human sensibilities, what I am going to do?"

"Must I remind you that we've lived together and slept together before? In the literal sense of sleep, of course."

"Must I remind you that I just humiliated myself like I had never done before, regretting all that?"

She did recall it, and it warmed her heart. "Thank you. I can't believe you turned my father around."

"I made it easier for you two to get along again. I knew you needed that. I know how important a father's approval is." There was a tinge of sadness in his words. It was the approval he'd never gotten.

"You're part of the family now. Your future father-in-law approves of you."

He chuckled. "Surprising, right?"

And yet, this was no laughing matter. Suddenly his insistence on not offending her father made a lot more sense.

"I'll go," she said. "You need to rest."

She was at the door when it hit her. She turned to River. "Did you feel that?"

AZIR SAT IN HIS OFFICE, trying to process everything. He hadn't asked much, perceiving how tired everyone was. Ursiana sat at a corner, a new, strange distance between them. And silence. The silence was killing him. So many unsaid words, so many questions.

He decided to break the silence. Most conversations started with stupid words. "Dragons?" He chuckled. "Can you believe it?"

She smiled and shook her head. "I guess... these things take a while to sink in."

"Dragon lords for me were a legend of times long gone, of magic that no longer existed. I had no idea they still lived across the ocean, and no idea they were actually dragons. I can't imagine Fel as a dragon. I heard the words, and yet…"

"He was very brave. They all were." She looked down. "I… apologized to your son. For not passing on his proposal to Leah. There was more to it. I guess someone falsified a note. I'm still sorry for my part."

He got up and took her hand. "If Ironhold was determined to marry your daughter, there wasn't much you could have done. I'm glad they didn't try to kill him—unless they did and failed. I know they haven't told us everything."

Her hand was still holding his, as she looked down. "So much to do."

He swallowed. *What now?* was the question he wanted to ask. Despite everything that was happening, he wanted to ask what of him and her. It felt real when they had been in the hollow, as if all their problems had been fixed, all their wounds healed, and yet now, when it was time to make it all real, all he felt was a creeping dread that some things could never be fixed.

Was he a coward? Perhaps the solution to his fear of hearing a *no* was simple. Instead of asking, he should just suggest something. "We'll… need to think about our wedding." All he could hear was his heart counting the seconds until she scowled and asked him if he was crazy.

"Wedding?" She smiled, though, a sweet, lovely smile. "We'll need to wait a few months. I'm still officially mourning my husband. I *am* mourning my best friends. It's not fair that so many evil people are still alive, while they… They were good. And now they are gone."

He held her hand tighter. "We can wait. What's a few months after twenty years? We'll need to tell our children."

She shook her head and laughed. "I don't know what Leah will think, frankly. It seems she knows, though. She knows she's a deathbringer, and yet, confessing to her my mistakes still fills me with shame."

"Shame?"

"You have no idea how many times I went over our night. That night. How many times I wished I had said *no*, how many times I wished I hadn't let you into my bedroom, how many times I thought that if only I had done things differently, I wouldn't have ruined everything. That blame... that fear... All I wanted was for her never to suffer what I did. So many nights I could only look back and hate myself for my foolishness, hate myself for being... a loose woman."

Her words were puzzling. "I thought you hated *me*."

"Hate is like love. There's always more where it comes from."

"So you thought I used you and discarded you, and you were blaming *yourself* for it? If anything, if I had really done that, you should be glad to get rid of me."

"But I was pregnant and would never be able to have a proper marriage again, never be able to find love again. Call me foolish, but you hear these things so much, eventually you believe them. Eventually you believe it's your fault."

"I'm sorry."

"It's not *your* fault. I could say it's my mother's fault, but she also probably heard it somewhere. It's self-loathing poison, Azir."

Tears were rolling down her eyes, and he reached out a hand to wipe them. "Most poisons leave your system with time. You just have to flush them well."

"I'm trying."

"I can talk to her," he offered.

"You'll have to. But so will I."

Her eyes were brilliant from crying. He touched her lips, then kissed her. This was real, not some hollow-induced hallucination. She was real, sitting in his office, in his kingdom, kissing him while the children rested.

NAIA WAS WALKING FAST to her father's office, River after her.

"What is it?" he asked. He had glamoured his clothes to look more decent, which made sense.

"I don't know."

She put her hand on the handle.

River frowned. "You should knock."

Naia rolled her eyes, pushed the door—and saw her father and the Frostlake Queen kissing.

Now, one thing was knowing that they had been involved, another thing was seeing them kissing. For some reason she had imagined her father never kissed anyone, which was obviously a ridiculous idea, but what could she do?

"So sorry," she said, before pushing the door closed as quickly as she could. "I saw nothing," she yelled, just to be sure.

River was chuckling. "Told you."

"How was I supposed to know?"

The door opened, her father standing there. "Naia, come in. River too. You're always welcome here." He pointed to the queen. "I was going to announce it later, but why not now? Me and Ursiana, we're getting married. In six months." He looked down, visibly flustered. "I do hope you get along."

Naia smiled at her. "Congratulations. I'm sorry for intruding, I really didn't mean to disturb you."

Ursiana smiled back. "You're always welcome."

Naia was pretty sure that she would not be welcome for everything, but it was obviously better not to mention it. Or think about it.

Her father then asked, "Is there something wrong?"

Naia swallowed. "The mirror, has anyone tried to—"

A light shone in it right as she said it. Her father rushed to the mirror and placed his palm on it.

On the other side was a young man, disheveled. "Where's Princess Irinaia?"

"She's here," Azir said. "Something wrong?"

"It broke. It broke. We're being attacked. She warned my father."

"Who's attacking you?" her father asked. "From what kingdom are you—"

"I'm prince Raymond, from Wolfmark. They are these things, like bugs, but they grow, they become bigger."

River whispered, "Fire should contain them."

Naia approached the mirror. "I'm Irinaia. You need to burn them."

"I'll have to set the castle on fire?" The prince's eyes were wide. "They're all over. Everywhere."

"Can I?" River asked her father, who nodded, and then approached the mirror.

"Are they round, big like this?" He put his thumb and index finger together. "And can look like a liquid when there are many of them? As if they were one big thing, like some dark oil that can climb on walls?"

"Yes," the prince said, then added, "My father's dead."

Naia was a horrible person, as she didn't feel the least sorry for the late king.

The prince trembled. "I... would you be willing to help us?"

Naia *could* help with her fire, but if it was just a matter of burning them, the guards in Wolfmark could do it as well. She looked at her father and River, who was looking down, deep in thought.

"We have a spell for that," River muttered. "These things are Kisilis. They could spread all over the continent if not contained." He closed his eyes. "The Ancient guards could get rid of them, but..."

"Offer them help," Naia whispered.

River walked to the mirror without bothering to glamour his horns and eyes, and told the prince, "Go outside, in the open, where there's sun. Carry a torch and fuel. Burn them. Tell everyone to burn them. I'm River, king of the White Fae, and I can help you. All I need is a guarantee that nobody will harm my soldiers. We'll get rid of these creatures, the kisilis, and leave. That's it. Can we go?"

The prince, who had been staring at River with wide eyes, blanched. "Fae? Yes. Help us."

"Go," River said. "Find a secure place. Tell everyone not to harm the incoming fae."

The Wolfmark prince severed the connection. In a second, River had a scrying mirror and found Anelise, telling her to send some soldiers to Wolfmark.

"Won't they be hurt?" Naia asked.

"No. Kisilis are easy to kill. Once you know the right spell. I don't think any humans can do it."

"The dragons could help." She realized she was saying something foolish. "But I guess the humans will be terrified if they see dragons."

"I'll contact other kingdoms," Azir said. "And ask if they're having issues." He turned to River. "Do you think you could send more men to other kingdoms?"

"Soldiers, yes, I can send them. But I need a guarantee they won't be harmed."

"You could have bargained for more," Naia said.

River shook his head. "Then they would think we were behind the kisilis. If we don't ask for anything, it will be harder for them to claim that."

Azir shook his head. "If people want to blame you, they will."

"I know." River shrugged. "But I'm not going to make it easy for them. Bargaining is an art, and sometimes it's subtle. Also, I don't want these things all over Aluria."

They contacted a few kingdoms who reported nothing, and where everything seemed to be fine. A few of them gave no answer, which could mean many things.

"Could you send glamoured fae?" Naia asked River.

He shook his head. "Few of us are good at glamour."

"They could wear hats, hide their hair and ears." It was a silly suggestion, but Naia found it hard to let people die and do nothing.

"Naia," Azir said. "You can't ask River to risk his people, especially without anything in return."

"No." River's eyes were unfocused, lost in thought. "We could try the hats. Reveal ourselves later."

"King River," Ursiana said. "Could you please send some of your soldiers to Greenstone?"

It was one of the kingdoms who wasn't answering, the kingdom where she'd been born.

"Of course," River said, then contacted Anelise again.

The Vastfield King then contacted them, reporting those kisilis, followed by the Varana prince. The king was already dead.

Naia covered her face in horror. This was all so fast. Finally River ended up sending soldiers to every kingdom, except Ironhold and Umbraar. He claimed Umbraar was safe. As for Ironhold, considering it was the kingdom where Cynon himself had established his throne, there was no reason to worry about it.

That until the mirror shone again, displaying Prince Venard, sweaty and pale.

"Is River helping the human kingdoms?"

That prince knew him?

River stepped in front of the mirror, arms crossed. "We are. Why?"

"I need help. Please." He was crying. "They're here too. Not only here, in my aunt and uncle's castles. They're killing everyone. I'll do anything you want. Just help us."

River looked down, silent.

Naia thought she had to say something. "Prince... Venard?" the prince nodded. "I'm sure you're aware fae can't—"

"I can help you," River told the prince. "But I will ask you a few things once it's done."

"It's fine," the prince said.

River ended the communication and turned to Naia. "*I* can go there."

"Alone?"

He took Naia's hands. "You haven't seen much of my magic..."

"I think I have."

"I can deal with that. And I can go to the Iron Citadel and whatever other monstrosity of an iron castle they have. Either way, I can't let the kisilis spread." He kissed her cheek. "I'll be right back."

Like that, he was gone, still glamoured over his ill-fitting human clothes.

Naia stared at her father, looking for an answer, a consoling word, something.

Azir's eyes were kind. "He seemed to know what he was doing."

"He's reckless."

Her father shook his head. "He sounded quite competent and wise, Naia. Perhaps he won't be king for long, but he's sure honoring his role."

"What if something happens?"

"You could trust his magic. Like I trusted yours."

32
FOREVER

It had been a strange week. Leah had woken up from her sleep that day to find out that all the kingdoms had been attacked, and that the fae had saved them. Of course, it didn't mean the humans would start accepting them that easily, but it was a good start.

Even Frostlake had been attacked, but the fae had been fast enough to prevent the strange creatures from doing much damage. They couldn't help with the damage from the dome and the creatures, but the city was withstanding winter and rebuilding, despite their losses.

Many people had died in many kingdoms, including most of the Ironhold family. Leah wasn't sure how she felt about Lady Celia dying. It felt too fast, too easy. Those were some nasty feelings. This was time to dissolve the stupid Ironhold Empire, annul her marriage, and try to find a peace alliance, not focus on a silly grudge.

The kingdoms had to meet again, but there would be no ceremonies or balls in this gathering. Everyone was too hurt or scared, so they were meeting in the portal hub in Frostlake. It meant that everyone would be free to make a quick retreat if necessary. Still, the Umbraars, River, and she were meeting with

Venard to arrange some details. That was how she found herself in the same room with Fel, Naia, River, Azir, her mother, and Venard.

"I will apologize for what my kingdom did," the new Ironhold King said. He turned to River. "I'll tell everyone they've been faking evidence against the white fae. Please, don't make me confess we're behind Formosa."

King Azir looked down and clenched his fists.

"I haven't made you do anything," River said. Apparently, Venard had acquired a debt with the fae.

"I know," Venard said. "But I'm asking. They used explosives. I found some documents. I'm not sure why they did it. It was my grandfather, not me. I grew up thinking it was the fae. I know that confessing it was us would help clear your name, but it would also create fear. In fear, they could want to retaliate. Other kingdoms could want to retaliate or punish us too. Everyone's dead but me, how can we be any more punished than that?"

River gestured to King Azir. "Ask the Umbraar King. Your family killed *his* family."

Azir grunted. Leah was coming to realize he did that a lot. He said, "An eye for an eye, everyone goes blind. I'll never forgive your family. But I'm willing to give you a chance to repent and start over."

Venard nodded. "Irinaia and Isofel are my sole heirs. Perhaps you should just kill me."

Leah was getting annoyed by his insistence on dying. "No. Your word confessing your kingdom's crimes is worth much more than anyone else's."

Venard pointed to River. "He could pretend to be me."

River shook his head. "There must have been a reason you were spared."

Venard only covered his face with his hands. "I'm trying. It's much bigger than me, and here I am, alone in the world."

"You have me and Naia," Fel said. "We're your family." It didn't change the fact that Fel still stared at him as if wanting to kill him. Perhaps part of him still did.

These words only made the Ironhold prince sink deeper in his chair. He looked at Leah. "I'm so, so sorry."

She hadn't exactly forgiven him for helping his monstrous brother, but she understood that he had also been a victim, and didn't want to carry anger in her heart. "Help me leave it behind, then."

"We should go," King Azir said.

They took two carriages to the portal hub, where servants had arranged a pulpit and chairs. It wasn't comfortable or ceremonial, but it was enough for now.

Venard was the first one to give a speech.

"I stand here, not to apologize, not to explain away my family's mistakes, but to state them clearly, so that they will never be repeated. My family conspired against the white fae. They blamed the accident in Formosa on them, they created illusions that the fae were attacking us, all for power, all so that they would have an Ironhold Empire. It was a lie. I wasn't part of that lie, but I'm still ashamed of their actions. They dealt with deep, dangerous magic, and brought death upon themselves, upon some of you as well. I know *sorry* won't bring back your loved ones, but it's the only word I have. Before you hate me, before you hate my kingdom, please take some time to see that I'm not hiding, I'm not lying, I'm not displacing blame. My family made mistakes, but they paid for it, and I don't plan on repeating those mistakes."

He glanced at Leah. "My wedding was a mistake. Not because Princess Leandra isn't honorable, but because it was forced upon us by my family. Marriage should be about love, not about alliances. We can still be allies without getting married. My wedding was annulled according to the laws in Aluria, but our alliance is still strong."

This was Leah's clue to come to the podium. She had practiced speaking in public many times, but still felt nervous. Her heart calmed down when she saw Fel, ever so handsome, standing by his father.

She took a deep breath. "My kingdom was betrayed. My father was betrayed by his own friends. It was Ironhold who attacked us, while blaming the fae. But they are dead now, so I guess they are paying for their crimes. This is not the time to look back at what happened, but to look forward to a new dawn in our continent, a time of peace. The fae have helped us, wanting nothing in return, but I believe they deserve a few words."

River came to the pulpit. "I am the king of the Ancients, or white fae, as you call us. All we want is to live in peace. Perhaps our scars run too deep for us to come back to our old settlements, but all I'm asking now is for you to stop hating us, stop fearing us. Yes, we killed the kisilis, but it was because we knew how to do it, and we live in Aluria as well. I hope that one day, in the future, fae and humans can shake their hands again as friends. For now, I believe most of you need to return home and heal your castles and your own wounds."

The Haven king wanted to speak, and told the crowd that some of his advisors had seen signs of dark magic used by Ironhold in Umbraar, when they had attacked them.

Then the Greenstone king came into the pulpit. "Isn't it a coincidence that these strange magical creatures came, and the fae were the only ones with a solution for it?"

Leah couldn't believe that man was her uncle.

"Not strange," Venard said. "My parents were dealing with old, dark magic. The fae know old magic and know how to fight it. They were kind enough to offer to help us."

"But they were hidden all this time," The Greenstone king said. "When they show up, this happens?"

River listened to it in silence, not even looking at the king. He had predicted that this would happen, and perhaps found it better not to argue.

Venard shook his head. "It was my family that locked up the fae. They knew they could defeat them. Perhaps you think they found freedom just in time as a coincidence, or maybe some evil plan. I prefer to believe in a greater plan, that there's a force for good in this world."

"This will remain to be seen," the Greenstone King said.

It would. And it was unfair. The fae were a little odd, for sure, but all they'd shown so far was good will. Then again, some scars ran too deep, except that fae were the ones with the true scars, and yet they weren't the ones complaining.

WAS IT POSSIBLE TO BREATHE? To believe it was really over? It seemed so. But Naia wasn't really good at breathing today. It was her wedding. The human wedding at least, since fae apparently didn't do anything special unless they wanted to, and River had been super busy. River and her. She was trying to be a good queen.

It wasn't that he didn't want to abdicate his crown, but rather that neither of his sisters wanted it. River wanted to become a diplomat, to try to work on a lasting peace with the humans.

Anelise had shaken her head. "Brother, if you want to go to human kingdoms and talk to them, go as our king. They will feel more honored and more important, and more willing to listen. It's also symbolic that you're marrying a human princess."

River ended up accepting the idea. His people were in the Ancient City, but also had a settlement in Umbraar, and a large area of Ironhold had become the Fae Kingdom. Venard, the new Ironhold King, had offered it out of his own good will. This kingdom was important not only because it meant that the Ancients had their own land, but also that they now controlled the area around Mount Prime, and could allow it to heal, and for nature to grow on it again.

Ancients were not great farmers, though, and would depend on some exchange with humans. For this reason they were building the Fae City, along a main road, which was meant to be a point of contact between fae and humans. It was there that they would get married.

It was part of his promise, to marry her according to human traditions, but also a symbolic political move, as their union symbolized a union on the continent. Still, some kingdoms allowed the fae to return to their old settlements, but River still didn't want his people to mingle with humans while unprotected. The memories of the war were still fresh in their minds, memories of innocent families killed for no reason, without an army to protect them. River wanted the Ancients to live closer together, at least for now, while these wounds were still healing. Naia hoped one day they would be healed.

Some of the dragons had come for the wedding. Naia was super happy to meet her dragon cousins. Soon she would need to study with them, especially Tzaria, learn more about her dragon magic, and maybe even learn to take her dragon form. She felt a thrill of excitement imagining herself soaring up into the skies.

River claimed he had seen her dragon form once, and that she was a white dragon. Naia would love to take that form one day. That said, Tzaria had warned her not to have contact with other dragons. They were still having conflicts, there were still Boundless in Fernick, and it would be dangerous for her if they learned she was an iron dragon. For now, she could have contact with Tzaria, Risomu, and her uncle and cousins. There was also a dragon that they had found in Ironhold, still healing, still unable to take his human form, and living in the mountains in Umbraar. Tzaria and Ekateni were taking care of him.

Speaking of dragons, they were going to help Umbraar reopen the seas to connect the two lands. Yes, deathbringers could keep sea-serpents away, but so could dragons, who had an affinity with the creatures. It would mean many changes for Aluria.

Naia looked at herself in the mirror. She wore a silver dress with embroidery bright like stars. It was a fae dress, and very beautiful. Leah and Ursiana were in the room with her. Naia was starting to like the Frostlake Queen. Not queen anymore—the Frostlake Queen was Leah.

Ursiana would soon be the Umbraar queen consort, but in a couple of months. Fel was going to wait a little to get married as well, which was silly. If anyone glanced at him and Leah, it was obvious they were in love. Then again, the same thing could be said about Ursiana and her father. Perhaps it was never too late to find love, and Naia was glad her father had dissolved the bitterness in his heart.

Leah smiled. "You look like you belong in a dream"

Naia raised an eyebrow. "Hopefully not a bizarre death-bringer dream."

Yes, the girl had weird, dangerous dreams, just like her father. They sounded terrifying. She would need to study about her magic with Azir. Leah's father too, except that the girl didn't want to call him that, as she said it made her feel like she was Fel's half-sister, which would understandably be quite disturbing.

"No, a good dream." Leah laughed.

Ursiana nodded. "It's a magnificent dress, but you're magnificent regardless. And you deserve all the happiness in the world."

Naia didn't want to feel emotional, so she chuckled. "Don't we all?"

THEY WERE DOING the wedding in the Umbraar tradition, so Naia had to enter from one side while River came in from the other. It meant she hadn't seen him yet. He was probably dashing and overdressed, likely trying to look as fae as possible. There were friends and family in the wedding, but also royals from other kingdoms, so there was an aspect of spectacle to this, and she knew River.

Or maybe Naia didn't know him enough. When she entered and saw him, she was stunned. He had tied the top of his hair in a ponytail, so that his pointy ears were visible. His eyes were brighter than usual, very visibly red. Glamour. Not only that, he had them lined in black. He wore two suits, a black one over a gold one, which looked strangely good. His crown was showing, and he wore long earrings with red stones. If his goal had been to look otherworldly and ethereal, he had done a fabulous job. Naia's crown was hidden, just because it would be too complicated to explain to humans why she was the fae queen before they were even married.

River was walking with Ciara, who had returned to the Ancient city and was now helping settle the Fae Kingdom.

No, it was Anelise.

The two girls were identical, but they carried themselves differently, and there was something just a little stiffer about Anelise, and yet she looked younger. Anelise, a sister River hadn't gotten along well with for most of his life. Perhaps he was trying to make up for that now. Ciara was standing near the front, her face lighting up watching her brother. Maybe this had been her idea. Forest was not there. Naia feared that he could eventually stir trouble, but his sisters claimed they were watching him and paying attention to any sign of treason. They were good leaders and brilliant strategists, so Naia chose to trust them.

Naia was walking with her father. For this occasion, he had decided to comb back his usually messy hair. Naia appreciated the gesture, except that she wished he had kept his normal hair, which looked better. Of course she didn't have the heart to tell him that. Not that he looked bad, of course. She was just happy that he was here, supporting her. In fact, he and River got along splendidly well. River's heartfelt apology had managed to soften his heart. And then, perhaps it was Ursiana softening his heart, making him laugh a lot more than before. It felt good to walk with him towards River, to know that her father was by her side, supporting her, supporting her choices.

Naia saw Fel and Leah, so cute and happy, her brother as handsome as always. She'd been missing him so much. He'd been spending a lot of time in Frostlake while Naia had been jumping between the Ancient City, Umbraar, and the Fae Kingdom.

She looked around to see if she found more guests she knew, and other than some kings and queens—not all—she saw Tzaria and Ekateni by her cousins. She hoped to be able to spend time with them soon. There was so much to learn, so much she still had to know about her family, her father, her origins. At least they were here.

They walked to a clerk, who spoke some words about love and commitment. This was a performance for Aluria, but it was also more. There was magic at work in words and contracts, especially for someone like River. Extremely fae-looking River, which was particularly gorgeous.

After that, they spoke to kings and queens, princes and princesses who were congratulating them. It was hard to know whose congratulations were genuine and whose weren't, but it didn't matter, they had to be polite to everyone.

A band started playing. They had both fae and human musicians, which had been a nice touch to promote peace and harmony between the peoples. It was impressive that River and the other Ancients supported all that. The truth was that the humans had acted much worse during the war, but then, they had been fed lies and hatred, especially by Ironhold.

River claimed that it was better to start over than to keep the cycle of hate. Of course, forgiveness would take time and a lot more effort from humans. And then again, the real enemy had been Ironhold, now defeated. What mattered was that at least now the Ancients had a place to live on the surface, not that it made it fair. This land had once been all theirs, and now they had to be confined to a kingdom, but then, it was better than being confined to a city.

River approached her and pulled her hand. Naia thought they were going to dance, but instead he pulled her to a corner, behind a tree.

He probably had something to tell her. "Something wrong?" she asked.

"Nothing wrong." He pulled her close and kissed her, a long, deep kiss that felt good but also inappropriate in that place, where anyone could see them.

Naia was about to push him, when she felt those tendrils of darkness around her, then opened her eyes and realized she was in the garden of their house.

The Ancient City had been unsealed, but this part of it, for some reason, was still only River's and hers. Of course they couldn't spend all the time here, but they came sometimes.

He stopped kissing and stared at her.

"Why are we here?"

He raised his eyebrows. "You break my heart sometimes, you know? When I first brought you, all proud of the house I made for you, you were complaining that it was just us two, as if being alone with me was awful or something."

That was unfair. And incorrect. "No. Completely alone. How quickly you forget you left during the day, River."

He scratched his head. "I guess."

"Why are we here?"

"Why?" He smirked. "What a great question: why?"

The woods around the house were still eerie and silent, still mostly dead. Some crickets chirping would have made this silence more bearable.

He caressed her face. "You know what just happened? We're married according to human laws. You know what that means?"

Many things. She thought for a moment, until she realized what he meant. "No more waiting."

His answer was a smile.

Her heart was speeding up, despite thinking she'd been ready for a long time. "Couldn't you wait until the end of the party?"

"It's boring. We'll talk more to everyone tomorrow." He glanced at her lips, then looked her in the eyes again. "Unless you want to go back. Nobody's in a hurry. I mean, I am, but..."

Naia pulled the ribbon tying his hair. It looked good, but she wanted him to look more like the River she was used to. "I *should* make you wait. As revenge. Torture you with wanting."

River kissed her lips briefly and had a mischievous smile. "Please do. Torture me until I beg."

For some reason Naia burst into laughter.

He frowned, but in a playful way. "Or maybe laugh at me."

"Or both."

He wrapped his arms around her, then they were in their little, cozy bedroom. She loved this place so much.

When she touched his chest, instead of fabric she felt his soft skin, as his suits disappeared. It was surprising. "You were glamoured?"

He smiled. "Genius, right?"

At least he was still wearing pants. It would be awkward if he had his stuff hanging during their wedding. Sometimes she still found him a bit weird, but the truth was that she liked that about him.

"May I?" He was gesturing as if to help her get her dress off.

Naia turned around. "Go ahead."

His fingers on her neck brought a chill down her spine, followed by a kiss there. Then he unbuttoned something, and the whole dress and her undergarments came out at once. Fae design. She should have suspected there was more at work than sparkly stars. He cupped her breasts with his hands while kissing her back. She loved his hands with his beautiful dark nails, loved the feel of them against her skin.

"You need to take off your pants."

"They're off."

"Am I mistaken in thinking you were in a hurry?"

"Take your guess."

He turned her around and laid her over the covers, then laid beside her. That dance of hands and mouths was not new for them. They'd done it many times, each time better than the one before, as they learned more about each other. His body was a map she'd been studying, every day finding a special treasure.

Their magic was blending, as they always did when they kissed and got close, and yet this time she feared she was about to burst on fire as she felt one of his hands on her tights, getting closer and closer, until finally he caressed her in that way that felt so good. He lay on top of her and kissed her, his hair around her face, the soft feel of the covers on her back, the wonderful touch of his skin against hers, that familiar, amazing closeness. Then he was inside her, their magic pulsing as one. Dragon magic, human magic, fae magic entangled together, becoming something more powerful, larger than the both of them, larger than life, imbued with the energy of love.

LEAH WATCHED her city through the window, her heart beating fast with the anticipation of what she had to tell Fel.

At least the city was healing, and now that it was summer, it was actually nice not to have that dreadful dome. The damage hadn't been as bad as it should have been, thanks to Fel and Ekateni, who had burned many of the creatures, and thanks also to Ciara and her shapers. Her shapers.

Leah had never heard of them again, even if she knew they were in Aluria. At least they were keeping their word that they would hide. Still, sometimes she saw a strange shadow move, sometimes she saw a movement from the corner of her eye, and could swear there was something else among them. But the shapers were benign, and apparently, didn't need to eat people. Hopefully they were happy now.

Venard had been keeping his promise to make up for his family's past mistakes. Leah had even found herself having to defend Ironhold, since a couple of other kingdoms were quite eager to retaliate against the iron kingdom for their own gain. As to Venard himself, Naia had told him that he'd been keeping his old beloved's corpse somewhere in the Iron Citadel, but Azir had verified the Ironhold castle, and didn't find anything like that. Leah's best guess was that Venard had given up on reviving her after seeing the effects of forbidden magic in Ironhold.

In the recent months, Leah had started to train deathbringing with Azir, but told him that she would never call him father. She couldn't. He was Fel's father. He accepted her decision. Still, he was a patient teacher, and slowly she was becoming more aware of her powers, getting to know herself more. A lot of what she had learned with her necromancer father was helping her, and she was excited to learn more and more.

Tzaria and Ekateni were in Aluria, spending time in Frostlake, Umbraar, and even the Fae Kingdom, helping Fel and Naia, who still had a lot to learn. Their cousins had come for Naia's wedding and were still here, spending some time and also helping Fel train and learn about his powers. Jacine was a dear friend, and Leah was quite happy that they were here. Things were quieter in Fernick. Fewer dragons had been converted to the Boundless, who weren't as strong anymore. Apparently, killing Cynon had actually done something, even if it hadn't ended all their conflicts.

Relia was still the Dragon Eye, not that Leah really understood what the position entailed. From what Siniari and Jacine said, it didn't seem that she had ever been influenced by Cynon. In fact, it was indeed unlikely that the woman had tried to poison Fel. Tzaria had her own reasons to dislike her, though, and hatred could be blinding.

Leah had hoped that maybe Tzaria and Ekateni would become a couple, as they had some history, but it didn't seem to be the case. At least they got along well enough to cooperate and teach Fel and Naia. And then again, the two of them were in Aluria, so who knew about the future? Perhaps their wounds were just taking longer to heal, or maybe their love story was meant to remain in the past.

Risomu had recently returned to Fernick with Kaneyo, who

had healed and was a magnificent brown dragon. He couldn't take his human form yet, but hopefully someday he would.

There had been no more voices in Leah's head, just the same old strange dreams. Her silver dragon was often in them, and had been getting stronger and stronger. Her hunch was that Fel would soon be able to swap forms again, but she didn't want to tell him that in case it didn't happen, as she didn't want to see him disappointed. The truth was that he missed his dragon form. She missed it too, but at least she could connect with him in her dreams.

Leah took a deep breath, then felt strong arms around her. Fel. Her heart beat faster, basking in the touch of her fiery dragon.

He kissed her neck. "Something worrying you?"

It was eerie how much he could sense her emotions. "Not worrying." She turned around and faced him. Was he ready for it? Was it too soon? The words didn't come easily. "Naia's wedding was so beautiful."

"It was wonderful." He frowned. "But why are you mentioning it?"

True, it had been over two months before. Leah fiddled with one of her curls. "Thinking about ours."

Fel kissed her cheek, then whispered in her ear. "Soon."

Leah closed her eyes. "Maybe it could be sooner?"

He stared at her and smiled. "Why don't you just say what you want to say?"

"I... The dress won't look good if my belly's too big." There. She said it.

"Leah... you're not gaining weight. And even if you were, you would still be beautiful, and the dress would still look great on you."

Oh, dear. He hadn't caught on. She sucked in a breath, then said, "I'm pregnant." The healers had been sure, and all the signs pointed to it.

His eyes widened in surprise, then he had a happy chuckle

and kissed her cheek. "That's wonderful news." He caressed her hair with his arm. "Why the worry?"

"I... we didn't plan it. And we'll need to advance the wedding."

Fel hugged her tight, so tight. "That can be done, that's easy. The important thing is that we're together. And soon we'll start a family."

He was truly happy, and she felt silly for her worry.

Fel then broke the hug and asked, "What magic do you think our child will have?"

"I asked Jacine for how many generations dragons would still be dragons, and it's a lot, so our child will be a dragon. Now... You're an Ironhold heir, so it's possible that we'll have an iron-bringer. Or a deathbringer, since you're the Umbraar crown prince. Finally, since we're in Frostlake, there's a possibility that we'll have a necromancer. And then again, the dragon magic bends the magical rules, so our child could have more than one kind of magic."

Fel laughed. "You really thought this through. So it could be a necromancer, deathbringer, ironbringer dragon?"

"It could."

He got serious. "Another iron dragon." His cousins made sure nobody knew where Fel lived, as he was still a target.

Leah shrugged. "Nobody needs to know that."

He kissed her lips softly, then said, "Can't wait to raise our little dragon."

They kissed again, a long kiss, a promise of happy days. So much hope, power, and love.

RIVER HAD NEVER IMAGINED he'd set foot in Fernick again, that he'd come to the place of the dragon temple, now abandoned. Here he was with Naia. The idea of going back in time just to do something that had already been done was a little strange, and yet, apparently it had to be done.

Naia had spoken a lot more with her family and Tzaria in the last year. It turned out that the staff River had stolen was the real Krittl staff, the staff of death. The dragons had thought it was a replica, meant as a trap for Cynon or his followers, but someone had switched them. It had been a dangerous object, and the dragons were glad River had destroyed it.

Again, this wasn't something other dragons should know, or they would try to take a closer peek into his power. Even River sometimes didn't understand what it was, or how much of it was just because of Naia. Of course it had to be her. Her father, blood father, had been the one to set the trap, and she could undo it because she carried his blood. Coincidence. Or maybe a greater plan? He couldn't be sure.

He wanted to try to establish peace with the Dragon Council, but Ekateni and Tzaria warned him against it. There were still Boundless infiltrated everywhere, and it was not the time for an alliance. Still, he was glad to be friends with some of the dragon lords, especially Naia's blood family.

That said, they needed to return to Aluria quickly, as Naia wanted to be there to see her niece or nephew be born.

Their dragon friends were securing the perimeter, while Naia and River climbed the steps.

"Aren't you anxious?" he asked.

"Of course." She made a voice imitating her brother. "I mean, make one mistake and rip the fabric of reality." Her voice turned back to normal. "You're right that it's not scary when the reality is crappy." She looked at him. "But now..."

"The dragons say it should be simple."

She laughed, such a lovely laugh. "They also say they had never heard of this amulet. And for some reason the old, strange, mysterious dragon, the First Mage, doesn't want to talk to us anymore."

River shrugged. "He must have retired."

"It's not funny."

Was she really chastising him? "You're the one who started laughing."

"Because I'm nervous!"

He held her hands. "I trust you. I know you'll do great."

They were atop the hill, standing on what was now ruins of that temple.

Naia took a deep breath and placed her hand on the amulet. "I hope—"

She simply disappeared. Not even black smoke around her, nothing. River closed his eyes, feeling his heart accelerating. If this went wrong, if this object had been a trick... There were so many horrible possibilities, and contemplating losing her was terrifying. And yet, all he could do was wait. Wait he did, an eternity of pain, until she appeared again.

He held her close, so close, so tight.

"River, you're suffocating me."

"I feared losing you."

"I'm here." She chuckled. "I had forgotten you told me you didn't have horns. It was a little odd."

"You see me glamoured all the time." As much as there were a lot of fae in Fernick, few had horns like the Ancients, and he didn't want to draw attention.

"I know. It's just... you were so young. Also, you were flirting with me. Really, River? You had never seen me and you were already flirting?" She was amused, but also curious.

"You're my life companion. Why would I not flirt with you?"

"You didn't know who I was."

That made no sense. "You think I wouldn't feel it?"

"Maybe."

River stared at her. "And you can't seriously blame me for flirting with you. You, who wanted to kiss me five minutes after first meeting me."

"After saving your life. It was romantic, River."

"Well, you just saved my life. Just as romantic."

"You looked at me like you wanted to strip me naked right there and then."

Obviously. "A normal reaction. What's the problem?"

Naia rolled her eyes. "Do you by any chance want to do it now?"

"Since you're asking... well, yes. The issue is that the dragons might wonder why we're taking so long and come check on us."

"We could be quick." She laughed, then changed her tone. "I'm joking."

River knew her well enough to realize she wasn't joking. She was daring him. He smiled at her. "Or maybe you got strangely attracted to the young, inappropriately flirty me."

"At least you know that was not appropriate."

He chuckled, then realized her amulet was gone. He touched her chest "It disappeared?"

She nodded. Now that his hand was here, he didn't want to move it away. Perhaps they could be inappropriate—and fast—before the dragons noticed anything.

The past had been restored to its right place. As to the future, it lay wide open for them. He trusted it now, and trusted that there was also good at work in the world.

AFTERWORD

Thanks so much for reading this book! I hope you enjoyed it.

If you'd like to know more about me or sign up for free books and news, you can find me at dayleitao.com

Also, reviews are super important for authors and readers, so if you have a minute, please leave your opinion on Goodreads, Amazon, Bookbub or any other site. It doesn't need to be long or eloquent. A short sentence like "this was fun," " I liked this but didn't like that," "good for readers who enjoy...," "reminded me of book so-and-so," is perfect.

Finally, if you enjoyed this book, you might also enjoy my other fantasy series:

Kingdom of Curses and Shadows

Portals to Whyland

Acknowledgments

Some books just jump into your life, the story almost ready, while others need to be pulled thread by thread from the confines of who knows where, perhaps the Eleventh Realm or somewhere even worse. This book was one of those.

I couldn't have done it without the wonderful support of the writing groups Tuesday Tribe and Apex Writers. Super thanks to the authors Loretta Torosian, T.F. Burke, Sharlene Healey, R. L. Perez, Allison Rose, Belle Luna, E. E. Everest, R. Dawn Hutchinson, and L. Wood, who listened patiently to me ramble about dragons, lost fae, weird realms, and bizarre magic. None of them is at fault if any part of this book sucks.

I'd also like to thank Donna Daigle and my wonderful beta readers.

Finally, I couldn't have written this book without my readers. The only reason it exists is because of those of you who wanted to know what happened to Naia, River, Fel, and Leah. I hope you appreciate their entangled, complicated stories, and this little window into a fantasy world.

9 781990 790034